SIMON & SCHUSTER
Rockefeller Center
1230 Avenue of the Americas
New York, New York 10020

SIMON & SCHUSTER and colophon are registered
trademarks of Simon & Schuster Inc.

Designed by Karolina Harris
Manufactured in the United States of America

10 9 8 7 6 5 4 3 2 1

Library of Congress Cataloging-in-Publication Data

Plesko, Les.
    The last bongo sunset: a novel/Les Plesko.
        p.   cm.
      1. Narcotic addicts—California—Venice—Fiction. 2. Heroin
habit—California—Venice—Fiction. 3. Criminals—
California—Venice—Fiction. 4. Venice (Calif.)—Fiction. I. Title.
PS3566.L45L37   1995
813'.54—dc20   94-22439
                                                          CIP

ISBN: 978-1-4767-9994-0

To Kate Braverman,
my mentor,
who taught me to write
and made this book possible.

One

From down in the street I see her hang out of my window, mouth open and screaming, her slim neck festooned with a single, pale crinoline lei the color of rose. Someone is holding the girl by the ankles. I run up the stairs. I see it's Gary who's trying to kill her or save her.

"She wants to fly," Gary says.

That's what we all want, I think. It's why I've come to this place at the edge of the ocean as far as I could from the opposite coast.

I only met Gary three hours ago, down on the walkaround street on the green-chipped-paint bench where we happened to sit side by side, remarking on nothing particular, crossing, uncrossing our legs. Somehow he managed to let me convince him that he should come up to my room while I went to the store for more wine. Now here's this girl out the window, a wild, alive wire. We pull her inside.

"I was just trying to scare her," says Gary, backing away from her gaze.

She straightens her soft, yellow dress that's torn at the hem and the shoulder. She purses her lips in a thin, bloodless smile.

"This, too, becomes part of my legend," she says. She stands like she thinks she's too tall, slightly stooped. Her pale skin looks nervous and cold. She staggers around in a tightening oval while running her hands through lackluster brown hair that's been chemically scorched with streaks of unnatural blond.

struck-sulfur smell of two matches she uses to cook down the brown powder she's spilled from the unballed small party balloon.

"Take the sash from my robe," she instructs, though it's mine. "Tie me off. When I tell you, let go. Remember that I'm always first."

I've seen this in a movie. I've read a book, it's not nearly the same. I think I've been waiting for something like this for twenty-one years. It's like being tossed in a pond as someone cries, "Swim." A door has been opened, I'm going to step in.

Cassandra teases and pierces a vein. Holding her breath, she pushes the needle, says, "You have to register twice." I watch the liquid turn rust with her blood as she yo-yos the plunger, hits up, pulls it out, draws more water, squirts pink on the rug in one long seamless move.

She's rubbing her face and exhaling. "I kept this from Gary, he'll kill me. Now hold out your arm, it's your turn."

I want to see everything now that I'm doing what I want to do. Her practiced hand gentles the spike. There's a tight pinch. A tea-colored murk clouds the dropper, a sudden blood bloom. Her thumb's on the plunger. She shoots me full of the dope. It begins with a flush in the back of the neck that becomes a vibrato, a deep-inside glow. The light in the room is too bright, then much whiter. I realize how everything's right, to the bone. After an insensate minute I have to throw up. It's not bad, a mere letting go.

I look at the room that's transformed. Cassandra kneels on the couch and stares out the window. She sways side to side, calm and cool. Outside, someone shouts about Jesus. Gray and white sea gulls wheedle and wheel in the blind summer sky. People are shouting vacation instructions, calling their children, carrying beer in Styrofoam coolers, patting their pockets to check for the keys.

"I'll bet you've never felt like this before," Cassandra is saying, running her nails on her face, on her arms. I understand what the fuss is about. She says, "Scratching is good," and it is. It kindles the high, makes it rise to the skin. I'm thinking I'm not the same as I was.

"Wait until the first time you're sick," she tells me. "That's something else, too."

It's happened so fast, then there's more. Next thing Cassandra is standing before me, her pose limp, unafraid, overexposed.

"It's best when the rush is half over," she says. "There's more we could do."

She leans down and kisses my mouth. Her lips are blistered and chapped. I haven't been touched in a very long time. I've never had this kind of needle-tipped high. I have to learn how to act, I've done nothing portentous until this day. I touch the flat of her stomach, see my hand drown in insensible light that's flaring and warning. Her skin feels moldy, she smells slightly unwashed.

"Don't be scared," she urges, "I'm not going to hurt you." Casually, she places her hand in my lap. Her long face is narrow and sallow. Her uncombed tangle of hair is the color of mud and straw. She slips the robe from her shoulders, lets it fall to the floor.

"It must be ninety," she sighs like a made-for-TV-movie actress. "We've got to lie down."

I think anything's possible now. Dust plumes rise from the bed where she throws herself flat. Her color is yeasty and pale from behind, with patches of skin lightly blotched, a sparse shiver of down on the length of her spine. Her thin legs are blemished all over with purpling yellowed contusions. She turns on her side, rests her head on her palm.

"Hurry up," she says with a voice like a pack-a-day torn-paper rasp. "Don't bother getting undressed. This won't take that long."

Then I can't believe I'm in bed with a girl with no clothes and she's touching my shoulder, that I'm brave enough and she's older, that now she's not taller than me anymore.

Languid, she studies my eyes. "Where you from?"

"College," I tell her.

"Some heartbreak apartment, no doubt," she replies. She looks at me closer. "No," she decides, "you've been mostly alone." She traces a line from my throat to my hollow of knees, to my groin. There's only the hint of a bare reckless grin on the edge of her mouth. She says, "If we do this you won't want to leave when it's over." Her breath smells like charcoal and etherized wine. On her wrists are thin slivers of suicide lines. Her tongue tastes like cotton. Her long, slow, rough up-and-down hand becomes fast. She says, "I know you already. You won't be denied." Her voice is the coax of a stone to follow it down as it falls in clear water. She leans on her elbow and halfway sits up. Cassandra says, "College, let's watch." She parts her indelicate lips, lets out a caught-up-in-it sigh. "I want to see how you look when it happens," she says. "You want to look at me, too. That's how you are."

I'd like to believe I don't know what she's talking about. I consider her narrowing shoulders, the slightly hipped curve of her sides, legs folded beneath her, the bitten nails of her quickening hand, the prickly skinned flesh inside of her thighs.

I reach for her hair, but she shakes her head no, says, "I won't be pawed," slaps my hand. "Hit me back," she insists, but I can't. She says, "I know, you won't go that far." On her drawn face, her slate gaze holds contempt, avarice, and longing. I sense a rumor, a fiction, and something she hides. Inside the pinned flints of her pupils is where an answer for every commission of sin resides.

She matches her breathing to mine. She says, "Christ, this is breaking my arm." I say her name twice. She shields her thighs with her palms as if for protection. I cover her fingers with white.

Cassandra is wiping her hands on the top of the mattress, the edge of the blanket. She keeps repeating, "I'm dirty, I can't get it off," many times.

After my breathing is normal we lie on our backs. Cassandra wills her eyes shy. We make steeples by touching our fingers together. We smell of each other. Outside, beach ball toss, bongo sounds, rise.

"I know why you're here," says Cassandra. "You want some excitement, adventure. You want to get into something that's over your head. Be careful, you might drown."

I'm thinking she's right, also that we shouldn't be lying in bed at this hour when Gary comes back.

He simply regards us, a trumpet in one hand, a dry wedge of angel food cake in his palm. Both of us look at Cassandra, knees drawn to her chest, not really surprised. Slowly, she stretches and shelters her mound.

Gary takes in the room, the kicked-off covers, my buttons undone, the black-bottomed spoon on the cinder block table, the robe where it fell, the needle unhidden, a shred of the rubber balloon on the rug, Cassandra's dress carelessly flung on the bathroom's linoleum tile.

He sets the horn on the floor. He says, "That was fast."

"It had to be done," Cassandra replies. I wonder what she means by this, but I'm too stunned and high for alarm. She's carelessly chewing her bruised, bitten lips that are sprinkled with tobacco flecks. She says, "It was time."

Gary sits down on the edge of the bed. His stained shiny pants are spotted with traces of mustard and beans from a can. He smells like buttermilk, Brylcreem, old clothes in a pile. I flinch when he pushes the long stringy hair from his brow. He wipes meringue from his hand on his unbuttoned shirt. He leans closer. He sees how my eyelids are lazy with dope. The tips of his hair brush my chest.

"So you're not cherry," he says, his voice measured, deliberate. "Whatever she says, don't believe her," he whispers distinctly, his lips to my ear, loud enough for Cassandra to make out each word.

"I've heard this before," Cassandra mentions offhand. She's rising and lifting herself on all fours.

Gary goes to the window, where suntan-oiled heat wafts in on a tenuous heavy wet breeze. "There's been enough resting, commencing and fooling around here," he says.

Cassandra crawls from the bed to the floor. "I can do anything now," she remarks. She climbs on the couch beside Gary. She touches his shoulder. He's putting the cake in his mouth. They both appear matter-of-fact, like they've done this in other rooms, looking down at an alley, a street, a door slamming, at nothing. She lets him play with her rings. He takes them off one by one, puts them back. She picks at a scab on his arm. I'm thinking that this is their way of forgiving each other for what she's just done and whoever they are. They're spacing it out, not hurried and feckless, entirely careless, just high. Or maybe they just want a room and a roof, to take over my life. They also won't be denied, I decide. Cassandra crosses the carpet, steps to her dress, lowers it over herself, unabashed. Gary turns from the glass. He says, "You have a car."

Two

Gary has said the role is official. I'm driving. The air in the Fair-lane is stifling. The sky is an orange soot poison that hurts to breathe in. Behind us the afternoon sun is profligate, bloated and low. My hands on the wheel feel infected and dirty, and what am I doing? There's no time now to figure it out. I tell myself what Cassandra has said, it's excitement I'm having, and leave it at that. The three of us sit side by side. Loose papers cover the dash, tickets and matchbooks, shopping lists, spiral-torn notes, a wedge of illegible map. Cans of transmission fluid roll on the floor in the back. The speedometer trembles and so do my arms. It hovers at twenty, won't climb.

This part of town is entirely sprayed with unreadable code on the walls, sides of trucks, trunks of trees, metal doors. Some of the squat flat-roofed buildings we pass are the color of jaundice or urine; others are pink, yellow, robin's egg blue. Abandoned railroad cars sit on the tracks by the cross streets.

Cassandra's explaining what she will be doing, how much she'll be charging. I should be appalled but I'm thrilled at the sordidness of the whole enterprise.

"This is what you wanted," Cassandra is saying. "Illicit and dar-ing." She's got the radio tuned in to Jesus returning. She's shielding her eyes with both seven-ringed hands. Gary is wearing a knife in a brown leather sheath on his belt.

"Turn here," he says.

We park by a thin copse of dust-covered palms on an unnamed dirt alley. I'm afraid to get out of the car. We walk toward a peeling red door of a bungalow crosshatched with gouges. There are too many radios on, large-voiced announcers calling on Christ also coming in Spanish, pumped through repeaters and echo machines.

It's tropical here because of the language. Two chickens are tied to a post. Men pretend to busy themselves under sprung steam-plumed hoods or in trunks with the spares and the jacks. Shallow burnt skillets are sizzling with fat, there's the pat of tortillas in palms. Mothers and daughters won't look as we pass. They know why we're here, who we are.

We're holding Cassandra's thin elbows so she can walk on the dirt in her heels. She catches me studying the side of her pale oblong face, how it's willful, disdainful, and glad all at once. She smells like the whole day we've had. I want to wipe at the edge of her mouth with a tissue but we have no time. We've come to a room that's releasing the sounds of a handful of men high on short dogs of ninety-cent screwtop green wine.

"I know what I'm doing," she says. "Don't stare like that." Cassandra shakes out her hair like she wishes it longer, jangles her five-and-dime charms, goes inside.

Gary pretends we couldn't care less as he sits on the stoop.

"We need anesthesia," he says. He's brought a back and forth bottle of bourbon to pass. He's inscribing Xs and Os in the dirt with the tip of his knife. We're listening for noises of who's doing what and how rough on a no box spring mattress that probably smells like fried rinds. I'm thinking men usually sleep in the room with their children and third-cousin wives. The air is the odor of rust, rancid butter, and lard. I study the clueless late grenadine smear of the sky. I notice all of the women's bright dresses are one size too tight. This is much more than I bargained for, but it has to be got through somehow, so I swallow and gag on the pint.

Inside, no doubt, from a yellowing wall, the Virgin is watching a hurry-up underwear tangle, bared bellies and thighs. Under a praying hands statue on top of a broken-drawered dresser, impudent, hard florid sighs come apart. There's elbow tattoos and groaning, insistent flat slaps that won't stop. There's curses in English and Spanish, both hers and the others'.

"You next. You get out of me now," we hear Cassandra demand.

Someone's throat catches and barks. Someone says, "Lift your knees higher," and then something harsh. I'm thinking muscatel wine might be spilled on her shoulder. She has to be shiny and trembling all over, her dress on the floor. She clutches bills in her fist, her head tilted back, neck exposed. Her chest is a stubble-rubbed mottle. Unyielding confusions of arms are around her. She lets out a no pleasure moan. Maybe she hears the birds' afternoon medley or sees out the upside-down uncurtained window the ginger blue apricot swell of the sun that's about to flame out. Nothing stops moving, limbs climb. The radios seem to get louder. A bottle is dropped. Gary is stabbing his knife in the ground.

I hate my hands that do nothing. I pretend I'm going to stand up and stop it, when Gary caresses my chin with the flat of his blade.

"Relax," he tells me. "Don't worry. She likes it."

Then everything pauses and seizes. Somewhere nearby church bells sound like a hobble of metal on sky. The orangy air itself stalls as Cassandra comes out. She's tugging her dress that's misbuttoned, exposing her navel. Her gaze is pale ash.

I'm going to touch her, when Gary says under his breath, "Don't fuck with her now."

She walks too fast to the car. We slide in on each side beside her. I turn it over. We head west on Olympic, the red sky bleeding to black. I glance over and Gary is counting the money, Cassandra is squirming around. I swerve when I look at the seat where a stain spreads beneath her from under her thighs.

Gary advises, "Don't hit a parked car." He switches the radio station to jazz.

Cassandra leans, turns it off. "There's been enough entertainment," she says. Her eyes are feral, her mouth set too tight. She's untangling her hair with a brush. Gary is scraping desiccated flesh from a burn in his palm with his knife. Ahead on the road is a puddle mirage. The horizon is strung with a scrim of low febrile white clouds. I'm wiping the sweat, all-day dirt from my hand, can't believe what I've taken a part in.

Finally the velvet exhaustion of sky meets the sea in a weary erasure of pleasure. I turn right on Oceanview and stop. I go around to open the passenger door but Cassandra is already out, running across the thin lip of grass toward the sand and the water. I follow, leave Gary behind.

She falls when she reaches the shoreline, her purse spilling out. She reaches around and starts throwing her tubes of mascara, flat plastic rouge, Clairol blond in a bottle, a Kelly Girl mirror. I kneel down beside her expecting her eyes to be damp, but she smiles.

"What drama," she says. Cassandra straightens her dress as she stands. She shakes out her hair. I find myself idled beside her. She studies her hands in the imminent failure of light. "I'm dying of intimate exposure," she says in a voice like a flower corrupt with its very last color. "In my head I'm not living this life." The surf sounds like twigs being cracked in the folds of a rag. Cassandra releases her top eyehook buttons as if to allow the light to anoint her. She says, "You can kiss me right now."

I shiver. We exchange the day for our dry, sullen mouths. She tastes like burnt matches, ammonia. Behind us I see our building scuttled in concrete and palm. The last pastel belly of sun is rubbed raw on the ribs of the clouds that are glazed to a violent burnish.

"My insides are that color," Cassandra says after a while.

Three

Evening arrives with its washed-out and filtered patina. We've returned to our room through its door with its shadow of 7 intact. We've admired the blue bulb that Gary has screwed in the bare ceiling fixture.

"It soothes" was his only remark.

It softens our skins, turns us aquamarine as if we're underwater. Cassandra's gone first. I watched her forgetting her name as she tapped the syringe, freeing bubbles so air wouldn't race through her veins and blow out her heart. I witnessed Gary in love with the paraphernalia, the tie in his teeth as he held out my arm that surrendered like butter to heated-up silver. Now Gary rests on the bed, Cassandra and I have taken our newfound regular comfortable place side by side on the couch.

"You ought to ask us to leave," says Cassandra, "before this goes further."

I shake my head. "Too much has already happened for that."

"This is nothing," Cassandra replies, "but you're right. Besides, it's two to one and we're bigger and stronger, we could throw you out." She turns around, taps the glass. "College, you're really in danger at last." She leans back and sighs. "So what do you want?"

"I want you to stay" is what comes from my mouth.

"To see what happens next," she completes my thought.

Yes, I am thinking, I want to abandon my previous self and become someone else. This is scary and heady at once.

Soon Gary's asleep. Cassandra is lighting a Lucky and tossing the match in the half-full glass tinged with our blood.

"I'll tell you a story. You like to hear stories," Cassandra assumes. "About how we hooked up." She points toward Gary's curled form on the bed, the trumpet held to his chest.

Cassandra remembers when she met Gary. He'd just pawned a trail of bad scrip and bald lies. As if we've known each other for years she leans on my shoulder. Her voice is that of an old confidante.

"It was Vegas," she says. "I had the best time." She smooths out her yellow trick dress and crosses her thighs. She bends at the waist in order to tell it better. Elbow on knee, she props her chin on her palm. The smoke from her cigarette rises.

"I was sharing a place with a roommate. We had a TV, went to shows with some guys. Could've smiled at Dean Martin except for my teeth. Spent some cash." She stifles a yawn, exhales, studies her arms. I can sense Cassandra's pleasure in telling, in having a listener who won't interrupt. This is a chapter of legend she alluded to when we pulled her inside.

"I was walking down Fremont, swinging my purse," she recalls. She stretches as if warming up, then folds her hands in her lap. "It was dusk. I was wearing a rabbit-fur jacket. I had rings on my fingers. The neon was just coming on."

She picks up the matches. "Gary walked by on the sidewalk," she says. "He must have said something. I said something back." She tears a match from the pack and lights it, lets it burn down to forefinger and thumb, shakes it out. "He picked up his horn. He played pretty bad." Her words sound rehearsed, like she's told this before, at least rehearsed it many times.

Cassandra is rubbing her wrists on the sides of her thighs. "He said he could get some good shit, but there was a problem with funds." She inhales more smoke, lets it out. "I opened my purse. I didn't think twice." She covers her eyes as if to help memory rise.

"He whistled. He told me he loved me. I knew what he loved."

Cassandra recalls they holed up in a pay-per-day five-dollar trailer, how they stayed high and he wouldn't stop talking, getting at something she could have been doing. She'd done it before, she knew what it was.

"Truckstop's the word he wouldn't let go of," she says, rubbing the tops of her legs in the blue that disguises her scars.

She recalls the doors of the rigs had names painted on them, DREAM LOVER, HOG HEAVEN, NIGHT RIDER. The mudflaps bore silhouette cutouts of girls. Cassandra says she knew all about truckers, the folded-down fake leather Kenworth sighs, the mother, wife pictures that crowded the dash. She learned "down in the kitchen" meant first gear through third. Deadhead was a word for no load in the back, not a fan of the band. She'd already heard about balling the jack.

In the glare of the store they sold chrome-plated lug nuts, furry seat covers, and souvenir spoons. She studied the T-shirts for sale and their slogans, IF THE MEEK SHALL INHERIT THE EARTH, WHO WILL DRIVE THE BIG TRUCKS? MY DAD IS A TRUCKER. I DRIVE WITH PRIDE. She bought sunglasses, makeup, and chocolate milk soda.

"That dope was too good," she recalls. "Gary said we couldn't quit. He was right. We got strung out."

It soothed the blank days and the fluorescent, halogen parking lot nights. They went downtown when flush. She fed nickel slots with casual panhandled change while Gary cadged drinks at the bar. Old guys with glass rings wore Key lime ensembles. Wide, cream fake gold buckled belts matched tasseled and ribbed canvas loafers and headbands of hats. Women in sneakers and kelly green stretchpants that rode up too high showing nylons were smoking and worrying quarters. The pinch-faced uniformed bar girls looked dipped in meringue. She says they had engagement-ringed, sucker bet hands and wedding band eyes. They tugged on their garters and pulled at the hems of their dresses but nothing fit right.

Cassandra is under her own spell, she sways on the couch. She says Gary dealt three-card monte on Flamingo Road in plain sight. He paid off the truckstop lot cops with his larceny money. Then, she says, Vegas ran down.

Those cabs got too tight. There were too many fading tattoos and CB eruptions. She had cramps in her calves and the backs of her thighs. The trailer was sour. They used up the veins in their ankles, the backs of their hands. They did it inside the soft of their knees for each other at last.

Her eyes appear bruised and unfocused. She says, "Gary got popped. He snitched the connection so I had a jacket. They all knew my face. I had to leave town." Under the blue light she's paling and holding my arms like she's desperate. Her tale is something that has to come out.

"He got ninety days knocked down to thirty. I must have been pregnant by then," she says matter-of-factly. "I kept throwing up."

I don't know whether to believe her or not. I remember what Gary has said about that. Whatever she utters could well be a lie. But what would be the motive for that? Maybe she knows the type of a story I want to hear, that I will be beguiled.

Cassandra opens the rest of her buttons all the way down. It's still hot, the sash of the window is raised, the blue of the room undisguised. She places her hand inside and over her heart. I'm thinking this is more intimate than what we did on the bed. She looks like she's come to her favorite part. She uncrosses her legs and looks down.

"I rented a room by the Amtrak," she says, her voice arid, stick-dry. The walls of the ten-dollar doss were stripped, split, uneven boards that let in the wind. There was a hand-painted chair, a porcelain bowl, the cold-water drip of a tap. Everything came to a stop but the trains and they shook her. She lay on her back and stared out the window's scratched glass at a wedge of bleached air for the length of the thistle-still breezeless white days without clouds. She came down with the sweats without wine. Her bones seemed to pull from their sockets, she turned from the wall without rest. Hours would pass as she studied the sand-colored sky. Cassandra lay by the window forgetting her name and growing her child. She let fear embrace her. She longed for the last of the light to remain but it leaked into dusk. Cassandra slept and awakened, heedless of time. At night she dreamed it was daylight. Sometimes the moon would be crossing the sky in the full bloom of noon as she curled with her fist to her mouth. It turned into winter at last. On somebody's unguarded clothesline she found a sweater, a pair of men's pants.

"Gary sent buddies from prison," she says. "They simply arrived."

She reinvented herself for each one on the floor, on the oat-colored blanket she used for a bed. They brought paper-bagged, waxwrapped mustard and cheese on white bread.

"You've got to eat," they would say, but they couldn't look at her eyes.

She only opened her lemonade cardigan buttons, lowered her slacks to her knees, and pulled up her dress. There were their own stories she let them tell. Their spent smell stayed on the silvering crust of her belly but she wouldn't wash. Cassandra was seized by the racket of trains and she couldn't care less. "By then the baby was showing," she says.

Cassandra bends over, holding her head in her hands. "I should stop. I should turn out the light. We could do something else," but she stays where she is. This is only a feint. She knows I want to hear all the rest though I know it is bad. I'm certain Cassandra's confession will bind us, that this is Cassandra's intent.

I tell her, "No, don't stop now," as a new lover might in another context.

"Gary came back," she says with a voice like a vesper.

At first Cassandra believed she only imagined him there in the alpenglow twilight. He pulled on her arms. "How long till it's due?" he asked, but she couldn't remember. He buttoned her dress. He fed her by hand. Cassandra was done with the window, the yellow-gray scud of the clouds, the last of the men who had recently come on her thighs.

She tells me, "I said let's go west, it was something Egyptian I read: 'To the west is the house of good fortune, to the east is a fire.

To the south you must sometimes travel, and as for the north, you better forget it.' Or something like that."

They passed Cheyenne Road, Fremont Street. They hid for a while inside Coffin Mountain, a crease of the Anchorite Hills. Then Gary declared they were hitting the pharmacy trail. He drove a white Cadillac without plates that was bartered for sex. They stuck to the smallest of towns. Some were unmarked, marred just by the sound of the Cadillac's wheels.

Cassandra says, "I wrote down their names." She searches her dress for notes on smudged pieces of paper that she doesn't have. She doesn't need them. She says they were called Beowawe, Weed Heights, the bald wilderness range of San Gorgonio, Hesperia, Phelan, and Twentynine Palms.

Soon they were tanked up on sweet muscatel behind clapboard, hiding in tin-roofed saloons from short knives in Ojos de Negros, the town of black eyes. She says she was cried-out in Yermo, where men wore checked shirts pulped with country. She shouted down Lemwood's cramped shotgun shacks.

On Minelda Road she was spying the local debris. Distended ribs of the clouds were crossing the sky, hauling their tarpaulins over the blue slake of Halloran Pond. The blanch of the heavens was colored a whaleskin-pale pasture, the air yellow with vegetable light. She scribbled more names that she stuffed in her bag, Imlay, Tenabo, Mendota. This was the hundred-mile start of the pharmacy trail that Gary had warned her about.

Gary busted the old-time docs' network, he knew the local patois, traced the route of the pharmacists peddling illegible scrip for the sake of nostalgia with blunt crayon lines on a map.

"Those places had drugs I never heard of," Cassandra remembers. She was made privy to almost-forgotten arcana of improvised outfits from droppers and soft rubber bulbs bound with twine. She choked on the odor of raw paregoric, was shown how it had to be squeezed from the tube to the spoon.

"Those guys saw us coming," she says. "We could have been carrying signs."

In those back rooms she let the old druggists touch her while Gary nodded outside. She didn't mind. Their tentative palsy of hands on her breasts felt like paper, their smocks smelled of ether, their breath on her face was a lingering formaldehyde.

Cassandra says she and Gary went into saloons without caution. She recollects the men's rooms sold condoms and combs. You could push a dispenser that sprayed you with sweet, sticky mist that smelled like an approximation of jasmine perfume.

"I drank red beer and Leroux anisette. I smoked Old Gold filters. I wore skirts over jeans and couldn't be bothered," she's saying. "I made men hide their eyes." In those bars she was traded for lamb shanks, roast loins, occasional cash, once even camping supplies. Because of the baby she'd lie on her side on thin wooden pallets in back.

"The dope we were shooting made everything seamless," she says. It was cut with mannite and something that burned but this didn't matter. It made the bodies she slept with feel merely like freshly washed sheets she would rub up against.

Picking at flecks of tobacco from her narrow mouth she says, "I'd like some wine."

I set the bottle on top of the cinder block table, hesitant that her story should pause. She picks it up, swallows long, cradles the liter, and sways for a while. I want more of this, to be inside her life, to be plumbing her thoughts.

"We weren't lost," she goes on. "We should have moved faster or slower. When we weren't high, we were drunk. Then we got drunker."

Not paying attention, Cassandra and Gary fell over the border. She whispers the names of those places as well, like coins of invisible realms. "La Bolsa, Coscorro, Jibarro," she slurs. She swallows some more. Not in the least disingenuous or ironic, Cassandra says, "Things became worse."

She threw up, ran a fever, got too sick to work. They recrossed north but the money ran out, the drugstores were shuttered. She held the last seven dollars for gas and fluid for the blown manifold.

They came to an army green tent. She was shoved from behind. Something was hurting so bad that she had to lie down in the dirt and curl up on her side. She couldn't breathe and she tried to imagine the float of a circle inside a triangle; that sometimes helped. Now the lines wouldn't hold. She pulled her own hair to divert the pain from where it was so large, where it stabbed.

Outside in the ocher of dust was a grapple about her with knives. She heard the flat tap of metal, smelled marijuana, sweat, vomit, and hide. She lifted her head, dribbled the rest of the no label bottle, and threw it aside. It was desperately quiet at last and everything swarmed, spun around.

Someone was there in the tent right beside her, she heard his hard wheeze. He said something dirty in Spanish. She didn't reply. Already his pants were bunched at the ankles, she saw his outline. He wrestled her onto her knees so her elbows and forehead were grimed with brown earth. She lifted her dress, exposing herself in the back.

He knew only memories of horses when he lunged inside. Her skin became rank with a carious grease where he touched her. He smelled of gasoline, cornmeal. She pushed back against him from habit, like she didn't mind. The rough scrape of her arms on the ground, the alcohol rocking, appeased her, it cut the hurt. She turned, tugged her dress higher, saw his jut-jawed upturned silhouette face. He grunted twice fast. He was done. It was over. He pulled out and wiped himself off on the hem of her skirt, left her alone in the flame-ridden, shadowy dark.

Cassandra rolled over and pulled herself tight. Outside was a pig knuckle rattle inside a raw leather gourd. Soon all sound stopped but for scramblings of hungry curs in the picked-apart trash. Gary still hadn't returned.

On the edge of passed out she felt others. She opened her eyes. There were three. One held a candle illuminating that forehead of scars. The women clutched strips of range-fencing and hay-baling wire. Red patterned scarves covered noses and mouths. Their hair was unbraided, let down in the flickering glare.

Soundless, they whipped her. Cassandra heard the swish of thin metal on air, the three-handed flagellant lash, but she wouldn't cry out, give them that. She covered her face, tasted salt, intoxication, and bile. On her uncovered legs she smelled leftover semen, the wet running odor of blood.

The beating suddenly stopped. The candle-wire women retreated. Through the left-open flap of the canvas Cassandra could see the night sky become pierced with a meteor shower. The howling dogs made her hair bristle. A desert sirocco swept the scorched gorges and rose.

Then something was tearing inside, coming out. She groaned, stretched out flat, raised her legs, arched her back. Everything jumped, came apart. The pain had a life of its own, it was tangibly separate and round. She says it was just before dawn she broke water, gave birth to a dead-limbed black clot on the ground. Dragging the cord in the blood-muddied dust, she heard herself scream without sound.

Now she tries to drink from her bottle but spills it. Under the blue bulb her gaze is a tremor, her fingers a panic on mine. I am suddenly chilled, revolted at what she's revealed and yet glad that she has. She says, "Please believe me. We dug in the dirt for two hours to bury it." She lies down with her head in my lap. She says, "Sometimes I pretend that baby's a fiction," and finally closes her eyes.

Four

Before I'm awake I'm in a place where what's real is uncertain. In the ways of these things there's something I ought to be doing but I'm interrupted each time by an out-of-reach phone, a letter from school on which I can't decipher the type. Something has to get done but time becomes liquid, some thick underwater abstraction that cannot be parsed. Someone is saying my name and instructions that I can't make out. There's only an aura of regret, an undefined loss. It is a sense of displacement I've had since I was a child, especially waking up in a place that's not mine, a free-floating, anxious aloneness. It's as if I'm incorporeal and weightless.

I know I don't own my own room anymore when I open my eyes. I realize I'm wearing my unbuttoned pants and plaid shirt pulled loose. Cassandra and I lie face to face on the couch. Her intimate details are exposed. I'm full of the places we touch, at our knees, our foreheads, the back of my hand on her belly, the other one cradling her black-and-blue arm. The alien-fissured geography wall turns from ash to dull white as I watch.

I'm afraid of Cassandra, her skin smudged by staticky grains of new light. Sleep enraptures her features, erases the difficult lines from the sides of her mouth. It makes her appear the young girl she's not been for a while. Cassandra is unguarded, slack. She stretches flat on her stomach, her arm in a trawl. Like this she almost resembles a boy. In her sleep, not counting money or spreading her ten-dollar thighs, Cassandra's unlivid, not coy.

I lean on an elbow and study her dream-fluttered eyelids, her fingers half curled, wrists cocked like a child's. She's using her yellow trick dress for a pillow. This is the first time I see her not frantic, sarcastic, but sober. I match her slow shallow regular breathing to mine.

I get up and look out the window, where pages of newspapers plaster the sidewalk and wrap around poles. The sky is a cloudless blue panel. Across Oceanview, a redheaded woman is filling a pot from a tap. Her room is pale tallow. She picks up a spoon and drops it on purpose. Outside is a barely heard lovemaking pillow-clutch cry.

I go into the bathroom and study my face in the busted-up glass. I bare my teeth, say to myself they'll never be bad as Cassandra's, scratch at the start of a stubble. I lean on the frame of the door, look at Gary's green bottle, Cassandra's fake rings, her beaded white purse, and her paper bag knickknacks on top of the kitchenette table. I ransack the bag for some clues. There's crayons, a scatter of buttons, torn and smudged pages of coloring books, telephone numbers scribbled on chocolate bar wrappers, and assorted coins.

Though I paid the rent I feel transient in my own room. Nothing is revealed by Gary tossed on the sheet, Cassandra's sleeping form. I've taken them in, but it seems the other way around. It's as if I've been baptized by all that has happened so far. Cassandra's confidence shared was a way of luring me in. We are in complicity now, a three-person commune. I have a sense of belonging that I'm not certain I yearn.

It is too soon to ascribe a motive for why we have become a team. It's got to be more than the use of my car, bed, and couch. It's not enough to simply declare this is something I want. Maybe it has to do with my being a student. I'm studying still, though this is an outlandish curriculum, not a learning by rote. This is real.

Cassandra coughs. The room turns to coppery gold. She reaches around for the blanket that we never used. She raises herself on her arms and stays neck bent and sprung. She gets up, unshy. Her eyelids are ringed with a permanent, sedative kohl. Her skin is the color of butter left out overnight and her dry hair smells like wine and bleach. She rubs up against me and kisses my mouth but it's only a game and she won't make it last. She appears vaguely denied, like she doesn't know me and I paid her money. She cradles my face in her seven-ringed hand. The tops of her breasts are flush with a roseate rash. There are pink indentations of sleep on her cheek. Once more I'm trying to decide how to act.

"Whatever I told you last night is a lie" is the first thing she says.

"I don't believe that."

"Believe what you want," Cassandra says, then relents. "No, I'm just kidding."

"About what?"

"Really, College, it's just my way of playing," she says.

"What's the game, *Truth or Consequences?*"

"Don't outsmart yourself," she advises. She goes to the table for getover dope and leftover cottons to pound. Before anything else there is nothing but this on her mind, I can tell. She sits down and follows the usual sequence I've now memorized, touches the ridge inside of her elbow, nudges its nugget of scars. Cassandra's so long-boned she crosses her legs on her arm like a vise for a tie. She sticks herself twice and together we watch the blood rise. The part of her venial lips is a ruin. She hits up and sighs.

"You're next. You've done it before," Cassandra repeats my own previous lie.

I could refuse but I won't. What am I going to do if I quit them? Enroll in some classes? Look for a job as a clerk? I look at Cassandra, her long, supple form, her hair in her face and her eyes half closed, her caustic imperious casualness I have now witnessed up close, and I know what I'll do, find out more about her, test how far I can go. Once I do this myself, our compact will be sealed, there will be no return. I pick up the needle that still holds faint traces of Cassandra's blood.

Then everything becomes peripheral. In bed Gary ruffles the sheet for his bottle. He pulls on his pants. I see the blur of him par-ing dead skin from his palm with the knife. Cassandra draws up her legs on the mustard-lime chair, nonchalant. She leans back, making room for me to sit down.

I'm drawing up water and squirting the pink on the rug. I fight a panic at finally handling the outfit, the curve of the black-bottomed spoon, completing the ritual of water and cotton and fire. Every move counts, sure as the struck-sulphur smell of the match. Each gesture must carry me through to the last.

The arm on the table is pale as a girl's and I realize it's mine. Cassandra hands me my striped bathrobe's belt and I cinch it tight, touch the muscle-dulled tip of the spike to the sore that's been opened up twice. I'm really going to do this, I think, then the needle is in. Inside it's gut-pulling, queasy. Gary is standing above me.

"Go slow and easy. Don't jerk it around," he instructs.

The mainline surrenders. The dropper fills up and I'm frightened and proud.

"Boot it. Let go the tie," Gary says hard and fast. Then I'm done.

"Not a virgin at last," Cassandra remarks. Gary says something I can't make out. I'm closing my eyes.

He says, "Jesus, don't nod, walk around."

I make myself go to the window, finger the hem of the still summer curtain, and pull it apart. Out there is a sky that's not blue but the very idea of that color, a brochure of sun and the travelogue crowns of the palms.

Five

The day is a stalled possibility. The idled light on the wall turns an amber shellac. Every singular thing appears incorporeal, apart from itself. The unvarnished blond plank of cinder block table is dusted with cigarette ash. The half-full glass of outfit-flushed polio water's congealed to a nicotine paste. Gary is pouring hydrogen peroxide into a wound on his palm. He said he got it in a knife fight but Cassandra coughed her harsh laugh. "It's a cigarette burn from a nod," she'd replied. We watch it froth.

We're inside that restless yet lethargic float when even the leftover fade of the sun is too much for our dope-weakened eyes. This is the time when everything dies and the smeared sky outside is a pink premonition of night.

For two days we've taken our turns on the bed, floor, and couch. Tomorrow we'll run out of cash. I've stabbed the tender skin of my arm seven times. Gary has once again said it's official, I now have a habit. I deny it. I could quit anytime, get a job, move away. I tell myself I'm only playing at this for experience sake, and I almost believe it.

For no recalled reason the kitchenette chairs have been tipped on their sides. Apparently this is the daily routine, a mere constant lying around. Gary says we'll buy an ounce, corner the local market, he'll one day assemble a harem. He'll drive a black Lincoln. He changes his mind, I can drive while he sits in the back.

Cassandra has no such illusions. We'll stay on this run until there's a bust, Gary goes to County, herself to Sybil Brand. Or maybe we'll OD, she adds. Her calm voice is frightening. It has a veracity that can't be disputed, but with the next shot, it will be forgotten.

She's painted her nails dime store fuchsia and shaken them dry. Smoking and squinting, she leans on the jamb of the closet. She's tried on and discarded each piece of our clothes at least twice. She pauses in Gary's blue work pants and wide-collared brown Antron double-knit shirt that she leaves unbuttoned.

"This room's too small," she accuses no one in particular. "There's nothing to do. We have to go out."

Standing takes a great effort. To get to the door we have to step over the pants, miscellaneous skirts, shoes, Cassandra has thrown on the carpet.

We engage the hallway's peacock wallpaper, its creepy constant dark. The fire escape window seems to be leaking a citrine piss. We're breathing hard as I pull the door closed. We don't take the wire-cage lift without lights. Its double grates have to be shuttered, its first-floor toggle has to be fumbled in darkness. We don't dare pause in the vault at the foot of the busted-rung stairs or we'd have to turn back to the cocooning safety of the room. It feels as if we've always lived in its womb, its dank smell, blue light.

But we are released to the street. The curb is dusted with small green explosions of glass. The late afternoon drag of a boardwalk is blowing with scraps. There are evenly spaced pagodas, a line of ubiquitous palms, along islands of sand and dry grass. A handful of leftover hippies in tie-dye and paisley strum beat-up guitars. Gary watches them with distaste. I turn and our building looks swollen from swallowing all-day-long sun. Its bricks are apple cream white.

The girl on the bench where I first met Gary is swinging her legs, aimlessly swatting at flies. She smooths the pleats of her blown-under glen plaid Catholic-school skirt as if nobody scares her. We watch a dog pull its withered hind legs in a hand-fashioned cart. She opens her mouth like nothing's surprised her until now.

Gary places a hand on my shoulder. He says, "She's got runaway written on her."

Perched on the top slat she shivers as Gary sits down. She tries to ignore him, looks left and right as if someone important's about to walk by. She spreads a hand on her heart, where her breathing appears to be trapped. I see how her wrists are too narrow for handcuffs, the width of a junior corsage. I can't turn away as Cassandra just stands there and smiles.

"What's your name?" Gary asks with a voice like a horn and molasses washed down with one-dollar twenty-cent screwtop green wine. His plans for this girl have to do with what went on behind the red door of the Mexican apartments.

I ought to warn her, but she says, "Maria," flipping her bangs from her eyes. The girl is so young. I have a presentiment there'll be one more in the room before long, that I'll aquiesce to this, though I know I should not.

Cassandra looks out toward the bulldozed ridge by the shore. The sand has been shifted. A man-made dune runs to the south. She sniffs the brine of the ocean that smells like it's having its bad time of month.

She cups her mouth to my ear like we're kids on a recess school yard. "This girl's going to follow my lead. We won't bother to save her. She won't remember a thing anyhow." I hate that I know what she's talking about.

Gary's hand brushes Maria's bare neck, follows the length of her spine. "We'll help you," he tells her. "We'll take care of you."

Cassandra covers her mouth with her palm, says under her breath, "That's a lie. He'll turn her so gently she'll think it was all her idea. He'll make her believe she thought of it all on her own, that it's something she wants."

The boardwalk stirs with a scatter of bottle caps, wishes, resentments, and leftover, paper-blown sighs. It is suddenly no longer holidaylike. The day is defeated. I smell mustard and strawberry musk. Quivery clusters of murmuring gulls crowd the tideline. The sun is a low ocher bloat on the seam where the pool cue chalk sea is sewn to the deepening sky.

Cassandra looks leery. Gary is running his criminal hands through his greasy black hair. He has specific ideas on his mind. I realize Maria is only a child. For no reason I'm tasting my palm. It's bitter and salty. The phosphoric filament stutter of streetlights flare on and I long to go in. I don't do well in the dusk. It is a time of abandonment, when premonitions lead to bad acts. My fear at this hour is like tangible death and it won't be dispelled. I'm certain it involves Maria, that I'll have a large part. She looks like she only recently surrendered playing with dolls, like she should be sitting on her bedroom's bedspread listening to Bobby Sherman on a two-speed mono phonograph.

I become caught in the pause of last light and the smallest of sounds, a late-inning transistor radio static, Vin Scully, the voice of the Dodgers, a tooting wood fife, a last-minute clamor of getting in cars. There is a lingering scent of patchouli nearby.

The moment is holding vague dread in the yellowing panes of our building. I shiver and turn from a fluorine breeze that stirs in Maria's dark hair and her loose, shoulder-slipped blouse. Gary settles a hand on her thigh. Her throat's so engorged that any last notion of leaving is mute in her mouth. She's certainly, finally arrived.

"How old are you?" Gary asks.

"I'm thirteen," she artlessly lies.

"I've seen this before. We'll do it just because she isn't," Cassandra decides. She spits in the shit-speckled scrub. I would as well but my mouth is too dry. She shakes out her hair with that look like she wishes it longer. Cassandra yawns, covering the wreck of her teeth with her palm.

I can see Venus, the gloat of an almost-full moon, the North Star. Somewhere nearby on a weak-batteried transistor the news of the war sizzles out. The daylight surrenders to indigo balm that I like. Thin tendrils of fog are peeled from the faraway purpling clouds.

Cassandra looks west past the breaker while biting her nails. Gary has gathered Maria into his tendon-strung, ropy-veined long bebop arms. Cassandra and I are doing nothing but standing around.

"You need a shower?" Gary asks; then, not missing a beat, "You ever get high?"

"Just pills and pot," Maria replies. Her tone is defiant but small.

Our outlines are sharply defined in the lavender glove of the on-coming night. Our building is lit with jaundiced, rectangular eyes. It seems to be taller, more bulky, in this kind of light. I'm thinking it's time to stop fooling around. Like children, we ought to be all called inside.

We take the stairs two at once past the knife-gouged wallpaper. Gary is leading Maria. Cassandra is grasping my arm.

"Here comes a do-or-die moment," she says. "You hanging around on the sidelines? Along for the ride?"

"I'm with it and for it," I say out loud this time. It sounds like I'm trying to convince myself. Gary looks over his shoulder, his features blurred in the murk of the hall with the blank socket blown out.

"We have to hurry," he mouths.

We look like we're breaking and entering a room that's not ours. Cassandra turns on the bulb and its blue dislocation's intact. She and I take the bed side by side. Maria and Gary ambush the couch. He shakes a bindle of dope that he's hid in his sock all this time, lifts the rig, pulls off its orange protective cap.

"You know what this is about?" Gary asks.

Maria leans forward. "One of my fathers used one every morning and night," she replies. This gets our attention.

Suspicious, Cassandra is propping her chin on her fists. "Which one was that?" She's lighting Luckys, passing them around.

Maria holds her cigarette between index finger and thumb. She looks like she's taking her first-ever drag.

Gary says, "Pull the smoke deep in your lungs."

Maria coughs, wipes her tear-welling eyes. "He was the next to the last. I've had five," she says matter-of-factly.

"You're making it up," Cassandra accuses.

Maria straightens the hem of her Catholic-school skirt, doesn't deign to reply.

"You ever been with a man?" Cassandra demands, changing tack.

"I've been with all five," says Maria, as if she's been rehearsing this line. We look at Maria in a new light.

Cassandra pretends nonchalance. She crosses her legs, her arms hugging the tops of her calves. She exhales smoke through her nose. "That why you ran?"

Maria appears as if somewhere a father is washing her smell from his fingers, a mother is folding up trays that ought to be stacked on a porch or inside a garage, as if it was nothing, her running away, no more than a thought come to life, acted out.

"Not this time," she simply replies. She leans and breathes in the chamomile stomach-churn odor of stuff cooking down.

Gary touches her shoulder. "We have to go into the bathroom," he tells her. "There's not enough light."

"Leave the door open," Cassandra is saying. "I want to watch."

The sudden white smear of ceramic tile is too bright. Gary sits sideways on top of the toilet-seat cover and lowers Maria onto his lap. He has to rest his weak chin on her hollow of shoulder and circle her arms with his own to draw up the scag. He tightens the sash of my robe.

Already I'm getting used to anticipating the dope, my body expects it. What's happening to me? Watching Maria becoming corrupted does not cause revulsion, as it would have last week, as it should. I'm curious to see it unfold. Her blood in the dropper leaves me dispassionate, cold. I only want Gary to hurry so I can have my turn. My stomach is hollow and churning, awaiting the high. I come to an understanding of what it means to be hooked.

Maria looks up. "Is it going to hurt?"

"Not this time," Cassandra repeats.

She catches her breath as Maria is stuck by Gary's steadiest hand. He punctures the crook of her elbow. He registers twice. Cassandra and I are rapt as he pushes the plunger. Just like a careful new lover he pulls out the spike. Maria stands by the sink and throws up,

wipes her lips with her palm. Her face is fit for singing, an oval surprise. She studies her gaze in the mirror, looks full of herself, as if beatified. As it began for me, so for Maria it starts.

"It feels good if you scratch," Gary says.

Then we're in thrall with the spoon, the flame, our scars in their
various stages. After the rote blood routine we all cram on the bed. I
feel no qualm about this, about what we've done. There's nothing
right now but the high, no past or future, no consequence or respon-
sibility for our acts. Inside the halt of the evening I'm changing right
now and it's nothing sublime.

Six

In the blue room Cassandra has come to the bed and she's sleeping beside me. I turn, run an afterthought palm down the small of her back. Maria and Gary are tight on the couch. The cerulean bulb still burns on. Outside is a dislocation of sky and a scatter of guttering stars, the ocean's dull thud and incessant shirr of occasional cars. There's only the four of us breathing, sometimes a moaning or cough. The rush is over, the heroin waning but steady, a humming refrain in the blood.

I have been thinking Cassandra reminds me of someone, not her expression or gestures so much as the wanton, nonchalant way that she's chosen to live. I realize it is my mother Cassandra calls up. All of a sudden, the loss of my mother is exceedingly, achingly present and real. The vision of her I like to rehash makes a sweet hollow hurt in my chest that I crave. It's one of my favorite pastimes. It is necessary for me to recall her, I need it as much as the dope, because without a past we are doomed. This is something she'd reiterate.

Memory is the aggrandizement of events, personal history remade, an interpretation of actual facts, my mother once said. Even the present will bend to the will of the mind late at night. What's tawdry and sordid is romanticized out of proportion. This affords a distance for not seeing plain truth, she proposed. It lets you gloss over whatever you want. The trick is imagining yourself as a character once removed. "It takes practice, it's hard," she claimed. Remembrance involves both cunning and rehearsal, you have to be willing to take liberties, to suspend disbelief. It must be culled every night from the edges of sleep. The trick is achieving a balance, coherence. Otherwise you have random events without mythology. The distortions, inventions, inherent in recollection don't matter, just that the essence of what once was should remain. This is the only way it makes sense and how it has to be. This is what my mother taught me.

Now I see how she was right. If you succeed you can do anything, drink bourbon while Cassandra's low cries are loosed from behind a red door, be content with observing the texture of light as Maria gets shot full of dope. Like Cassandra's tale, the past can become a balm or a bedtime story. It is the salve of warm sweetened milk before the last light is put out for the night.

I remember an eight-millimeter home movie I watched in my brownstone walk-up one subway stop from the Common. A webbing of light from inside the projector was smearing my brow. The sprocket caught, a flaring of orange flames stuttered the wall. Then there was the luminous black and white face of my mother. "The only correct tint for Europe," she'd said once of those monochrome hues. She lifted her arms and waved from a snow-dusted, wide cobblestone boulevard. Behind her an electric trolley's guide wires were sparking the overhead lines.

Hanna's eyes flirted southwest of the lens to where I stood beside her. She ran both her hands through her peroxide hair and bent over to button the jacket I wore with the fake-fur seal collar. I caught myself playing to the camera as Hanna adjusted my silly Tyrolean hat.

In that paper and book two-flights-up room I watched the amateur cameraman pan to a one-stroke, twelve-horsepower bike. He lingered along the chipped curve of each fender, circling the front and rear hubs until I knew where his sympathies lay.

It wasn't my father in love with the slush-covered scooter. He was already dead by that time, the man Hanna said she had met on a headlong-west Budapest train hurled toward Lake Balaton.

Hanna had told me she met him on summer vacation. Where she was headed men rolled up their sleeves, younger men removed their shirts altogether. On raw, sunburned patches of grass they gathered for Tokay wine, bloodwurst, pinochle, and soccer. They'd toast fatback and bacon strips skewered on tip-whittled sticks over slow, open fires, catching the drip of the lard on flat caraway slices of rye. Someone would play a guitar, ocarina. All the old songs from the war would be sung too drunkenly one more time.

But Hanna was caught by the insistent steam hissing under the lurch of the side-to-side carriage, the unceasing cadence of ratcheting wheels on the track. She must have told me the man in the opposite seat didn't take off his wide-collared, off-season, gray-speckled coat. It was warm in July in that car. He drew it closer.

If she didn't mention the rest, then where did it come from? I believe now I could have pieced it together from Hanna's demeanor, the essentialness of her, or from mere fantasy. The tale was implied in her gestures, curls from her cigarette smoke, and sighs between the lines.

It was too lush outside of that train, almost rank, the air choked with verbena and sage. Too many thickets and orchards streaked by with their willows and alders and birches and lanterns of hives hanging low in their crowns.

My mother had to turn from the window and study the ringlets of dappling light that trawled up the sides of the coach. She noted my father's nicotined fingers and breathed in his cheap local smoke. Hanna saw how his eyelids were weighed with regret. His hair was like ash. Amidst all that summer she thought he was longing for some other season long past.

At first she pretended she couldn't care less. She was only nineteen, after all, she wore her third-ever new dress.

She said, "Aren't you hot?"

He shrugged. "Do you smoke?"

His sleeve rode up as he offered his pack. Hanna was slapped by the blueing tattoo revealed on his forearm. She shuddered. It couldn't be helped. She hated those numbers, she'd seen them on others but she was too young. It wasn't her fault. They caused it themselves, she'd been told, and sometimes she even agreed.

There was something she had to decide. She must have felt similar to me as I picked up the needle. She might have believed this was her own inevitable destiny come calling. We both had to answer a summons. I think we come to these interstices because of a schematic engraved within us we don't know about until it's revealed in full bloom. The hidden internal design of our lives propels our arrival. We are impelled toward squaring the circle, setting in motion the decisive action. She'd had hers, now I have mine.

For Hanna the option ran out for admiring a tan, for a game with a ball by the shore with a boy. She marked time with the coda of rails and cross ties through Kápolnásnyék, Várpalota, and the rest of the towns. She traced her thumbs on initials of lovers rubbed smooth by successions of hands on the glass. Droplets of light converged on her face like a welter of tears.

Hanna lifted her eyes to the delicate pouches under my father's, their color and crinkly texture a salmon's dull white underside. She leaned back in the seat and stared at a wedge of raw sun that pierced the whole length of the car. He became blurred in her vision, the six on his arm became zero, the eights turned to threes and dissolved. Their contrary, parallel histories shimmered between them and inside her new yellow outfit she burned.

Hanna was sure if she touched him the train wouldn't stop, he wouldn't get off, so she willed it. She uncrossed her legs. She stood and he stood up, too. She placed a hand on his chest. He smelled like stale, blunt nonfilters and West German gin. He stirred her hair she'd dyed blond for something entirely different or perhaps exactly for this. She ran her fingers all over his face, traced its creases. She caressed his knuckles, first felt his tongue on her teeth.

"A secret is hidden not once but each day. I won't tell you what happened," he told her, and Hanna was grateful. She unclipped her ivory barrette, loosened her hair plied with sun as the train picked up speed.

She figured out not to speak, even whisper, to never reveal all that she could not understand. In turn, he wouldn't mention his grip on a shovel, how hectares of bones that he buried again and again kept breaking the soil, split, bleached femurs and thighs snapped and pushing themselves through the loam. That was the bargain they sealed with their lips and their hands, at first hesitant, furtive, and anxious, then gradually becalmed.

Memory is illumination, Hanna once told me. The past is the proof of our presence. I have taken this axiom to heart, nurture it shamelessly. She said he was her proof, that she'd remember his saltpeter hair every day if she could, the man in the peppercorn greatcoat the color of pigeons and soot.

He taught her to brew chamomile tea as he liked it, to never hum Schumann or anything German. In turn she recited the poem that went *death is the mother of beauty*. He didn't believe it. How could he? Hanna said she'd always be mining that place where the difference between what is and what might have been was revealed. When it comes to my mother, I do the same thing.

In his room with the curtains all drawn, in the part of the city most bombed in the war, her tongue traced his brand of blue circles and lines until the numbers were grafted inside her and wouldn't come out.

She got used to removing her clothes with a casual languor in all kinds of light, carefully draping her pale underwear on the back of the single wood chair. At first she was cautious approaching his narrow wood cot. Eventually she learned bold. Her voice became hoarse with his smoke and his name and his belly on hers. Are you sad, do you love me, when will you be leaving were obvious questions she didn't dare ask.

That man couldn't take too much pleasure. Hanna was certain she was his final allowance and gesture. He barely permitted himself the luxury of her yellow hair in his grasp. He denied her full-throated brazen insistence, the sight of the part of her thighs from behind, her black market nylon-clad back-clasping legs, her slight smell of fresh marzipan.

He must have known what would eventually happen. He understood history, had it seared on his skin with a brand. It would be a morning much like the others, its surfeit of gray and its oatmeal birds speckled with sulfur, but he would realize a piece of sky come apart. It would be too large to contain him at last. The clouds would be crowded with faces he'd try not to conjure but this couldn't be done. They wouldn't be stopped. He wouldn't know how to hold them all back. They'd tell him his story had ended with them, on a plank near the chimneys that never flamed out.

He'd recall the pills in the sock in the drawer. After my mother would finally leave him he'd put on his favorite white shirt with the overstarched collar. He'd sit at the table and wash down each pill with a swallow of smuggled-in gin and tepid tap water. Maybe he'd lie fully dressed on the bed in his shoes, now it wouldn't matter. He might think about leaving a note but not nearly enough could be told. Though he loathed God with his face always turned he would offer a just-in-case, last-minute prayer.

Then he'd be not in the room but a barracks with slats and never-extinguished weak bulbs. Everyone would whisper Hanna. He'd rise from his pallet and walk undetained to the wire, spread both his arms, cross the fence, and step forward to meet her. He wouldn't be able to see her. Nevertheless he'd know she was wearing her dress, bright like the light in the coach of that train in the immodest, indolent blush of that summer.

In the film it was snowing an afterlife white, I remember. Hanna was lifting her hands to the overcast sky as if waiting forever.

S e v e n

Something wakes me. It feels like the worst of the night, the dead haul of three A.M. dragged toward the warning of five. We're under the blue bulb that's never turned off because Gary's afraid of the dark. I watch him sleep in the space where he's slipped between table and couch. Maria lies on its cushions, her hand in her mouth. Except for the icebox's drone, the dull metered porcelain drip of the tap, the pungent, sharp crack of the surf, and the occasional gargle of car on Speedway, there isn't a sound.

Cassandra's in the bed beside me, her unbuttoned tousle of blouse untucked from her tiny hot pants. She reveals a belly flat as a runaround boy's. I like the idea of her here in the bed for the night as if I was a man and she's mine, how lying down she's not taller than me anymore. I put my face in her hair that's astringent with shampoo and vomit, ten-dollar sex, Silver Satin. Her cracked lips are freckled with specks of tobacco and flaked skin like lemon-lime rinds. Even asleep she looks so much older, defined. I think she has to be earned, not found or found out. That will be my goal, I decide.

The air in the room is a redolent sickly sweet breath of crude oil. Flushed hot from the ground, it's forced through the pipe of the derrick outside to our south. Cassandra wakes up. She appears fitful, like unwanted memory has stirred her and opened her eyes.

"You like to see me in danger," she starts. "That's how you are."

She leans on an elbow and touches my mouth. "It's all right. With you I've got nothing to hide."

She has cut to the quick of the matter between us. It comes as a shock that Cassandra is right. I get a sad pleasure from seeing her troubled and she favors showing her scars like a badge.

"You're a watcher," she says. "You want to see things unfold, to be shown." Cassandra sits up, lights a Tareyton filter. "It gives you a thrill, but this can't be done. It's not fair to the person observed."

I light my own smoke. "I'm only trying to learn."

"It's all right with me if you want to be in my thrall, but get too close, get involved, you'll get burned." She studies my face. "But you long for that fire."

What she says makes me shiver.

"What were you thinking before," asks Cassandra, "when you were pretending to sleep?"

"About all this. About you. And my mother. I feel like a strange courtship's begun."

"That's all a bad sign." She pauses to search for the bottle of wine that she'd earlier set on the floor. "You want to grow up and you want me to teach you. Here's the first lesson," she says. "I'm going to reveal everything, but you won't believe any of it or you'll get it all wrong."

"I'll try to," I say, "but you undercut what you tell."

"Don't second-guess me. Stop trying to figure me out. If you get into that game, you can't win." In Cassandra's forthright demeanor, the resemblance to Hanna is plain.

"I'm not sure I can help it." We're shoulder to shoulder, passing the bottle and wiping our lips.

"I'm trying to help you, give you some tips about how to survive. It'll come down to that."

"Why bother? What do you care what happens to me?"

"If I knew that . . . " Her voice trails off into silence. "Maybe it's about how I want to be viewed," Cassandra says after a while. "It's like this," she continues. "I'm an exhibitionist and you like to watch. And I have a need for control."

"But you have Gary."

Cassandra lets out a small laugh that is more of a grunt. "No one has Gary. You notice he sells me?"

"He told me you like to be sold."

Cassandra sighs. "How much is a matter of choice? That's a big question, you know. You'll have to answer it before all this is over."

"I can't think about that."

"No," she agrees, "it's too soon." Cassandra leans forward and covers her eyes, then removes her rings one by one. "You're not sleepy now," she says, and it's true. "We have nothing but time, so I'll tell you why I'm a whore. I'm sure you'd like to hear about that. There are psychological theories about it and I fit the profile."

She proffers her now-ringless fingers. "Smell my hands, they remind me of childhood," she whispers. Her sudden new voice is phlegmy and cracked.

"Whatever it is, you don't have to tell it," I answer.

"I must, and you're dying for me to begin. You're so distracted, your cigarette's going to burn your fingers."

It's true I crave the whole dirty secret. I toss the butt in the glass of water by the bed.

Cassandra turns slightly sideways and scrapes at the wall like it's some sort of intimate map only she can decipher. Its fissures are a clueless cracked landscape, a trick of the dark.

"I was wearing my small yellow jumper," she says much too calmly. Outside, the chaff-colored morning back then was glazing the sky.

She says it was already hot. It was that kind of summer, like now. She sat on the edge of a little girl's bed in a house with a yard. She stared out the window into the daylight's unbearable bright. She heard boots hit the floor in the room on the opposite side. Cassandra followed the sound of a hacking dry cough, the limp down the hall of her uncle's slow step-and-stop drag.

"I looked at the clock. It was nine," she mentions, like it was a usual day without wind or intent and not an incongruous season at all. The sprinklers arched over the burn of the hedge. It was no more or less of a day than the *zee* of the gnats, the Dopplering drone of a plane overhead, and the regular buzz of the bluebottle flies.

Our skin is too close in this guilty blue light. On her face is a large apprehension she knows all about. When she moves closer I flinch from her touch, unsure why. She wraps her leg on my waist, rakes her teeth on my brow. I taste the char stumps in her mouth that ought to be coated with camphor and tincture. I place my hand on her breast through her blouse.

It's when she pushes me off and abandons her last-ditch embrace, when she says her uncle called her, that I see she's never been so afraid. Cassandra is once again mired in that all-around yard as a child and can't will herself back.

Outside she was swamped by the ringlets of light from shade trees that stippled the ground. He kept up the calling her over, at first almost tender, then feigning a calm, finally pleading and petulant, mad. She took a step, then another. There were other small houses nearby but no one came out.

She suddenly noticed her uncle was gutting the rabbit they'd bought, like it was supposed to just happen, as if it was of no consequence. Cassandra thought it was a pet. He sat on an upended milk crate, wiping the gore from his hand on his shirt. He repeated, "Cassandra." She was enticed with the sound of her name and that violent smell.

To save her own self she recited, "American Beauty, Damascus, Maiden's Blush, Henry Navard." She beseeched the grace of those roses that her mother, Daisy, had planted in scatters of coolant and lube on the thistle-strewn car-part-flung lot.

The air was a tinder all set to ignite. There was a gamy aroma of blood like a thick humid rust. She thought about running or screaming and willed herself absent but knew she was not. Everything crowded itself in her mind, turgid, enormous, amorphous, and bad. She had to get closer to figure it out.

Like dishcloths left under the drip of the sink he seemed ripe and sour. There was his plug-of-tobacco-chaw breath, his clench on her jumper, his blunt, bloodied fingers undoing his pants and her front-to-back snaps. Her uncle was recklessly tearing her Babar the Elephant panties with his warm rank rabbit-dipped hands.

She says there was this: He lifted her onto his lap by her waist so she had to face him. She raised her palm to her mouth because she might throw up. Cassandra looked past the fence at the break of tall trees where she could have run earlier. She took in the yard as it changed with her hand in his lap she knew nothing about.

Sweat dropped from his brow to his chin and clung on his lip before falling. He was large on the place Daisy had warned her not to show or touch. He squeezed her too hard to cry out. It couldn't go on but it did. Nothing would help her. Not "It's time for school, Daisy's back, there's my doll." She couldn't fit a shape to the thing he was doing inside of her legs. He pulled back and she saw the red swell he had grown from his thighs. It barked a quick butter all over her jumper, hair, hands. Then it was done. He shuddered, pushed her from his lap. Dirt stuck to her palms when she fell. She rose to her feet and stood very still.

Cassandra heard the three-note screech of her swing, its links ribboned with buttercups, tendrils of vines. She noticed the mop that she'd waltzed by the purposeless pole that anchored the hull of the yard. She saw where the wood with the maggots was stacked, the crushed coolers, the bent picnic table where you couldn't eat, legless and listing too far to one side.

She studied the limbs of the largest of elms, its rough russet treehouse ropes trawling the ground. It crossed her mind how her uncle had built it last fall as if she was a boy who would climb, and she had. She wouldn't allow herself this kind of thought, that he waved, that he might have been proud and she might have been glad. Then, so she'd remember it all, just to be sure where everything was, Cassandra once more looked around.

"Now you know, you're the first one I've told." She's trembling and wiping the back of her hand on my shirt, on the sheet, on the wall. I recall she's done this before.

I'm guiltily glad to have been the witness for something no one else has been told. Cassandra registers this, though I try not to show it. It is the repugnant relief after masturbation. By having confided, Cassandra has made me a party to her defilement, as she has intended.

"It feels like a sin to have listened," I say. It is how she draws me closer, until I won't be able to separate my world from hers.

"That's right," she replies. "Now you're also stained."

I dare touch the tops of her cold narrow thighs. She moves my hand to the cloth of her blouse, underneath, leads my palm where she's wet through her shorts from behind. I know she can tell I'm afraid but I also want everything now. She raises herself on all fours as I lie on my back. She pulls her shorts wider and lowers herself with deliberate calm. She's purposely willing a change on her face until I wouldn't know if she lied.

"The absence of love makes me clumsy and sad," she remarks. "I'm your own little girl and I want you inside."

She pushes down on my shoulder, her mouth forms an *ah* of what might be an unguarded pleasure, she lets go a mere exhalation that's not quite a sigh. She says, "Pull my hair. It's good if it hurts. It makes me believe I'm worth it. Pull harder."

I'm not sure I can or want to but make myself do it until from her throat comes a painful refrain of my name, her head tilted back, face parsed and smiling through tears in a sliver of golden streetlight. Her brooding sloe-eyed gaze seems to be staring past mine into her childhood's yard. I watch her as I come undone, and she watches me, too. There is a dispassion about her that dares me to stare, says it doesn't matter. Carelessly, she wipes me clean with the sheet. Her eyes search the room for her cigarettes, lighter. "College," she says, "we always get what we want, what we fear, which is the same as what we deserve." My mother, Hanna, could well have spoken the very same words.

Eight

I'm taken aback at the moment of waking. I'd forgotten Maria was here. Cassandra and I look out the window at the latest perfection of morning. We lean over Maria and Gary, who's joined her on the couch. They've just begun stirring. The sky's become pinked, the horizon banded with smog. Though it seems a long season, it's been only days since I moved to this room.

Her skin revealing its honey to violet bruises, Cassandra walks to the closet, poking the haphazard pile of our clothes with her toes. She slides off her shorts with one hand, steps out of each leg using nothing for balance. She holds them up like a prize and tosses them toward the table. Then she is fluffing her thinning hair with a seven-ringed hand like auditioning a walk-on bit part. Her cock-wristed pose is tragic, then comic as she leans on the frame of the door. Like Hanna, Cassandra appears dismissively unrepentant for any evening she's had, for last night. She pulls on a sheer cotton skirt daubed with cherries embossed on a faded blue field, reaches behind her to fasten the straps of a rhinestone-swept halter she says is her favorite. Each day it's another. She wedges her feet into four-inch-high heels and hobbles around for her beaded white purse. A cigarette bobs in her lips. Finally she sits on the edge of the bed to pull on her bracelets, slips her rings back on her fingers, bends down to fasten a thin ankle choker of feathers she's found.

Gary remarks, "Quite a show."

I climb back into bed and lie with my head on my arm. The sun cuts a swath on the wall and the floor. Naked, Maria has stepped to the bathroom. She's hefting Cassandra's trick dress that's the color of button-heart daisies, the wetted-down shimmer of expiring wasps. She brings its sheer cotton marigold cloth to her mouth, turning and hugging it, squeezing it into the cleft of her thighs with the heel of her palm.

Maria is raising that shivery enticement and then she's in it. She's as surprised as I for no reason except its skin-clinging brightness. There's a bruised kind of smile on her mouth and some defiled delight that smudges her uplifted eyes. She tries out a venal, dangerous smile she's already learned from Cassandra. The dress has transformed her into someone else. I can tell she's in love with its seductive tightness, its history of bought-for-cash ardor. That dress would let you call her a whore without slander, could let her play the part without qualm. It might make her not mind.

Gary is watching her, too, with a tight little grin. For approval, Maria turns around and around. I have a knot in my chest at the scene, a pained look Cassandra must notice, since she misses nothing.

Cassandra says, "Get up, College. Time for the next lesson. Remember? You ready to learn? Today we're all working the park." She points toward the kitchenette table. "There's your getover. Later, we'll really get high."

I give a weak nod in reply and get up. "Let's do it," I say in the tone of a pep talk. Cassandra and Gary just stare.

I'd rather stay but we've run through the options. The lull of the room holds an intimacy that I fear. I've always had my own place and in college I lived alone. But it isn't only the press of the others I find unsettling, it's who they are, what we've done.

Cassandra and Gary are passing a bottle of MD 40/40. They're grappling over its dregs. I suddenly want them all gone, but maybe Maria could stay. This is a strange errant thought, I don't know where it comes from, I don't know Maria at all. I'd like to mull it over but there are other more urgent priorities, my spasmy muscles, the knot in my stomach.

I go to the table and pick up the needle. The spoon is still warm, then I'm fine. A benevolent aura surrounds us. Down the hall there's a third-inning transistor radio on, a baseball highlight. Hank Aaron has beaten Babe Ruth for the overall record of hits. The *Apollo 15* has come home from the moon and splashed down. I look toward Maria, who studies the stir of the curtain, how it's turned creamy and whey, the float of the blond-dusted motes. Because of the dress Maria appears resolute.

Cassandra walks over and hands me my shoes. She looks at Maria, bends close. "Don't try to protect one more cheap prostitute." I'm amazed by the cold of her voice, the motive for her warning. Then we're all standing, performing a dance of picking up brushes, combs, cigarettes, coins.

We hurry the stairs. Outside, we stall, squinting. Cassandra and Maria whisper something that I can't decipher and look up the block toward the park.

Gary says, "Lend me your watch. I just want to borrow it."

Cassandra gives him a look like she knows he will pawn it. I slip the high-school graduation present from my wrist.

It doesn't matter. Time is irrelevant here anyway in this woozy seaside enchantment that's nothing like Boylston Street, where I lived, its bakery and tailor and Old English script on doors with their lacquer burned black. There's no Blue Danube Restaurant, where I'd eat my supper, kielbasa, red cabbage, and bull's-blood-red wine. I used to study the peasant embroideries, the pictures of overthrown monarchs, high-valley plains in gilt frames. I'd let myself think about Hanna, of how it would be if she was there. She was my secret companion. I pretended to show her whatever I saw. I won't do this now, I could not, I'm ashamed.

Then it was easy. There were hand-painted plates and clusters of rust-plastic Tokay grapes on the walls, like we'd had on ours in the Budapest apartment. I'd sit with my arms propped on tablecloths

etched in red stitching and savor the violin music. The vague sentimental regret that it culled still remains. Now there is also the
heroin high that obliterates hours with its chemical refrain.

If I were in Boston on a day like this I'd be reading or pacing and
smoking and waiting for nothing. If this was last summer I would
have been going to work, past the model train window display. I
would have checked out the fit of my shirt in the glass. Later I'd sit
in a theater longing for something that's now come to pass. There's
no room for that fashion of moodiness here, only the present, its
slim alternatives, scoring or scratching, our lowered lids slowly opening, closing.

Here runnels of greasy gray clouds are streaked on the blown-
apart blank of the sky. On the lawn surrounding the nearest pagoda
it looks like a pillow exploded white feathers all over the grass in the
night. There are only the smallest of sounds, a bicycle ticking, a low
wooden gate being latched, the *whee* of the black-speckled birds on
the telephone lines. A red and green tattersall kite has been trapped.
A pair of blue high-top sneakers hang by their laces beside it.

"A local tradition," Cassandra muses.

Oceanview is littered with miscellaneous papers. Pigeons peck
imagined crumbs. The raw bricked apartments echo our clip-tap advance. Gary's in front with Maria. I'm following behind Cassandra,
watching her hips barely shift. She appears pleased with herself, casually swinging her bag by her side, paste rings on each finger, her hair
unbrushed, zipper not all the way up in the back. I run to catch up.

Some of the buildings are sturdy red brick, but others are ply-
wood and look on the edge of collapse. The windows are draped
with mandalas and flags, crocheted hanging decorations that flap.
There are bird feeders and beads hanging down, the crumbling
arches of a bathhouse, a cracked door with a palm reader's sign.
Graffitied facades, occasional tie-dyed-sheet curtains, pole-stapled
rock concert posters suggest a fair always pulling up stakes that will
never leave town.

Draping an arm on her shoulder, Gary straightens the straps of
the trick dress Maria is trying to wear with aplomb. She's nodding

her head as he talks, her small hands crossed over her heart, a gesture I notice she has that I like very much. She's flanked by Cassandra, who tells her, "Don't do anything I wouldn't do." Cassandra
then has a bout with a laugh that's too harsh, raises her hands with
her bracelets' accompaniment to cover her black-toothed-grin
mouth. Maria holds on to the sleeve of Gary's T-shirt that says LIVE
FREE OR DIE.

We're unprotected and blinking, not good in this heat and light.
I fleetingly think of my street with its bookstores and tall brownstone bowers, its orderly trees, its Colonial tones and ten-steps-
down-from-the-sidewalk martini-tight bars. I convince myself how I
hated it there in that wintry, pacified town. This is nothing like that.

We're not holding hands but I'm thinking we should, for protection at least. Already the air is blinding, sharp, fervid, a high sun reflected in windows we pass. Cassandra is casual, Maria figuring a
regular gait to her arms. Gary pretends to be playing the horn, head
bent, fingers curled. I touch the damp back of my neck.

We've come to the one-square-block hummock of grass known
by turn as Oceanview Park, Dogshit Park, Hooker Park. Gary turns.
He says to me, "You see a cop, you say, 'Man on the line.'" Already
Cassandra is vividly waving at cars that make five-mile-an-hour left
turns and come back. Men lean out the driver-side windows. She
breaks for the bus-dusted corner. They know who we are.

Gary is holding Maria's bare arm. "Keep your eyes on that piece
of street trash and do what she does," he instructs. Then, disingenuous, he changes expression. His voice becomes sly. He tips her chin
with fingers thick, split-skinned, and blunt. "Do it for me, just this
once." He rakes his hands through his hair. "I'm going to the Post
for some wine. When I get back you'll be inside a car, am I right?"
He doesn't wait for Maria's reply.

I watch her. I mimic her lips as she counts the thirteen trees here
one by one. She looks like she's willed herself absent without camou-
flage. She's smoothing the dress that Cassandra told me has swept
past Las Cruces, southwest through Alamagordo, Nagadoches,
towns that held promise in only the lilt of their names. She's watch-

ing Cassandra, who's flaunting herself on the corner, and trying her
gestures, practicing hands on her waist and her elbows akimbo, jiggling her wrists as if she, too, wore five-and-dime charms. She appears tentative, slight, unsure if she has to be older at once. She's
touching the hem of the dress Cassandra wore in a doss house in
Sanger, a flop outside Fresno, the booth in the back of a bar.

I know what to think about this. It is wrong. But I lack a direction
of action. Now is the time I might change what will happen. I don't
rush down the hill when she flags down her first errant husband and
father. I don't yell stop or come back when a schoolroom-beige
Pinto pulls up. Maria lowers her hands to her side and raises a question mark face for advice I don't have. There is a wavering plea in
her eyes that is also resigned. This is no game, we both realize. I
watch as she weaves to the curb with a tremble of uncertain calves
as if shoved from behind. Maria leans in the window, then goes
around, opens the passenger door, climbs inside. My weakness will
extract its price.

I lower myself to my knees, rock back on my heels in the dry
burned-up grass. Where does culpability start? I'm not responsible for
Maria. Events simply unfold. I tell myself it is Gary's and Cassandra's
fault. I recall Maria's look when she put on the dress, like she could
hardly wait for all this to begin. Why did Cassandra think I would try
to protect her? From what, her own self? I think about Hanna, how
she'd go away after dark, but I never saw money change hands. Don't
dwell on it, there will be a next fix, is my mantra. I watch the blueing
exhaust of the car dissolve to a shade paler than sky.

I can't get my mind to shut up. Maybe right now Maria is thinking
the john reminds her of one of five fathers, the man in a pair of
plaid slacks and a lime crewneck sweater, his hair greased with pomade, cheeks after shave slapped. She might be eyeing the broken
door handle, the unraveling fake-leather steering wheel cover. They
must park in the Supersuds Laundromat alley. That's where everyone goes, I've been told. She may be smelling the breath of his nervous Kamchatka half-pint, moist vented Clorox and Oxydol soap.

Last I saw where she's gone the lot blew with scraps. I noted a hub-cap bowled on its side, a long gray-haired woman bending and tying her Red Ball Jet high-tops, spray-painted brick that read WASH 25¢ and JOY FOSH PLEASE WRITE.

I'm thinking Maria has no purse, the trick dress no pockets. She must be squeezing limp bills as he tips his seat all the way back. She'd have to turn from the flushed bloated pink of his alcohol eyes. He might be touching her breast through the fabric. Maria uses her left hand for balance when she takes him out, gentles his skin up and down.

I cannot know any of this, I can only imagine. It is like playing at recalling Hanna. The characters move on the scrim of my thoughts. Hanna would say that memories have their own stories to tell, validate what is random, give context to chaos, a shape to disorder. Dramatization is also an objectification of both the present and the past. It is giving form to desire. To imagine the worst is to prepare for its happenstance.

The man's hands are surely in Maria's hair as he pulls her head into his lap. She can't help inhaling the yellowing sheen of his bleached, graying shorts. There's not enough room in her mouth for both him and her tongue and she gags but she figures it out. He reaches under her goldflake and buttercup shift and she has to bite down hard enough, not too hard.

I hope she's a girl who's good at removing herself, who can hide for a very long time. Maria might call into memory the first man she chose not a father, if there has been one. There might have been a blue van, a shirtless blond boy whose tattoos and intentions she could decipher. In an X-ray grain parking lot light she might have believed if she slipped the Econoline latch her whole life could start.

Led Zeppelin should have been playing too loud, the van filled with the odor of ten-dollar Mexican grass, shirts and pants for a bed on the floor in the back. She'd lick the side of his neck, taste his pulse, run her hand all the way down.

She could be recalling the glow of the cast-iron lamps from outside in the halogen night, that she was frightened and happy to take

off her clothes, to lie on her side and learn how to make him breathe
fast. She must have thought she knew everything then when he was
inside her at last, as they moved on each other first awkward, soon
right, then too fast, as she pulled him out just in time and he
smeared his relief on her belly and thighs.

Then she could sleep, dream his CYA knuckles, Wayside Correc-
tional shoulder with dagger, the juvenile lockup blue puncture of
Christ with his thorns on his arm. They might have offered the
quiet required for hiding and soothed her at last.

That boy might have made up her mind about running away. I
see her folding a twenty three times. She could have counted down
from seven and started walking. She took a step, then another. It
wasn't so hard. I think when she ran, she followed the vines to the
end of a driveway that spilled to a nothing of road one car wide. The
whole day was heavy and sweet with her leaving. It made her think
of baked clay. The thistle and palmetto tarmac burned her bare soles
but she couldn't care less once she knew she was actually on her way.
She might have turned on her heels and the house was an absence
at last. There was only the slight downward curve of the road and a
whistle of air as she walked with no underwear on. Maria glanced
back for a truck or a car. No one was up but the chickens, and dogs
chained to stakes in the clutter of yards used as auto repair shops
and graveyards for disemboweled washers and dryers.

The Catholic-school skirt that she rolled at the waist to make it
look shorter surrendered to billows of wind. The air itself sighed
thick with promise, imbued with her fleeing. The tips of her fingers
were tingling. She found a stride that suited her. Each step became
surer. She was no longer thinking it over. There were two miles of
heat marrying dust until regular houses and sidewalks were found.
She might have turned left and left again from a low break of trees
until finally she reached the fastidious grass, the fizzing of sprinklers,
each house the same style, set back from the street the same number of yards. She might have wondered if stay-at-home fathers were
watching her pass.

There would have been traffic at last, an orange and black fume exhaustion against a pale sky. She didn't mind the pavement's glass. Maria was used to bare feet on all kinds of ground, swung her shoes by her side. She found the right bus, became lost in its roll and the murmur of Spanish around her like water on stone in a river. She touched the cool metal bar with her palms, heard the fare-box coin coda, smelled the brilliantine cream in the silver-gray hair of the driver. Maria studied his fold of pinked skin on the blue of his uniform collar. She rode for three hours, switched buses twice.

Where she got off, which was not far from here, terns were diving for scraps. Maybe she ran to the edge of the sea, took in its crashing. It was the height of the day but she unbuttoned her skirt from the back and stepped out, lifted her arms, freed herself of her blouse.

Maria looks like the kind of a girl who would have folded her clothes just so on the sand even then. Gulls rode the lukewarm eddies of wind that came off the waves and stippled the tips of her breasts. Small plovers were rushing the ebb and flow shoreline again and again.

She seems a girl who'd wade right in and it wasn't so bad, the cold whitecapped jade only tightened and prickled her flesh. The seaweed confused her. Tendrils of kelp swam between her legs. The tide going out seemed to strum her insides.

Perhaps in the Pinto Maria remembers ducking her head in the foam. She swallowed a mouthful of water. Salt froth stung her eyes, but she made for the breaker. She paddled away from the fathers, the noises they made, how one of them covered her face with his palm, how it tasted of transmission fluid, tacos, and stale cigarettes. She forgot the elbows and what fingers felt, the perilous skin and the intimate sweat in the wrack of the bed. "*Bocas de tristes muertos,*" I heard Maria saying last night in her sleep in her Catholic-school skirt. "Mouths of sad dead men," where did that come from? A poem read by one of those fathers?

This is no more than conjecture, but it cuts the taste in my mouth that is bitter. It's soothing pretending I know all about her. I curl in a fetal position, close my eyes on the lawn, and dream of a dreaming Maria, Maria who longs to remember her name but her mouth is held fast. In her sleep by the ocean Maria is climbing through earth's thick brown loam, its belly of fire, boulders the size of curled corpses, bones piercing the soft of her throat. So much soil has to be swallowed in order to breathe. Histories of sequoias press on her breasts. The ruins of mountains turn sand. Up from the bottom she comes where old bones don't stir, past weapons in clay and burned grasslands, scorched savannas, coals turned to diamonds, lands shaped with reptile and mineral schemes.

She longs for protection while rising through creepers too full of themselves in a jimson-choked stream, diaphanous, bottle-green water. She struggles up through a peat of deep sleep where crustaceans nibble pale meat with soft beaks. Maria is trembling with petals of black on her lips. She's gathering strength as she climbs through forests and feathers, past sulfur through earth to a verdancy of moss embracing the trunks of tall trees, their abundant confusions of roots. She straddles a rain-bloated log swollen with rings of deciduous sleep. Fires have burned. Pebbles of sand grace her cheek as she calls her own name because no one else will.

Lie still, say the echoes of fathers. Her chest is caked with dirt and the wings of small insects, her thighs scrape the bark. Her clothes are in shreds among flowers. Maria cries like the child that she is, compact in her tears. Finally garlands of light appear in the sky as she wakes.

Rising from my dope-induced swoon, I see a picture of Maria scanning the line of the sea where it spilled onto sand. She stood wiping grains from her dress. Maria realized she'd really escaped.

She walked under a pier to a boardwalk and sat on a bench. Soon two men and a woman approached. The woman was frowning and whispered something to the younger man. It gave her a thrill because she was sure they were talking about her. She said to herself if mistakes were about to be made, so be it. Perhaps Maria was thinking of fleeing and considered crying. Nevertheless, when the taller man touched her and asked her a question she knew she would stay.

Now behind the Supersuds lot Maria is digging her nails into the pale curled-hair flesh of the frenzied-gasp john. He sounds rabbit punched, says, "Don't stop," stiffens, comes. She jerks away too late. Her throat becomes flush with his almondy salt. His smell of ammonia mixes with whiffs of hot clothes in a red plastic hamper.

Maria straightens her dress, wipes her silvering cheek. "Take me back to the park," she requests, sees the sky become turquoise at last. Perhaps there's a patchouli van and a blue-tattooed boy on her mind.

Or maybe it's nothing like that.

Nine

It's like this the days pass in the balance of summer: On a typical Tuesday Gary and I sit in the Fairlane. The back of our building's inflamed in the afternoon sun. We pass a Four Roses bottle, just slightly drunk as we wait for the girls to come out. They're up there exchanging their graces for crumpled-up singles and thrice-folded fives. Inside the room the removal of clothes has begun.

Thick fingers must loosen the buttons. Creased Key lime pants hang on the back of the kitchenette chair in the drench of the light. Black and blood oxfords and chambray-sheathed pumps have been thrown to the ground. There's only the sound of the names they've made up for each other as heard from a stranger, the tussle of limbs, and the murmured requests that all have to be answered somehow.

Men lie on the girls like anxious confessions. I try to imagine the hair, the no hair, what fingers feel, and the quick exhalations. I see Cassandra in bed and her head off the foot of the mattress, the pale of her belly revealed, and how all but one stay of my favorite dress is undone. There must be the part of a thigh or a mouth, a bent hand, the rise and fall jog of her arm in a troll on the rug, her knee slightly crooked, and her casual legs splayed apart.

Maybe Maria is watching and trying to mimic the languorous lilt of her head. It's all she can do to hold on to the side of the bed so she won't be bucked off.

"I know what you're thinking," says Gary. "Don't think about that."

"What's all this about?" I ask him.

He gets my meaning, looks up. "They like what hurts them," he answers. "It's what they want and I just turn them out."

I wonder if this is a disingenuous statement, or if Gary is really naive enough to believe it. Even I don't. Gary is only absolving himself, I decide.

I study the grime on my hands ten and two on the wheel as I figure my part. I hear a distant accordion sough, the sea-borne breeze stirring small twisters of dust that spin like disorganized tops.

"And me? Where do I fit in?" I'm afraid to ask.

He places a palm on my shoulder. "You're the mascot, confessor. You're someone to tell," he confides. "Anyway, Cassandra likes you," he adds. "That's not necessarily good," he amends.

"What am I, Cassandra's pet?"

"You're her witness," he says.

"Is that how you see it?"

He shifts in the seat, an ambiguous smirk on the side of his mouth. I must have sounded offended.

"She's got you," he says. "I can tell by the look on your face." He is shaking his head solemnly side to side, a parody of bad feeling about having to explain this. "It's a shame," Gary says in mock earnestness. "One way or another she'll kill you. You won't even know it, you'll think it's suicide."

I shift in my seat to more closely regard him, to see if he's kidding or serious. "So how come you're protected?"

Gary displays what may be a hint of a rueful smile. "I'm immune, College. I'm already dead."

He caresses the bell of his trumpet and whistles the half-recalled notes of a long-ago cover, as if in condolence for what he's revealed.

"My father wrote that on the road in the car," Gary says. There's a slight contrite tilt to his head. "You've seen him but I haven't pointed him out. He's the guy pimping rainbows on Hampton and Seacrest, the one with the cart."

Sure, I've caught a glimpse of that man, his discarded rayon and double-knit limp on the rung of a fire escape ladder. Bisected by sunlight he paused as if caught in a bright amber aspic surprise. He gripped a cheap throwaway lighter, the cellophane crush of a pack of Old Golds, his other hand meshed in the double-turn tubes of his horn. He looked at it slyly, then down at the two-story drop.

"For him it was always 1929, Oklahoma," says Gary. I know he is purposely changing the subject. I don't really mind. "He couldn't get over he made it across." Gary flexes his fingers, testing his own trumpet stops.

When Gary was seven, he tells me, he'd long ago found all the needles and run his small hands on the knots of black scars in the crook of those ropy veined arms. Gary remembers he watched as his father dealt solo, casino, and beggar-my-neighbor, beneath his cane rocker the blond cigar box with the stash and the paraphernalia, beside him the heavy brass smoker that never went out.

Gary says in that house outside Fowler off Route 99 there was nothing to hide. He stares at a shadow of stunted palmetto that's flung on the blaze of our building's blank wall as the day lengthens out. He rubs his face with the last of his doped-open palm and swallows the dregs of our pint.

"My so-called mother made Cream of Wheat sweetened with Sue Bee honey she let me lick from the lip of the jar," Gary says as if memory slapped.

He tells me how he and the common-law wife of his father drank all-day-long pitchers of pink sugar water she carefully doled from a stainless steel ladle rinsed under a cold-water tap. He says they ate Milk Duds for supper and napped in the afternoon hall. It was cooler inside of the bottlefly buzz as they spooned in the dark on the runner of worn hardwood floor.

Gary lifted his head from her stiff jet black hair wound on flesh-colored curlers. He saw tar-hearted sunflowers tilted like drunks in the yard where the liver-red Rambler was parked. On all fours on the mange of the living room carpet his father was spreading a shot-and-chaser-stained, thumbed, split-seamed poster announcing his second-billed name in a three-junky regular combo that played its last gig in Lemoore.

"He taught me some lessons," says Gary. "Never keep outfits in pockets. Keep stuff in your sock by the quick right-hand ankle. Carry ID in your shoe."

He looks like he's hearing the syncopate snapping of his father's fingers swollen from nicks of the seasonal pickwork and piecework he found them in Tipton and Shafter, the random aluminum tap of the kitchen's screen door

As Gary leaned on an elbow, he already knew he wasn't the genuine child of the woman who lay beside him, smelling like talcum and harsh yellow soap. They never quite told him in so many words. It was something that he figured out on his own later on in the night when you had to be sure.

Outside the light became doused, no more than a sear of pinked char. They must have known he heard every word as he lay on his mat, unable to stifle the sounds from the opposite side of the wall. In fact, he craved to hear more.

No one was spared between slaps meant to redden hot cheeks and raise tears, to pick off the usual soft pliant scars. Each of their small bar late-bebop communions were hashed out in their afterglow room. Someone named Tonio Roca was blamed. Then what about Becky, Conchita? his substitute mother accused.

"The boy is the issue of that," Gary says she kept shouting. "I almost knew what she meant." He made out the slap of his father's hand.

He flattens his palm on his forehead to smooth out its chevron of creases. He says, "This is a gesture he used that she liked."

Inside the car becomes dipped in the goldenrod pollen descent of the sun. "What happened to her?" I ask Gary.

He hefts the empty Four Roses bottle and tosses it back among bell-bottom Levi's and discarded tank tops, wax paper cheesy with pickles and ketchup, a scatter of tampons. He looks at the butter-brick wall of our building like she might appear there in fifties chiffon.

"She threw herself into the flood control channel," he murmurs so quietly that I have to lean toward his mumbling mouth. "She didn't drown, though. They put her in Plano, the state hospital." He pauses and swivels to glance at the bottle. "I hardly knew her," he says, by way of dismissal. "It's you who has a mommy thing. Cassandra told me. As for myself, I like institutional care."

He looks like he's thinking fondly of jail, that place he prefers. In there was cigarette money to spend on tight pinners of scag cooked down on filched metal-shop wire. "You dribbled it into an improvised outfit of rubber and string and a whittled-fine safety pin," he recalls. Sometimes it took half an hour but that was all right. There was nothing but time to squeeze on the pacifier plunger, to let the dope drip to the open sore you had to maintain in the crook of your arm.

He learned to distill Aqua Velva through bread behind opaque cream mesh as he squatted on tile, to stay still for the length of the sentence in Reedley, Dinuba or Earlimart, Blythe. Each kitchen smelled just the same and yet different, the odor of scouring ammonia. He knew the schedules for starched prison blues, where lights out was welcome or warning, how each face-down pillow had tasted. "Some of the old cons remembered my dad," he concludes.

He flexes the lucky third stop of his horn before tonguing the gunmetal mouthpiece like once again tasting a woman. Then there's the invention of sound. It's like being touched by a hand after too long without, like pigeons released from their coops and their clay upward beating of wings a gray sky under sky. Gary now plays that the crowns of the palms are dragging southwest in a breeze and their song is an olive green solace, a pause on a B&O siding, a hay-scattered field overripe.

The girls have to hear it, this late summer afternoon haul that's like sidecars uncoupling and rolling. They may be shielding their faces from elbows and sighing when it's the right time. I look toward the room, where Maria is combing her hair and arranging a just-about-used-to-it face in the cracked bathroom mirror. Cassandra is standing and wiping the skim of her man with the hem of her sunflower outfit tucked inside her thighs from behind. They might be tugging the eyehooks of unfastened clasps, bent from the sash of the opened-out window, gleaning the blow of the horn like a shuffle of forty-eight diamond-backed Bicycle cards. I see Cassandra flouncing her curls to the sizzle of flat scrub, bald tires, a burr that's a crossing of border through Idabel, Hugo, and Hope, Oklahoma, a languid decision inscribed on a shifting white cloud. She knows this sound.

Maybe Maria is smoothing her Catholic-school skirt, the trumpet an insistent push of a wood-handled shovel inside a brown loam of just-overturned earth. Under this serenade they could be making it up to each other. Maybe Cassandra is placing her hand on Maria to make her feel safer. It calls for stalling and tasting the breath of the wind in the curtain. It exhales American cities, Sheboygan, Des Moines. It offers the sight of the buttercream calves of a girl on a sheet spread outdoors in a blue August glare, someone calling her first and last name, a slow definition of how far away is Seattle via the Southern Pacific freight train.

Gary releases the minor chord riff of a '29 fireweed plain, wide-collared shirts on a line and how they appear from a brilliantine-scented barbershop chair, a rough B-flat callus of farm-hardened hand on the face of a boy who is going away. His half-step declension declares a new span of time without time that's deleting itself as it passes. It tells us we're nearing the knell of the season. It shows us a sunset smudged midway at dusk in the fallible light of a final town fair. I'm thinking I'll recall his horn when meeting a lover somewhere in a city where we've never been, our hands on our sleeves at a sidewalk cafe in a rare summer rain.

Ten

Fall is a dangerous season and a dope disaster has happened. Gary's been busted. Last I saw he was preening and jiving outside the pagoda, soul-shaking hands, a Baggie of reds in his sock. He was selling a nickel of pills as the metros pulled up. We watched the arrest from the window, kneeling side by side on the couch.

Cassandra just sighed. She'd been practicing gazes, lowered her Kelly Girl mirror, buttoned her organdy blouse. "All bets are off," she had said, plunged her hands into the couch's deep rent, where we hide the stash.

Cassandra was right. Now there are no more scams with boys new to Venice and looking to cop. "Tomato gangsters," Gary had called them for some obscure reason. They were typically searching for downers, speed, scag. If they were looking for grass or acid, he'd pass. He'd say, "That's lightweight hippie crap." Gary could spot real drug need in a shambling gait or a furtive expression. "You're looking for me," he would say. "I'm the man. How much money you got?" Then he would take it and score, but for us. Cassandra would stay as the hostage. She'd linger along the boy's side, maybe touch his thigh.

She'd get them to tell where they were from, about mothers, girl-friends, left behind. She'd let them chain-smoke her Luckys or Tareyton filters as they paced the boardwalk, trying to look unperturbed, attempting an unperspired swagger. Cassandra calmed them with the run of her braceleted, silver-ringed hand on their arms. She had the same down-turned glance as for me the first day. I saw, because I was the decoy.

"I have to go pee something fierce," Cassandra would say after too many minutes had passed. She'd point to the public restroom behind her. "It's just over there, I'll be back."

Those boys were simplistic, naive. I didn't feel sorry for them. I wondered how they would appear if they stayed on the beach for a month.

I'd idle by, sit on the backrest of bench where Maria had sat. The tomato gangster's stare would be fixed on the concrete oat-colored restroom encamped on the spit of dry scrub.

"You're waiting for that tall, black-haired guy," I'd say to distract him.

"Am I getting ripped off?" he'd invariably ask.

I'd angle him toward our building, giving Cassandra the chance to slip off unobserved. "Nah, Gary's cool. I know where he lives, right up there, I'll go find him." Then I, too, would be gone.

I was surprised there were never any recriminations about this. We'd often run into a guy we had burned later on the street, in the course of a subsequent deal. Often as not, they'd pretend not to know us, that it never happened. Gary explained. "They're embarrassed because they were chumps." If by chance the matter came up, Gary would simply shrug, Cassandra would preen. "We've all been beat," he would say. If Gary could sense an exploitable character flaw, he might invite one up for a taste. Together they'd scheme to rip off someone else while the guy made eyes at Maria. "Leave her alone, she feeds my habit," Gary would warn. Some of the gangsters would hit on Cassandra if they were especially brave. She'd say, "I don't give it away."

But with Gary gone we've turned lazy, play hearts in bed until noon. We haunt the street corners praying to find a connection, for late inspiration, not wanting to think that we ought to be paying attention. Cassandra has taken to wearing diaphanous dresses. I've found a straw hat, Maria a nearly sheer nylon lace blouse. We've become part of the local distraction. We're hanging around with only one desperate reason. For money Cassandra is carelessly pimping Maria, trading her own body at fire sale prices. It's simple to follow the daily routine, the dashing between room and park, easy to watch the girls adjusting their skirts or tucking in blouses. I have accepted this way of commerce without reservation. We never discuss it. I think of it only late at night, in the doubting hours. During the day, the dope provides absolution.

By trial and error we worry the corners, practice dime-bag cons. This involves cutting half the dope, which is weak even further with baby laxative. We peddle the shit in tied party balloons we carry tucked against our gums. We plan ahead by increments of no more than an hour. The rent's overdue but we're not concerned. The girls don't bother removing their clothes when they sleep with the johns while I wait in the hall. They make no sound of pain or feigned pleasure. I drink Silver Satin while biting my nails. I hold a soiled kitchen knife in my lap and I try to look rough. If the men take too long I pound on the door with both fists. After they leave, if we've made twenty-three dollars we rush to go score. We share dull outfits that clog, with rubber tips on the plungers that often come loose. We crowd on the bed that lingers with sweat, after-shave and play make-believe.

"I could be a beautician, open a salon," Cassandra might say.

"Someday I'll be a nurse. I'd look good in starched whites," Maria chimes in.

Cassandra says, "College, you'll be a professor, in front of a class with a pointer, explaining something no one cares about."

"If I had my druthers I'd rather own a bookstore," I reply.

Time surrenders itself on the sex-smelling bed. Outside are the usual bongos, guitars, the autumnal strains of occasional flute. Sometimes there are cries, breaking bottles. We don't bother to get up and look. We are content with hearing the hum of our blood in our ears.

•   •   •

We are nearly lost in September. The three of us sit in the front of the Fairlane, Maria in the middle, me driving. Cassandra has urged me to sell the car but I won't. It's the last tether to the actual world.

"There's nothing to eat," Maria remarks.

"You can't be hungry, it's reflex," Cassandra replies. "There's M&M's in my purse." She lights a cigarette, coughing and watching the billows of smoke.

Maria squeezes the chocolate-filled buttons until colors come off in her fist. Cassandra is passing a bottle of blackberry brandy. She's slouched like she'll never get used to her height. Though it's not cold she's got on a too short sleeved inside-out fur. Her face appears moony, dream-bound. Biting her nails, she lets out a sigh. All the car windows are down. We're slightly drunk, cruising the glass-dusted corners of mattress-strewn alleys. We're underprepared, we're on hold. In the leftover light we look like suggestions of selves.

"Gary likes it in prison," Cassandra is saying. "He gets to play with his homies in there."

I miss him, his hand on his trumpet, holding his bottle and buttermilk carton. It's good for digestion, he claimed. He'd wash down the sour milk with wine. He'd button, unbutton his shirt, look out for that man on the line. He's already becoming larger than life in our recollections. It was Gary who offered protection and did all the talking, the shopping, dope-running. We're not good at it.

The wind's begun rising and knitting the clouds into thick-fingered gloves. They appear lusty and full of themselves in the new autumn sky. It's late afternoon when everything's stalled, compromised.

We've swapped each others' clothing. Cassandra has rolled up the cuffs of my checked chef's pants without pockets, revealing scabbed ankles, bruised calves. I've got on Gary's pimp velveteen jacket. The trim of its sleeve and its collar is fake silk and shimmers as if it were wet. Maria has fastened my plaid flannel shirt at her throat. There are small kindnesses we have bestowed on each other, a shoplifted comb, a five-and-dime cameo brooch. Despite everything, we have become a family of sorts.

"I had a Ford just like this," says Cassandra. "Saw it crushed on the way to the dump." She's in one of her lighthearted moods that is liable to instantly crash. There's a Pollyanaish air to her gestures that she has only when she's at the cusp of her high.

She says the rusted-out '61 four-door was parked by the Stardust, Experience Room, Motel 8, Friendship Arms. Her cigarette hand out the window she tells us they parked behind bars. "Betty's Pistol Dawn, The Driftwood, The Nest, Two Drops of Scotch, Limbo Lounge." Cassandra remembers Gary would nip at a pint of Four Roses while she worked inside.

She lights me a Tareyton filter and passes it over. I blow out smoke, feel adult. This is a great pleasure somehow. I try the heater to see if it works since last winter. The smell of small New England towns, Scituate, Ashland, and Weymouth, blows warm as the breath of a child. Memory induced by an odor's the strongest. It calls up the best of a reordered past where the tint of the light is just right in the flush of the fall for roaming back roads with the radio on in my paid-for car. In truth I was typically nervous back then. It was this time of year. The third year of Boston U. was ahead and I still had no major picked out. I was going to school only to escape from the house, to grow my hair long, to think about finding a girlfriend, about joining a commune perhaps, heading west. I was at odds with myself. I hadn't decided on anything yet. Now Massachusetts has become a fiction wrapped in the gauze of pollen released from the Fairlane's vents.

As we cross Deep Grotto Lane, Cassandra's recalling her and Gary's history of automobiles. The little Toyota that couldn't. The Lincoln hand-painted by roller. The no-handled, roan-colored suicide Pinto, the Buick Electra that only ran backward at last.

The sky becomes bruised with the oncoming night. We're easing the bridge over Linnie Canal. Its buttresses are pasted with handbills. A carcass of Styrofoam cooler is floating below us on algae and rainbows of oil. We pass a natter of ducks. Maria is counting our change, making small sucking sounds with her teeth and her tongue. Her expression is Catholic and calm.

Cassandra willfully slaps out the coins from her palm. "What the hell are you doing? We don't have enough. Why bother with that?" Her frivolous mood has just snapped. She turns in her seat, her lips tight, her face pinched and white. "Well? Pick them up."

Maria stares straight ahead, she's nonplussed.

I manage to say, "That's enough," surprising myself with the tone of my voice. I haven't heard this timbre before, it is sudden and harsh.

Cassandra raises her eyebrows, swats smoke from her face, quickly shrugs. "It's only a game."

Maria slumps. There's a lingering essence of baby shampoo in her hair. She bends to pick up the coins from the floorboard and Cassandra does nothing to stop her this time.

"You want to protect her?" Cassandra says over Maria's head as if she wasn't present. "Maybe you feel a tenderness for her because she's so innocent, young. Unlike me, by contrast." There is a malicious squint to her eyes. "It's not an emotion you can afford to indulge."

"There's no need to be cruel. I don't see what you're so pissed off about. I was just . . . " I reply, when Maria shouts, "Stop!" as she covers her ears with her palms. She looks at me and Cassandra, then carefully climbs over the seat to the back. "Don't fight about me," she is saying, "just pretend I'm not even here in the car."

Cassandra tugs at a shock of her own hair that's been chemically fried, brings it up to her mouth. "All right," she says, smells the brown strand she then brings to her mouth.

"Daisy would rinse it," she mentions, twirling her curls between a forefinger and thumb. She seems intent on distracting both me and herself from what's happened, pretending it didn't. Something between us is changing and she doesn't like it. She didn't think it could happen. It's made her nervous. Biting the ends of her hair she starts talking too fast.

Cassandra says she remembers the acid peroxide steel-wool-tinged aroma of Miss Clairol coloring lotion, the bent-over porcelain sink in the bathroom, the slick rubber gloves and too-cold rinse tap.

She recalls a day much like this one, a late afternoon. Daisy was sober, not swaying at some checkout counter, her cart piled up high but with money for nothing but vodka.

"I was almost your age," she twists in the seat and says to Maria. "I just got returned from the home."

I glance at Maria in the rearview mirror. She's been leaning sideways, eyes closed, but she opens them now. We're watching Cassandra revert to the self I had seen in our bed after telling the tale of the dirt-covered yard, of the Indian tent, her gaze abstracted as if willing herself until she's back in the scene. A thin spittle forms at the edge of her lips. She needs to tell it and by implication we need to hear it. She can't recollect her dumb tales without an audience present. It gives the story credence to say it out loud. It is as if she's rehearsing a set piece, polished by many tellings though she'd swear it's being revealed for the very first time.

Cassandra says she couldn't stand how much Daisy had swelled in her absence. A long cigarette in her mouth, her mother looked larger than ever, like loaded with melons. She was leafing through half-off ham offers, past-due utility bills, fliers for dry cleaning discounts, YOUR NAME HERE labels, an ad for a country charm wall clock ensemble, a government notice. She wore her going-to-market cloth coat. Slumped down on the couch, beguiled by a free-chip trip sweepstakes to Vegas, she squeezed out her feet from the rabbit head slippers she wore.

Cassandra was sick of the living room littered with cheap plastic brushes and porcelain fishes, plundered containers of Jim Dandy chicken, a warm cup of booze with the president's face, and the portraits of Jesus. A dull light was smearing the walls. The curtains were drawn. The radio pleaded for money and mercy and each door was closed.

"Daisy was making a welcome-back gesture," Cassandra recalls. "We went for a drive."

Cassandra remembers herself in the rust and cream Rambler, in back of the wagon, the seat folded down. She was wearing her taffeta dress lined with lingerie crepe. She lay on her side and rested her face on her arm, watched the pole to pole swoop of the telephone lines. She played her secret doll game in her mind.

There was an absence of clouds on the orangy sky, a green PALM-DALE 7 MILES sign. Cassandra leaned over the seat to see Daisy reach under and pull out a flask of Kamchatka. It was flat and so clear in her palm. She pried off the cap with her teeth, spit it into her fist, tipped her chin. Some of it ran down the side of her mouth.

Cassandra counted the gnats and the palmetto bugs that smeared themselves green on the windshield. As was Daisy's habit, they drove by turn too slow and too fast.

"It smelled like my mother," Cassandra recalls of the bargain bazaar where they stopped. She's lighting her next cigarette from the butt of the last. She says they sat on the swiveling stools of a Formica counter, Daisy's dress like a guernsey brown tent in the fluorescent light. Cassandra observed Daisy ogling the lidded protection of lemon meringue, the magnet-backed letters and numbers aslant on the stained menu board. A propped by the register felt pen thermometer drawing announced the results of a blood drive and how many pints it would take to save one more life. She couldn't care less.

Cassandra was drawn to the cluttering murmur behind her. She compared its subdued blue-talcum-smell clamor to lunch in the board-and-care home. She thought of the tins on the knees and the elbows, the pulled-hair conspiracy whispers, the curses they both gave and bore.

A hurried-up frosted-haired waitress heady with grease and perfume set a child's plate cheeseburger before her. She shoved it aside. Cassandra leaned over and kissed the inside of her arm as if it was a boy.

Daisy said, "Think of starvation." She flashed a bib of a dishcloth she'd brought from the kitchen for just the occasion. She wiped off her silver and tucked the rag into her collar. Cassandra was watching her chewing a rasher of bacon, layering her shudder of fried egg yolk sandwich with Miracle Whip and potato chip curls.

Cassandra was painting with Gulden's mild mustard and Worcestershire sauce on her plate with the flat of her spoon. She peeled off her sweet pickle circles and folded them into her napkin. That's what she'd save for the big-bellied, yellow-eyed magazine children with flies in their eyes who looked like they ate bugs and dirt.

Cassandra let everything sit and congeal. She knew Daisy would finish off even the wilt of the useless limp parsley. She watched her mother lick the tip of a finger and daintily dab at grains of the left-over sesame seeds.

Then Daisy leaned back and let out a satisfied gas. Cassandra looked down at the floor.

"What's wrong?" Daisy asked. "I guess you want a toy."

"I don't play anymore," Cassandra replied. If she did it would be with a too-loud snare drum, an electric guitar, a chemistry set to make poison with fingernail polish and powder. Cassandra would savor the smell of the fumes as they flushed down the drain.

But Daisy was pulling Cassandra along by her elbows past shelves lined with calamine lotion and liniment cloth, ingrown toenail tincture, salves for corns, bunions, and warts, enema bags with their dangerous tubes.

They skirted the five-and-dime bin labeled NOTIONS and made for the heap of a table with flesh-colored stretched-waistband panties, buttonless corsets, marked-down irregular bras.

Cassandra noticed how under her shift Daisy's breasts rolled like logs in a sack, how her nylons were bunched at the knees. Daisy stood under the NO SMOKING sign buried up to her forearms in Antron and rayon, a lit cigarette in her lips.

She was not really touching the pile. She thought inside it were hairless dead mammals and Cassandra said, "What are these, used?"

Daisy squinted and swatted the smoke from her face.

"For God's sake, Cassandra, they're only unwrapped," she replied through clenched teeth.

Up front in plain sight of the cracked green glass doors Daisy offered her bulky diversion for pocketing lipstick, a thin pack of razors, a pair of dice earrings, and rouge.

Inside the Rambler it smelled of old go-nowhere summer vacations near lake beds long dry. They sat side by side licking Frostee Freeze ice milk that melted all over their fingers, sticky and soaking the wafer-taste fifteen-cent cones.

Daisy handed Cassandra the bottle. "You're old enough," she insisted. "You might as well get it over with now." She started the car.

Cassandra could sense the cold whiff of the booze. Her stomach tightened. Still, she couldn't allow such a moment to pass. Brazen, she swallowed, again and some more. It burned her throat but she looked at Daisy and smiled.

"It tastes good," she insisted, wiping at tears.

Daisy was holding the wheel in both fists. She only nodded like that was that. Cassandra leaned from the window too far, made dolphins on air. She waved at the boys and the men that they passed.

"You fall out I'm not stopping," Daisy was saying and swerving.

Cassandra yelled into the wind, "Where we going?"

"The boneyard" was Daisy's amazing reply.

Three gulps was too much. The no lunch ice milk and vodka came up on the side of the car. Cassandra was wiping blowaway strands of white froth from her hair when they rocked to a stop.

It was dusk. The trees were too sparse. The first thing she saw was a birthday balloon on the grave of a child, but she wasn't sad. Cassandra was staggering and making like choking. She picked up a pinecone and threw it as far as she could. She stepped on a branch for the sound of the snap.

"Let's pretend we're dead and we've come to visit ourselves," she suggested.

Daisy seemed not to hear. She tippled the last of the bottle, reclined on a plaque from which lawn mowers had sheared off the name and the years.

Cassandra lay down, her back to her mother, her head on the soft of her arm. She noticed a headstone the shape of a tree trunk, a quartzite limb lying beside it perpetually severed. It was pathetic, she thought. She studied the plain HERE LIES markers arranged in a scattered relief. A weak smoke-laden wind skirted the hedge concealing the yard from the one-square-block streets. It was the size of the glade at the home.

In the last of the palpable light, trees cast their shadow agendas, black branches like hands that could cover her face anytime. The stars were eclipsed by a thin slush of gravy-gray clouds. The brood of a dull aureole surrounded the half-halo moon. It was open and dark. She felt overexposed. Something held and released her, sure as the fate of a stone once it's thrown.

She turned toward her mother and studied the folds of her rise and fall thighs, the wattles of flesh on her arm that were pitted with granules of pocked cellulite. Cassandra checked out if Daisy was really asleep. She matched Daisy's breathing, pretending to breathe for them both. She pulled herself close and touched Daisy's thighs where they met from behind. This was a thing she knew she would do in her mind.

It was unlike Cassandra imagined yet still the same. She tried to imagine her hand was a man's and shifted it higher. Farther up it was dangerous, stipple-skinned, warmer. She thought of a used-to-be Daisy out on the lawn, clothespins stuck in her teeth, hair braided in two coiling loops. Cassandra saw Daisy was hanging her yellowing jumper to dry in the lack of a breeze. She heard a warning, a whisper. She saw a crate in the yard, a sewing room door that locked from inside. Something was nearby the color of white root and worm with the feel of a peeled-off brown scab. She tried thinking of nothing, but everything came up at once, each interred enigma a desperate, deep water cipher, a little girl feint. There was no way to forgive it, forget it, or leave it alone. Her fingers felt coarse tufts of unpleasant hair. She shoved her hand up as far as she could.

Daisy coughed, shifted, and woke. Cassandra jerked loose. They sat up at once, regarded each other. Cassandra could tell Daisy knew what just happened. Wary, drunk, silent, they weighed the options together.

Cassandra was quicker. "You got a government notice. You're not fit to parent," she shouted. It's what she always said when they played at scaring each other, but now it was worse.

Too late, she saw Daisy's hand with the bottle. She barely had time for the castaway thought that she'd never seen Daisy move so fast before. It glanced the side of her cheek but she didn't go down. The glass broke behind her on stone.

"Look at you. Stupid and fat. You'll never sleep with a man" came out of her mouth. Her whole jaw felt loose.

Daisy was swaying like she might fall over, her eyes a dull blur. All of her body was shaking. "You're not the child of your father," she cursed. "He was thrown from a truck, run over, a man overboard."

Cassandra was suddenly standing, unwrapping the Wilkinson blade she'd stolen from the store. She held it up like communion in church. She tested the steel on the flat of her tongue. She snapped it in half. It cut her thumb. She touched her lips with the smear and stepped closer to Daisy, bending and bloodying her brow with a kiss. Cassandra pushed the blade into the crook of her arm, pressing down, breaking skin.

Cassandra now stretches to turn on the dome light. The car is a womb, a weak, yellow dopesick insomnia. We've pulled up in back of our building. I park without thinking. It's getting dark. The streetlights come on. There's the surf, its abstraction of waves.

Cassandra lowers her hand to my lap. She says, "Go ahead. Touch it."

Maria leans over the seat and we run our palms up and down. We say nothing, don't look at each other. Our fingers massage the hardened black squirm of her tracks, the thin raised white welt of the scar. We stare at Cassandra's contusions, purple blooms, the texture and color of flesh marred from missing the veins many times. I am thinking of my own skin, which will eventually be just like hers, and Maria looks like she's got the same thing on her mind. I understand this is a necessary communion, a healing rite that Cassandra has thought up so we can go on. Eventually she rolls down her sleeve. "There," she says quietly, more to herself, "we're a family again."

Eleven

Cassandra has gone on a ten-dollar errand and hasn't come back. She has a private, discriminate life she won't let us near. She'll reappear in time with a down-turned smile, a new bruise she's not had before, a new blouse. "I've been with some guys," she might say, or nothing at all. Even Gary didn't know where she went when Cassandra would willfully disappear.

Maria's asleep in the bed by my side. We don't touch and I don't find this strange. It is better for us to stay chaste, otherwise it would complicate things. It's past noon and the morning getover's run down. We're out of money and dope and I know what has to be done. The sequence about to unfold is inevitable. It is not a matter of guilt and regret, or that Maria's too young, it's about being sick.

Except for the inbred hysteria of gulls it's entirely quiet. The room is a place indistinct, without form, without sound. I look around and see how our commonplace things are discarded, the misbuttoned shirt, dress and jacket, odd shoe. The "famous striped bathrobe," as Cassandra calls it, is thrown to the rug.

The place where we live has surrendered its last pink-tinged glass, torn pants, rent skirt, bent and black-bottomed spoon. Outside the window the light is transparent and tacit, static and gray like a radiogram. Someone breaks bottles methodically down in the alley. I'm guessing it's Tuesday again. It makes no difference. I have arrived in a place where the concept of calendar time has long fled. I'm no longer mere guest or witness, I've taken matters in hand. I'll walk Maria out of the room and down to the park, where I'll watch her flag down a car. There is no other way it will unfold, I have been a party to it all along.

The day is too large, the blue bulb doesn't soothe. Beside me Maria seems tossed. She wakes looking rapt, her wrists sprung, arms over her head in a sprawl.

She says, "It doesn't feel like I slept at all."

"We have to go out," I say as if she didn't know this.

"I don't want them to touch me." She sits up and shudders, hugs herself tight. Skin doesn't lie and Maria doesn't want sudden confessions. She looks afraid for herself while pretending indifference. I study the door as if miracles happen, a dream of found money with music for which we can almost decipher the score.

"Nothing I say would make any difference," I tell her.

"That just isn't true," says Maria. "We could stay here in the room."

"Sure, and throw up in the sink, come down with the sweats."

Maria studies my face. "No, it's something else," she decides. "You get excited by this, of us being working girls."

"You've been listening to Cassandra again."

Maria is staring me down so I have to look at the floor. "I got a brain, I can think for myself."

Of course Maria is right, I'm drawn to the vileness of it, the criminal allure. I want to touch it, get more than close. It's an opportunity I won't refuse. I raise my hands. "Maria, I have no excuse."

"Okay then," she says. "As long as you know."

Then we're arranging and straightening our clothes. My joints feel tender and swollen. The pain in my gut is a permanent dull hollow burn. I get up and go to the couch, see the bellicose overblown clouds, the sky like a lake bed of clear winter ice. I turn, see Maria buttoning her dress with regret, brushing hair from her brow with a

sweep of habitual gesture. It seems to assure her and renders a delicate calm to her face like a stone tossed in water, concentric ellipses
lapping a shore.

She looks around like she's fixing the place in her mind. She sees
how the room cannot help her.

"This place is used up," she says. "I thought I could hide here, be
safe."

I look at the room we have never cleaned up, this refuge for no
more than fixing and sleep, the unwashed sheets coming apart on
the bed, the bottles and cans, the roaches bold even in daytime that
scatter at night when the light is turned on. I tell her, "That's what I
thought, too."

"Oh, well," says Maria, shrugging and tossing her head with a resigned and dismissive gesture that actually hurts to observe. "I've
been in worse places before."

We tread the marred narrow stairs with their wobble-toothed
rungs, push past the double doors heavy and wide as the planks of
an ark. Oceanview gathers its vapors that seem to be culled from the
cool floating hearts of the clouds, pale and bland as the street-corner
regulars' sugary wine. Towels are draped from some of the windows.
The air is wet newspapers, urine, flat tires.

Maria places one foot in front of the other, precise and yet careless, like nothing matters. Her gait is clipped, unadorned. I'm walking in step beside her and holding her arm. I wonder about her, the
little girl named for a saint, after all. Instead of what I've been urging
I should put my arms around her, buy her a guitar, a cute, not-too-
short miniskirt.

"You ought to be flirting with sixteen-year-olds," I tell her. "Kids
driving their first cars and wearing peace symbols, just learning to
smoke."

"Yeah, right," she replies, but sounds wistfully pleased at the
thought. "And you ought to go back to school."

I don't want to talk about me. "We've taken your childhood," I
tell her.

She looks up and touches my cheek with a hand that she quickly removes. "It was lost long ago." Maria places that hand on her heart and I feel like I should be crying. "About what I said before. It's not your fault, we're all doing what we have to do."

I fumble my dirty shirt's buttons. "It's not a good enough reason for this."

I feel the last of the dope strum inside my ears when I swallow. I want to name places and things so as not to forget them and lose who I am. I long to be in a room set back from the streetlights, inside its yellow lit window that others regretfully pass. I see myself eating roast beef from a can with a spoon. A bourbon half-pint is set back in the cupboard but just for the cold because I'm in control. The ceiling has one single fixture, a bulb on a chain. The walls must be bare except for one picture, a scene at a beach. This is a game I play, rearranging the past and projecting it forward, imbuing it with what I've since learned. It's like that wish to relive what's happened, but knowing then what you know now.

I touch the things in my pockets for luck, loose coins, paper-clip, a maroon Afro comb, a tube of pink passion lipstick, a marble cat's eye, my out-of-state license and library card.

"If we were back east," I say to Maria, "we could drive out to Lake Winnipesaukee, rent a boat, fishing poles."

"I don't know how to row."

"I could teach you."

"I won't touch a fish or a worm."

"I hate them, too."

"So much for fishing," Maria says, wiping her nose on her sleeve.

I compare the light to all of the light that I've seen, but it's singular, different. It has a dull iron tint. Trembling, I look at the clothes that I'm wearing, a patched madras jacket, the checkered chef's pants without pockets, the joke of my shiny white shoes with black heels.

"It's as if I'm walking beside me," I say to Maria, "like I'm my own guardian angel."

"That's happened to me," Maria replies. "Also sometimes I feel only ten, sometimes twenty-one. Now I just ache every place."

"We're coming down, that's what happens." A sliver of spit drools its way to my chin.

To quell my nerves I make a brief list of the things that I like: the odor of smoke from a Lucky, the must of car heater, my arm out the driver-side window rolled down, Maria's aroma of baby shampoo, its No More Tears script on the bottle, its scent like its color of gold. Cassandra undressing under the blue, carelessly tossing her clothes on the floor. A silent library in late afternoon.

"Things haven't turned out the way I thought they would when I rented the room." My face twitches, my legs start to shake.

Maria appears on the verge of losing her balance. "How could they? You couldn't have known."

"I want to be rescued."

"No one's gonna do that."

"If I left here would you come along?"

Maria is nodding her head like she's giving it serious thought. "And give all this up?" she asks.

We cross Main against the red light without looking. In the park, birds are swelling the crowns of the diffident trees. She tugs on her dress in the lye-colored glare. I touch the small of her back but don't stop her from what happens next. The taste in my mouth is of queasy betrayal, like bile might come up.

"Cassandra would say 'Let's just do it,' " she says, begins waving her arms as if inviting impending drama, then steps toward the curb. She offers an over-the-shoulder blank turned-down-mouthed smile without guile. She wears her disquiet like slow water rising or upside-down flies in a jar. She doesn't stumble or falter this time. It's she who must cross all alone to a passenger door of the car that pulls up, get inside, watch the hand put the shift into drive.

From what I can see of her face through the glass she looks like she's going to throw up. Again I don't run down to save her. Once more I've allowed that option to pass.

The nauseous stir of the wind on my skin is like hundreds of un-welcome slaps. I want to fall comatose, forgetting Maria, recalling the blue line that runs toward the school. This is the shape that my self-rescue takes.

There were seasonal flowers and small towns nearby, Ashland and Swampscott. I once held books of significance in my hands. In truth I despised college, my backpack was heavy, the blue line was crowded, but it's better remembered like this. I'd like to sit in a bar where over the counter on TV the Mets are relentlessly beating the Dodgers in a late twilight shutout at Shea. Then I could go for a walk, see a French movie, eat popcorn, drink powder-creamed coffee. Later, I'd sit in the car, remove shoes and socks wet from the snow, turn the radio dial back and forth. There'd be jingly pop, a lesson on how to broil chicken, the news. Except for the baseball results, it's hard to believe at this remove that I've done all these things. Nevertheless, some vital essence was absent, something was unresolved. It was an unfinished lapse that Boston U. couldn't cure.

The answer, I'd thought, would have to reveal itself far away, maybe by the opposite shore. There would be blond lithe young girls hitchhiking on Sunset Strip, rock and roll. We'd lie around in a crash pad, smoke dope. Somehow money and food would simply float from the roof.

It hasn't come out as imagined. I've just led a girl on the verge of her teens to sell herself so we can score. It is a remarkable fact when put plainly like this. When I was Maria's age I slept with a transistor radio under my pillow, read World War II history books, rode a bicycle wearing my Tenderfoot Scout uniform.

The only way not to dwell on what's happening here is to return to my mother, to our last autumn together, when I was old enough to begin remembering coherently. It is like dreaming of food when you're hungry, the gauze of that self-contained place. It is a retreat. If you tell yourself something often enough, you begin to believe it. It becomes inviolate, a safe refrain.

I wore lederhosen and black patent, open-toed shoes. It was hard to step up to the streetcars when carrying a pack with schoolbooks. Our building was filling with anticipation and Voice of America.

Hi-fi squelch rose from the courtyard. Everyone played Hungaro-fone records and polkas. My father was absent. My mother had taken to riding the trains for her memory's sake.

I see Hanna pare crust, salting and buttering slices of caraway rye she called soldiers. Her eyebrows were scant and she'd burned her hair blond. I think of small tortes, eclairs smothered with glazed marzipan, the air a wet wool. Someone was always leaving her, wait-ing for her to return. She had a look as if harboring a secret, an ex-pression Cassandra might wear.

"Who'll remember me three years from now?" she would ask. It is something Cassandra could say after telling a story at night. Hanna was already the far side of twenty, a ghost in a laudanum bot-tle. She wanted to sit with a man in a bar. Then they'd go to his room and shut off the light. She liked it best languid, not fast. Then she could dream her husband's blue numbers, how they repulsed her, excited her after a while. She would remember the gray hair that dusted his chest and his arms.

I have a need to remember my mother this way. She couldn't be merely selling herself, it must be a desperate act that she did for my sake. I've nurtured this version of Hanna too long, and why not? She's my mother, and gone after all.

Anyway, I wouldn't swear to the veracity of remembered events. They become crystallized incidents, highly compressed, a mix of emotion and memory, their structure created to accommodate yearning, strainings of the heart. Our childhood is where we are al-lowed the creation of gods. It's where our beliefs and wishes are strongest, where we are innocent still. Our memory of that time, whether cobbled from bits or entirely imagined, is boundless.

I lie on the damp lawn and go back to when my parents were both still alive. What I recall are barren horse chestnuts lining the wide cobblestone boulevard. I stood by the window, looked down at the sparkle antenna electric streetcars. The air was the color of nut-meg and pigeons. The weather had turned. Down below, men and women were pulling on long sleeves of first winter coats. The ortho-dox bells were declaring the start of a Catholic night.

My father and I were waiting for Hanna, who hadn't come home all day long or the previous evening. He stood wide-lapelled, turned toward the tall parlor mirror. The flat charcoal tablets he chewed for digestion rubbed off on his thumb and forefinger. They turned his tongue a dull black. There was no sound but the porcelain ticking of one spigot sink, our breathing, and so barely heard it might have been imagined, a young girl's soft persistent cry. Or was that the echo of chimes?

Outside the day turned to copper and sepia from high-clouded secular white. The sky became slush with the darkening soot of the clouds. On the opposite sill a housecoated woman was sprinkling a planter of gone-to-seed violets with rust-tinted water. She squinted because of the clenched cigarette in her mouth. The chipped umber can caught the last of the light.

I saw how my rare visitation of father was holding a half glass of water, the difficult set of his shoulders. He studied the Grundig hi-fi as if waiting for some certain sound to come out, crisp BBC stutter, perhaps.

We heard Hanna spilling her purse in the hall on the bright-buffed parquet. He always helped her when she was like this but he wouldn't now.

"This is a test," he said out loud. He meant it for her. My father leaned down and placed a conspiratorial hand on the small of my back. He shouldn't have touched me like that. There was something I should have been doing. Somehow it would even have been allowed. It would have been right.

Instead I listened to Hanna stir earrings of genuine onyx and silver, her rabbit-hair brushes, the flat half-moon vial of lilium water she dabbed on the top of her breasts and sometimes just inside her thighs. I'd watched her do that.

My legs became baby unsteady as Hanna managed the latch. I felt my face tug in an odd kind of smile as she stepped inside. She wore our favorite fox-collar jacket unbuttoned. She brought to the room the faint traces of black market whiskey, flawed nylons, ostmarks, and American cash.

Hanna pretended that she wasn't swaying. My father told her you're drunk without speaking. She carefully lowered her black patent bag on the unadorned mantel's shined sash. He took one step forward, she counterstepped back as if choreographed. An essence I couldn't distill passed between. Then I was inside of their secret: He could forgive her but she disallowed it. She kept her fists clenched by her side.

She said, "I might be guilty but I won't be tried."

My father turned to conceal something furtive he did with the backs of his hands to his eyes. Hanna studied my face as if it was her right. She sought out his similar features in mine, the same blood-less mouth and the wandering eye.

"Don't ever do this to the boy. Don't make him take sides." She looked at me like it was my fault.

That was the first time I sold out my mother, I realize now.

Everything changed after that. My father was mentioned so rarely he might have passed into an afterlife white. Then I wasn't told he had died.

Even at six I knew there was something new going on, yelling, gunfire, outside. "Stay away from the windows," Hanna would warn. I'd just started school, then it was called off. The newspaper head-lines read "Russians Go Home," Radio Free Europe was unjammed and it said to hold on. My mother counted her cash every night. She packed a valise for herself and a small suitcase for me that she placed in the hall. "For when things get worse," she said ominously. Despite Hanna's pleas I would look out the glass. There were tanks in the street.

"It's not going to hold," Hanna said. She'd been absent on er-rands for hours every day and often into the night. She'd said to keep the lights doused, so I'd sit in the dark with my thumb in my mouth, watching flashes of bright on the sky. Then she was washing her very best dress in the sink, smoked all her hoarded cigarettes, said, "We have no choice but to try, it's all set." I didn't know what she was talking about but could tell it was beyond anything that had happened so far, portentous and large.

Hanna and I later stood in the hall of a building not ours, its wall-paper burnished with weak orange stains. Hanna was wearing a short tartan plaid skirt, a long white-sleeved blouse, a corduroy jacket extravagant blue as her eyes. On her face there was bombing and singing, a folk-song-filled upright piano that had played all night. She appeared weavy. She said, "We need papers, more money. We have to get out." She straightened my silly Tyrolean hat.

All day long there'd been difficult stairways, anchovies in cream sauce, kiclbasa, and too many shots of plum brandy until I became sleepy.

I overheard Hanna make promises, fountain-pen street names and contacts on small scraps of love letter paper, saw how she suffered the last-minute kindness of bills being tucked in her bag. Then we escaped from red lipstick kisses, from "Button your coat," "Where's your mittens?" unasked-for advice, and the damp over-heated hysteria of saying good-bye.

Soon, I could tell, she would be with a man. It was the plain silver pin in her hair she'd burned buckwheat with bleaches and lyes that gave her away. The light-headed linger of lilium water betrayed her.

We walked. Wind smeared the rain on the windows above us. The sky was like film negative when exposed to the light. Fistfuls of snow clumped the ground. There were high, wide dark clouds as if someone had dreamed them, tumescent across the night sky. Singular pinpricks of drizzle were falling but we weren't looking for shelter or running. Her breath was warm vapor, her skin marzipan.

A tractor was dragging the corpse of a mare in the street. A man recently called by first name in the down-the-road tavern now spun from a lamppost, his neck an irregular comma, his mouth a perpetual vowel. Someone ran by with newspapers on fire. Carbine-clad men ankled past.

We skirted the trash-fire smudge of the crowd that was swelling the dim Boulevard of the Martyrs. Strangers were milling and holding up lanterns like censers. Around us in shadows and out in plain sight they were trading flat, imported watches, powders for sleep, and dark, bittersweet chocolates, silk scarves, themselves, and each other. Timetables for steam locomotives that no longer ran were littering the ground. Upwind by the bend a just-from-the-country collusion of horses were hauling a driverless, high-slatted, sack-laden wagon around and around. Down by the concrete abutment the famous blue river ran brown.

Under a busted-out wood and brick covert Hanna located a laudanum vendor. She hefted a handful of near-useless forints, their cash value measured in weight. With open corruption, not bothering to hide it, she swallowed hard from the small bottle cupped in her palm. Her hand shook. She told me it made her feel shivery like late winter wheat outside Saturday Place, towns named Sainted and Jeweled, her hair like chaff ready for combine blades, scythes. I wanted her touch but she clutched the hem of her skirt with both hands to her side, hugged her waist.

Some of the stores had been looted, the plate glass punched clean. At Jozsef Benn Circle a column of students came toward us with bottles and rocks in their fists. Two middle-aged women hauled bricks in an awkward bump cart with three wheels. A bottle-bound troika of local militia were boozily cursing and tearing the epaulets, hash marks, red stars, from their shirts and peaked caps in the breeze. A light-armored lorry was flying the last war's defeated tricolor. I saw Hanna's eyes were exceedingly bright as she started to weep.

She shook out a pink handkerchief from her purse, dabbed her cheeks. Then she wiped mine, though I wasn't crying. Lilac and lavender powder brushed my cheek. It put me in mind of our leaving.

Castle Hill was lit up in the distance. Its clusters of gathering fires bruised the sky. The rain turned to snow gummed with ash. Our steps made that cereal sound, much like Hanna's clasped bag when its leather was cracked. We went down some stairs in the sidewalk that I hadn't noticed before.

"It's a secret jazz bar," said my mother.

Inside the long, narrow foyer she shook off her jacket. Her blouse in this light was indecent, a transparent ivory and salmon too bare for the season. We sat in the back in a cigarette litter of Cinzano ashtrays, drained snifters, and clear soda spritzers. I pushed my fingers through scattered curled cheeses, sprinkles of caraway seeds, rinds of rye.

"I know someone who can help us," she said, her voice brittle and tight. Hanna stood and stepped into the blue. She would not be denied.

Then I couldn't wait any longer. I crossed toward the stage through the jittery press of the crowd. Here everyone promised and pleaded, mouths stuffed with ridiculous wishes and unrealizable lies.

A tall man beside me said, "Now we'll have something to eat besides slogans."

"I doubt it," somebody replied.

I hugged the wall with its peasant embroideries of overblown daisies and stylized, overwrought vines. More men made bolder pronouncements. Out loud they rewrote the textbooks and mocked up the placards, ripping down, running up, flags in their palinka alcohol minds.

Everyone yelled about money and who manned the border. Women were singing the national anthem and drinking like it was their last one forever. Virtual strangers were leaning together, hands furtive and dark under shadows of tables on crinoline dresses and soft cotton trousers, shoes kicked off and bold. Their clothes were releasing last-minute sausage and trapped, risen smoke. The air was imbued with unbearable yearning undone by cologne and smuggled West German perfume.

Behind the fust of the curtain I stood among mops, ocarinas, a snare, and the props for a juggling act. I looked in the dressing room door left ajar. There was an oilcloth-draped table, an ottoman shiny with use. Beside it a vanity mirror was strung with dead sockets and unlit, irregular bulbs hanging loose. The room was singed citrus. It reminded me of pancake, vanilla, and encore dried rose.

Someone sat in an armchair of no recognizable color, striking a hesitant question mark pose. Hanna's black handbag lay unclasped, exposed by his feet on the floor. He leaned forward to touch her.

"They've retaken the radio station," he said.

I moved to see better. Hanna was kneeling before him and spitting her gold wedding band in her palm. She'd moistened it first before gentling it loose with her teeth and her tongue. She wrapped
her bloodstone, her mother's black opal, her amethyst, garnet, and
silver in royal blue velveteen paper and handed it over.

"The shooting. He would have enjoyed it," she said.

"Your husband?" he asked her.

She looked him over. Hanna had said she liked men who were
spare, somewhat sad, unadorned. She studied the wall as if there
was a window and my father floated outside. Hanna stood, straightened the seams of her stockings, and paced out of sight.

"Something to drink?" he asked as he turned. He saw me. He
kicked the door closed.

There was a rapid staccato of small arms fire popping and furniture rubbing. I watched the thin strip of yellow from under the runner for clues. I heard drinks being poured.

She swallowed, said, "God, this is awful. I'm doing this just for
the boy." Her high-heeled steps rang on the hard parquet floor. I
heard the fall of his shoes. Hanna said, "Please," nothing more. A
palpable silence preceded a gasp, a clasp or a belt coming loose.

"Let's pretend we're on a train and it's summer," I heard Hanna
whisper. "I'm wearing the new dress I bought. Go ahead. Lift it. Put
your hand there," Hanna urged. There was a tousle of fabric, a low
orchestration of couch spring and sighs.

"That's right. Do that," Hanna said.

I sifted the wavering surges of glasses and shouts from the bar for
the mere distillation and essence of Hanna inside of those words.

"I want to be scared now, go turn out the light," she ordered distinctly. There was a three-short-step clop to the door. We were
plunged into dark.

The man said, "Where are you?"

"Find me fast," she replied.

I heard what I thought was the scratch of her skirt over nylons,
the click of the clip of her garters, the small restless breath of her intimate laughter.

After a while I could make out the shape of my hand in the black. The beat of the couch was insistent against the far wall. Something fell to the floor among wheezing and skin-on-skin slapping. He said something indistinct, harsh. She let out slow moans of a thankful surprise that grew high-pitched and closer together. She said, "Don't stop now. Go faster." She uttered the name of my father. She cried out with relief like a long hollow hurt turned to pleasure at last.

A clapper released a late-note appeal from a bell tower nearby. The tolling was golden, it rolled. Then there was an unsteady walking, a cough, the strike of a match. The bright band of doorstop startled my eyes. I heard the raspy condolence of clothes being hastily zippered and snapped. One of them righted what had been knocked down.

"It's not summer at all," she remarked. She sounded too close. There was nothing to do but draw back as I saw the knob turn. Hanna was bathed in a circumspect, cold yellow light. She shielded her eyes, looked around.

"What are you doing?" she asked, unconcerned, not really wanting an answer.

She took my hand, pulled the door closed on the room like what had happened in there didn't matter. She hauled me past shouting and tables tipped over, tablecloths twined in the legs of the knocked-aside chairs. Hanna stopped and leaned closer, exuding a briny ammonia aroma like alcohol, yeast, just-turned earth. A roseate sheen flushed the cleft of her neck and her tantalized, uncontrived face. It rose from the wedge of her legs between nylon and skirt and everywhere else she was bared. Because of a plate being dropped in the din and a violin playing lieder I couldn't quite hear her

I read her bruised lips say, "I got us a visa."

We stepped out of there. Fires had turned the sky tamarind. The air was tinged charcoal, it had the feel of wet clothes.

Hanna was saying, "If anyone asks any questions, don't answer."

At the apartment we gathered our bags. I fingered the just-in-case-I-got-lost paper that Hanna had cribbed with a name and address in America. We didn't linger or dwell on the things we were leaving behind. I held tight to the miniature child's suitcase she'd packed. She rested her hand on my head as we walked. The permanent cigarette held in the other was blunt and burned down. A runaway Skoda and two smaller scooters lay mangled beside trolley tracks. I realized I'd lost my Tyrolean hat.

The station was shuttered and mobbed by the time we arrived. A sallow bulb swung from its precipice vault and blinked on and off. The regular tremor of ground was familiar. We faced with the others toward tendrils of dissipated steam from the east, border-bound. Burned leaves and cinders were gracing our hair, leaving a bitter ash taste in my mouth. The platform convulsed. Hanna looked rapt in the stuttering green X-ray light of the tinted-glass cars flashing past. The might-not-stop train had arrived.

The Dopplering regular clatter ground down with a metal-on-metal white whine. The pistons released small cloudlets like breathing in winter, the color of ice. Everyone surged all at once. Hanna's hands lifted me onto the gunmetal steps. We stood side by side in the narrow conductorless corridor, our tickets a fiction, our destination a rumor, conjecture passed down the line.

Someone beside her said across the border was Weiner Neustadt, a new start. She let out a hiss, tossed her hair, rolled her eyes. Bottles collided as we lurched and I fell against her. Pulling her skirt I caged reassurance but she didn't care about that. There was nothing to hold but a cold metal runner of rivet-stamped studs at the height of my arms held straight out, nothing to do but stare at the men rushing runaway rungs. One clung to the legs of another, who tried to both shake him and climb. Mothers with babies were stranded and pleading among the abandoned belongings strewn across the ground. A carriage, an ebony dresser stood out, a lamp in the shape of a spectacled owl. We noticed a man with his hat in his hand throwing up on a bare patch of ground.

"He's sick with fright," Hanna uttered out loud. "This is fate. See it good. Take a look all around." For everyone's benefit Hanna said, "See how we're all civilized." I could tell from the way she blew cigarette smoke into rings she was drunk. "Later you'll think of all this," she remarked with a sweep of her arm.

She turned and spoke sullen in German to someone with dirty blond hair. The man shook his head, looked away. There was nothing to see but occasional indistinct flickers of light in the pitch. I guessed we passed over water because of the more hollow clatter. The finger of river below us was spread in a dark inky stain. I breathed the damp talcum thighs, the other discriminate odors that rose, the alcohol flush, and the anxious chill tremor of nerves.

People were intently smoking and drinking the last of whatever they had. Those who weren't leaning on shoulders were swaying, straphanging and stunned. Others were watching for outlines of harrows and steeples, searching for their birthplace visions of towns like where Hanna was born. Her small gabled house had a swing and a ball in the yard, a low-lying hedge, and an incessant rooster next door, she had said. The road that passed before it curved into a forest of alders and tall poplars trembling with bees. Everyone's vision was rendered more real by the black that the windows gave back and the syncopate drum of the wheels.

We brushed by a milk train, a rolling stock wagon. An uncoupled club car sat sidetracked and glowing. Inside it torsos were rising and falling.

Hanna bent closer and straightened my schoolboy blue sweater.

"He shouldn't have missed this, your father," she whispered.

"Where is he?" I asked and hoped for a lie. Instead she told me the very same answer I'd cobbled together from rumor.

"I won't spare you now. You should know. He died by his very own hand," she replied. She studied the camouflaged countryside as it passed, lit her last cigarette with her next-to-last match, crumpled and let drop the useless brown pack.

The train shuddered and stalled with a steam-soughing gasp. Her smoke in my face and both Hanna's palms on my shoulders, we single-filed out. I sank past my knees in the snow, Hanna up to her calves.

"You're too old to carry," she told me, but lifted me out, looked around for firm ground.

I buried my face in her goldenrod hair, its butterscotch fragrance. I noticed the slight meringue of softening lotion she rubbed on the nape of her neck and inside of each arm every night. I wrapped my legs ankle-clasped tight on the small of her back. I looked around like she'd said, as if for the last time.

Clear implications abounded. Half sunk as if tossed from a height to the crystalline powder were boxes and busted-out wicker, clothes wrapped in brown paper and twine, trunks broken-clasped. They cast oblong shadows and glowed in the wan empty stretch of the railroad cars. They reminded me of a graveyard, each stone with its sanctified candle enclosed in a tiny cupola of glass like a small lit-up house.

Beside a deadwood-tipped grove was a red and green stop-and-go signal with both bulbs alight, a soft clicking switch box, a narrow-gauge slant turnaround. The startling wedge of a guard tower searchlight imprinted a halo of useless white oval upon a blank spread of wide sky. Hanna put me down.

"This is it," Hanna said as we ran. We stumbled on sticking-up roots of a vineyard plowed under. Some kind of soldiers were standing ahead but it didn't matter, they, too, were deserting the land of their birth.

Hanna said, "Soon we'll be exiles." It was the first time I'd heard that word used. We rushed the limp pole-strung barbed wire toward a ragged-edged freshly cut gap. I thought those loose metal tendrils would gouge. I was pushed against somebody's belt, being shoved from behind.

Despite the crush it was eerily quiet, the trample subdued, a sublime practiced practical habit learned standing in lines. I clutched my case and the note with my name and address in a language that I disavowed. I'd heard it spoken by someone to Hanna, loud and abrupt, too plaintive and crowded with vowels.

There was gunfire and panic, a low grind of half-tracks and snowtired trucks. A girl my age reached out her hand toward mine. I turned to show Hanna but it wasn't she who was clutching my shoulder. The woman with bangs cut like my mother's looked just as surprised. Then somebody lifted me up. I was passed overhead hand to hand. I saw my mother. She stood too far back, both palms were cupped to her mouth. Like in a dream there was no way to reach her. A bullhorn declared they were sealing the border. She shouted but couldn't be heard. There were tears on her face. Her blouse was untucked, her hair wild. That was the last time I saw her. It was the compost and fertile brown loam of nostalgia. Then I was set down on the opposite side.

Twelve

It's been a while since Maria's been gone. How long have I been daydreaming? Sometimes it's good for an hour or longer. By constant rehearsing I must have created the details I couldn't recall. How accurate is memory at six? It doesn't matter. Remembrance has its own story to tell. Over the years I've sewn a coherent webbing that won't be dispelled. It is a blanket, a keepsake, a treasure. For me it is like meditation, it lets me rest, allows calm. The present is hard, immediate, harsh. There are too many choices, a right or a wrong way to act. Later, when this is all over, there'll be Cassandra as well as my mother, Gary, and Maria to ponder. This park, the room, and the boardwalk are the breeding ground for tales to relive in the future. I close my eyes, almost soothed by this thought.

I awake from a dream of Maria by her real-life self. She is standing above me, dress furled in the breeze. I'm curled on my side on the itch of the lawn, focused on singular blades. Nearby is a saw-pitched insistence of bottlefly drone. I stretch and lean on an elbow as Maria crouches to show me two yellow pills in her palm.

"You know about these?" she asks in a childlike singsong. I shake my head no. Maria is pleased that I don't. "They're Dilaudid. I scored them myself, all alone. You crush them up, cook them down just like stuff." Maria is happy and proud she's been brave. She says in a hurry, "The guy took me back to his place. Look at this." She pulls a small wad of bills from the top of her dress, smoothing and fanning the money bouquet.

I'd planned to tell her I'm sorry what's happened but it's not an appropriate response. Now that Maria has done it without any help she seems self-assured. Just as Cassandra predicted, she thinks the idea of all this is her own. I ought to slap her and straighten her out, shake her by the shoulders so she'll figure out what she's become.

She throws herself onto her back and flings the bills over her dress. "They're wildflowers, pick them," she says.

Dutiful yet uncertain I harvest the singles and fives. Once more I wonder my part. Should I pocket this money or hand it to her? I'm truly her pimp if I keep it. You can't have it both ways. I tuck the bills in my shirt.

Maria stands, pulls me to my feet. Revealing more than a hint of impatience, she's smacking her thighs with her fists. I'm plucking nettles and burrs from my clothes. I realize there's no time to plumb subtleties. She's got those pills in her hand and if we don't do them we're going to be sick.

We ford the bulge of the park with its patches rubbed raw like a hide, brown and coarse. What's left of the feeble sun's orb appears drained, enervated, washed out on a sky crowding with Teutonic cumulus clouds.

I notice Maria's newfound willful stride. A hand-sized stain spreads on her dress where it clings to the back of her leg. She reaches behind her, pulls the cloth loose, makes a face. I see how she wants to be older and harder but her expression reveals she's not ripe for the task. At curbside she bends, inhaling the gutter's leafed mulch. "It smells like old rags," Maria remarks.

I take her hand, hear her counting each step as we cross. This is a little girl game that she plays every time. She trips, almost falls. "I ought to know how to walk," she says, giddy and light.

Our fingers entwined, we race down the rest of our block as if we were kids. In a way, I believe we still are. Above us the whaleskin-tinged sky becomes denser with spiraling flutes. Ahead, the three-crowned pagoda's deserted. A bottle of wine has been set on a bench by a single black boot. Under the eaves of our building's dank entrance a lone pigeon pecks itself dry. From one of the windows a phonograph scratches a vapid pop tune.

Maria is taking the lead as we climb to our room, past thuds and thumps behind the wall, cued laughter, a talk show's applause. Inside I part the curtain, lean, and look out at a gray band of smog that's been blown off the coast. I turn and watch Maria tearing a matchbook in half. She creases the close-before-striking square cover and places the pills in its fold. Deftly, she inscissors them into powder.

"Where'd you learn that?" I ask her.

Overtly casual, she shrugs. "I just picked it up."

Maria taps the sluice of granular crystals into the spoon, flushes the 1 cc insulin needle, lights matches, and fires the tablets to piss-yellow froth. The liquid's odor is tangy and bitter.

"If you don't mind," Maria is saying, "since I did the work, I'll go first." She says this with a tone like Cassandra might use. She pinches the cotton, drops it in the concoction, and intently draws up the dope.

"I'll hold you off," I offer, but Maria shakes her head no, looks around for a tie.

"I'd rather do it myself," she replies. I vaguely recall it's a commercial's punchline as she finds the sash of the robe. She swipes the hair from her eyes with a gesture not gleaned from Cassandra. Maria tightens the tie with her teeth and gentles the spike into the tenderest part of her arm. The base of a half-inch-run scar on her mainline accepts the hot silver tip. She lets go the sash.

I watch the shivery eel of thin blood in the dropper. Like some practiced addict she boots the orangy liquid inside the syringe, making it fall and rise. Maria plunges it, wincing. "It burns," she exclaims. She pulls out the rig, licks at a hairline of red that snails down the pale of her delicate skin. She leans back on the couch, just sits there, her mouth hanging slack. She rubs her face with both palms. "It hurts going in but man it feels good getting down. You want me to fix you?" she asks, sounding much like Cassandra my very first time.

In Cassandra's absence I see how Maria tries playing her part, the mimic of her lank demeanor, even to the cynical smile. But then she says, "Please, College, let me," and ruins the act. I hold out my arm.

"Wait," she says. "I have to dump." With touchingly needless decorum she runs the faucet to cover the retching and flush. She comes to the couch, runs her thumb over my scarred brown line. The joints of her short dampened fingers are still a bit baby fat plumped. Maria sits sideways, her legs tucked beneath her, and readies the paraphernalia again but more slowly this time, her eyelids occasionally closing, her head bending forward, then suddenly snapping upright.

"Don't miss," I tell her, though I can see from her difficult, doped concentration she won't. She repeats the ritual procedure.

She's right, the Dilaudid's a sharp, subcutaneous fire. The rush isn't heroin deep from the spine but much lighter. It seems to rise from the chest through the throat to the scalp, where it tingles and throbs. Not bothering to pull the bathroom door closed, I also void my insides.

We sit on the couch, the light from the window a whitewash of bright on her face. There's something I ought to be doing for her, if it isn't too late.

"I dreamed about you in the park," I tell her. "It was snowing. You looked like you wanted to be anywhere else but outside, but you didn't know where. There was something about you I had to settle but couldn't put my finger on."

We found ourselves walking. "The incline we climbed was the same as our park but strewn with white stones half the size of our palms." Pebbles like kernels of soft yellow teeth were all scattered around and they melted through the ground's permafrost.

"We weren't dressed normal," I say. I was pulling my unbelted

beige college raincoat around me but I wasn't cold. "You'd fashioned a thistle tiara you wore with aplomb. You were naked beneath
a man's knit green sweater covered with holes."

Maria says, "Oooh."

And I haven't mentioned the wind. I heard myself sound like nar-
ration. It reminded me of grass-bound blown reeds carved of scav-
enged white bones.

"We were rapt about balance. We stumbled. I said, 'Hold on to
my arm, watch your step.'" Disembodied, the words seemed to
float, became scattered in whirls of fine shavings that settled onto
our faces and burned like the dope we'd just shot.

Maria pointed down at a swarming of gnats from a denuded
cedar that floated in a still scum-ringed pond. A tern sparked its
cover. A crane dipped its beak in the algae that we hadn't noticed
before. A sparrow's torn wings were laced in the clustered dry twigs
of an alder.

"Ahead was a stand of resilient, arson-blacked firs." I go on. "We
couldn't help but run toward the spires despite what we knew. Inside
that forest your bad secret fathers were waiting." They were bared to
the waist, clutching long rudimentary tools. Out of breath, panting,
they leaned toward a freshly dug gouge in the earth. "Nevertheless,
we entered the place where your childhood had gotten loose."

There's a pause and a southerly shift to her gaze as Maria considers the dream. "Jesus, College," she says. "That's what they call psychological, right?"

"At the least."

She's picking a speckle of something that's stuck to her lip. With
slow doped disgust she wipes it off on the edge of the couch. She
says, "I'll tell you about those five fathers. But don't repeat any of it
to Cassandra." She looks toward the wall, where shadows etch bi-
secting lines. "She'd use it against me somehow."

"She wouldn't like that you told me and not her," I admit.

"She wants you all to herself and she's jealous," Maria declares.
"Like when we were driving on Linnie Canal."

"But now she's not here, we're alone. It's the first time, I think."

"Yeah, and it's kind of exciting," she says, and then, "You're turn-ing red." She smiles, tilts her head.

"About those fathers," I say, feeling flushed.

"All right, you coward," she says, tries a serious face. "I've lived in a lot of small homes," she begins.

Maria recites the names of her streets, "De Soto, Valjean, Mari-copa."

Maria remembers she had her own mustardy-brown Peechee folder, her three-holed blue-lined notebook paper. She recalls her hand pencil sharpener's guillotine blade, her White Front sack full of loose jigsaw pieces and five-and-dime charms, a red plastic snap-apart choker, a pink Eberhard Faber eraser like I used to have. I can almost breathe in the waxy nostalgia of schoolroom Crayolas, the must of a Dick and Jane coloring book. Wielding her crayons she'd smeared kids crowding dogs, climbing slides. Maria colored the arms and the legs all cornflower, the short pants and dresses a lime. She painted the eyes a goldenrod wide and gouged on red brick for the mouths.

She says she lived in a house by a canyon, a wash, an arroyo. She could count on a stone patio, a tarred barbecue grill in the yard. Maria is lighting a Tareyton filter and tossing the match on the rug. She still looks too young to smoke. She says in those houses raised up from dry mud there were pictures of Jesus, his muscular arti-choke heart in his palm. Nylon clotheslines were sprung from rain-spouts to poles in the ground.

Men drove her in '52 pickups and Plymouth Rancheros on rides in the charged Santa Anas. The dry valley winds made spaces inside her. It hurt to inhale the perpetual summer. The hot plastic seats burned her thighs.

Unsure what to do with my hands, I lean closer. Maria reminds me of burnt jubilee cherries and umber. It's nothing like Cassandra's wine and ammonia. I want to find a way to be soft with her.

She says in one of the houses she played with a red rubber clown that went limp when you pressed on its base, a green make-believe nurse's kit that held dirty white tape, suntan lotion for ointment, and rust-colored scissors too dull to cut.

"That was on Sylvan Street, no, Etiwanda," Maria recalls. "The mother was Esther. We called her Estrella sometimes," and she frowns. "That's where I learned how to whistle," Maria remembers. "The trick is to hold down your tongue."

I think she practiced all day once she got it, whistled the bedpost, the lemon rinse sheets, the door's brass unlockable knob. She would have run to the bathroom to see how it echoed, rushed through the lawn to the dry copse of lean tilty trees and tried piping the birds from the transplanted pines.

She stares past my shoulder as if the wall is the scratched back room window she used to look out. Dryer-scorched sheets hung limp on the line. There was a pair of disorderly trees, a washer, a Dodge with no tires propped on blocks. She summons the fry of tortillas cooked over the burner, the snug of her favorite retreat by the kitchenette table pushed up to the cupboard. There it was quiet and cooler. That's where she kept out of sight.

"I had my bed in the room with the babies," Maria goes on. She is indulging her habit of spreading a hand on her chest when she talks. She seems deliberate, spare, a girl who keeps secrets and knows how to hide for a very long time.

At night in that house without clocks the too silent hallway was indistinct, sooty, obscure. The tipped-open door cast its shadow agenda and there was an unannounced crack from the bare hardwood slats of the floor. The desiccated limbs of a tree scraping glass made it seem like the house was a nest raised up high and about to ignite.

Doves didn't fly from the peeled dry wallpaper though she thought they might. Above her short bed too narrow for sleep Jesus stayed crucified. There was a stripe of sick light bright enough to make out his bandana of thorns, his eyes upcast, spaniel, enamel. Outside she could see the full moon eclipsed by a low slush of waterlogged clouds. She lay in her man's nightdress T-shirt, uncovered by blankets, her bag safely under her bed, her third father's hand on her mouth.

He spoke in a slurred secret tongue that could not be ignored or denied. There must be rules for what he couldn't do with his fingers, she thought. Practiced, he pulled up her gown. Beside her the babies were squalling. He took himself out.

She tried to turn to the wall but the weight of his arm held her down. His cheeks were Aqua Velva, his breath smoke and Woolworth lunch counter sweet pickles and rum. His matted chest hair was pasty yet rough. She had to surrender. Her skinned knees were blundered apart. Everything happened too fast and yet took too much time.

There's no more here than the ignored accretion of moments as Maria pauses, nothing to do but listen and wait for the end of the high. We don't stir. Maria is lost in the scent of those fathers. I'm discomfited by the sight of her so undone, revealing a dispossessed gaze, distracted by some dialectic she couldn't yet name. What does she think of? What's been done to her? How does she get her mind around that? How does she live in the present in lieu of the past? She whispers the name of a father who taught her jacks, another the smell of turned butter and lye, of flypaper, tallow, and synthetic leather.

She says to her all the five fathers are one, except for the next to last. She won't talk about him, electing to keep that memory unspoken, intact. They're no more to her, she insists, than eight blundering hands, seven eyes, and the last with a dull opaque blindness that tugged her insides. Maria claims those men were nothing but swelled ruptured parts spilling seed everywhere, on the tops of her legs, in her palms.

Maria considers her hands, so innocent, calm. What does it mean that her fingers are guileless, despite what they've touched? They're so smooth, small, demure in her lap. What about all the tool-chested pickups, scrap metal, baling wire tossed in the back among severed-topped bottles?

She thinks of the trucks that were littered with pried-open cans, armatures sparking the torque of large gargly motors, torsion bars aching with weight as her fathers adjusted the pinch of their pants at the crotch. When they drove away, were they really gone?

"Tell me a single detail about each of those fathers," I ask, hoping I'm not pushing too far.

"I'll try," she says, "but it's hard. I'll pretend describing some other girl's life." She brushes the hair from her eyes. "All right, College. One wore an animal vest rubbed with butter to keep the hide soft." Another, she says, stressed plaid shirts and felt boots with spurs. The third father buttoned himself in a hunting ensemble, draped a low-slung bandolier on his shoulder. Maria says, "He liked hunting me down." She had to hide while, not calling her name, he tracked her through the yard's unmowed underbrush.

Maria most hated the chicken coop where she hid from that man, its sneezy feathers and feed in her hair, the oil from the truck on her dress. That father would unzip his trousers, commanding, "We'll do it right here," as he aimed his gun.

The last made her carry a sample case she had to lug with both hands. It was heavy and scraped at her shins. Sardined inside it were sturdy brown sandals and shoes, a shoe scale and horn. He wore a pocket protector, where he clipped pens stamped with auto part, gas station logos. He took her on rounds, as he called them, and made her disrobe between stops. Though he did no more, this was as bad as the fathers who touched her, to be so exposed.

"What if somebody comes?" Maria implored.

No one, of course, even slowed. They couldn't be seen from the broken-striped road. With the radio silenced on afternoons torpid with summer, the strum of approaching tires could be heard in the distance a quarter mile off. They'd be stalled in the space between towns where they parked by a construction fence near untended plots zoned for town homes that hadn't gone up.

Maria knelt on the crackly split sun-fired leather that scorched her knobbed knees. Her skirt would be bunched in his fist as he stared at her quickening breasts, the sparse brush of her mound.

They would maintain this tableau for the length of a twin-engine plane as it traversed the tipped bowl of sky.

Sometimes they'd pull over next to a sewage drain project. There'd be stacked half-shell pipes, a furrow so wide she could have easily disappeared in it if she found a way to get out of the car.

Once they had parked by an abandoned factory. Bent metal wedges whose purpose was lost still littered the ground. "Please look at my eyes," the man asked, but bare and appalled she stared at the cream of the wall as it soaked the abundance of light. It glared with a high yellow color, obscuring the sky with its height, bathing Maria's unguarded flesh to a brazen gold bright.

As she might have then, she shudders and crosses her hands on her heart. How did each of them know they could take what they wanted? Why didn't the mothers speak out? Maria decided it must be a plot.

She'd sifted the lilt of the afternoons' tortilla-grease kitchen babble for clues. The Spanish was as easy to mimic as swallowing water. Clear-as-glass Indian names were repeated in each of the homes, Huehuetenango, the coarser Zacapas. She pondered the thread of the trail they recalled leading north. That was what bound all her fathers, except the next to the last. "He was the weirdest," she says. "I won't get into that."

According to her, the rest were the end of a march, a migration begun before roads, after the ten years of spring and the juntas. Then one cousin sent for another, a nephew, a brother.

Maria says she had an image of them in a clearing as thorns bled their feet. Against the horizon past vinegar grasses was lightning, for clouds had joined up in the blue to burn what they could. Everyone hid from machetes, on their hands and knees, the fathers shot at or shooting or running away. She says she pictured a delicate rain, the after-shower flowers, a rumor of singing, desertion of gestures, worms in the water, loose teeth, doused fires, enclosures of wire. She heard the inexplicable words "full tin cup" on everyone's lips.

One of her sisters once said, "You were bartered." Maria did not understand.

"Your real parents traded you for a Chevy Impala," the girl took pains to explain.

Maria can still see her so-called sister, what was her name, Ilena? Inez? That girl stood with her arms akimbo, head tilted, foot tapping in taunt.

Maria looked up the word during recess at school, memorized it exactly: exchanging one commodity for another. That led to "commodity." It meant a convenience, an article of commerce. So that's what she was, her skin a shade lighter than that of the others, as if during all the exchanges some of her pigment had worn.

Maria remembers a picnic one time on the coast, a bucket of Pioneer chicken, crushed cans of Budweiser strewn by an insensate father, his belly distended and taut as he snored. He shifted and opened his eyes, one directly filthy-intentioned and black, the other filmed over, a mute cataract.

She says the eye centered her dreams. It had a weird second sight that followed her sleeping and waking. It could read her mind. That side of his face betrayed nothing benign.

"Where was your mother?" I ask.

Maria replies she wished her drowned in the backwash of tide. She stirred the crumbling Styrofoam cooler where melted ice water turned brown sloshed around. She wanted to flee from disorder, the gulls' caws that sounded like swings gone too wild. The chop of the ocean was nauseous and cold but she became drawn to its slap.

Her stringy redheaded mother was pulling a streamer of kelp on the sand. She said something rapid in Spanish that Maria couldn't make out, sucked in her cheeks, put her hands on her hips, turned around. Maria noticed how off in a corner of concrete and tar the stumps of the palms had been slathered a creosote white.

Later they climbed in the pickup her father liked to drunk-drive. That truck had no glass. The emergency brake made do for full stops, wrenched all the way back.

"The license plate said it was driven from Juárez, BC," Maria says now, "but that was a lie. It was stolen, picked off a Duarte construction site."

How her father drove was by tilting his head to one side. She liked that he cut his losses. She wasn't scared of his swerving. He used up his ride. The mother screamed, clutched the rusted windwing's broken arm.

"Baby," he said to the henna-haired woman. He busted her flush on the mouth.

Someone's down-the-hall radio startles us free with the shout of the news up too loud. I hear that the Pirates are leading the series, the Beatles broke up. I'm thinking somewhere fall semester has started and no one is thrown from a window or missing or circling the park with her head in a lap for a six-dollar yellow pill shot.

Maria's plain face seems abandoned. She moves beside me and hugs herself tight.

She says, "I bet you think about running away from this place all the time."

Like ready to marry I tell her, "I do."

We kneel on the couch and look at each other. Outside gulls scream and nearly collide. A man in an auto shop shirt and blue cap tosses crumbs from a red and white Wonder bread bag.

Maria leans over. The taste of her mouth when we kiss is a warm sour milk tremor. She parts her lips wider. Her tongue is the texture of paper and stone rubbed together. She gathers her skirt, tamps it into the crease of her thighs.

"Are you scared, too?" she asks.

"All the time." We don't move, we don't attempt to rise.

"About this?" She points to herself and to me in the awkward failed light. I realize I'll have to love her to save her. There will have to be some sacrifice. We are caught in a defining moment that must not go further. I will not sleep with Maria, not here, not now.

"Especially this," I reply.

Thirteen

Cassandra is framed in the door and graced with a gasoline odor. She says only, "I'm back. Don't ask." She leans on the jamb, her head tipped, trying to figure the puzzle of me and Maria spooned on the undersea blue of the sheet. "Here's something new," she remarks, bending to scratch at a scab on her shin, "you two are a lovey-dove sight."

"We haven't been sleeping together," I say.

"It's nothing to me if you fuck her," she answers. "There's no need to hide anything. You can do what you want."

We're tucked side by side only for gentle protection but I don't argue. There's no use trying dissuasion when Cassandra has made up her mind. She's wearing a strapless white jersey knit dress woven through with gold filament strands. It's her shortest one yet, it looks ironed on. In toeless black heels, her gait out of kilter, she walks to the table to pick up a cigarette pack. I notice a brand-new purple contusion that blooms on the side of her neck.

"What can I tell you? I fell." She mumbles like it doesn't matter, it happened to somebody else. She looks us over like passing a sentence, able to own the whole room with merely a flick of her wrist. I see that Cassandra is high.

"You still like to do it with clothes on," she mentions offhandedly. Her tone is the kind Hanna often used when talking to men she had

recently met. It has a casual come-on and taunt laced with innu-
endo and threat. It requires a clever response I don't have.

Annoyed, trying not to awaken Maria, I climb from the bed.

Half turned to the window Cassandra says, "I want to go out. I've
been sick. I slept on the floor of a van."

I glance at Maria curled in the trough of the mattress, her thumb
in her mouth, face creased from the pillow, feet sticking over the
edge.

"I don't want her to wake up alone."

"Come on," says Cassandra, tapping her foot, "she'll be fine."

"She looks like she ought to be clutching a stuffed animal."

"There's no need to feel guilty about her. Anyway, she's not so
young. I've seen worse," says Cassandra.

I cram my fists in my pockets. "I haven't."

"That's right, College," she says. "I always forget." She reaches
over and casually grazes my face with the back of her hand. I shiver
and shy from her touch.

"You're running a low-grade dope fever" is her diagnosis. "You've
had your fun, I want mine. Here's extra money I made."

Cassandra shows me a twenty she pulls from the V of her cleav-
age. "We'll spend this together," she says. "It'll be worth your while."
With that, she turns and walks out. I can't help but follow her steps.

I'm almost used to the ominous taint of the hallway, the hand-
prints of blood on wallpaper. Fleas come alive at our tread on the
rug. The stairs genuflect but we pass.

"I'll summon the plunge box," Cassandra is saying. "I need the
excitement."

Inside the cage we're lit by no more than the emergency button's
red warning dot. I click the toggle for down. We descend. It sounds
as if ingot-filled buckets are slamming around. Cassandra is pushing
a knee between mine as the governor, counterweight, roller guide,
tear at each other, the weak cable flaying the length of the shaft. She
puts her tongue in my mouth.

"There's no time," I protest as she pulls me against her, her back
to the grimed, sticky corner, a cigarette pack in her grasp. She

thrusts my hand in the cleft of her thighs as we rock to a stop. She pulls up the front of her dress and rubs her long stomach on mine.

Cassandra is saying, "The absence of love makes me clumsy, remember? I haven't done this in a while."

She's lying outright. I sense it on her, that damp yeasty bittersweet odor. She fumbles my zipper, says, "You've got no underwear on."

She pulls her dress up to her waist and I see she doesn't, either. It's hard to maneuver, she's taller and she has to crouch. Her hair still smells chemically scorched. I brace the sides of the car for composure. It sways on its wires, releasing a tolling like dozens of wrenches on pipes.

"College, you know I can't come," she says between gasps. "Can Maria?"

This makes me go faster. I want to bruise her. She slips her hand under my shirt, scraping welts on my back.

"That got you meaner," she says like she's hit the big prize. Cassandra lowers her head to my shoulder. She says with a harsher inflection, "That's right. Do that," her words echoing Hanna's. I think of lyrics to a song by Sinatra as a way to hold myself back.

"Pull my hair. Pull it harder," Cassandra demands. I can't help but do what she asks and it doesn't feel bad.

"Jesus, don't lose it. Make me believe that I'm worth it. Go faster," Cassandra calls out. She's giving back all her old lines. She somehow takes over and stretches it out. Drawn to the flog of her belly I cup my hands to the jog of her haunch, feel her wet from behind. Her hips are unhinged. Our skin slaps.

"Why don't you bite me?" she suddenly asks as she parts her legs wider, bends into it now.

I know what she wants, a sudden stun like an off-and-on hundred-watt bulb, a hand in the flame of a candle, a permanent startle to wake her and make her eyes wide. I tighten my teeth on her cheek and clench down. She buckles. I let out a spittle-filled whine. A weak-kneed, unguarded collision, we lurch to conclusion at last.

I think how this isn't invented, remembered, made up. Maybe

it's how Hanna felt in the car of the train when she knew she was living at last. Cassandra is straightening her dress, pulling the grate, stepping out.

"That pays off the price of admission," she's calling over her shoulder. I tug on my pants and try again to decide how to act. Should I be full of myself, nonchalant? She crosses the checkerboard tile. From this vantage Cassandra seems vagrant and sad. When I reach her I see she's nothing like that. Instead, she's wearing a febrile, insufferable smile.

"You won't take the stairs for a while," she predicts, and she may well be right.

There is a daytime quaintness to Venice that disappears during the night. When the sun's out it's flutes, hippies, bongos, guitars. I can imagine its heyday as a summer resort. Women wore knickers and bloomers, a light rail line ran to the shore. Replica gondolas cruised the canals; Ferris wheels, tilt-a-whirls, crowded the pier, which eventually burned down. Then came the war, the tracks were ripped up, some of the canals were paved. Nevertheless, a carefree blithe essence lingers on bright afternoons, a collective dream memory of the amusement park place as it was.

The evening appears opalescent. In darkness this place holds a menace. The air is expansive. Wet clouds ply the radiogram of a sky. The streetlights are singular, tacit, like I'm on acid, which I tried in college one time. The blond sand seems lit from beneath by a buried round moon. The concrete enclosure that hides the oil derrick is painted with flowers and eyes. The palms are sparse sentinels, the pagodas damp and exposed in the finicky light, with weeds pushing up through the stone that is littered with empty beer bottles and miscellaneous trash. The inky black puddles we skirt appear forced through the ground.

Cassandra refuses my hand as we walk. Because of the sheath of her dress and the height of her heels she must take careful steps. She's awkward, long limbed, her shadow stretched toward the base of the even-set palms. She studies her chipped purple nails in the halo of each cast-iron lamppost we pass. There's only the slight pick-tock tap of her heels on the abandoned boardwalk.

We near the Townhouse. The *T* and the *N* of the marquis are gone. "I have a wild-hair idea," she announces. "I want to get drunk in that bar. Let's make a grand entrance and drown."

She stumbles over the runner. The regulars squandering their government handouts pretend to be blind to her stride. We stake our stools near her favorite bottles. The mirror is still decked with cheerless blink last-Christmas holiday bulbs. The dust bowl pallor of boilermaker, shot and chaser dimmed patrons slouch in the TV's electrical sleet. We sit where the light is crepuscular. Cassandra doesn't remark on the bartender's wig he's dyed shoe polish black.

"Look, they have Four Roses," she sighs.

We give ourselves time to adjust to the sour, subterranean amber. I stare at a backlit Olympia beer diorama, its hypnotic mimic of waterfall urged by the trick of a bulb and the turn of a roller inside. Soft pickled eggs float homunculus-like in a jar by a punchboard. A fast clock hums toward the time to collect all the 1:50 glasses. A deer head stares off into space with a gimme cap cocked on its horns.

"Two bourbons straight up. Then we don't want to be bothered," she tells the bartender. "He doesn't remember I rolled him one time," she says in my ear, palm shielding her mouth. I look at his tremulous liver-spot hands, the dead cheap shag rug askew on his crown, and I'm not surprised. "It was after his payday," she says. "I got him drunk in the back. Didn't have to blow him or nothing. Got his whole roll. Three hundred dollars." She shakes her head in bemusement. "That's the most money I ever made at one time."

Everyone's leaning on elbows and tiring of red beer and pretzels. They're bearing an old silent wind, Oklahoma, perhaps, that blows through their clothes. It tousles their short-sleeved checked shirts like a wagon wheel churning the dust of a prairie, a ten-year-old patched hand-cranked Ford as it exhales the dirt of the migrant-run road.

Cassandra swallows her drink in one gulp, tips the glass so an ice cube rolls into her mouth, nudges it with her tongue, makes a lump.

She looks around the dull tawny smear as if for the first time, like she's never heard the 45 jukebox start up, seen the waterfall neon come on. Cassandra stares at the bevels of brown-dusted bottles, obscure brands never tapped. She's mumbling their names like the liquors' rare colors, the yellow of long Galliano, berry-tinged sloe grenadine, the wood smoke Metaxa, the crisp bite of peppermint schnapps.

Just for an instant, Cassandra wears an expression like Hanna lost in thought, after my father was gone and before the revolt, when she was submerged in the past and the future was a wish unformed. Maybe it's the bar's pallor. The resemblance is so close I start to say something about it, but then Cassandra's face hardens. Whatever ignited that look mimicking Hanna's has flown.

A light casts a widening stripe on the floor, climbs the wall to the shelf lined with varsity swimming team trophies. Its tint suffuses an oil-on-felt toreador. We watch a water bug fording the rubberized nodes of the back-bar glass drainer. She lights a cigarette, hacks, cranes her neck as if anyone cares, and bends near.

Squirming like something is squishy, Cassandra says flat, without rancor, "Bastard, you came inside me." Still, no one turns. She undoes her top eyehook fasteners, allowing the light to anoint her. She's shaking her hair she constantly wishes was longer, leans on her stool like she's going to fall underneath it, and orders another. Smoke rises up in her face.

"About Maria," I start, but she cuts me off with a pat on the hand, a provisional smile.

"It's not time for that," she advises. "Just take it one drink at a time." Smelling her fingers she leans on her elbows in puddling change, limp, soaking dollars. Tammy Wynette starts to hurt from the juke. Cassandra raises a hand to my shoulder. "Come on, College, let's dance."

"I don't know how," I insist. Nevertheless, I follow her onto the waxed parquet section of floor and she hustles me close.

"Put your hand on the small of my back," she instructs. "I'll lead. You just shuffle around. Pick up your feet every once in a while."

We begin turning ellipses, Cassandra's dress scratchy, her skin where we touch slick and cool. "We reek of each other," she says, and she's right, it's like bleach and damp wool.

"I was sixteen when I ran. Four years older than your girl Maria," she starts, as if carefully testing the words.

"I thought you said we should let that alone. And she's not my girl."

She pulls away, looks down at me, coy. "I'm sorry if I'm mistaken. I was just going by what I observed." In this honeycomb gloom her face is as smooth as a bottle.

"You want me to sleep with Maria, but just to make trouble."

Cassandra dismisses this with a wave. "That little shit's good for nothing but some extra money. She isn't even a very good whore."

"Because she's so young?"

"No, because she doesn't have the right attitude. She doesn't like doing what's wrong, doesn't relish the sin." Tinged with a boozy hysteria she says, "Forget Maria, I want to talk about me. Anyway, I got further than her. The Salton Sea, do you know where it is? That's where I chose to hide."

As if just for me she recalls the bellowing cattle, how squat pens of lowing were scattered around in the mulch. The cow calls were murmurous, dumb, and insistent, too close to the ground. Ahead was a buckshot CALEXICO 40 MILES sign. Beside her the tear-tasting under-sea-level stench opened out.

She says, "That place took over my mind."

Burned yellow bundles of hay bound with wire clumped the sod. The water though dead was too bright. It couldn't be quit, that rank open lake, its weed-choked embankments of citrine rye. Among all the salt and manure she couldn't hold out.

Cassandra noticed the men hauling flatbeds and trailers were obvious about her. Wistful, she whispers, "They just about crashed."

South was the Bay of All Saints, where she'd taken some rides in a powder blue taxi too crowded with Mexican cousins and smeared with orange flames on its sides. The meter was off, her own fee was flat, twenty dollars for four in the back.

Everyone passed around bottles of muscatel, port, sometimes Burma Shave lotion. They got late noon *cojones*, sang ranchero songs. She didn't mind that they threw up almost shy against stucco or pounded out tin when they parked. She kept on swinging her purse by its strap. When they passed out she would have to hitch back.

"That's how I learned about trucks," Cassandra declares as she guides me around. In front of a gas station mirror she'd put on her violent lipstick, her darkest mascara. "You're so good," she practiced before it out loud.

Then she'd be wagging her thumb toward Kenworth, Freightliner, Peterbilt cabs, their framed, unframed pictures of wives with fat arms. She says in late summer inside of those sleepers the air became pungent with marsh and the sea never lapped. Incessantly, country and western was playing or nothing at all. Her turquoise-braceleted ankles were usually propped on the dash.

She got to say things like, "Hold on," "Not so fast," to study the working-tan biceps and hands in her lap and breathe in the fine red sand blowing inside.

She says, "Time's quality changed. It slowed down."

We, too, are virtually still in a clinch. The music has stopped. We're propping each other. Cassandra is slurring a little, though her recollection's becoming precise. She says it was early October, after the last darkened truck, during the first of reliable light.

"This looks like Fresno," she said out of habit when she was let out with a pat on the rear and a ten-dollar bill in her palm.

Cassandra dry-gulped a double-cross benny and tried not to gag. She had to decide what she wanted, more pills, extra money, or wine. She swiped at her soft cotton dress that was wrinkled and spotted, at the knees of jeans underneath that were tucked in her scuffed tricked-out boots.

A rabbit lay caked in itself on the side of the road and she shuddered. Cassandra glared at the chemical surf, indiscriminate sun. She shaded her eyes and saw the refinery that never flamed out, its constant tongues lashing the sky, far upwind where the birds wouldn't fly. There was a vague gasoline smell, some far-off harvest, a hacking brown clay, as she started to walk past a ROAD WORK AHEAD yellow sign. She made for a picket of stunted brown trees. Cassandra knew she could go anywhere that she pleased.

"Ocotillo was west, El Centro southeast," she recites. "I could have climbed the Chocolate Mountains where no one's allowed."

She might clamber up Mount Superstition, walk barefoot there on Carrigo, the gunnery reserve where Cassandra imagined spent shells the size of her thighs reverberated and glowed in both daylight and dark.

Where she walked was no more than a marred unmarked strip of jaw-breaking potholes and tar. Cassandra figured she must be on Wagon Wheel Road near what once was Fort Yuma. She says it's important to get the geography right. She smelled the stink of the hundred-mile lake, stopped where the path met the spur of a B&O cattle car feeder. Above her the sky was a seemingly innocent pasture. She placed a dime on the track.

"Bring me luck," she called out to no one, and no rolling hopper came piggybacked by. Cassandra followed the trestle that veered from the shore and hooked back. A slight torpid breeze rose and touched her all over.

"I had a place I could go," she recalls.

Outside the bar, no more than a shack made of weathered boards haplessly clapped, she stomped her heels in the gravel. Cassandra picked off stray grass from her clothes. She pulled a face like she'd not be revealed, went inside.

It was dark but for startling runners of white from the gaps in the wood. An unvarnished plank made do for a counter. The This Is It sold only one brand of beer and homemade corn liquor, but you had to ask. Cassandra stole two pickled eggs from the jar by the sign with the usual motto IN GOD WE TRUST, ALL OTHERS PAY CASH. This was placed next to a plastic collection container for someone named Shorty with cancer. It held steady at seventeen dollars, she knew. She'd been here before. Cassandra had tried hard to think of a way she could skim those limp notes.

The Salton Sea spilled its unsubtle feminine odor. She shrugged herself onto a stool, ran a hand through her hair. Because or in spite of her most recent favor the bartender eyed her with intimate malice or ardor, she couldn't be sure.

"Mind your own business," she said with contempt, her first addressed words of the day.

He swiped at the bar with a T-shirt the color of vomit. He leaned toward her petulant face. "This business *is* mine," he replied, "and you can't drink here. You're underage."

Nonetheless, he was placing a long-neck Budweiser before her. Cassandra crossed her legs high as she lifted the bottle and hefted the hem of her skirt to wipe off the dust from its mouth.

She said, "I don't have to pay, that's the case," but unfolded a crumpled-up bill anyway.

"Some kind of clown," he said as he snatched it, rang change.

Cassandra washed down the last of her bennies with dregs of her foamy first beer, made too much of an ah, smeared the back of her hand on her face. She ordered a shot of the special kept under the bar.

Everyone bought her a round all at once, all four men there. The bartender lined up the ounce and an eighths. Cassandra stifled a false nervous yawn. The speed itched her teeth. She felt a flagrant hint in the tight, grimed saloon, a mid-game stalled clatter of quarter-up snooker, but what did she care? She flicked a tapered brown cockroach off the counter. This was the best kind of dare.

Cassandra knocked back each glass in succession. The men tried to look and also to hide in their beers. Did they think she would daintily sip? Maybe cry? It was no big deal.

The alcohol hit her at once. That white lightning liquid was faintly like antifreeze, tallow, and damp underclothes. It cleared her completely. She looked around. A nonchalant overage biker was testing the edge of his knife on his tongue.

"Tough chick," he told her.

"No one can scare me or tell me a thing," she replied. "That's the truth."

Cassandra might simply have him, she thought, or maybe the

boy who came out of the bathroom adjusting his belt as he belched. Maybe both. She felt her eyes roll with a motion both too fast and slow, like a swoon. Though inside her mouth was entirely dry she dabbed at her froth-spittled chin.

She got to her feet. Her skin prickled clammy and cold and she needed relief. The air turned the color of pumice and soda, her vision obscured. Then someone moved laterally beside her, too close.

She made out distinctly, "Cassandra, you whore."

"Then buy me another," she managed to slur, or was that some other girl's voice?

She had to get out but a guy in a Harvester cap was talking right to her and blocking her way.

"Ain't you got some kind of ride?" His words seemed a cartoon balloon.

"You don't see one waiting outside," she replied, raising an unsteady arm toward the door. She took a step. Her foot caught on nothing. She let herself fold.

"Glory be Jesus," she heard.

This is all right, Cassandra was thinking, it's safe, oddly comforting crouched on all fours. She could have stayed just like that, she believed, for the length of an hour. Dropping her head, she had to laugh, saw her dress was undone in the front. It was alcohol stained, pickle-juiced. Cassandra studied her breasts swinging loose as if they weren't her own. Someone was prodding her ass with the tip of his boot.

"Sway perfectly still," she heard herself say.

This thought ran around in her mind like some kind of elaborate pun. It was so clever she'd tell the others. But by the time Cassandra deciphered the sequence of speaking, the words, whatever they were, had long flown.

Instead she was looking at caps. They'd rolled her onto her back. She saw the men try to decide by side-glances who got to go first.

It was the Harvester man who ended the stall by lifting her under the shoulders. She yelled any words that came out but they had her. It was past parry or question and answer. They carried her out

through the back and wrestled her down among patches of cardboard, old tires. Hands pulled her pants, spread her legs.

"No underwear on," someone said in surprise.

The boy with the belch, his belt loosed, cried out, "Let me look."

This kind of thing, she fleetingly thought, always happened to
her out of doors.

Cassandra warded off some of the blows. She bit where she
could. By some extrication she pictured herself standing off to the
side once removed. It wasn't her feeling the maul on her stomach,
the elbows, the lunges, the skin upon skin. It wasn't her tasting the
blood and the bile, the overwrought swell, the shuddering jerk and
familiar tang in the back of her throat. She wasn't bracing herself in
the dirt for the tug up inside, for what seemed like dozens of hands
on her breasts, the wrench of her knees thrust apart. She didn't feel
how the frenzy of moments collapsed on itself and yet spread itself
out. That thrash of a girl on the ground pinned by limbs didn't care.
She liked it, deserved it, Cassandra was sure. She was no more than
a very young girl in a small yellow jumper, a doll in her arms while
her dog jumped around in the dust of the yard. Cassandra was
merely a child who was uselessly calling her mother, the girl to
whom everything happened too fast and too soon. She realized it always came back just exactly to that. Then as before she could name
all the roses, and part of her remained unsullied, intact.

Later she crawled to the scrub or was dragged. Listless, exhausted, she slumped uninspired. She used her fingers to pry open
the crusted-shut pastry-thin lids of her eyes. She jiggled a tooth that
was loose though it hurt to open her mouth.

Cassandra demanded attention but no one came by. She wanted
an eighteen-wheel diesel to find her and put her together. She had
to go to the bathroom and thought this was a good sign.

Far in the distance she made out obsidian buttes. Up there in the
thermal pool, sulfur hot water forged travertine spires. A tattered
formation of sand cranes and whistling swans flew in the line of her
sight. Nearby a power saw tore itself through two-by-fours one by
one. Country music continued to leak from the slats of the bar. The

twangy guitars and the sight of her feet sticking out from the brush made her dizzy and ill, like something could not be made right. She knew if she stayed where she was the moon would eventually rise and become her own cream shroud.

Cassandra stood and it wasn't so bad, brushed stickers and straw from her dress that was torn down the front. She gathered a few of her buttons, reached in her pocket, and thumbed her square silver-backed mirror still somehow uncracked. She fingered the three wadded singles left over, enough for a downer perhaps. Her hand came out daubed with a Benzedrine residue powder she rubbed on her gums. She studied the pulp of her face in the mirror and wondered if lipstick, mascara, could still make her over, restore her.

She took a step, then another. It sounded like walking on fistfuls of crumpled-up paper. She walked by mud flats, a hatchery upturned, blown around, a lean-to about to collapse. There was no cover whatever. Here was a place if you let yourself go you could linger forever, Cassandra thought as she breathed salty brine. She stuck a hand down her throat, clutched her gut, and threw everything up.

She aimed herself vaguely toward State 111 and followed the line of the track. Cassandra would cut north through 20, northeast to Twentynine Palms. No Santa Fe Special, no Rock Island Line, shook the ground. She wouldn't lie low after all, she decided. Maybe she'd try out her luck in Las Vegas, that thin-mustache pomade-hair town she'd heard so much from Daisy about.

Fourteen

Inside an aimless gray afternoon it feels good and American to be driving. Maria and I have punched all the leftover cottons and leached them so clean that we're all right for now. We left Cassandra behind on the bed.

"What's with Sleeping Beauty back there?" Maria asks as I aimlessly crisscross the canals. "She barfed the whole night."

"Way too much fun at the Townhouse. We closed the place, then she wanted to swim, said she had to be clean."

"Did she tell you the Salton Sea story? She said the same thing when she told me, drank a quart of tequila, got in the shower with clothes on."

"That's what it was," I say, only mildly surprised. "You remember the details?"

Maria is squinching her eyes to aid in the recall. " 'I got further than you' is how she started. To make me feel small. Something about truckers who almost crashed, the Bay of All Saints, a blue taxi and ranchero songs, how she learned about trucks where the sea didn't lap. And there was a rabbit and speed on her gums, a bar with some bikers in Harvester caps, white lightning and her on the ground on all fours and finally spread on the scrub."

"She must have the whole thing memorized."

"Then at the end, she said the whole thing was a lie."

"I didn't get that, not this time."

"She just wants to be bigger than life," says Maria. "It's you I wonder about."

"I'm just an ex-university guy hanging out," I say, flippant, offhand.

"It's not true. It's not the College I know. You could be doing something else."

"What're you, my wise older sister or something?"

The car fills with disquiet. We pass spray-painted V13 walls, an appliance repair shop SHORELINE CRIP–tagged. Maria gets on her knees, rolls up my sleeve, and looks at my tracks.

"It's no fun to argue," she says in a plain, somber voice.

I realize Maria and I have defined how we act with each other. Our intimate routines are jelling, we're better rehearsed. She chooses my clothes from the floor of the closet, I brush out her hair every noon until it shines. When riding she always sits sideways, legs tucked beneath her, propped on the passenger door. I let her pretend to be older. She has a wry just-for-me smile. When we fix I hold off her arm and gently swab any blood with a cotton ball damped with my spit.

Today Maria is wearing her trademark plaid Catholic-school skirt, plain scuffed flat mouse-colored shoes, outsized man's pullover sweater. She bends and her straight bangs obscure her delicate features. She's spreading a *Herald Examiner* in her lap that she bought with change we can't really spare.

"Tell me a thing that you learned in that college," she asks.

This is what we like to do when we're together alone.

"Somniloquy is the word for the language that sleepwalkers talk," I recall.

She shifts on the seat. "Tell me more."

"Cartographers call the blank spaces on maps Sleeping Beauties," I answer.

She plunges the cigarette lighter, says, "I wouldn't have quit if I was you."

Impatient, she waits for the pop, dabs the glow of the coil to her

Kool menthol filter. Maria has finally found a brand that she favors. She leans from the window allowing the mist to anoint her. As if still practicing smoking she exhales an exaggeration of blue.

We know the season from watching men pasting cutouts of pumpkins and witches on windows of stores.

"Let's go trick-or-treating this year," says Maria.

"I'll go as a junkie, leave the needle sticking out of my vein."

"Funny," she says. "I'll borrow Cassandra's trick dress, mascara my eyes, pretend I'm a child prostitute." I look at her face to see if she means what she said as a joke, but her features are foreboding and dark like the small, sullen storm that is threatening to break.

The wind begins rising, stitching the clouds to a peerless white backing. They turn indigo, gunmetal, kohl. In summer, who would have predicted these hues? The air is corrupt with the mulch of the gutters, the nearby sea heady and crisp. I notice the leaves here don't really change color, they mostly stay green.

Maria has tuned in a Mexican weather report. It sounds like a poem by Neruda, a divination by hen entrails, blood, and small bones. The clouds become rent by each other and thunder and let go their wet meditations on concrete, wood, stone. We're skimming the tops of the streets slick with water and oil. It's as if another's foot nudges the brake and the gas, some other hand guides the wheel.

"Don't hit a parked car," Maria advises. She sounds like Cassandra. She's playing a giddy insistence of hiding her face in her palms, her fingertips damp, orange, red, M&M-smeared. She counts down from seven and opens her eyes. Disappointed, she says, "I still know where we are."

"Andalusia," I read the street sign. I like how it sounds, a name for a three-masted ship in a gale sinking down. I imagine it carries the romance of Venice, but as we drive by I see it's no more than a grimed, narrow street lined with beat-up sedans, an occasional hippie van, bicycles bolted to posts but stripped to their frames.

"Where are we going?" she asks.

"To play the piano" is my out-of-left-field reply.

"You can do that?"

I reach over, touch newsprint. It seems like an illicit pleasure. I glance at the headlines. Pat Nixon went shopping at Sears and the war is still on.

Outside it's the kind of a late offshore squall when the lights in the houses all come on at once. The rain causes bubbles in puddles. A chain-link fence holds nothing in on our left but an auto shop sign on the ground. A junkyard car garden gleams bright on our right.

"I'll look up our horoscopes," says Maria, rustling the pages. "Here's mine." She follows the words with a finger. "Show you have poise. Be most careful in speaking." She frowns. "That's not the future, it's only advice."

We bump over the creosote planks of a bridge wide enough for one car at a time. There's merely the hushed-babble Mexican station, the welter of drops roiling Linnie Canal, and the hiss of our tires. I know where we're headed. There's a Colton Piano and Organ on Lincoln nearby.

Maria is biting the edge of her lip. "You're a Capricorn, right?" She pulls herself straight. "It says, 'You'd better get at that work only you can perform which is your own particular trial.' What's that about?"

I think it's a clue for how I ought to act. I'm vexed at the words, their explicit command. I suspect the horoscope's meaning has something to do with Maria and me. "Never mind, read Cassandra's," I tell her. I know Cancer's been softened to Moon Child to make it benign.

"It says, 'Assist a good friend. You'll get to bed early tonight.' "

We laugh but I notice her trembling hands as she folds the paper and creases its spine. Maria is trying to figure how soon she'll be sick, her throat tasting bile.

She says, "We ought to make plans." She's etching a Mickey Mouse portrait, fingertips rubbing a high nervous squeak on the steamed-over glass. She yearns for an Emenee organ, to become a rock star perhaps.

"Make plans. Sure. What do you want?"

She pulls up her knees, tucks her skirt in the wedge of her thighs. "To have twenty-three dollars," she ventures, the price of a shot. "A color TV. To be sixteen and legally drive."

"Think bigger," I tell her. "Let's pretend we have unlimited cash." We do this sometimes.

She mulls it over, fiddling with the radio dial. Maria looks like she ought to be wearing pajamas and taking a nap.

"We'll get a phone with an unlisted number," Maria decides.

"An answering service," I urge her.

"A sewing machine. I know how to sew."

"An ounce and a scale. Toy balloons. Our own library cards."

"I'll make Gary a suit. We'll bust him out, buy him a velvet pimp hat."

"A fedora," I tell her. "We'll open up false bank accounts."

She says, "You can buy him a gun."

"He'll be the enforcer."

"We'll go to restaurants together. We'll never get popped."

"If wishes were horses, then beggars would ride," I tell her. "Now I understand what that old saying's about."

Maria is sniffling and coughing, wiping her nose on her sleeve. We're more hooked than I thought if she's already coming down. I'm thinking how constricted my vision's become. This is our grand design for the future. We can have any grandiose thought that we want but settle on being small-time dope-dealing punks. There's a paucity to even our most farfetched desires.

We've arrived. The Fairlane gleams wet, alabaster. Puddles reflect the dun sky. Maria's afraid to get out of the car. She tugs on my arm but I'm already pulling the handle, releasing the latch. The plate glass of the store is dark as a lake in a storm and too wide. There's movement inside. I see our reflections belie that we're corporeal. We've turned into shadows, suggestions of selves.

"If anyone asks, you're my little sister," I say to Maria. We open the heavy brass door.

A clerk takes a few mincing steps, then he halts. He's eyeing my fa-

vorite jeans that Maria has patched with brocade-and-silk paisley, a
knit terry square on each knee, a pink satin heart on the crotch. Maria
is drenched in patchouli, stands tiptoe, hand cupped to my ear.

She whispers, "We don't belong here."

"Let's wing it," I say, "pretend we own the whole place," though
Maria is right. We are estranged from the world at large. Seeing this
store, I realize how far we've gone from the everyday, commonplace.
It is an unnerving shock to be so removed from life as it's commonly
lived. I turn, look around. "They have everything," I remark. I sit on
the rubbed-walnut bench of a Bluthner. I say to the hovering clerk,
"I hear this sounds richer than even a Bosendorfer '48."

This calms him somewhat. He nods, backs away. Beside me,
Maria scoots up so her thighs make the polished bench squeal. Her
feet barely reach the pedals. She presses the one that makes echoes,
the other that dampens the sound, the third that has little effect.

"One of my fathers could do this," she says, "the one who shot
speed, the next to the last I wouldn't tell you about."

I lower my hands to the keys, begin Chopin's *Barcarolle*. I don't
play well, blunder my favorite notes. I clutter the bass-line, tangle
the treble, manage a doomed major chord. Maria raises her hand to
her heart as I run a shaky arpeggio. I lack the mathlike precision required, the timing that ought to be subtle yet bold.

It's a difficult piece, plangent and fitful, blind to its own melodrama, full of false denouements and premature minor reliefs. Nevertheless, it peals with an essence of waves, long gondolas loosed on
calm rising waters that lap against barnacled cobbles and mortar-
bound shoals.

Because of Maria's foot on the pedals the notes toll from hollow
and liquid to mute. They're like silver fish cast from a net. Some are
reborn in the salt of the ocean, others twitch dull on the shore. I let
fall cadenzas like globes filled with pale light and oil. It sounds like
the shower outside, lamps sparking alive, the blink of the stoplight
in mist and its overbright regular orbs.

I look at my arms in their flannel-clad sleeves, how they tremble.
I imagine them bared, their mar of brown scars over thin, collapsed

veins. How long will they last? What happens when they are burned out and I've used up the ones in my hands, feet, the backs of my legs? I pierced them deliberately but blame the tones culled from wire and wood, the milk tooth white drip of the scales. I blame the rain.

I try to remember what clothes I wore only last winter. What were the names of the hardcover books with their sense of proportion I carried and how did I hold them? What kinds of things did I say? It seems so far away.

Last year I heard silence transmute to the cellophane crunch of my heels on the glaze of fresh powder, a crumple of cigarette pack, a refinement of sound at the edge of the spare university park. I can recall the particulars: In a robe, on a buckle of porch, a dark barefoot girl lifted a dairy-scarred bottle, held it to the light. She twisted the tight paper cap, touched the cold milk to the tip of her tongue. She glanced around guiltily, as if observed, and she was. She bent, put it back. It made that familiar rattle of glass tapping metal as she eased it into its rack.

The lemon-scent wood of pianos is singular, like the university library had. It had leather-bound doors with small portholes. Its walls were covered with wainscot to rafter armadas of paintings with nautical themes. Lamps shaped like bells ringed by porcelain chalices hung from long chains. I sat by a window and fingered the nearly translucent gray paper of outdated Hungarian news magazines. I tried to decipher the meaning of long-ago twelve-letter words tight in five-column type, the consonants rushing each other, accents and umlauts, stress marks adorning the vowels. I searched the text for a handful of names like the one I had owned. Abetted by ivy, stone, snow, by my age, too, this was my favorite sad, melancholy pursuit, to dredge up the past, make it glow, to practice an intellectual mien, pretending a world-weary attitude.

The university library was the crucible where my mother's shimmery image was once again forged. Hanna was beatified in the long, cold late afternoons. I was thin, consumed by fashioning a narrative that would hold from the tanks in the street, from my father's pills, from Hanna's laudanum and gin and her wayward pursuits.

Then, dizzy with imagination and print, I walked outside under uplifted crowns of bare boughs. It was the kind of a light that made you widen your eyes to take it all in. I sat on a bench in a green overcoat, history's secret agent disguised as a student, breath quietly rising and falling, my useless hands limp and ungloved.

Words seemed to be waiting it out until someone could hear them. I felt imbued with an answer I couldn't decipher. The breeze meant as much as the season that held it. My undefined notions grew larger. The reasons for learning by rote became shrunk to the size of the new winter finches, the paper cup blown here and there among tufts of grass pushed through the frost.

I bought the car parked outside for just two hundred dollars. I drove with the windows rolled down past windbreaks, raked lawn fires of wood smoke and ash. I rode past buckshot-pocked deer crossing signs and boarded-up Frostee Freeze stands.

Forests gave way to sloped lawns abandoned to trash and silent corrals. Houses were peeling on burgundy fields of aluminum siding. A whole wood seemed dipped in a pale verdigris. Under a flattened-out vestige of sun in an ocean of white calla lilies I saw split boats collide.

I witnessed lakes frozen over for skating just thirty yards wide. Unruly pines nudged half-collapsed porches. Green slatted houses with awnings and swing sets tilted in clearings. I passed abutments of hand-hewn stone retaining walls, a toll bridge, a forest floor russet with five-pointed leaves, a waterworks boat house scrawled over with unexplained sevens and nines.

Three saplings weaved on an islet beside a man-made bird perch. A trawler named *Salt Shaker* eddied away from its berth. The air was so bloated and charged it pulled in a high-country radio preacher who sizzled a nasal New Hampshire alarm from the dash. It started to snow. I tried to imagine a girlfriend I might have been leaving behind. I rehearsed the decision to close up my room, practiced driving west. Why not south or north? Because west was where music was from, where the ocean was warm. It was long hair and girls. It stood for adventure, escape. Not so much a geographical place as an icon comprised of vague, idealistic beliefs, a cliché culled from movies and TV, and it was far. It was a fantasy willingly burnished by me every day, like dipping a stone into water again and again so it won't become dull as gray slate, so it keeps its sheen.

In the funereal showroom I play the penultimate notes of the *Barcarolle*. They sound like the splash of a gondolier's pole striking shale, the prow of the boat making wavelets like tender hands clapping that rise and converge, disappear, released in the final twin hammer of chords.

I get up from the bench, take hold of Maria's damp hand. We practically run from the store.

Inside the car we're giggling and laughing at what we pulled off. We stop at the International House of Pancakes to celebrate.

I've almost forgotten how to behave in a place like this. There is the awkward business with seating and water and silverware. I haven't had a real restaurant meal since we started all this. The sizzle and smells are making me ill. Maria plays with the setup of A.1., salt, sugar, Worcestershire sauce, the cream tin. Across the table, she arranges a battlement of these things. The stiff plastic menu bears glossy pictures of perfect food, as if we didn't know how to read. The waitress comes by blowing loose strands of hair from her face. I'm trying to decide between Vive Le French Toast, Banana Nut Waffles, order puddings instead for us both.

I try to picture us through the waittress's eyes, the vantage of her middle age. Black circles ring Maria's lids, there's grime under our nails. Who is Maria to me, the waitress whose name tag says CLARISSA might guess. My sister? Too brown, I'm too large-nosed and pale. My lover? Disgusting, maybe she should call the police, but this is the seventies, who cares, and she leaves.

Maria looks like she wants to say something, scoots up on the mustard-brown seat of the booth so the fake leather squeaks. She twirls the jelly-jam condiment holder, says, "I'm not used to this, I can't handle it." She splashes the front of her blouse with the water when she tries to sip, sniffs, wipes her nose on her sleeve.

I say, "We're simply having a meal."

She shakes her head, stares at the Formica table, the paper place setting. She doesn't mean the piped Muzak, the clinking of glasses, eggs frying. "I'm stuck," says Maria. "I can't go back home, I'm too young to leave here. Can't drive or rent an apartment, could be picked up just walking around on any school day."

"It never crossed my mind," I say.

"It wouldn't."

The pudding comes. It has a chemical taste. "I never think of us being a part of the regular world," I amend.

The people around us seem alien. It's hard to believe all this exists every day with its separate momentum, its rules and order, its prescribed ways to behave. It comes to me they are all sober and how can they stand it? Maria would need a mouthful of constant excuses each day to get by. She can't exist without allies. This means me.

I say, "Now I see how it is."

"No, you don't really," she says. "To you, all this is exciting, I bet. And you've got a way out. Tell me something, College, you have a choice, why did you choose this?" She doesn't mean the piano store or restaurant but the rest.

I think of an answer that's easy and facile. "Because I hated school, I was bored."

Maria peers over the edge of her glass before taking a sip, sets it down in its puddle. "That's not it," she says.

I try, "It was because of a movie I saw."

There's some truth to this. Not so long ago there was the white of the snow turned to sludge at the edges of roads by the plows. There were the finches of winter, my breath in crystalline clouds. Soon spring semester would end. There were summer classes I'd have to take to make up my grades, which were falling. Whatever momentum had carried me forward was faltering. There were only my un-opened textbooks, Kraft cheese and tuna on toast in the tiny apartment, cool wind through wind-wings on drives through the nearby townships.

I'd stopped attending my Boston U. classes, sat through double features instead. The routine was a downer and blackberry brandy washed down with a Sprite. The films were a gauze. I was into the third week of this when the screen caught my eye, a documentary about L.A. junkies.

It was the details I found intriguing, the insular world with one goal. I studied the handwork with paraphernalia, the face-rubbing nodding. I was amazed at the sky bleeding pink, purple, black, behind tops of tall palms. Though the theater was cold I was suddenly warm.

I'd always had a vague predilection toward the subject. I had read *Junkie* by Burroughs, Algren's *Man with the Golden Arm*. I thought it was all so romantic. I guess this happens to college boys studying literature who still pine for their mothers. The film was a lesson, it beckoned. I yearned for a loss of a self I deemed inconsequential.

I decide to tell her a little. "I wanted adventure," I say. "To claim an experience as my own, a do-or-die thrill at the edge of America, to live through something large like my mother, to find myself in a circumstance that was out of my hands."

"And you bumped into Cassandra," Maria says, twirling her spoon. "She's gotten you good."

"Her pain is what I want her for" is what comes from my mouth. Maria's eyes widen and I'm also surprised at my very own words. It is exactly Cassandra's extravagant hurt that I crave.

"What about me?" asks Maria.

"You're nothing like her. You simply stumbled onto the scene of the crime."

"You make it sound bad," she says, "that I'm not larger than life like Cassandra." She folds her small hands. "Anyway, College, I knew what I was getting into when I came up to the room."

"Then why did you do it?"

Maria is tearing her straw's wrapper into confetti-sized flakes. "I told you, I can't be just wandering around. I needed a place. And you know everything that's happened. All this is more of the same."

I play with my fork and spoon. "You're young, you could do something else."

Maria is folding her napkin into triangles and squares. "I'm way older than you if you're not counting in years."

If Gary and Cassandra were here, we would not be discussing this. Instead they might try the check-switching game. Gary pretends not to know Cassandra, they sit apart at the counter, as far as they can from the register. She orders coffee, he a large meal. They exchange checks under the table. Later he pays for the coffee, she protests the amount of her bill. It only works, though, if you don't laugh or trade insults as you drink and eat.

Maria and I are not brave enough to try it. We merely play with our silverware.

I ask Maria, "What's going to happen to us?"

"We go on," she says. Her voice lacks inflection. She could be telling the time or reciting the day of the month. "We're already coming down. Soon we'll be crampy. You'd have to work a regular job for eight hours just to get us well."

I tell her, "At least it can't get much worse."

Maria carefully sets down her knife and fork. "You should never say that, it's a curse."

I take out my money. There's not enough for a tip.

"Look at the weather," Maria is saying as we step onto the parking lot. "I feel like everything's changing."

The rain has relented. We're frightened to look at each other, our fever, our sallow perspiring weak shivers. We get in the car. I put it in drive, unmindful of scenery, the leftover runnels of clouds. The radio's playing a cut from *Sticky Fingers*, "Dead Flowers," a song about heroin.

I don't want to think about what Maria will soon have to be doing, exposed on the mound of the park. I think of the slow-moving left-signal turn of the cars, my horoscope's meaning. I want to put off the moment we part, the sequence that ends with her exposed skin. Cassandra says she likes to be sold. Maria, I think, should be spared, so I'm stalling. We'll be at the park soon enough.

We arrive at the beach, cross the sand that seems eerily lit from within, pale as the blanch of the firmament's blubbery hide. I take her arm and the wind blows our clothes.

Today the sea is a jade, its froth-peaked caps legion, an expanse of turmoil that reaches the low blank horizon. We near a wide huddle of sea gulls. They squat as if autumn-bewildered, genetically stunned. I fear their immutable memory. I hate them. I lead Maria toward the nattering beaks, the speckling murmur, the dirty muttering wings.

I say, "Let's make them turn."

"Another surprise," she replies.

"It's something to see. Don't be scared." But she isn't, I am.

As we approach, the line of the gulls folds over itself like a gray-flecked live viscous blanket. In slow queasy waves the nearest birds scuttle, rise, float to the rear. It pains me to dare get so close. It physically hurts, a palpable ache in the bones of my wrist.

Suddenly, the quivering mass of sea gulls explode and take wing, a malevolent sky under sky. I gather Maria under their tattered, dissolving umbrella. We're trembling and holding each other. Maria looks rapturous, her cheeks glazed with a sheen of sea mist. It's only after the cover is clear that she speaks.

"It was a great present," she says, leaning close. "The piano and this."

Her voice is blown thin by the wind. She clutches my sleeve and studies my eyes as if I might betray her. "Don't tell Cassandra. Somehow she'll use it against me. It's my birthday today. I'm thirteen."

Fifteen

There's nothing to do in the room where we live in debris. I lie in the bed on my back and study the moon crater ceiling. I've turned off the blue bulb, I've never much liked it. I've made a mistake coming here, but I had to try it to know this.

It seems like the first time since summer that I'm all alone. To test my own presence I take measured steps to the window, kneel on the couch, grope the secret-stash rent of the cushions for cottons I'm certain we've used. I press my palm to the dew of the glass, wipe it clear. I turn and pretend I've not been here before. This is a way of enhancing the present, of rendering it into a fiction of sorts. It is a way to distance myself from what's happened.

Making a game, I ask the most obvious questions: How come the water brimming the cup on the table's tinged pink? Why's the bulb blue? Whose is the soft yellow dress crumpled and tossed in the corner, the oversized boots, the synthetic shirt on the floor? Who bent and blackened the spoon and what for?

I stop cold. The dissociation won't hold. I realize I'm no longer a witness but one of the characters we have cooked up in the spoon.

I go to the bathroom and study my face in the cracks of the mirror. My skin is sallow, slick, sheeny like it would come loose if rough-thumbed. It puts me in mind of bad meat. My eyes are rheumy, red-rimmed. I touch my sparse start of a beard that will never grow out, run my hands through my dun-colored hair that's matted, sand-flecked. I run my thumb over the slight straight scar I've somehow acquired on my cheek. I can't be this sick. I go to the bed and lie down, itch in my third-day same clothes. I take stock: Gary's in prison, Cassandra is once again absent without an excuse, Maria is out in the cars making left-signal round-the-park turns. Our aimless days' patterns have come down to this, nothing more. I know it won't change, there'll be more of the same. Gary will come back, get busted again, I'll keep taking notes in my head, Maria might make it to fourteen years old.

"You don't have to watch out for me anymore," she had said when we got to the park and I left. Even while walking away it felt ominous, wrong. I'm trying to ignore the warning that I should go find her. I tell myself I'm too dopesick to move.

I search the room for the things that I owned when I came, but they're gone, my elbow-patch corduroy jacket, the "famous striped bathrobe," the squat stack of English lit books. The parchment-thin *Norton Anthology* pages made the best toilet paper when crumpled and smoothed. I close my eyes, rendered still by the ache in my joints.

What I've been mistaking for quiet's a subtle, insidious din, cumulative, much too close. There's the mutter of indistinct voices through walls, thumps and odd footfalls, scraped silver on plates, the dry moan, moist gargle, of pipes. Other apartments release the chime of *The Price Is Right*, a radio touchdown's thin staticky cheer, Miami creamed by the Patriots at last, the dumb thump of Top-40, "Maggie May." There's never any classical music or jazz.

I smell boiled cabbage, our tart musty pile of used clothes, Silver Satin's faint ether. Eggshell and spilled coffee grounds odors rise ripe from the sink. My own acrid sweat stinks on the sheet. There's a linger of old cigarettes and Cassandra's sweet Joy perfume.

It might be Tuesday. My concept of time is undone. I say my own name and the names of the others. Still, no one returns. I want to be out in the hall with a one-minute future, to push through the tall double doors to the glass-busted bottle cap alley, to turn from our building's brick fascia and leave. I lie to myself that I would if I wasn't so ill.

Maybe things will change. Gary will get out of prison and marry Cassandra, who'll get a job as a waitress. I'll be a clerk at Hunter's Books. Maria will sign up for junior high and learn how to play guitar. We'll rent a house on the canals, plant marijuana and flowers. Come off it, I say to myself.

Then I'm given a gift, I'm removed. This is what happens when there's no way out, it's a trick of the mind I have learned, a retreat, a way of escape. The memory door opens and I step inside. The past from its pocket of silence delivers my New England childhood. It's a no school afternoon. The light is filtered by closed curtains. I hear an echo of "We'll be back soon" and a slap of screen door. The Plymouth Ranch Wagon tires crush gravel as it backs from the drive, pulls away from the curb. This way to retreat is the trick that I've learned. It's my way of escape.

My new parents' forbidden bedroom was talcum. Its afternoon walls were sliced with thin angular stripes from the blinds that were tricky to lower and raise. I placed my hand on their bed, where I didn't dare sit.

I gave in to the urge to rummage the lowboy, the dresser, to scavenge for secrets that objects like penknives possessed. I searched for legible postcard surprises, engraved enigmatic vacation mementos, the bracelets and charms in the jewelry box, zirconium rings, fake pearl chokers, hoop earrings.

I ransacked the miscellaneous drawer, with its napkins and matchbooks from restaurants, highball swizzle sticks, car-emblem key chains and torn movie stubs, buttons, a compass, protractor, slide rule for clues. The foreign-tongued names in the worn address book on the bureau were mute.

That house offered nothing. Nor did the rest of the tract subdivision, a prefab-carved thirteen-block grid of three-styled, three-color-schemed homes. They looked like they came from a kit. Ours was bumblebee yellow, black-trimmed. I sat on the bed out of spite, turned on the TV, adjusted its rabbit ear tin-foiled antenna, watched flickering shadows of cowboys. A slow wagon train was pulling a Boraxo twenty-mule team.

My new mother saved Blue Chip Stamps that paid for the couch. The catalog rested on top of the wire-mesh stand by the pink princess phone. I was still having trouble with some of the words. I thought it was "old rotten" instead of "au gratin" potatoes. I confused "monster" with "dinosaur."

I used to repeat to myself what I knew: "I live at seven-three-eight East Ashland. I go to Sacred Heart School. My name isn't really my own." I breathed the lingering smell of the husband's mechanical pencils, mimeographed blueprint scrolls.

Sometimes he came home with after-work beer on his breath, once in a while something else that only the wife could detect in his hair, on his clothes. That's when the house got too small for them both. Then I would have to shine shoes in the ill-lit garage by the flame-fired bulk of the black oil burner that looked like a large diving bell without ports. The ovals of Kiwi shoe polish had difficult butterfly snaps that dug into my quick-bitten nails.

Before I arrived I always imagined America as a place with broad streets lined with awnings, atomic clocks on the corners, chrome outdoor tables peopled by tall men and women in space-age tight-fitting suits. They would be smooth, knowing, concerned, wrapped up in earnest discussions, tilting deliberate, delicate thin-stemmed tall glasses to full blood-red lips. I'd thought they'd be quick with rejoinders, well-chosen retorts. Hanna would be there, drinking and smoking, wearing a cool linen suit. I would be her factotum.

This tricked-up American dream was no more than a mere distillation of indistinct wishes, collective desires imbued with vague romantic notions. Everyone had their particular version back there in fifty-six. Each had a particular runaway Budapest palinka vision of what our own barbed wire and rubber stamp fate had conspired to conceal.

Not one of us could have imagined how it really was, how modern but common, inconsequential, suburban, amorphously casual. Where I had come from nothing was allowed but everything mattered. Here it was reversed.

I carried my *Sky King* lunch box. Inside without variation was wax-paper-wrapped diagonally sliced bologna and cheese on white bread. The sandwich was tinged with the smell of the Raleighs my new mother constantly smoked. They had coupons of their own. Beside it were twin-digit cellophaned Twinkies, loose milk-money coins.

They were still printing in school. Though I already knew how to write, this wasn't condoned. My longhand was straight up and down while theirs leaned. It was called the Palmer Method. I had to relearn. One time I stood on my seat in the classroom and sang out the national anthem, our old one, not theirs. I wasn't forgiven, any more than my accent, a strange aberration for which during recess I had to pay. "I'm from a country that's Communist, though not by choice," I tried to explain. "Truman lied. He promised to save us. It's your fault," I claimed.

This would elicit blank stares or a provincial fear. By merely saying the Red word out loud, away from the context of radio, newspaper pages, I became instantly tainted. I realized these students' geography stopped at the cow-bellied Florida-pizzled map of the states we recited by rote every day. I learned to keep quiet about it, to not bring it up anymore.

As a concession, because it's what all the boys did, on Sundays I cut out the Dick Tracy Crimestoppers Notebook. I couldn't make sense of the slang or the jargon of what it conveyed. My two worlds wouldn't mesh. I daydreamed about Hanna instead and how it would have been if I'd stayed. This was my most common ploy, as necessary as breathing to cobble artifacts, a collage of the past. It was a jigsaw puzzle I made out of air.

I rehearsed my return toward the direction from which I had recently come. I'd go back, conspire to find her. This part was vague, but the rest was exceedingly clear.

We'd sit in a city cafe recalling our dreams. Hanna would stare with her laudanum gaze at her fluted glass half full of purse-hidden gin. Across the street is a pigeoned cupola, walls bullet-pocked. A streetcar sparks by on electric antennas. The conductor's steel punch is revealed in the cold snap of afternoon light as he turns toward the cobblestone square.

It isn't so cool, though, that Hanna would button her fur. She's wearing my favorite white dress with its red patent belt that she's loosed.

"One too many eclairs," she says, merely tilting her head to summon the waiter, who brings a new spritzer of soda. My mother is sweeping her careless, imperious hand on the checked tablecloth, brushing crumbs from the edge of her plate.

Across the renamed Boulevard of the Martyrs a storefront reflects us. We both smell roast chestnuts wrapped in newspaper. Hanna crinkles her nose at the thin blue exhaust of incessant-burp Skodas. I can detect the yeasty cheap soap in her hair that she washed in the sink bending over. "It's in my eye, get a towel," she called and I handed it to her. Water was splashed on her slip, everywhere. There was the sharp chemical bite of the mystery liquid she dabbed on her curlers, the tang of her lilium eau de cologne, the tender aroma of slight pancake base she applied to the tops of her breasts, her unadorned neck, and her face. I breathed in the whiffs of that cream she would squeeze from a tube and rub in the hollows of elbows and knees. She always offered to share.

"Not for me," I declined. "I'm a boy."

"Then you shouldn't be watching," she'd answer. Still, she would not make me leave.

Hanna would never have lived in a house at street level. She wouldn't have bothered with moistening stamps twice a week on a sponge in a bowl. She wouldn't deign to push a shopping cart loaded with six-pack canned beer, cereal boxes bearing cartoons, frozen foods. Hanna would not have been caught in a loose-threaded housecoat, worn pedal pushers or shorts, tennis shoes. She wouldn't be seen with a man with his T-shirt untucked or chewed gum or served meals on trays that unfold.

"That's what they make tables for," she would certainly say.

She hated God for what he allowed. She'd never have let me get close to the clutches of Jesus' brides. Instead, I could have eaten what I wanted, read Jules Verne in bed until I fell asleep, at whatever hour that was.

In my new parents' room as a boy in my Catholic-school shirt I recalled icemen once came. They hefted the blocks with their tongs. I remembered the stove with the ash box and its sliding grate. Each noon a sixteen-note buckle of bells pealed from the Budapest towers. Hanna and I would walk hand in hand by the city-bound lily pond lake. There was not one fastidious lawn to be seen anywhere. In that squat Brockton house I discovered the birth of the past as a wish for the future, its bitter yet sweet synesthesia I now smell and taste.

Sixteen

The afternoon's desperate. Occasional cars arrive, pull away from the curb. Drunk curses rise from the street. I sit up too fast so that everything tilts, break out in a sweat.

The room is a vague dislocation and squalor, murky and dim as if seen from a deep bathyscaphe. Shadows advance toward the ceiling, the light on the walls seems to shift by itself. I crack my knuckles, run both my hands through my damp, matted hair. I look for the longest butt in the overflow ashtray, wipe soot on my pants. I'm thinking the day can't go on, when Cassandra and Maria return.

"You haven't been paying attention," Cassandra is saying. "You misplaced this." She's holding Maria's left wrist.

"She said not to come, to wait here" is my stammered excuse.

Cassandra hisses, releases her hand. Maria sits down on the edge of the bed, pulls the blanket around her, not meeting my glance.

"College, you've been a big disappointment," Cassandra is saying, her eyes narrowed, grim, elbows akimbo, her back slightly stooped. "You can't leave her out all alone."

"I'm not her keeper," I mumble, but know that I am. I stare at my nicotined thumbs that are nothing but plungers. When Cassandra's like this it's dangerous to say anything.

"You two hurt to look at," Cassandra continues. She seems to suffer our presence, turns toward the pull of an oboe foghorn off the coast. She crosses the room and sits in the kitchenette corner, removing a cellophane packet from inside her boots. Cassandra bends to the paraphernalia she takes from her purse. My mouth turns entirely dry as she fizzes the water and stirs in the powder. My stomach contracts at the strike of the matches, their sear on the black-bottomed spoon. Inside my head I hear me repeating, "Not yet but soon."

I've seen this before but each time it holds an allure. Cassandra is holding the rig to the light, then tapping its side. She holds herself off with an arm wedged inside her crossed legs, flicks hair from her face. I can't take my eyes from the drama of Cassandra clenching and pumping her fist, forefinger tamping the length of her scars, slowly, methodically piercing herself. I wait for the usual ah from her mouth as the needle reopens a hole and slides in. Instead she doubles over, tosses the works to the floor.

"This is bunk," she cries out. "I've been burned." She curses, kicks over the chair, dashes the glass with the polio water into the sink, where it breaks.

It's as if flat, oval coins are placed under my eyelids. I can't take a breath. There's a pressure and sound like a scooped-hollow conch being pressed to my ears. I realize there won't be the regular sequence of getting me saved. So *this* is the one-minute future, I think.

Cassandra starts counting her loose coins and leftover bills. "There's not enough to re-up. We'll get drunk, turn more tricks." Maria looks like she's been hit.

Outside a weak, sluggish wind chills our bare, unwashed necks. The daylight seems blurred, rough and scratchy, too heavy and full of itself as we head for the Post.

Abandoned, drawerless dressers and torn-apart car seats are cluttering the street. The random constructions of wood, brick, and stucco look tight, dirty, mean. From up in an opened-out window comes slight raspy coughing, a P.M. news radio Teletype clacking, the eye-in-the-sky traffic pilot announcing the 405 sig alert's cleared.

"We'll get something stronger than wine," Cassandra is saying. "It's the only way I can bear this."

Inside the mom-and-pop liquor and deli we're carefully observed. Nonetheless, Cassandra manages boosting a man's pocket comb, a handful of Reese's Peanut Butter Cup miniatures.

We idle inside the Supersuds laundry, passing a flat pint of peppermint schnapps. It smells like a pine-tree-shaped car Odor-Eater. It burns going down and hits us at once. Cassandra is drunk, so she takes off her blouse.

Maria points to the sign. "Can't you read? It says keep your clothes on."

Cassandra shrugs. "That's not meant for us."

Maria goes to the bench by the window and sulks. "Why can't we behave like regular people?" she asks.

Cassandra is taken aback. "But we're not. We're stone junkies," she says. There it is. Her skin where it's bared is unhealthy, slack, maggoty white. Her bell-bottoms are too-short high waders, incredibly tight. The feather ankle choker is tearing. Her hair needs a wash. She's twisting the detergent dispenser until the lever breaks off. "No more Tide, no more Cheer," she sings. Then she pummels the change machine, sits on a washer. "This feels good on my pussy," she calls, "you should try it, Maria," but Maria turns away.

"Don't be a baby," Cassandra tells her, then saunters over to me. "Do something, College, for God's sake. I can't stand that liverish look on her face." This has become my permanent job.

I go to sit by Maria but she averts her gaze. "You're on her side," she says. "Stay with her."

Cassandra is bored with the show. She reties the Dacron shirt cinched at the navel, redons her ripped, puffed-sleeve coat. She weaves to the pay phone, her gait lackadaisical, tilty. She's calling for someplace to score. I watch her fumble in her purse for telephone numbers lipsticked on insides of Hershey's bar wrappers, eyeliner-penciled on unfolded chewing gum packs. Squandering the last of her dimes she feeds change, stomps her foot, repeatedly slams the receiver into its cradle. She tips her brow to the glass before making a wandering, blundering return.

"Gary is out. Someone's seen him. We have to find him," Cassandra says through clenched teeth.

Maria sits down and moans. We pull on her arms. We make her get up.

Unmindful of stepping on slivers of bottles, we stagger, supporting ourselves against curbed, dented cars. We come to a sewer grate graced by a fly swarming carcass of sea gull. Cassandra teases the corpse with the tip of her shoe, flips it onto its back. Its beak is missing, the head has been chewed. A nugget of gullet lies like a pit by its side near a primary wing torn in two. Cassandra starts kicking it hard. The bird comes apart in soft, mushy clumps and her heels become mucked with slight wisps of feathers embedded in clots of dried blood. I can't help but stare as she wipes at her ankle and foot with a Kleenex where some of it sticks.

Maria covers her mouth and leans over. "I'm going to puke," she announces, and does. Cassandra offers a strip of the tissue but Maria grimaces, holding her belly and letting a liverish dribble drip from the edge of her lip until it drops to the ground. She shakes her head, straightens, and swabs at her chin with a sleeve. We go on.

The boardwalk's deserted. The palms appear stunted, the lampposts impervious, cold, as if bodies might dangle matter-of-factly from their tops. The verdigris empty pagodas we pass release brackish odors. The lights that are already on in the windows cast yellow and glutinous hues. Dead patches of grass poke through windblown, packed eddies of sand. The darkening palimpsest sky etched by tendrils of clouds holds a blue and gray shivery taint. We walk fast but without destination. The imminent night is too close.

At Seacrest we abandon the boardwalk and lean against brick. Cassandra is looking me over. "You're less than useless. If you were a man you'd find the connection, get even," she says. "Look at yourself. Your shirt's hanging out, your collar is torn."

All I can answer is "You ought to see yourself first."

She's wearing an oversized inside-out fake rabbit jacket that's deracinated to strips, a scraggly teal feather choker wrapped tight on her neck, those bell-bottoms blotched with spilled wine and what could be motor oil stains.

"What are we doing?" Maria is asking, her voice halting, meek, eyes sunk in themselves. It could be a general, defining question. She could be guessing if we have some long-range plan or a contingency that might cover the next half an hour or week, but we are reduced to the minute, at best the next.

"Shut up. We're waiting," Cassandra replies with an edge of abandoned hysteria.

We're not good at this. I'm wishing us hidden like children, surrounded by summer again. We walk back to Speedway and Breeze. We stand by the NO STOP IT sign in the alley awaiting a rumor, relentlessly hoping and hugging ourselves. We return to Ocean Front Walk. Cassandra is striding so fast it's hard to keep up. She's repeating a litany, takes large, awkward steps. "I know we'll find Gary. Why doesn't he come? God damn it, I hate to be sick."

Maria is wiping her nose on the cuff of my plaid flannel shirt she wears over her wrinkled school uniform skirt. I'm shivering inside her pullover sweater, my pocketless checkerboard pants and cheap plastic shoes. If we saw ourselves as observers we'd have to look twice before turning away.

"We're being avoided," Cassandra is saying. "It's some kind of game." She looks toward the open-gape door of the restroom and swipes at her dress. "Before we met you we used to shoot up in there. Even in daylight, you know how dark that place is." She's taking a perverse pleasure in talking about this, the thing that we crave.

Cassandra says inside the last cubicle she and Gary had crouched on their heels. The flare of a match revealed vomit and piss on the concrete, a lidless bowl gutted with cardboard rolls, excrement-smeared.

I've been in there. The vented slats high in the wall let little light leak. You can hear the sea lapping and drips. The unlit bulbs in the ceiling are wrapped in steel muzzles so they won't be broken or stolen. The neglected skylights are obscured by detritus, brown rot, dead leaves.

I see Cassandra step to a porcelain sink, fill a cap, bring it back, hear the tear of a cigarette filter, the strike of the matches that mimics the pronunciation of sulfur. I smell the simmering broth and its chamomile. I can imagine the dropped-in balled smidgen as it swells with moisture, Cassandra's stick work. I see her and Gary collude in a circle of glare in the stall in the corner that no one would dare to approach.

"Know where else we did it?" she asks. "Headlights by the side of the road. We borrowed your car. Did you know?"

Why is she taking it further? I don't want to hear any more. I want to hold my ears, don't believe her, think she's making it up as she goes.

"It's true," she insists, though no one has called her a liar. "We got lost in Mar Vista. We couldn't hold out any longer. It got dark too soon. "

Cassandra is overexcited, as if this was some perfect adventure. Whitening spittle collects at the edge of her mouth as she rushes her words.

She says they pulled over and searched the rear seat for an outfit she'd hidden. They tossed Valvoline, brake fluid cans, in the gutter, shards of a dinnerware setting, a note that read, "Back in a minute, don't ticket," a Grateful Dead album missing its cover. Cassandra came up with my GOLDEN GATE BRIDGE engraved spoon. Inside a peacoat's left pocket, next to a brush choked with hair, wrapped in a wedge of a road map that lingered with Brut aftershave, she claims to have found the spare works.

"There was no water," she says, "but I had an idea."

The hood latch was stuck, then released with a click, a raised groan. The radiator cap wouldn't turn. She pounded it hard with her shoe, broke her nails until it gave. Gary looked on, his arms patiently folded, faintly amused.

"I need a long pointy thing," she exclaimed. By feel Gary found a coat hanger, unwound it. Cassandra dipped it as deep as she could.

It came out slick with a thin sheen of water she dripped in the spoon that she'd set on the grille. She dipped it again. It was taking forever. Crying and shaking, she knocked it to the pavement and had to start over. Gary made no move to help her. Finally there was enough in the spoon.

They balanced on haunches, lit by the unbusted headlight to see. It blinded them, caught them like breaking and entering thieves. The first book of matches was damp but the second one flashed, held its flame. Cassandra could not find a belt, sash, electrical cord, for a tie. Gary gripped her just under the bicep. She dug in her arm for an uncollapsed vein.

"Better not clog the outfit," she heard Gary warn. The needle was flaring incredibly silver as Cassandra hit, registered. Inside the dropper the liquid turned russet. She booted it, eased the stuff in, hoped the cooking and leeching through cotton had sopped up the rust, burned the dirt.

Their half-moon backs curved. The insistent, anthracite blackness around them had weight and a physical force. Cassandra's pinned-pupil lazy-eyed stare as she finished and pulled out the spike was caught in the beam. Her forearms were covered with oxidized metal. Streaks of grease smeared her forehead and cheeks.

"That was as good as it gets," she declares, shivering and wiping her perspiring face.

It's getting colder. We've dragged ourselves farther. We stop at the parking lot spread at the dead end of Rose Avenue. I take in the tarmac cluttered with curlicue-sprayed hippie buses, mandalas, flag-bannered breakdown encampments of modified pickups with wood camper shells like miniature gingerbread houses.

"Someone saw Gary close by," says Cassandra, shielding her eyes, staring south.

I take a long useless look up and down. No one is even remotely nearby on the boardwalk, not even a dog. A sheet for a curtain is flapping, a trailer door slaps.

Perhaps if I conjure his stride in my mind Gary will appear, lanky, jerked by his belt buckle's clasp as if tugged from the front. Maybe if I picture him running his hand through his greased jet black hair of which he's so casually vain, he'll be here. I find it scary and strange that I miss him, his spare, loping, ominous presence. I wonder if he thinks of me where he is and decide he does not. He lives in the now of his circumstance, nothing else. For him I am only the person attached to a convenient room, a toy for Cassandra, a baby-sitter for a teenage whore.

I straighten Maria's collar as she wipes her nose on her sleeve. Cassandra is making long, sizzy sounds with her tongue on her teeth. She settles herself on a creosote log that borders the lot, crosses her legs, props an elbow on knee.

She says, "It's like cause and effect. He'll show if we wait." I'm thinking that's not how it works but I hold on to a hope.

The wind picks up, shepherding clouds. A moderate breeze raises dust and loose papers, making the power lines sway. The screaking of terns for whitefish and scraps is the realized sound of my thoughts. We're being expelled from even the small world we've fashioned. It's a big little game and we're stringing it out. We're completely exposed. There is no protection and no place for me, no safety at all. I think we'll be blowing away soon like bits of confetti and ash.

A coal and salt rise of liced pigeons alights, banks, glides, settles upon a pagoda's three peaks. Under cupolas they're burbling and moaning like couples in cramped stuffy attics in coitus who can't reach relief.

Cassandra studies Maria. "What's wrong with you?" she demands. Maria responds with a wan, kind expression that shimmers and threatens to break.

"Don't stare at me like that," Cassandra says, livid. "You look like Miss Lives of the Saints."

Lately I've noticed Maria's face has turned angular, its flesh unattractively slack, pimples pocking her chin. Her placid demeanor barely disguises a startle-eyed cringe. Once so idyllic, her gaze is perpetually martyred by some premonition she mustn't reveal. A virus of unguarded panic has festered and bled through her peace.

I wonder what Maria thinks about this, our hair-pulling waiting for Gary, the sickness and cold-tap-soak washcloth of wind on her papery skin. What must she make of who she has become at thirteen?

I'd like to have Maria's thoughts, if just for a moment. Then I'd know the corruption of shadows in rooms faint with light, the yammy touch of a hand, gamy breaths of chorizo and wine on my mouth. I'd know how to speak Spanish, the taste in the back of her throat. "Como sangre," she'd said once. "Like blood." Obscuro means dark, azul is blue, negación de la luz, light denied.

In that span I might feel the wrench of her gut from someone inside. Maybe she thinks of the lamps in her houses, a still silhouette of mantilla draped over the bulb. There's the tension engaged in the night that has not been resolved.

Maybe to her, every vignette has become compartmentalized. Here is the room with the castanet, cymbal, guitar. Here is the pantry and larder, a pickup's cracked Leatherette seat; there, weeds overgrown in a yard.

Maria must have had a wish for a doll, a dress of a particular style. There was a place where faint praise was bestowed for a project at school, later withdrawn with a slap. Here is the girl who looked pretty in church, hair pink-ribbon-bound, the one who was struck with a length from the plastic clothesline. Her name means bitter, she's told me, it's in Ruth 1:20. It means one with whom the Almighty has dealt very harshly. Does she see herself being someone different next month or next year? What does Maria dream?

If I knew what she knows, my breathing would seize. It would be forced down my throat by the taste of small pickled onions, pimientos and peppers, chimichangas rotting between unbrushed teeth. There are hands the color of pumice, red clay, pushing onto her shoulder. Now there's no dope to absolve it, to hold it at bay. Maybe to her all of this, the rides in the cars, the room with pants draped on chairs, bunched at ankles, is merely what's commonplace.

I search her eyes for a clue. What exactly compels her? Is it a thought of the Chevy Impala returning? Maria might see herself washing her hair in the front yard's rust spigot, spitting water and soap. A couple climbs out. They resemble her. "We made a mistake," says the man, "we're sorry we left you. We had to." He flings the car keys to the ground. "It's all right," she says as he gathers her into his arms. Her hair soaks his collar. She tells him, "It wasn't your fault, I forgive you." Her mother is lit in the radiant fallout of sun and there are tears in her eyes. Her father is there to protect her. "No one touches my daughter," he tells her. They're leading Maria out of the yard that's lost all its power to hold her.

This will, of course, never happen. It is my fantasy for Maria, my wishful invention that keeps a small part of me cushioned, intact, from the truth.

We form a triptych of waiting. Maria's arms hang at her sides like tacked-on afterthoughts. She doesn't look left at the meaningless sand, the coiled and dashed crashing of surf, or right at the windows that pop one by one into yellow rectangles above her. The lights are revealing a pastiche of vague lurching forms, a head turned and mumming, a hand holding a plate, releasing a lamp cord, encircling a waist.

Cassandra is lighting a Lucky, blows undulant doughnuts that rise and disperse. She curls a limp strand of dry hair on an unringed forefinger and studies the street for a scene of life-saving reprieve to unfold. She's scanning the boardwalk while biting her nails.

I can't stand the sour, withdrawal smell of my skin. If it had a color, it would be a tender, bruised jaundice. The light doesn't fade so much as it's squeezed from itself. The air is a tonic of battery acid and mist from the sea. I'm grinding my teeth. Maria has moved to a thin wedge of grass, where she's shredding straw tufts from the bark of a palm. I'm pacing in front of Cassandra, awaiting salvation, as if on review.

"Jesus, you're making me nervous," she says. "Go walk somewhere else."

I step to Maria, who's humming some indistinct tune and shies when I near, embraces the tree. She presses a cheek to its hide of no comfort, her eyelids half closed. I pry her arms from the trunk. She doesn't resist, holds them limp by her side.

I tell her, "It's bad," as I pick brown-filament strands from her clothes, from her bangs and the side of her face. She doesn't reply, looking dazed, in retreat, gazing into an infinity. Maria starts singing her counting down ten to one on her fingers. She looks like she ought to be slapped in the face to make her snap out of her trance.

Cassandra is saying, "Be quiet, hold on," though we haven't spoken or budged. Then even Maria looks up at the singular loose-lug-nut roll of a van that's cruising the lot.

It isn't peace-signed or antiwar-sloganed, bedecked with spray-painted flowers or rainbowed, paisleyed. It's tar-grunged, black-splashed, S. C. Edison Water and Power utility green underneath. Incredibly, Christmas lights swing from its busted-out panes. Its motor mounts grind as it rocks to a stop. "An omen," Cassandra declares.

The driver side window is tinted, I can't see who's behind the wheel. Its engine block ticks as it cools and its grille exudes overheat steam. The door facing the ocean opens and someone climbs down from the passenger seat.

"It's Gary," Cassandra calls out, her voice manic. She hurdles a creosote log, starts to run but her heels catch on something. She sprawls, pulls herself to all fours.

In this incarnation Gary is wearing steel-framed reflecting sunglasses, a tan leather vest, a bandana tied on his brow. He's clutching his knife and a fifth as he sways, drops the bottle that shatters and splatters his oily blue jeans. His steps through the shards sound like walking on frost.

Hands on hips, he considers Cassandra. "Here's something I've seen before."

Gamely, she regains her feet. "I heard you'd been sprung," she says nonchalantly, wiping at pebbles of gravel indenting the mounts of her palms. She rubs her scarred, knobby knee through the new tear in her bell-bottom pants. They study each other like casting indictments, late-getting-home accusations, blaming each other for beery-breathed, strange-perfumed infidelities.

Cassandra says wryly, "So, we're a nuclear family again."

Gary tries on a weak smile but it doesn't wear well. "Can't you take care of yourselves? You all look like shit."

"Thanks," says Cassandra. "And how was the butt-buddy service in jail?"

Gary raises an arm to backhand her. "You calling me punk?"

Cassandra won't flinch. "Thirty days up the ass. Must be sore."

It looks like they'll strike at each other. They've missed this, I can tell. His prison yard gestures, his taciturn poses, reveal why Cassandra favors his presence, why in her dismissive fashion she hangs in with him. Cassandra articulates that part of Gary he'd claim doesn't even exist. If she was a man Cassandra would be a more grandiose, dangerous Gary, I think.

Caught in longed-for melodrama, they don't notice Maria, who's sidled beside them. She looks like she's ready to take first Communion, her fingers entwined, rapt. Cassandra turns, startled to witness her prayerful stance.

Maria stares up at Gary. Her face appears otherworldly. "I want to die, I can't stand it, please kill me," she begs. Her imploring tone has a tremulous ingenue lilt.

Cassandra bends over, gingerly teasing a gash on her shin where a scab has come loose. "We are. It takes time," she replies, tears off the beef jerky oval, flicks it to the ground.

Gary is mulling the options. Maria grapples the knife from his grasp. Like a Catholic ecstatic, she doesn't wince though she's cut. I see the thin rivulet's drip. She shifts the hilt to the palm without the stigmata, warning Cassandra away with its tip.

Maria raises the hem of her skirt and presses the blade between her bared legs. Slowly, she nudges it higher. The steel tip snags the cloth. The insides of her thighs are stippled and white. The flat of the blade rests against her lemonade daisy print underwear. She slides it coyly back and forth.

"I'll do it, I'll cut myself," she proclaims, preternaturally calm.

"You sound just like me at your age," Cassandra remarks. To Gary she says, "Our baby has snapped."

I don't dare move, make a sound, uncertain how to forestall the momentum of what has begun. Maria is shifting her gaze from Cassandra's to mine. Her eyes are unfocused and without resolve, a doe rushing toward headlights. They rest on Gary, who casually leans to his boots, extracts two glassine packs, holds them out.

He asks her serenely, unblinking, "Is this what you want, Joan of Arc?"

Maria releases the knife. It clatters on blacktop and looks like a stiff silver fish she's expelled from her womb. She turns and keens into the wind. Her hands on her chest beat like gulls.

Gary turns to Cassandra. "Now what?"

Cassandra nudges the Bakelite shaft with her toes and just shrugs. "I guess this time she gets to go first."

S e v e n t e e n

Once inside the blue room we do the dope and regroup. Gary, Cassandra, and Maria half nod on the bed. I take the kitchenette chair in the corner and stare at Maria to make sure she doesn't pass out. The dope is too good after so long without.

I want someone to tell me what happens next. I want to be led by the hand to some other scene, one with promise. I also want to stay just like this, perpetually noddy with brown heroin.

I've chosen the place in the room that's the farthest from the three of them. I watch their faces and gestures, detached from the spell they've woven around me, the hazy cocoon. Gary is blathering on about stealing a porterhouse steak from the Ralphs supermarket by shoving the meat down his pants.

"So where is it?" Cassandra is asking.

"It fell out as I ran," Gary says.

She lets out a snort at his incompetence.

"Why didn't you stop, pick it up?"

"I was being chased."

It scares me to see how easily we fall back into step, the casual way we revert to the routine of needle, match, spoon. Cassandra and Gary quickly resume their usual poses. He pats her behind, says, "I got us a brand-new connection. He'll front me a quarter to sell. From here on we shit in tall cotton."

"I'll believe it when I see it," she says. "We'll shoot it all up, then he'll break your legs."

He gives her the "better shut up" kind of look she especially favors. He plays at bouncing the tip of his knife in the space between fingers outspread, misses, cuts himself, wipes his hands on the hem of her bell-bottom jeans. "It doesn't hurt much," he says as she sucks the blood from his cut. It's as if he never left.

I used to think of Cassandra and Gary as worldly but this isn't the case. They've never flown in an airplane. Gary was proud when he told me he'd not ever read a book. They have not seen a play, or acted in one in high school. They've never joined the debate team, played Scrabble, or sat in a proper restaurant, led by a maître d' to a white-covered table. Cassandra and Gary have never seen a river as wide as the Danube, copied their palms on a Xerox machine, learned to type in a classroom, or filed pink, yellow, goldenrod forms, the carbon smudging forefingers and thumbs. Gary says he's not held a job, had the pleasure of cashing a check earned, not stolen or forged. They haven't sat in a tiered lecture hall, heard the multiplied snick and snap turning of pages, watched one hundred students take notes. They've not written "PAR AVION" on a striped, bordered, thin envelope, mailed it to an address from which no answer has ever come, the recipient doesn't live there anymore. I think they have never seen snow.

Maria has pulled up a chair and she's sitting beside me. The hysteria with the knife on her thighs is forgotten. For now, she is cured. It may resurface one night when the temperature drops.

"What was it like growing up?" she is asking. "When you were thirteen?"

I contemplate how the dope opens memory, though I realize no story is fiction as much as the one that begins, "I recall." It was a time of infinite blandness and intense boredom. I moved through a fog in the corduroy brown and long-sleeved white shirt of my Catholic-school uniform. I read *The Rise and Fall of the Third Reich* and listened to news radio.

"I was forced to go on picnics," I say. "My new parents had a favorite place on Cape Cod."

"You could do something to help," my replacement father had said as he loaded the car. He looked toward my ersatz mother. "The kid's still in pajamas," he told her.

She sat on a torn folding chair on the lawn, searched her purse to make sure she had enough cigarettes for the ride. "So put on your shorts," she said in my general direction without looking up.

Then there was the ritual of checking the house, making sure all of the windows were closed, the lights doused. Finally the father ground the ignition, the Ranch Wagon eased from the drive.

I watched the black hairs on his arm on the rim of the rolled-down driver-side window. He looked at the woman I had to call mother. "What did you leave behind this time?" he asked.

She lit her third Raleigh filter. "I don't know. Stop the car. We'll go back." I covered my ears but this didn't block out the sound. The mother remembered forgetting to bring the Scott tissues and started to cry. Her hair from behind was a helmet of stiff VO5. I thought if I touched it, its strands would cut flesh; its texture brought to mind Brillo pads. The father let out a long-suffering sigh. He lit a dime store Corona, handed the band to the mother. He saved them for a prize.

I lay in the back among insect repellent, thick rope for some unlikely towing, the red ice chest crowded with hard-boiled eggs, three-bean and potato salad, soft, tasteless buns in their mushy packets. Swathed in a coarse Pullman blanket and tucked to the side was the thirty-aught Remington usually hid in the ironing board cupboard.

The father said "Nature!" too many times. A tinny treacle of Mel Torme leaked from the radio speakers. I wished I were back in my room with my books.

"Our family drives were excuses to fight," Maria breaks in. She is cured. "The fathers held beer cans inside their thighs so they couldn't brake very fast. Someone was always caught in a lie. It was me who got slapped."

I say, "My folks didn't yell, they just seethed."

The familiar land ran with moraines and igneous taprock. We passed signs reading SAGAMORE, SCITUATE, SHARON. I knew where they'd appear before I could make out the white-lettered plaques. The parents were bickering quietly in front. "That subject's closed for discussion," I heard.

I hoped a gust of nor'easter would blow us from the road before we arrived at the no trespass patch that was hidden from water and sight. This was unlike my picnics with Hanna. Then there was a small man-made lake in the heart of the city, ringed with cast-iron benches and well-tended flowers. Hanna always dressed up for the occasion. She wore black market hose that had seams up the back. Her dress, cinched at the waist by her favorite red belt, was the yellow of bleached buttercups. The rolled blanket tucked under her arm was almost too small for us both. The air was fresh but not cool, still Hanna wore a white sweater that buttoned in front.

"It's not decent to show your bare arms in the street," she had told me before.

I had on the black patent shoes that I hated but Hanna liked, so I wore them for her, shorts with straps and a buckle in back.

"Next year, long pants," Hanna said as she began to unpack. From the hand-woven wicker she removed two thin crystal flutes, a steel-nozzled spritzer, and her flask of gin. Her hair was freshly dyed, loose and unribboned, reaching the tops of her shoulders. Her hands almost steady, she poured. Slivers of light reflected through glass, emboldening the red of her nails. I tried the spritzer and freshets of soda were sprayed everywhere. Hanna teased a bright bead from her lips with her tongue. She said, "Give it here. Just like your father, all thumbs." It was the first time she'd mentioned him in a very long while.

The day became warmer, she shrugged off her sweater, revealing the pucker of inoculation on her upper arm. Her teeth clinked the glass as she sipped. There was an uneasy, disquieting aura about her. Hanna lifted a crust-pared rectangle of caraway rye, bit into it gently so as not to let her lipstick smudge. I closed my eyes so when Hanna spoke her voice came from no one particular spot.

"Your father hated me pregnant," she said. "He was afraid and repulsed."

I opened my eyes in surprise.

"What am I doing bringing this up? Hell," she said, "you're only six." She refilled her glass, made a careless small gesture like she couldn't help it, the drinking, the telling. They go together, I later found out. "It was because of his past," she went on. "He could not take a chance." Her voice became brusque. "Are you following any of this?"

"How could I?" I asked. Hanna and I were both startled. It was as if someone else, older, had spoken that line.

"Of course," she replied. Her face flushed. A slight skein of sweat had broken out on her forehead and cheeks, from the gin or what she'd just said. Her breathing was harsher than it should have been. Her heartbeat was made manifest as a tic of her eyelid.

Later I looked for that lake on a Budapest map, but it was not there. The dead do not efface themselves, I have read. It is we, the still living, who betray their memories, or make them our own as we embellish them.

"Come on," says Maria. "You always do this. Lost in the ozone again."

I try to not think about Hanna and focus instead on that later picnic of heat, dust, and flies.

"By the time we arrived," I continue, "the other couple was already there. They had a daughter, she was two years older."

The girl was squeezed into a one-piece swimsuit adorned with a useless pink skirt. I knew she hated her name, which was Margit, that I was to call her Darlene, but I always forgot. Sometimes just being close to her skin that smelled slightly of aloe would make me confused.

Her mother wore dull orange stretchpants she rolled at the waist. Her father was obscenely shirtless in ill-fitting lavender shorts.

My father said to my mother, "Behave," nothing more. We got out of the car.

The fathers socked shoulders, the women shared diffident hugs. Margit and I were unloading the back of the wagon.

"We brought the rifle," I said in Hungarian.

"Don't talk to me in that language," she warned. "I hear enough at home."

Later we wandered the glade, whacked a come-apart chair with a switch, punted a sawed-in-half bottle of bleach, lifted a boulder, made pill bugs roll up. We climbed the wreck of a Harvester tractor on blocks, scrunched in its saddle-shaped King Kong–palm seat. We watched our fathers' back-and-forth boasting, our mothers' indelicate preening, adjusting their lipstick even there by the sea in a forest clearing. They were already into a jug of red wine. Margit-Darlene said, "Next year I'm getting a car and I'm leaving," and I wished I could. We were stunned by the heat. The parents were laughing and wiping their chins. She said, "Let's find some shade."

We aimed toward a stand of scrub. Behind us the ritual shooting at tin cans began. We straggled away from the shouting and rifle-pop clearing.

"This is where Miles Standish landed," I said.

She couldn't have cared, looking nonplussed and bored, tore a bough from a sapling to nudge a dead bird, raised a bluebottle cloud. The air was a furnace, its smell a damp mold. Then she said, "Touch my breasts."

She stared not at me but off into space, her gaze elsewhere but focused and tight. I did what she asked. Smoke from the fire bore whiffs of charred onions, wedges of fatback, bell peppers, on sticks in the fat-spitting flame. Her small breasts had a give, were resilient, not hard as I had expected. Above them her dank misted skin was blotched pink. Her nipples stiffened, our breaths became quickened. She said, "You better keep this to yourself." She was breathing a little bit hard. Then there was a rifle retort and a high, endless scream that swallowed and silenced all sounds in its wake.

My so-called mother lay curled on the ground, ankle-shot. The father actually said, "Stand back, give her air."

Of course we crowded in tighter to ogle the raw dime-sized wound, some fatty white stuff exposed, a slight yellow ooze leaking out. The mother sat up, seeming pleased at this grist for the nuptial

mill. "You shot me!" she cried. "He shot me!" she repeated in case
we missed it the first time, her tone weighted with incredulousness,
then, "I can't look, I'll throw up," and did both.

"I only grazed you," the father shouted. "It's just a flesh wound."
Margit-Darlene would not meet my gaze.

"That was the last picnic," I say to Maria, "and I never saw that
girl again."

She remains silent, fallen into a reverie of her own. I'm brimming
with mothers and fathers, with childhood. Our room is adrift with
no more than the sum of its meaningless objects. There is no substance to it anymore. It is a collection of litter, a place for nodding
and deep dreamless sleep.

As for myself, I'd rather hide wrapped in gauze. I'm tired of this
place. I'd like to stay in bed with the blanket pulled up, to never
leave. Not in the bed here but one from the past, with my mother
nearby and small sounds of housecleaning routine. I'd like to believe
that back then it was so comforting.

I recall something we recited in grade school: What are the fruits
of this region? Cattle, stone, poultry, and lumber. And what does our
city produce? We make sturdy shoes. But that was in Brockton, and
I have a need to go further, to hide in the Old World.

How much is remembered at six? I distinctly recall Hanna's
American longings, the tracks of a toy train on the living room floor.
That she often couldn't be bothered. "Go play with your toys," she
would say, slam the bedroom door. Or she would be out, leaving me
alone. Then I would think, why wasn't my father around?

"He makes me guilty and angry, and mad at myself for the guilt,"
Hanna had said once by way of excuse. "You look just like him," she
had added, turning away from the stove. Could she have been purposely cruel? I don't want to admit this, even at a fifteen-year remove. Hanna is more than the sum of her gestures, what she did or
failed to do. She is the childhood I claim as my own, the repository
of when all was seemingly good. I think for maintaining control, I
must not let this go.

I'm thinking of HO-scale narrow-gauge trains I had way before. It was harder to couple the sections of track that were curved, tricky to connect those precision-milled slots, so difficult to place the groove of the half-dozen wheels on the twin spines of track so they all fit at once. I recall the bite of the cordite aroma the power pack had, the regular click of the engine, caboose, and coal car completing their tireless ovals.

That toy was smuggled, cost more than just money would buy, I was sure. It was only October but we couldn't wait until Christmas to open the box. We tore at the brown paper wrapper, the sealed cellophane. I tugged at the new revelation of Styrofoam innards we'd save to show neighbors while Hanna would whisper the price. We sat on the floor, our legs tucked beneath us, the parquet cooling our thighs. I wore my scratchy school uniform shorts, Hanna her late-assignation cream pleated skirt and matching light velveteen blouse with its top two buttons undone.

She gingerly handled the passenger coach with its jewellike windows reflecting the room's upright lamp. Hanna peered into the car as if seeing its corridor, cabins that ran on both sides, and the sway of its metallic straps.

"I'd like to be in there," she said. I thought she might cry.

"Where would you go?" I asked her.

She clutched the train in her fist, her other hand straying inevitably toward a flute of clear gin that by now was always no more than arm's length from her side. Not picking it up, she rubbed its stem as if teasing herself with its imminent taste in her mouth.

Hanna said, "I don't know. Maybe to the West." Of course, that's the direction I've traveled instead. She lifted the glass to her red glossy lips that left permanent stains everywhere, on my clothes, on her sheets. I had checked.

"Your father taught me to like this," she said, staring into her drink with a lopsided smile.

I kept my eyes on the circling cars, afraid she might reveal about him the thing I had already guessed. It was deduced from words whispered in hallways I tried to put out of my mind. Nevertheless, they rose on the edge of tossed sleep from the mouth of the gargoyle adorning the ceiling-high bookcase that menaced the foot of my bed.

Hanna shrugged something loose from herself. "Come on, let's play America. Here we are getting closer," she said.

She nudged the caboose as it passed by her nylon-clad calves. Hanna dismissed the Atlantic Ocean, but this after all was pretend. "Where would we live, in New York? Disneyland?" She tamped her skirt in her thighs, lit a cigarette, sighed, drank again.

"We'll buy an automobile," she went on. She never exhausted this topic or tired of it. "A Studebaker. A Citroën sedan."

I never reminded Hanna that that make and model was French.

"You'll teach me to drive, to speak English," she said, ignoring that I was just six. "I'll get the phrase book." She started to stand.

I watched her climb to her knees, supported on wrists, ignoring the train as she clambered and rose to her feet. Hanna tottered across the slippery waxed cherry wood floor to the bureau where she kept her American things. In there were a Realistic transistor radio with a plug for an ear, a Timex, a *Life* magazine, matches from someplace called Hilton, a red star patch printed with TEXACO on it instead of the usual Cyrillic print. I never wanted to find out from whom or how she had procured these things.

Wistful, she rummaged the drawer, returned rifling pages she'd study at night down-comforter-tucked, propping the book on the upside-down V of an uplifted knee. She said she could not memorize any more than a sentence or two.

She sat as close as she could. "Read along with me. 'How far is the train station? How much is the fare?' "

The paper was clean thick white vellum, not yellow-gray, thin. It smelled disinfected, the typefaces modern and spare, not crabbed, tight, and crowding the page. I complied for Hanna, reciting the words. That difficult language was truculent, wide-mouthed, too long-voweled, and crude.

I search for sense in the hurried-up consonant tongue I once spoke from habit, not translating as I went along. All I come up with are words for my god and my school.

It must have been some other boy who unplugged the train, uncoupled the cars, stacked the tracks and the rest in the box, looked up at the curtain-part window, said, "Look how it's starting to snow." This sentence comes up in that language, unbidden and primal, *Nézd hogy kezd esni a hó*. The letters fall into place like some in-grained code. I turn them around in my mind until they don't make sense anymore.

Eighteen

People come in all the time, since the door doesn't lock anymore. It's all right, there's nothing to steal. Once when I returned from the Post, there were six junkies sprawled on the bed, couch, and floor. Someone was heaving their guts in the bathroom, another was nodding on the kitchen tile, his back propped on the wall. "Who are you?" asked a girl with a face tight and sharp as a fox. "I live here," I said. "Is there any more dope?"

Gary is always watching for people who come to Venice to score. Now he has brought another stranger to the room.

"My man," Gary says. "Give up fifty clams, I'll go score."

I watch the guy fumble his wallet.

"It doesn't cost that much," he says as he counts the limp bills. There's a vague familiarity to him I can't put my finger on.

"It does today if you want it right now," Gary says.

The guy wads the money into a roll. "I could find someone else."

Gary looks at the door, gestures toward it with his palm.

Hesitantly, the guy extends his hand. "How do I know you'll come back?"

Gary snatches the bills, spreads his arms, looks affronted. "This is my crib. I wouldn't desert my girls." He vaults over the clothes on the rug, then he's gone.

The kid settles himself tentatively on the edge of the couch. He doesn't know where to direct his gaze, though it tends to drift toward Cassandra, who sits on a kitchenette chair, undemure in her trick dress, legs crossed.

"It must be great living so close to the ocean," he says, his tone brittle and high.

Cassandra lights a Lucky. "A regular fun-fest." She uncrosses her legs, revealing a hint of her tan underpants.

"I mean, you can walk to the beach, lie around, get a tan."

Cassandra sneers, turns it into a yawn. She exchanges an eye-rolling look with Maria. "We never go down there," she says. "There's nothing to do, the sand gets into your clothes. Besides, junkies don't tan." She makes this sound like a physical law.

"So you're working girls," the guy stammers on, trying to stay conversational.

Cassandra gives him a weary, contemptuous glance. "We're free-lance hostesses," she says as Maria laughs into her fist. "Listen," Cassandra goes on, "you don't have to talk. It's all right to be quiet sometimes."

The boy nods. How old is he, nineteen, twenty-one? He fiddles with his fingers, entwines them, makes a steeple he brings to the point of his chin. Then he tugs at his shirt, folds his hands in his lap, brings his hands to his mouth.

Cassandra walks over and settles herself beside me on the bed. "College, this guy, he remind you of someone?" She speaks into my ear but the room is so quiet he must overhear. "Check out the way he keeps sneaking peeks over here. He thinks I don't notice. Look how expectant he is, how educated and neat he appears, how he's afraid and yet brave about this."

"I don't get it," I say, though I've got a hint of what Cassandra might mean.

"Dummy," she says. "This kid could be you the first time we met."

I watch him fidget, trying to take in the shooting gallery scene, put myself in his place. He looks toward the small mound of com-mingled clothes near the closet surrounded by wrappers of Peppermint Patties and Snickers, darts his gaze toward us on the disheveled bed with large stains on the once-green gray sheets, away to the bathroom door hanging off its hinge. He stares at the green panorama of a half-dozen Silver Satin empties scattered across the floor, then up at the stove top grimy with overboiled beans. He looks like he wants to reach for the cotton balls, cans of Coke, Gary's knife on the cinder block table. I wonder what he would make of the ceiling pocked with the steel tips of outfits, if he'd figure out how they got there, from forcing clogged syringes until their points exploded like miniature rockets, tiny Cupid stings.

Cassandra breathes in my ear. "Ask him if he went to college, if his mother or father is dead, if he's ever done this before."

"I don't want to know."

"You're afraid of what he might say. He could replace you, you know. When you leave."

"Where did that come from? What makes you say that?"

Cassandra just smiles, pats my knee. "Go ahead, College, ask him anything. I want to hear if he sounds just like you."

I move slightly away from Cassandra, place my palms on my knees. "Seen any new movies?" I ask. Beside me Cassandra makes a tisking sound on the roof of her mouth.

"James Taylor in *Two-Lane Blacktop*. *Clockwork Orange* was good."

"Who won the World Series?"

"The Pirates beat the Orioles seventh game two to one." He pauses to wipe at his brow that's perspired with waiting, with everything. "I guess you guys don't get out much."

"We don't have time for that nonsense," Cassandra calls out.

I wave her off. "What about the Super Bowl?"

"I'll take Dallas over the Dolphins," he says. "It's finally their year."

There's so much more I want to ask. What's happening in the art world? What' new with new realism, anti-object art? I'm even curious about what books top the best-seller list. The other thing I want to know is why is he screwing around with this shit? It might be like asking myself. I want to lecture that it's not a game, grass or acid, it's serious stuff, look at us, but then Gary is back.

I know what he's done, bought two balloons, hid one, shaved a third off the other he' already fixed, and he'll still have the gall to ask for a taste. Gary rips at the balloon with his teeth, spits the rubber to the rug.

"Roll up your sleeve, this won't hurt."

The boy's arm is a curiosity, it's so bare, marred with just one small black dot. Cassandra has moved into position to hold him off. Gary slaps the crook of his elbow to raise the mainline. We're staring intently, it's never routine. I'm thinking we're not at fault, since it's not his first time.

When Gary is done we let out a sigh. The boy tips his head, his mouth wide, inhales once, twice, then stops.

"Jesus H. Christ," Gary yells. "Hey, kid, wake up." We're all standing at once. Gary says, "Grab his arms, make him walk." Careful not to slip on the bottles, we drag him around.

Cassandra opens the window. "Let's throw him out." Her face is alight with a passion like this is the most fun she's had. She looks like right after I saved her when I first arrived.

"Not in broad daylight, that's crazy," says Gary. "Let's take him out back."

I'm curiously disengaged as I pull the limp body around, unthinking, serene, lost in the sequential action. "Just like you said," I tell Gary, "they really turn blue when OD'd."

"If he kicks off it's manslaughter," Gary reminds me. "That's four years each for you and Cassandra. I get a dozen, Maria gets CYA till she turns twenty-one."

I realize I only care if he dies as it relates to us, that this doesn't seem repulsive at all, it's not even a sobering thought.

We somehow muscle the body into the rusted elevator cage. Gary clicks the toggle for down. The boy's head bounces against the metal wall of the car with a hollow melon clunk. We drag him out over the checkerboard tiles into harsh afternoon light.

"Too much to drink," Gary says to someone walking by on the

Oceanview sidewalk. We make it to Speedway, the lot. We set him down on a spilled pile of cardboard, rusted cans, soiled diapers, crimped mushy telephone books.

"Now what?" Cassandra asks.

Gary turns up his palms.

"His shoes look about your size," she suggests.

"I'm not walking in no dead man's shoes," Gary says.

"In a way, you already are," she replies.

Gary looks at Cassandra, the body. "Jesus, you're cold. Why don't we take his belt, shirt, underpants, socks?"

Cassandra studies her nails. "I've done it before."

The guy opens his eyes, sits up in the trash, says, "What am I do-ing outside? Who fucked up my high?"

"We saved your life,"says Cassandra. "Plus you get to keep all your clothes."

We've fixed the rest of the dope and the room is a definition of en-tropy, absence, though it's occupied. Cassandra, Maria, and Gary are reduced to serial gestures, scratching, face rubbing, tortuously slow-motion smoking and exhaling smoke. Gary's repeated what has just happened three times, as if we weren't present. The three of them cross, uncross their legs with deliberate attention, with eyes at half-mast. They're scrunched so close together I think anytime they'll start grooming each other for fleas. Maria sips 7Up from a can through a straw. Gary is playing air horn, Cassandra refusing to look. She picks her nose, her gaze fixed at the empty foreground, licks the snot from her fingers and shivers, disgusted at what she's just done.

There's something I ought to be doing, the inertia is stifling, too many blank minutes without new ideas about how to proceed. I kneel on the couch and look toward the thick, greasy clouds. Lean-ing out the window, I take in a squat gull encampment, a strip of brown grass. The sea is a white-tufted gunmetal jitter domed with a scatter of low-skimming terns. I hear the steady refrain of the inces-sant ocean that sounds like erasure among hieroglyphics of arrow-shaped webs on the dull yellow sand. There's no visitation of inherent meaning revealing itself on the scrim where the sky rubs the water. The genetic scavenge of gulls offers no secret answer in nature, its cause and effect. We're composed of no more than reflex, I think. The light turns to striated bands from detergent blue through a chroma of unsubtle greens to an unsettling feminine pink.

We start to come down from the rush. Cassandra gets up, lights a candle. She looks at Gary scratching his groin through his pants.

I look at him bending and worrying a bunion. Sometimes I wonder about him. I want him to fit in the puzzle of us. He's told me a little, a bit of his history that, as is my habit, I've made him divulge.

Maybe he's thinking of prison, a round Cadillac with sloped fins and fenders like thighs of large unafraid girls. Or maybe he's back when his father sang just in the car, just for him. He taught Gary chess but it's long been forgotten. Gary had misplaced the knights playing horse in a San Joaquin roadhouse in Raisin, then they had moved. His father replaced them with furry pipe cleaners he bent into similar shapes. Gary consented to tell me this much.

His so-called mother would shout from the kitchen to turn up the bebop so she, too, could hear. She'd tap her feet, rock her head side to side like when she was "smacked back, jack," she called it. She'd stand in her slippers embedding Jell-O with tangerine wedges, chunked pineapple slices, and miniature marshmallow squares. Later she'd leaf through an out-of-date film magazine she had swiped from the laundry and used as a wishbook to pick out men, locales, and clothes.

Into his day's final nod Gary's father would tamp at his pipe with a burned, callused thumb, magisterial, slow It didn't matter. He didn't need the scarred digit for playing his horn that was by turn packed or pawned. It used to be rescued at last from places with wire-mesh cages behind which the tallyman casually smoked, his ashtray full, head tilted aside with a smile for the wheedling plea in Gary's father's voice.

If there was money left over they'd go for a scoop of vanilla ice cream dolloped in tall cherry Coke. Gary liked stirring his with a long paper straw, which grew uselessly soggy and limp. He'd palm the glass until the tan goop turned malty and needed no spoon. His father would insert the stem of a round berry Popsicle into a bottle of Nehi lime juice. He'd swallow and suck it together. Gary had tried it—too puckering, tarty, yet cloyingly sweet, all at once.

If they had a car they would simply sit in it. If not, they would stick out their thumbs. His father pushed Gary forward, well onto the blacktop. This was to elicit sympathy, hasten a ride. He'd told him to do this when he had a child.

If they were lucky and inside a broken-spring coupe or a bald-tired pickup he'd tune in the late farm report. The static precision of recited bushels assured him.

"That's four pecks," he'd say without fail. He'd hold up his fingers to highlight the numbers and drive home his point. His psoriatic right wrist would be bent on the cracked steering wheel. His horn and flask between his knees, he'd be rubbing the red dermal flakes that dusted the seat.

"A peck is eight quarts and a quart is two pints, which is never enough," he'd maintain. He'd said this so often he spoke it mellifluously, with a nursery rhyme lilt.

Gary's dad kept a grease-penciled tote of the local abundance on waxed butcher paper rubber-banded to strips of stiff cardboard. If yields were to suddenly fall or foreclosures were tacked to barn doors, if some charged, dry wind came rising, he'd not be surprised, they'd be gone. This time he wouldn't be caught with no more than scorched tin pots, a hammer, a trowel, rusty shears, and a tied-with-twine parcel of shiny World War II demob suit. He'd have something better to wear on his feet than worn sole-split Little Rock foundry cork boots.

His father would reach for the Old Grand-Dad bottle tucked inside his rubberized jacket's right pocket and recall the road. Inside the car he'd rehash his trial by highway, the two thousand miles of a narrow dirt spine that wanted to throw him, but he had hung on.

"I was seventeen then," he'd begin. "Had a wife with a cough who was older than twelve, I was told."

He said she'd cut his hair, always this, that they traded the scissors for two wormy pippins in Clinton. In Alva they fought a wild granary fire with nothing but buckets of dirt. He pulled a blue baby girl from out of its straw-clutching mother. That was in back of a cart they had towed past what now is called Guthrie. The car broke in Gymon, due west.

"I didn't own it," he'd always amend. It was a miracle ride flagged down one dawn near a hand-lettered sign by the side of the road that said ARKYS MOVE ON. The metal plate with the name of the town had been torn from its post and flung upside down in a lot choked with dust and parched weeds.

He said, "Nobody had any use for a horn or could pay." His wife, "Carnation, if you can believe it, it means flesh-hued in French," took consumptive from breathing the air. He pawned his first trumpet to buy a wood box to lower her in. He paid for an unordained traveling collar to mouth a few words, throw a handful of dirt, spit TB phlegm while not bothering to turn from the grave.

He'd told this tale so many times it assumed the proportion of legend. Even he wasn't sure of its truth anymore. By its conclusion the bottle was usually drained, the windows were fogged, the walnut groves woozy with glare in an afternoon haze.

Gary would think of his father's rough voice as a sepia print turned to low blurry notes. He'd hear the trumpet blurting at midnight, playing to the vines to succor their harvest of sweet Thompson Seedless green grapes.

His father allowed him to rub along scars on his arm like a map through the drought-beaten states. The soft of his elbow felt to the touch like a rubber eraser worn to a graphite-smeared nub. "Be careful, she's jealous" was all he would mention about it, no more than this worn-thin cliché.

At night in the bathroom Gary would practice, tying his arm with the cord of the curtain he'd have to stand on the folded-down lid of the toilet to reach. He'd point his index finger to the places where his father aimed the syringe, the hollows and crooks of blued veins. He'd let go the make-believe tie and gasp in a meek imitation, bending his head in a pantomime nod, scratching himself like his father. Gary repeated his words to his common-law spouse, "It was always the first one I loved best of all." Whether he meant the first wife or first shot, Gary couldn't be sure.

He'd go to the room where his father sat head tilted back, open-mouthed in the rocker. It reminded Gary of chicks begging food. His mother would sprawl in an after-shot second-year habit's light swoon on the remnant of carpet beside him, black crinkly hair in her face. If they had money the turntable scratched through the last dead-air grooves. Gary undid those pipe-cleaner-fashioned chess pieces and made them as straight as a spike or as curved as a black-bottomed spoon.

"Remember that trucker I rolled outside Nagadoches?" Cassandra asks, breaking my reverie about Gary. "The one with his bottom tattooed with his mother's initials?" She holds the candle in both hands like offering a brief votive prayer and studies its flame.

"You didn't do that," says Gary, looks down at his boots. "It was some other girl I turned out. Someone I told you about."

As if he hadn't called her a liar, she raises her eyes toward mine. She says, "It was Vegas. Remember? You know."

Not bothering to cover a sneer, Gary says, "I was there. It's not true."

"We had some adventures," Cassandra insists, unperturbed. She sets the candle on top of the cinder block table and stands on one leg, unsure where to sit. "We shot up all over. The tops of our hands, in our ankles. The backs of our calves, behind knees, between toes." She touches these spots on herself as she talks, not bothering to wipe at the sliver of spit that hangs from the edge of her mouth. Like me, Cassandra is nurturing her legend, romanticizing the past in the telling. This way she can think of herself as a woman whose name is spelled in all capitals.

"I did the most dangerous vein," she goes on, placing a palm on the side of her neck. "Here, right near the carotid. One slip and you're gone."

"It was me who did that," Gary says. "You just watched." I finger my artery there but can't locate a pulse.

Gary is pulling the front of his shirt from his pants, exposing his skin. He nudges his belly scars garnered in lockups and street fights he claims to have won, at least fought to a draw. Idly, he's running his fingers from one to the next as if playing connect the dots. It's some counterpoint to Cassandra's spike marks, a contest to prove who's the baddest and bravest, who's done or been done the most harm. Gary believes what James Baldwin has written, that no man is a villain in his own heart.

Cassandra and Gary start trading a list of the people they know who have recently died. Cecelia, who walked in the ocean. Dewey dragged from the bushes at dusk. Myesha beaten with pool cues and stabbed near the heart.

I consider the implications. Why this obituary? Is it for me or Maria? Are we supposed to be learning some lesson about what will happen to us? Or is it mere chatter, an attempt at filling the silence that makes them both nervous and glum.

Cassandra slow dances herself as she hugs her own arms. "I'm tired of arguing and it's too spooky discussing the dead," she declares. "I'd rather tell a story. Which do you want to hear next?" she asks me. "The uncle? The baby? The Salton Sea bar?"

"I've heard all of those," I tell her, resigned. Gary yawns, closes his eyes.

Cassandra is watching me studying Maria. She sighs as she steps to the couch, delivers herself to my side with a put upon calm.

"Don't look at her, look at me," she commands, touching my face with the flat of her palm. "You want to help the one who's most hapless. That's the allure you most like. You're repelled yet drawn, fascinated. Though it scares you, you like the adrenaline rush I provide. I told you, I know how you are."

"You're right," I say. "You've got me figured out."

"Yeah, but I'm bored by the whole enterprise," says Cassandra, looking abstractedly past the window's glass. She appears to be thinking of places she wandered, high desert towns whose dwellers forgot the street names, the end of a trail with no more to chew on than pebbles and air, nothing to drink but the smell of hot beer.

To stop is to die, she told me one time. That's why she'd never grow old. Cassandra daydreams the excess of road where all possibilities dwell. I know she courts it. This is what drives her, motion for the sake of itself, relentless and fevered. It substitutes for a set of beliefs or a genuine purpose. Cassandra daydreams the excess of road where all possibilities dwell. She has to retreat in her memory, to repeat the tales. Then they become like a movie, a third person fact.

I see how she so wants to re-create the past. Cassandra is nourished by heroin lore patched with wishes, intention-embellished. This is revealed in the self-possessed Giacometti half smile she now conjures at will.

Her eyes are consumed with herself and what's happened. They are exactly like Hanna's could be when she thought of her nineteenth summer, when she tippled her gin before going out for the entire night. Cassandra's eyes are freed from their cunning belligerence, mining the place that's the difference between what is, what might have once been. Her slightly filmed irises reflect and double the guttering candle. Her pupils have swallowed the blue of the bulb and the darkness that rises outside.

I know what she wants. "Go ahead, tell whatever you like," I say, and lean back.

Cassandra relaxes against me, her shoulders go slack. We fit best together like this, when she talks.

"The first time I did it," Cassandra begins. Our room is enshrined by the flickering wick of the candle. "This was in Amboy. No, I only made it to Baghdad," she says.

Cassandra is buttoning, unbuttoning, her blouse, running her hands through her hair like she's wont. The blue bulb burns on. I sit slumped against her, not drinking or smoking, my hands held still in my lap. I look toward Maria, who's curled on the bed, to search out a twitch of her rise-and-fall breath. I feel paternal toward her, then it passes. Maria beside him, Gary has fallen asleep on his back, his trumpet held close to his chest.

"It was a piss of a town, the kind of place paroled rapists are sent." Cassandra bends forward, her legs tucked beneath her. She shifts and scratches the backs of her calves with both hands. "I got a ride in a pickup from two guys named Bob. It was night, just like this," she recalls.

They had come to a stop, out of money and gas. Hands on hips, she stood on the gravel, a little bit drunk. She surveyed car hoods stacked by a corrugate fence. Nearby was a telephone pole on its side. Sentries of portable outhouses queued at the edge of her sight. Unexplained elbow-curved pipes broke the ground. An unattached placard read WINE BEER & ICE. Moon cactus bloomed all around.

Cassandra moves closer and touches my hand. Her skin is too hot. She knows that replete with remembering like this is how I like her best. Once more, she wears Hanna's look, her eyes recklessly wide. There's nothing at all subtle in her expression. It is totally open and wide.

She says, "It was cold out. We went in a shack."

One of the Bobs lit a lantern. There was no table, chair, mattress, only a half-gallon clear plastic jug and a bare carpet scrap. There were gaps in the fiberboard walls like the This Is It bar. She thought this was not a good sign.

She wore her torn dress. She still hadn't washed. Somehow her jeans had got lost. A punched-out pie wedge of the roof revealed a scatter of stars. Cassandra says she tried to remember the ones she could name as a child, Pleiades in Taurus, Cassiopeia, Sirius the dog. Likely as not she rubbed her thumb in her pocket on torn scraps of paper, those small town reminders of nowheres she'd already passed. She moved barely sentient notions around in her mind.

Cassandra leans close to my ear. "I took off my clothes. I thought that's what the deal was about."

She says one Bob actually laughed. They were involved with a furtive removal of wall. From what she could see they then busied themselves with a spoon and a bindle of powder, a match. Finally the other Bob moved to the lantern-cast halo beside her. He mo-

tioned for her to sit down on the remnant of rug. He held out an
outfit he'd made from a needle, thread, pacifier, and dropper. She'd
never seen a real one before. It was filled with brown liquid the color
of tar.

"This is a rig," he announced.

She shrugged, dismissive, pretending she couldn't care less.

"Pay attention," he said. "It's important. There's steps."

Cassandra nodded. She got it. "They showed us a movie about
this in school," she said.

"So you've never done it," the squat Bob accused.

"Not yet," she admitted. "So what?"

She could afford the whole truth when she didn't wear clothes.
Cassandra wondered if this would be similar to codeine or downers,
the slur of a Quaalude, that's what she'd heard. She watched him
tighten a length of surgical tube on his arm. He teased the tip of the
spike to the end of an inch-long brown scar, worked it in and out. He
was tender and careful. It took a long time. His head bobbed to his
chest for a full count of ten. He expelled his breath.

"Only this once you go next," said the boy.

Cassandra resented his tone. She saw in his unlocked expression
that this was no pill, cheap smoke high, no Strawberry Hill, Annie
Green Springs, or Boone's Farm's dull stun.

"Make a fist. Pump it," he said.

"Will it hurt?"

"Not now. By the time that it does you won't care anymore."

Cassandra flinched as he slapped the inside of her arm.

"It raises the veins," he explained as he knelt before her. Gripping
her bicep he poked with his finger. "You got some rollers," he told
her. "See how they slide? Can't use them. They shy from the spike."
He tapped the syringe with a flick of his thumb. Small bubbles rose
to the top. "Your mainline's strong now but you'll burn it out."

Her breathing was shallow, uneven. Her heart beat too fast. It was
no more than the feel of a pinch or a nick when he slid it in. She
watched her blood enter the dropper. He made it rise, fall, rise again.

"Have to boot it to make sure you hit. Miss and you lose the rush, raise a lump," he said as he squeezed the rig's nipple and let go his grasp. "There, that wraps it up," he said with a voice like a pediatrician.

Cassandra reeled where she sat. A knot in the back of her skull that she hadn't known to exist dissolved with a soft velvet tap. She stood up and staggered around. It felt like an igneous liquid irradiated her spine. The Bob with the bliss in his fingers retreated back into the black. There was only herself, no outside. She squatted and fished in her dress for her vanity mirror. Cassandra stood by the moth-battered web of the Coleman and held out the reflecting glass. She thought she'd discover her body in square-inch installments to see how she really was now, before the phenomenon passed.

She says, "I wanted to look myself over, to see myself new, the first time." She couldn't care less, both Bobs could watch her all night if they liked.

Holding the glass at arm's length, pointing down, she made out the vague knobby shape of her cracked, split-nailed toes. Cassandra had painted them ocher, her favorite color. She looked at a grimed dirty ankle, its anklet's fake gold. Cassandra noted her shins were unsubtly bruised, saw how her knees were infected with razor-thin welts that felt good to be rubbed, so she did. Her thighs were pale, unremarkably bland yet so smooth. She thought of her thin hips as inconsequential but for that reason entirely comely, noticed her stomach was flat as a tree-climbing boy's.

Cassandra noticed the leftover map of snail tracks on her belly and scraped off the silvering crust with her rings. She shifted the mirror and followed the line of her arm to its newly marred hollow of elbow. She moved the glass higher. Once more she saw how her right breast was just slightly tipped to one side, a little more full than the other, its hard nutmeg eye and stippled dense oval of tight aureole. She skipped the stoop of her shoulder, moved the reflection along her soft neck, where she wore her red plastic choker, the present that Daisy had bought her before she was banned from the house.

Cassandra paused on her obdurate mouth that was blistered, lips set straight, peeling and chapped. She bared her teeth that were already yellowed and blackened from long-ago Kool-Aid, sweet suckled water, and what she believed was the manifestation of lies.

She took time to study her flame-fired gaze, which was nonetheless sunk full of dark doped surprise. She knew how to make her expression give nothing or everything back, to guarantee invented passion or its utter lack. Rueful, then smug, satisfied, Cassandra thought she could make herself anything other than kind and how this was just right. It was important to know that her stare was precise. She tried on discriminate features, alluring, beguiled, by turn falsely glad, touched with lust, disconsolate, petulant, slapped. Savoring each face, she went through the whole repertoire one more time.

With almost an afterthought gesture she lowered the glass to the V where her thighs came together, tufts of stiff, matted hair sticking up. It seemed no big deal but she knew she could get anything that she wanted when this place applied. Cassandra crouched and parted herself with her fingers, spreading her legs to allow the full sight of where she was defined. She was slightly sore, dry. To make herself damp she ran the heel of her palm back and forth on the ridge of her mound. She clenched herself, watching the folds of pink skin contract then relax. Cupping the mirror beneath her, she let herself linger a while, her half smile perhaps like the one she wears now, the one seemingly borrowed from Hanna, bemused, sentimental, detached.

Cassandra thought of the word genitalia, how often allusions to food were used to describe her, sweetmeat, peach melba, she'd been called one time. It was nothing like that. She smelled her own yeasty aroma, like salt mixed with butter left out on a counter all night. She brought her hand to her tongue, licked her own viscous tart sticky brine.

Her blunt inventory concluded, not aiming, her volition slack, she tossed the mirror aside. It fissured with a crack that hung in the air long after it actually passed.

She went outside, threw up. Heedlessly naked she looked at the high desert hardscrabble verdure. The earth seemed lit from within. It had swallowed the moon, she was certain. Cassandra lay down on the ground that was warm from inside and stared at the come-apart sky.

In her head she expected a picture vignette to unfold, flat, like a cartoon perhaps. Instead, a deluge revealed every detail that made it coherent. Cassandra thought she lay still on a clean and wide bed by her window and not on rough granules of sand. Outside was the plot of hibiscus and clover that Daisy had planted and tended, a circle of water on asphalt, still-wet late-summer sheets on the line.

She recalled the caramel Rambler aslant in the drive. The ceiling above her was brazed with gradations of soft yellow light. Gold runners angled the walls and made stripes on the sandalwood floor. Head-high sunflowers swayed in the yard like top-heavy drunks. The curtains were blowing and lush and the room smelled like wax. She breathed in the sour copper of six lucky pennies she held too long inside of her perspiring palm. The air was aswarm with blond motes. She clutched a doll she pretended to like, closed her eyes, and feigned sleep when Daisy came in.

"Quit faking, you're too old to nap." Daisy pulled back the cover.

Cassandra abandoned the penitent smile she'd been nursing, sat up, rubbed her cheeks.

"I'm going to get lunch," Daisy said. "Want to come?" Squinting, she sat on the edge of the bed. "Take your hands from your face," she commanded.

"I'll put out my eyes if I want to," Cassandra replied. Daisy's open-palmed swipe grazed her chin.

"Don't use that tone. It makes you sound like your father. You're just like he was," Daisy said. This was a worn theme.

"I'm running away," Cassandra exclaimed, her usual refrain.

Daisy was putting a More cigarette to her lips. "Go ahead. Go. That's what he did." She made an exaggeration of smoking, said, "Get up and straighten the room." It was always like this.

Cassandra could not help but stare at her mother's nightdress beneath the torn housecoat. It was spattered with barbecue sauce, smudged with ashes, and alcohol-blotched. The fabric was sheer and revealed the white rolls of flesh underneath where it touched her skin when she moved.

"Don't burn down the house," Daisy said as she stood and slammed out.

Cassandra considered this option at length. At last she heard the tap of screen door. "It had holes from where we both kicked it. It was boredom that did it," she says.

She packed her essentials inside a brown Fedco sack, pecan halves hidden precisely for this because they didn't spoil, her Club Special Bee playing cards, Maybelline, L'Oreal, Nivea cream. Then she had a better idea.

Cassandra took off her Red Ball Jet sneakers and plain faded jumper. She changed to her favorite yellow checked sundress. She'd show her. She went into the bathroom and pulled down the Ready Set spritz, the Vaginex feminine douche, and the Oxydol powder.

"I don't have to live," Cassandra says she decided. She'd make Daisy pay but there were no razors. Instead, she picked up a lipstick and covered her forehead with ocher, her favorite color. She ran through the house, pulled the blinds, locked both doors. Cassandra went into the kitchen, tugged open a drawer, stirred the knives in the cutlery bin. She picked them up one by one, tested the edge of each blade on her tongue, threw them down on the black and white tile.

She walked to the living room grasping the serrated holiday carver. She tuned in a radio gospel that covered the Antelope Valley between Adelanto and Harold. There'd be lots of blood, she'd make sure. The preacher was shouting about fornication. Cassandra knew what that was. She looked around at the half-dozen aspects of Christ that Daisy had found in a firesale box and crookedly hung on the walls. She feared and hated those eyes that constantly watched with their pitiful, silent reproof, the only begotten, the incarnate son, word made flesh, lamb of God, son of man, Nazarene. The radio taught her those names. When Daisy was drunk she'd prostrate herself on her knees before each one and make-believe pray until it got too scary and real.

Cassandra was standing and holding the sharp silver steel to her wrist. She pictured Daisy come back from the store with no hands for the keys. Her mother would cradle the Jim Dandy cardboard container, a bit-into couldn't-wait chicken breast lying exposed on wax paper, an on-sale half-gallon of Kamchatka vodka she'd finally set on the floor by the Formica table. After she let herself in, Daisy would scatter her purchases across plastic place mats emblazoned with bleached reproductions of Americana, farmers with hoes, a loom and a kettle, a Lincoln log cabin, a quilt and a rocker, a churn and a hearth made of stone.

First things first Daisy would uncap the bottle and take a long pull, mush the sopped mashed potatoes and beans, figure the house all shut up as she tossed in a dollop of butter and scooped out the paste with a wedge of a roll, licked each finger clean.

Then she might think to turn down the AM revival, and where was Cassandra? That's when she'd notice the two unshod feet sticking out by the couch. Daisy would jump, maybe scream. She'd take in the clotted red spread on the carpet, her little girl's knees slightly bent and the dress riding up, her only baby wearing the choker of snap-apart beads they both liked. Already the skin on her daughter's cheek would have turned sallow and taut, her eyelids drawn closed like a detective magazine pose.

Daisy could try CPR like she'd seen on the police and medical shows, but it would be too late, of no use. Cassandra would be like the angels you made by raising and lowering your arms as you lay in deep powdery snow.

Then it was over. Cassandra sat up on the ground in the desert and shivered. It wasn't warm after all and she shook herself loose. She didn't know how much time had elapsed and there was an ache in her joints.

She got to her feet. There was a faint smudge of purple against where the horizon would be very soon, the tentative keck of first birds. She wiped at the pebbles and stickers that stuck to her thighs, touched where they'd pitted her bottom. Cassandra could walk if she wanted, she knew. She took a step, then another. This sequence had happened before and it wasn't so hard.

The rough-hewn board door of the hut was ajar. Inside, she barely made out the shape of the huddle of Bobs in the corner. Cassandra put on her dress that was ripped down the middle, straightened the hem best she could. She bent, picked up her small pocket mirror from where she had thrown it a seeming light year ago.

She asked, shy, "Is it time?" It scared her to hear the plea in her voice. Cassandra said in the dark that was tinged with a raw charry dawn, "I want more."

Nineteen

I can hear from the sizzle of the tires on Speedway it's rained. I lie on the couch and look at a sky that's distilled, a sheet lightning seafoam bicarbonate screen. Cassandra sits by my feet in no more than a longing for clothes, though it's cold. Gary's intent at the kitchenette table pounding the cottons and melting the getover powder. Curled in the bed, Maria is murmuring, her back-and-forth forearm sweeping the tangled gray ruin of sheet. A loud down-the-hall radio can't believe Vince Fregosi's been traded. The announcer's incredulous forty percent of Valley State's students admit having tried marijuana. Johnny Ukelele is dead, he intones with a note of false grief. Outside, someone's swearing in Spanish, a car engine grinds but won't start, a garbage truck dashes an upside-down bin on its fork's double tines. The room feels cramped, crowded. I should have wakened alone in a high and white place near the Common, before all of this. We're three too many in here.

At last we follow our usual life-saving habit.

"This is all we do," Maria complains. "The morning getover, pounded from cottons, the pop at noon and at dusk. Except for the park there's no time for anything else."

"Would you rather we take knitting lessons, sign up for the Girl Scouts?" Cassandra asks.

I say, "She means there's no long-range plan. All we care about is not clogging the outfit."

Cassandra furrows her brow. "College, you're taking her side again."

I watch Gary drinking his sugary wine and looking at us, back and forth. "I'm just making a point," I reply.

"Well, keep it to yourself," she says as she finishes shooting her share.

Gary's next, then I let Maria go before me to make Cassandra even more annoyed. Once we've queued by the toilet, our purgative routine complete, we can breathe easily again.

Cassandra and Gary take over the mattress, ankles hung over the edge. He's riffling a fake leather wallet. "Look what I boosted," he says.

Cassandra takes the bottle of wine from his side. "You found that in the trash." She turns to Maria. "He's the worst thief in the world."

"Am not," Gary says, petulant, rubbing his face.

"You've got no cunning, no patience, finesse."

Gary frowns. "I could tell you some stories."

"That's what they'd be," Cassandra cuts in. "You overheard them in the lockup. You couldn't even hold on to the can of sardines you tried to steal at the Post."

It's Gary's turn for a shrug. "What can I say? So I dropped it."

Beside me, Maria's unraveling the sleeve of her oversized sweater, pulling the threads with her teeth. Her other hand squeezes my wrist.

"Sweet," says Cassandra. "Why don't you kiss her?" She's lighting a Lucky and carelessly tossing the match on the carpet.

I shrug, pick at pennies and nickels suspended in candle wax puddling the cinder block table. "I already have."

"Really?" she asks. "Where was I?"

"You were out. You said you were sick, that you'd slept in a van."

"Whose van was that?"Gary asks.

"Just a trick," Cassandra answers too fast. "Anyway, you were in jail." She turns in my general direction. "College, you have a big mouth."

I shrug. "You started it."

Maria says, "Children," but Cassandra gives her a withering glance.

Cassandra decides on the safety of changing the subject. "Since you're being so smart," she says to me, "tell us again about something you studied in school."

"What do you care?"

"I want to know how the other half lives. To get a different perspective. It provides a contrast of sorts to all this."

"Whatever I tell you, you'll ridicule it anyway. All right, I'll take the bait. Philology. There. Now make fun of that."

"What's that? I forget," she asks, conversational, offhand.

"I told you before. It means casting light on the history of culture through language," I answer. "It's how the past achieves permanence." Out loud I recall a Germanic proverb I read: " 'More's done with words than with hands.' Obversely, words won't feed cats, the Italians say." My tone is insincere, haughty, just as she likes it.

Cassandra slips forward, props elbows on knees, chin on fist. "I enjoy when you sound like a book. And what did you learn about the subject?"

"I wasn't paying attention," I answer.

"That's still a problem." She takes a puff, blows twin streams of smoke through her nose.

"I watch. I know what's going on." I think it's the one thing I do well.

"All right, that's enough," Gary says. "We're not going to lie here all morning yacking and bickering. We've got to make money, re-up." He rubs a palm on his widow's peak, raises his feet in a cavalier gesture, waits for Cassandra to pull on his boots. It's a sign that we'll go to the park when she does what he wants.

Gary stands, gathers his trumpet, the wine, his cooled-on-the-sill buttermilk. Cassandra is tying the ends of a lemonade blouse in a knot on her navel. She has to lie down, arch her spine to tug Key lime stretchpants past her hips. They're one size too tight, the taut fabric revealing her intimate crease. She tucks her feet into blue denim platforms, arranges her mussed, mousy hair, flicks ash on the floor, and jingles the seven charm bracelets she wears.

"They make hand jobs sound just like Christmas," she says.

I shiver, straighten the same clothes I've worn for three days, search for my white plastic shoes I find under a kitchenette chair. Provisional, stalling, I pick up the keys, sit next to Maria, who still doesn't stir. Outside the window there's heaves of black clouds on the lye-colored sky, a leftover drip from the eaves.

Gary says, "I'll go ahead, reconnoiter."

Intent on intimate commerce, Cassandra weaves to the closet in heels unevenly worn. She glances over her shoulder while plucking her torn-collared fur.

"Don't do anything I would," she chides. "Hurry up or we'll do your fix," then she steps out the door.

I want to find something to say to Maria and put her at ease. She ought to be practicing smoking with bubble gum candy, licking her lips from its sugar, crunching its cherry-red tip. Maria looks like she wants to be crying but thinks she's too old. It's as if she's waiting for someone to come to her aid, to protect her, make sure she's untouched. I could be wrong but I'd like to believe Maria desires a place where she could find ease, dance to a phonograph record, cut pictures from fan magazines. There would be no one unzipping himself in a car, making a bed creak.

"Okay, let's do it," she's saying, smoothing and straightening her Catholic plaid skirt. She slips on her rent-at-the-toe espadrilles. We take the stairs gingerly, as if our tread would splinter its rungs.

"I'm not coming," I say. "I'm sick of you all."

Maria turns, looks surprised. "What are you going to do, then?"

"I had a life before this that you couldn't imagine. I have to relive it a little," I say. Maria shrugs, walks away. I don't even consider offering her any alternative.

I get on the number two bus that dead-ends at UCLA. I have a plan, to read the New York Times from cover to cover, to visit a bookstore. It isn't too much to ask. I'll crack the crisp spine of a novel and smell the fresh ink.

Now here is the bus with its fifty-cent clink and a seat in the rear with the fumes leaking in. It passes facing churches on Hill, one a reserved Presbyterian, the other Dominican revivalist, loud on Sunday with guitars, tambourines.

How pleasingly innocent everything seems. There's a rocking lull comprised of the jog of the ride, bright yellows and pinks of stucco enhanced by the hide-and-seek sun, the driver intoning the names of the streets where there's stops. Pigeons land and alight from the Newberry's sign undeterred by stone owls. Wind ruffles the spiky green tops of the evenly planted short palms. The dishwater clouds have dark undersides.

I watch the backs of the slight weavy heads, the varieties of headgear, flower-print kerchiefs, baseball caps. An Indian child with green plastic round lenseless glasses gets on with her mother. "What time do you have?" someone asks.

"Ten-thirty" comes a reply and several people look at their watches at once.

The child talks to itself, staring out of the glass. The woman across from my seat has large bruises under her eyes. She's incredibly pale, with tears on her cheek she doesn't bother to wipe, a pronounced overbite. Her hair is unwittingly touched by the man behind us outfitted in unmatching patterns of plaid.

"My fault," he says.

"T'sokay," she replies.

We're passed by a tandem formation of jockeying blue and white meter maid carts. There is assurance and calm in the regular squeal of the brakes, the engine's hypnotic accelerate whine. The weepy girl is falling asleep sitting up, listing and catching herself just in time. There is a shy expectant mien to the people about to get on.

Outside, the shapes of the clouds are reflected across the façades of the towers. I look down into cars to see how men and women are handling the wheel, the things that they have on the seat by their sides. I try holding two simultaneous truths in my mind, the world as it is and the one that I have. They won't be reconciled.

How would it be if the blood in my veins could be changed? Would I go back to school, live alone in my fantasy room? It is the

color and odor of apple peels, cinnamon powder. Plenty of light but
an unremarkable view, an oval throw rug, hardwood floor. A chair
and plain table, a narrow cot would be fine, the chair straight-
backed, the table blond. The white plastic AM radio on the sill
would be tuned to the classical station, its tenor tinny, the volume
low. Imagination could fill out the notes. I shake my head, make the
room disappear. The fact is, I'm going to be sick in a couple of
hours.

The bus has turned off Wilshire into the VA compound. I drove
here before with Maria. Here's the same narrowing road where we
made the right in the heart of the summer, the street lamps like
props from black-and-white movies where all the men still wore
hats, sheared acres of dusty dry grass that smells like a dry chaparral
with its hint of sage and lupine.

I like this place's aura of defeated quiet, the sharp slant of the
sun that makes the stone buildings look livid, the air subtle and sad.
The blown creamy veil of the sky is shot through with twin silver
contrails, its wide rounded clouds are the color of bran.

Maria had said, "Let me drive."

She was really too young to be behind the wheel, even when only
parked. She wore a copper bracelet she wouldn't remove though it
stained her wrist green. Her eyes were dry and the skin underneath
seemed daubed with gunpowder as she nudged the gas.

"Be careful," I warned. "We're on federal property now." We
chuffed by the multidenominational chapel. I said, "It's Victorian in
style."

A white strap of Maria's bra was exposed. She said, "This place
creeps me out."

"The street that we're on's named for Douglas MacArthur," I told
her.

She grasped the wheel with both hands as if it might come off.
"What else do you know?"

"He ordered firing on three hundred World War One vets on the
steps of the Capitol. They wanted their pensions."

Maria glanced over. "He shot his own men in America?"

"He got a medal."

She thought about this. "Maybe we'll see someone missing an arm or a leg," she said after a while. I have to remember we laughed about that. We still could have quit. Our habit was light. No, I take it back, we could not.

Then I'm in Westwood at last, get off at the newsstand as planned.

I hear myself say, "New York Times," just like that.

The vendor replies with a lit cigarette in his lips as he takes my change. "The Jets need a miracle defense," he says. "I'll take the Colts. What do you think?"

I am nonplussed. No stranger has spoken to me about anything except dope for months. "What's the spread?" comes out of my mouth. It isn't hard.

The man blows smoke from his nose, his Jersey accent is harsh. "Fourteen points."

I lift my shoulders, spread my palms-up arms. "That says it all."

"You got money on the fight." It's an assumption. Not really a question.

"Gotta be Clay. I mean Ali." This is banter, I haven't forgotten. Did I used to do this all the time?

"The Great White Hope, they're calling Frazier." I must have overheard this somewhere.

I head for the Ship's Coffee Shop, sit at the counter, and stare at the paper, amazed at the eight columns of type. It's sunny and cold in New York, the low 27. Castro is visiting Chile, school prayer's been disallowed. The Mylai trial is on. Does Bernadette still live near the Common? Could I really go back?

She lived two floors below me. We studied Chaucer together while doing our once-a-week laundry. "Whan that Aprille with his shoures sote/The droghte of Marche hath perced to the rote." It sounded absurd, yet there was something soothing to the words.

On Bernadette the sixties had not left their mark. She favored pointelle knit blouses with round frilly collars, knee-length dresses with flats. She'd actually blush when folding her pale underwear.

She invited me to her apartment. I watched her placing her clothes in the drawers, separating each layer with scented tissues. It was a delicate touch I admired.

There was a cafe nearby with bad modern art on the walls, twenty-five-cent Signet paperbacks showing lantern-jawed men turned toward women bent at the waist nearly spilling from décolletage, muted jazz, Turkish coffee with silt at the bottom of demitasse cups. We thought this quite cosmopolitan. Hanna would have approved.

Bernadette had a way of sitting with her calves tucked under her thighs I found comely, but I never said this, did not dare. I thought her too pure and reserved. She had a slight nasal accent, she set her curled hair herself, usually kept a number two yellow pencil tucked behind her ear. Her only curse word was "pisser" and this could connote both a good and bad thing. For all that, I loved her a little, I think.

We used to go for long Saturday drives in her car, the eight-track playing Cat Stevens, Neil Young. She read Dylan Thomas out loud when we parked and we never kissed once. We watched the dissipate fog of our breaths and, wrapped in winter clothes, we didn't touch. Neither of us seemed to mind. Bernadette was content with "the stars falling cold, and the smell of hay in the snow, and the far owl warning among the folds, and the frozen hold flocked with the sheep white smoke of the farm house cowl in the river wended vales where the tale was told."

This newspaper vacation is finite. My nose is running, my coffee is cold, and I'm coming down. I hurry to Hunter's and look at the titles. They have *Being There*, Tom McGuane, *Rabbit, Run.* I pick up the slimmest, most hideable, novel, John Gardner's *Grendel*, slip it between the newspaper's fold, nervously bolt from the store.

The bus ride return to the park is not charmed, it's not fast enough. Now all I can think of is getting the brown liquid shot that will unclench my guts and my joints. I get off before the park stop and walk.

I pretend I've never seen these particular buildings, try to imag-

ine not having been here before. I attempt distraction by architec-
ture. It was my new father's work. I study the slight fenestration of
crenellate glass, wide fluted columns, a classical cornice, horseshoe
arch, fretted tile, the egg-and-dart pattern of molding. In some of
the windows I glimpse televisions and regular furniture. Paintings
are enhanced by apricot light. Ferns hang from ceilings. A sense of
decorum, proportion and order anchor these rooms I'd like to believe are nothing like ours. Of course I wouldn't know how life is inside, it's just my impulse, like Hanna, to fantasize.

Maria stands at the edge of the park. She's distractedly smoking a
Kool, whipping her head so her hair clears her eyes.

She says, "Cassandra's not happy you took off. She said she
wouldn't let you get high but I made her say it would be all right."
Maria pauses to wipe at a stain on her dress. "So where did you go?"

"Remember the VA? I went through there, to a newsstand, a
bookstore. I talked about sports with some guy."

Maria is underwhelmed. "A load of excitement," she says in a
harsh tone like Cassandra might use. "Did you bring me a present at
least?"

Reluctantly, I hand her the book I just stole. She, too, hesitates
before taking it from my grasp. It's no gift for a thirteen-year-old.
"You didn't buy it for me, but all right. You hold it, I still have to
work. Tonight, in the room, you can read it out loud."

Maria does not want to go. I'm comparing Oceanview's apartments to brownstones in Brockton when Maria says, "Tell me about
the first girlfriend you had." Sometimes memory is prescient. It sets
itself up for its own recollection. That's where that first girl and I met.

"She wasn't really my girlfriend," I answer. "We never dated. One
thing's for sure, no money changed hands."

Maria looks up as if she's been struck. "Why did you have to say
that?"

She's right, it's a heedless, flip comment, a defense against what
we're doing.

"Did you go all the way? Did she bleed? Was she cherry?" Maria's
already forgotten the slight.

"She'd done it before. She said her friend had just ended, you know, her period," I recall from I don't know where.

"She called it that?" Maria squirms, pulls a face, hugs herself. "What was her name?"

"She wouldn't tell me. I thought that was weird. She didn't let on to too much. She'd gone to Saint Vibiana's for girls. Told me the sisters had made them kneel down for skirt length inspections in class."

"I know about that. There's tricks you can use. You can loosen the threads around here," says Maria, thumbing the hem of her skirt.

"I'll bet the nuns knew them all."

She nods. "It was for the brainwash effect." The breeze ruffles her bangs. "So, was she older than me?"

"Older than me, and I was sixteen."

Maria is twirling a twig she's picked up from the ground. "I must have been eight, then, or nine. I lived in Pomona. We drove to horseshows, and auctions, barn dances on weekends. That Mexican music," she muses, "lost *novias, lágrimas, besos.*" She tucks her hands in her sleeves. "I wasn't pure by then. If you know what I mean."

To this there's no proper response.

We're passing the Kool back and forth. The wind sounds escaped from the alleys. Above us attenuate strands of dark clouds blow in armadas due east. We climb the thirteen-tree slightly damp rise. I spread my coat on the ground. We sit facing the Post in case Gary comes back. Cassandra is absent. She must have collared a ride. Maria is nervously checking the slow-left-turn cars. She appears to be hoping no one will pull to the side, demanding her lips or her palms. Maria wants no empty pint, no kid's Big Wheel tossed in the back among toys and loose Pampers, no man with specific ideas and his shirttail untucked, no catch in his throat or the sudden surprise she'll have to wipe from the back of her hand or the edge of her mouth. A beige Pinto rolls to a stop.

Maria gets up, picks at nettles and scalpels of grass, turns away, takes tremulous steps to the curb without looking back.

I consider chasing her, rescue arms wide. I tell myself what she does is a matter of necessity, nothing else, but I don't really believe it. I don't practice expressions I've picked up from Gary like cop a mope, jab-off, or man on the line. Instead I lie back, ignore the damp lawn, close my eyes. To forestall the anxious wait for the high, to put Maria out of my mind, I make an effort to recall when I was sixteen, that first time.

What I liked to do was drive my own car away from my adoptive parents. I always made sure to point out this family distinction whether or not I was asked. My father smoked dime store Corollas, saving the bands for a prize. His wife, whom I had to call mother, stayed home to straighten, sweep, order her matchbook and napkin collection. She wore her hair in a bun so severe, when she bent to housework the veins in her temples would purple and bulge. She favored polka-dot aprons and fuzzy white mules, culottes rolled at the waist. She'd decorated the house in Blue Chip and S&H Green Stamp Colonial. They were immigrants, too, and she wanted to fit.

Plastic protectors covered the arms of the couch and the monthly installment recliner where just the provider could sit. A sepia portrait of her great-grandmother was propped on the leased-with-an-option-to-purchase piano. They couldn't play it, but I was beginning to learn on my own.

I owned a rust-speckled, cream-colored '58 Buick Special with fins, a palm-burnished necker's knob screwed to the wheel. I'd bought it myself from a job mowing grass, washing windows, scrubbing car leaks from asphalt with TSP powder, filling in for the maid at the Ashaway Inn. I was licensed, pink-slipped, unobserved.

Back there it was also this season. A light snow had fallen. My tires mushed the slush as I steered through the curves. I rolled down the window and turned up the heater that let out a tart singe of melting electrical wire. Raked leaves smoldered in sweet, acrid piles on the lawns. As always, I would have been nervously bored. I dressed in dark corduroys, plain white Sanforized shirts, a blue jacket patched with the Carmelites' celibate seal. I drove without

destination. The radio picked up a Boston rock station that sang to
go west. I'd seen pictures in *Life* magazine and I wanted long hair.

I kept a loose-leaf binder beside me to write down impressions for
cobbling verses, though I didn't know where to forward the poems I
composed. I'd try to translate to Hungarian what Hanna might notice, the New England Market's torn awning, an orange-bud hedge,
factory windows on hinges, and sentries of portable toilets. I made
note of tractor hoods stacked on burst palettes like metallic dinosaur
wings. A cluster of people in wet, yellow slickers were waving a passenger coach through a station. A girl on a narrow back lane in an
army green jacket leaned over and lifted a bonneted child from a
canopied stroller, holding her high in the air. I sifted the images
Hanna might cherish if she had been there. Already I was adept at
heightening the present so she would be worthy of joining me in it,
making it clear enough so she could be by my side.

I glanced at the books on the seat and thought about stopping to
read *The Sorrows of Young Werther* or Lawrence Durrell. I picked up
the notebook and flipped to the page where I logged words that recently came into usage, telemetry, space walk, beach bunny,
flashcube. These lost their meaning when transliterated to my for-
eign language. I tossed the binder in back. Sometimes I felt as if I
was living a memory exercise.

Then I might have parked in a town unlike Old World train stop
destinations with specific meanings for events that had taken place
there, Regretful Bridge, Hill of Tears. I wanted historical context,
not Pawtucket, Nantic, and Swampscott, those nonsensical Indian
names. I'd visit a library, sit by a dry winter fountain, and stare at the
girls. I'd walk in a glade, eyes closed, face upturned, guessing if I was
in shadow, in dapples of sun. I'd get in the car and drive on. I was
having that kind of mood year.

Outside the A&P stood a girl in a long dark tweed cutaway coat. Her
rhinestone-flecked muffler caught pinpricks of afternoon glare.
We'd seen each other before.

She jiggled her change in one hand, the other clutched thick-fingered gloves. She wore a pea-green twill skirt that stopped at the tops of wool socks folded twice over scuffed lace-up boots, carried no purse, and rocked heel to toe on a striated marbling glaze of cracked ice.

"Buy me some cigs," she asked, although she appeared more than legal. "Any brand. The kind that you smoke," but I didn't as yet. Her inflection was flat, upstate, nasal. Her face bore a longing for something to happen, like Hanna's before the revolt.

She took the Marlboro hardpack I bought. I waved off the quarters she offered.

She looked toward my car. "Go for a ride?"

I was stuck between clever and shy, I was mute. I nodded, held open the passenger door.

"Mind if I drive?"

I said I guessed not.

I studied her hands ten and two on the wheel as if testing its fit. Her nails were clear-lacquered, her hair permed in ringlets she blew from her brow as she shifted from neutral to first. I watched the speedometer arc, plunged the lighter, plucked out the hot metal coil. Then I was coughing and wiping first-cigarette tears from my cheeks.

She seemed bemused, asked how old I was. I told her, "And you?" but she squinted from smoke, her own filter lit in her lips, only shook her head no. She leaned forward to dial through the static across the AM radio, turned it off, and sat back, elbow propped on the window, tilted the cracked rear-view mirror not for the traffic behind us but so she could see how she looked.

Snow had been falling all night and most of the morning. The blacktop was recently plowed, frozen slush heaped in a high dirty row. We drove by the pig farm and junkyard in Ashland.

"Here's where I live," she said as she waved toward a haphazard tract of dun homes.

I was shaking. The air from the wind-wing was cold and I tugged it closed. The car became choked with the scent of her talcum, her heady perfume. Like Hanna she'd also subverted her hair to a dish-water wheat.

"Let's park and stretch," she suggested.

We leaned on the passenger door and breathed mulch, trailing gasoline, fir. We threw our butts in the mush, heard them sizz, watched them glow. As if it was nothing she turned, shoved her knee in my legs, tucked my hand in her coat, kissed me full on the mouth. Her peach-flavored lipstick was waxy and smooth. She tasted unlike popcorn, Milk Duds, or Bazooka but older. She seemed like a girl who could live all alone, sip top-shelf sherry, smoke one last filter while checking the lights, step casually through a front door. I put my face in her coat. It smelled of milled shavings, lathed metal, lubed bench press, and slim rows of drawers that held drill bits and bolts.

"It's my factory work," she explained.

I moved my hands under her sweater. Her voice threat and promise, she cautioned, "Not here, I know a place we can go."

I got in beside her, her scent on my clothes, in my hair. I brought my hands to my face. She rolled down her window and let her sleeve soak with the tire-spun sleet. She told me about her brother who drove a truck for Saint Vincent de Paul, another who'd joined the Holy Cross order to avoid the war. She wanted to run off to Frisco and dance in a cage in white go-go boots or else be a nurse, to run west, California, did I want to come?

I thought if Hanna was driving she'd resemble her, deliberate feet on the gas, brake, and clutch, the same posed wrist cocked on the wheel. I wondered if Hanna's seductions were similar to this, so emphatically charged.

The girl said, "Show me your house, then we'll stop."

My mouth was dry, my fingertips itched. The familiar streets looked entirely different with her by my side and me in the passenger vantage. The place my friend Izzy got hit by a blue Barracuda, the hill where I sledded on shovels, the pharmacy where I shoplifted sunglasses, got caught with a hand in my pocket, all seemed from some other boy's life. I pointed. She slowed when we neared.

I saw how the square lawn I watered, obsessively shorn in the summer, was frost-scorched and scabbed with raw earth. The only resilient elm that had taken a decade to grow was bent in the trucked, tired soil.

That was the year television went virtually full color. My father might have been tapping the afternoon paper and yearning a Mercury Cougar, picking the odds on anyone else in a fight except Cassius Clay. I glimpsed the TV antenna's tin-foiled rabbit ears and briefly pretended the girl in the driver's-side seat was my wife, me the husband in there. Even at this sublime crux of a so-nervous moment I couldn't stop my usual game, to create something else from what was at hand, to present it as an offering to my mother.

I witnessed the house as if new in its bumblebee colors, watched as if somebody else once stepped from the car in the drive in suspenders and shorts. I recalled the plane change in Frankfurt, the cards in my lap with their rudimentary phrases typed red in Hungarian, black letters in English. "I'm going to Fiorello La Guardia." "I'm lost." "Call this number and tell them I'm here." The card with my old and new names.

I'd never tasted machine-sliced bologna with ketchup or seen a built-in clothes washer before. I thought it was not up to par with the guns on the corners, the taunt of wired border, the refugee shelter with hospital cots on round casters we raced down the halls. I recollected the hung-sheet partitions for walls, the steady spring screech they allowed in the night like a swing in a yard in a storm, at-last gasp sounds like someone was glad to be hurt, the selfsame cries Hanna released that I'd once overheard.

Then we were past. I could breathe. The sky turned a gunpowder taint. The sun breached a tear in the berm of horizon and streaked spears of light through the ice-blackened trees.

"We're almost there. Think of a name you can call me," the girl suggested. I realized she'd never said what hers was. She drove fast, now, intent on the road, patting the dash as if this would add speed. I blushed with excitement and shame, I knew instinctively and immediately who she'd be.

We pulled up by a frame-busted cottage. She said, "No one knows about this except me." She paused, studied my face to measure my worth. "And now you."

Cement blocks propped the sag of the porch. A garden hose twined with torn scraps of rags was coiled in a leaf-choked bird feeder. Stiff tufts of loose mattress ticking sprouted from inside a tipped-over front-loading Laundromat dryer. We climbed out under a denuded maple, dead twig and feather nests high in its crown, its foothold-bruised bark smooth as ivory joints. A felled beech blocked the path to the ragged-edged punched-in screen door.

The cabin, no more than a room, was damp, chilled, unweatherproofed. It smelled dank, moldy, closed. A creased travel poster of Greece was Scotch-taped to a wall. There was an unvarnished armoire with one missing grin of a drawer, a checkered wax-cloth-covered table, a backless round stool. Kelly green chintz curtains, honey-hued flypaper strips flecked with shrunk insect casings and bits of diaphanous wings didn't stir. A jumbo-sized Cheerios box lay spilled on top of a mute Frigidaire that she pushed me against. She said, "There's mice behind there." Strawberry, pineapple, cantaloupe magnets fell to the floor.

"Who am I?" she asked, bending close. Her coat released a redolent odor of attar and eau de cologne. It put me in mind of lilium water. I took a deep breath, went ahead with my plan.

"Hanna," I sinned.

She looked me over and tried out its sound. It was too breathy, obscene from her mouth.

She said, "Are you sure?"

I nodded. I sealed the deal. As if she knew what I'd done she turned away toward a spiderweb corner, then guiding my elbow as though I was blind, led me to the low cot that defined the room. It was narrow, uncovered.

She said, "There's no heater. We'll have to keep most of our clothes on."

We lay side by side and tried to adjust. She was taller. Her skirt scratched my thigh where my pants got undone. She lowered her own underwear that was torn at the line of elastic, meringue-colored tricot lace patterned with rose. We touched where we could.

"Wait," she said, fending my hand with her palm, sitting up. She bent, reached under the palette, opened a curved plastic case from which she extracted a small rubber cup. I watched amazed as she licked it all over, said, "No Vaseline," as if it was my fault. "Don't look," she demanded. Of course I did as she spread her knees wide on the edge of the cot and slipped the protection inside, well-rehearsed. She tugged off her skirt.

I wondered if it was all right to just reach for the smooth of her skin. She rearranged herself with a wrist for a pillow, the other hand pulling my shirt. She must have said something that meant to begin. Uncertain how, I let myself sprawl.

"Lift yourself up on your arms," she advised with the grace or the guile not to mention that she must have noticed I'd never done this before. I didn't know whether to put my legs outside or inside of hers. She helped me solve my dilemma of limbs by shifting herself in suggestions, lithe hints. She opened her coat, raised her sweater, her cotton blouse slight for the weather, revealing a gooseflesh pink belly, a mole by her navel, a wormy appendectomy scar that ran underneath. A crucifix pooled on her wet indentation of chest where I saw her heart beat.

She said, "Repeat my name," in a low singsong whisper like her namesake used. It was a bad guilty game, and I did.

"Keep going, you know what you're doing," she urged, hands braced on the side of the cot and inciting our hips.

I dared to image her then as Hanna beneath me, cramped on the bench of a hurtling train at nineteen. I thought the girl couldn't guess, but nevertheless. Then I didn't think anymore.

I couldn't maintain my usual running description. I let myself

breathe her slick, loamy yeast, and the moment was no longer hidden, abstraction, not gossip or rumor or anything written. It was direct, its own definition. I witnessed the bloom of her latent
expressions, insouciant, coy, fey, determined, abandoned, and reckless by turn. I had seen all these looks on my mother before.

"Not yet," she said as I finished. She turned on her side and covered her face with an arm.

The bough of a tree scraped the glass. I lay in the darkening room
feeling shamed but exceedingly glad. I wanted to do it again, this
time lazy, protracted. She wiped herself off with her sleeve, yanked
the tattering cord of the bulb that hung bare from the ceiling. We
straightened our clothes. In the wan yellow light she looked sallow,
exposed. I saw how, like Hanna, she had a mien as if something at
stake could be won and lost many times over, that she wasn't careless, that this was all planned.

Her gaze was a sentiment meant as a salve for a soon-to-go lover,
one who might last the first week, at best two, who had never arrived, who had died by his very own hand. It was private, the same
as a prayer. Her eyes were entirely dry. As if she'd taken a risk and
now weighed the price, she wore a reproach for us both. I thought
she was afraid of and for herself, too, frightened of what she was capable of. That's why she sought risks with strangers while gauging
the cost, as Hanna used to. She held an unrelieved, sad, pleasured
glance of nostalgia for something that I'd never know. It culled a
conspiracy vow. Her eyes willed a closeness that held its own lingering, intimate distance, the enduring secret of who she really was. In
her silence I found what I most feared and wanted but would never
own. You can't sleep with your mother.

"Stop staring at me," she said at last, a pale simulacrum of
Hanna. "Just take me home."

Twenty

We are back in the room, we have fixed. Gary and Maria have gone to the Post for wine, candy, and Cokes. The rain reads the Braille of the bricks on our building, describing its shape, splashing the eaves like hundreds of applauding hands. Bubbling, it sluices the parapets, rushes the dormers. It offers a chorus of garbled protection that drowns out the hollow-blow regular foghorn and whitecap-swarmed ocean's roiled tubular swells. They're dashing themselves onto pocked lunar sand in a silvery foam.

If I could grow into this cocoon of sound I would rise, become swept to a Budapest courtyard, a bullet-gouged apartment eight flights up. This regression in time always comes at the fading edge of the rush. From up in our large apartment I'd witness the rivulets flung against glass in bold finger-thick streaks. The Grundig hi-fi might be leaking a Chopin prelude. There'd be mints in a bowl by the door. On top of the clear low glass table in front of the window I'd arrange my molded lead soldiers, the battlements, hand-painted steeds. My late-day long lamp-enhanced shadow would stretch, climb the wallpaper patterned with watermarked pheasants, their stylized feathers, spread wings, and spiraling tails. Outside the rain might be turning to mist from sleet tapping the glass with occasional tight clumps of hail. The cumulonimbus Cook's tour of tall clouds would blow out to reveal a sky that's the blanch of a sheet.

My shirt would be lingering with delicate whiffs of persistent al-
mond, Hanna's sweet scented perfume, the heater releasing its dried
leather smell. The past is always a piece of perfection when willed to
appear. Even the bad things that happen are graced.

My mother would stand in the kitchen, about to go out, her
gabardine greatcoat inheritance draped on the back of the upright
wood chair. She'd wear her gypsy print scarf carelessly tied on her
hair. Hanna would sprinkle a pinch of hard-bargain granular sugar
into my sleep-making skim-membraned milk warming over the
cast-iron range. Then she would bend, squint from the smoke of a
cigarette constantly held in her lips, straighten her black nylons'
seams. With anticipation she'd look at the clock, at the door. She'd
heft her patent high heels by their straps and absently polish them
on her rust skirt. The scrape of the after-work trolleys and shouts
from the call-across corners, the solicitations of aproned flower ven-
dors, their red and green carts bright with leftover moisture, would
climb to the room in a comforting din. She'd slip on her shoes and
hobble the breadth of the handwoven rug as the cherry wood
creaked. She'd lie about where she was going, implicate herself with
a slow sidelong glance that allowed disbelief. Hanna would say some
kind phrase with my name in the middle. Or maybe it was actually
something disdainful that would make me cringe. It doesn't matter.
All that counts now is remembering the mood. She'd turn to the
mirror, drape the coat over a shoulder, smooth down the front of her
blouse, and attempt to look sober. Then she would leave.

I'd hear the finality of latch clicking, count down the seconds it
took to descend in the wire-mesh cage of the lift. I'd press my brow
to the window and watch her step through the portal's wide beams.
She'd look left and right, adjusting her shawl, start walking at first.
Hanna would increase her pace as she crossed the tracks, cautious
not to let the grooves catch the spikes of her heels. She'd clutch her
purse to her chest and break into a head-bent slight canter, then disappear around a tight corner, finally running full tilt.

I'd go to her bedroom and lie on her talcum-scent sheets fully
clothed, open her diary, try to decipher the words Hanna crabbed in

her secret-code script. I'd stare at the high blank wide ceiling while marking the metronome *sick* of the grandfather clock in the foyer, trying to stay on the edge of awake in half dreams until Hanna returned, and sometimes she would.

"Come in here, College," Cassandra is calling.

I know where I am, this is Venice. It's late afternoon and Cassandra is taking a shower. The moment is rare. The dope that we're shooting makes water repellent, unsettling. Gary discourages washing. He has the specious idea it dilutes essential oils from our skin that ward off infection, bacteria, disease.

Across Oceanview I see an inverted star-and-stripe curtain that snaps in accompaniment to the power lines flayed by directionless wind. Occasional headlights are parsing the water-drenched street. Maria and Gary haven't come back from the store. Maybe they're actually cooking up some kind of plan for what happens next, though they're probably slipping around the canals, smoking and aimlessly drinking instead.

"Hurry up, join me," Cassandra commands from the burbling stall.

Inside the bathroom she's lit several candles lined up on the rim of the sink. The halos of flame cast the perspiring walls marmoreal and dim, the orange tongues throwing my fluttering form into stuttered relief. It looks like penance, redemption, and church. The run of the shower mimics the weather that batters our room. The air is sodden with steam, hard to breathe. Behind the grimed plastic curtain Cassandra's slim silhouette shifts. "You ready?" she asks.

I step from my clothes and into the shock of hot water, unsure what to do. Cassandra studies my uncertain stance, her hair plastered flat, skin flushed pink.

"You're even thinner than me," she observes, lifts my arm, runs my scarified veins with her thumb. "Looks pretty bad," she remarks.

"It couldn't be helped," I tell her.

"No one was holding you down," she replies, dips her head in the prickly stream. "Even if somebody was, we're responsible not just for our acts but those done against us," she says after gasping for air.

I consider this. Up to a point, Cassandra is right. Hanna complied with events on the train. It eventually led to the border. Maria made a conscious decision to run, to come up to the room and extend her bared arm. These circumstantial events were actually acts of the will, they've exacted a price. I've been in thrall with the thought of a scattering hand as my guide, though this isn't the truth. It's not blundering chance but a latent wish made manifest that's the reason I'm here. For Cassandra it didn't start out quite this way.

"Your uncle wasn't your fault." My words echo waterlogged, dull, somehow lame.

"Maybe not," she concedes, "but the rest." She pulls me close so we stand on the drain. She lowers her gaze, moves my hand on her slick gooseflesh belly, up inside her legs. "In any case, let's not debate it. Just touch me," she says.

The skin of her thighs is stippled and rough as if she'd shaved with a blunt razor blade. Her tuft is coarse, matted, sparse. Cassandra tears open a free sample packet of liquid detergent she pours on herself.

"Rub up and down," she insists, moves my wrist to show me how fast she prefers.

I try to subsume myself in the act, to discover the right attitude, a nonchalant passion perhaps. I see ourselves at a remove, my rapid hand skimming her cleft. We appear awkward. Cassandra leans on the tile, head tipped back, nipples erect, thrusting her sex to my hand.

"That's right," she murmurs. "Do that."

I look at her face to catch a resemblance to Hanna, but Cassandra's eyes are unbetrayed, sunk in themselves, her motives submerged in the water, its rush on her rise and fall drip-beaded breasts. Propped on the cool wall the color of butter we kiss. Our teeth clink. "You're still clumsy," she says. Her fingers open and close on my shoulder, her ropy hair clings to my cheeks. I wipe it away, ply it from her brow to the nape of her neck. Even now I'm thinking of how this will play in the future when I'll recall it. I can't help myself.

It's as if the shower is singing, the stall turned a honeyed bell jar that's translucent, opaque. I put my mouth to the soft of her throat, where her distended vocal cords hum on my lips like twin tines of a tapped tuning fork. Then I don't wonder my role anymore, become lost in the steady cascade. For the moment it's only this. Cassandra reaches up, clutches the shower head fixture, her knees slightly buckling. Suspending herself, she utters a low, hollow moan, twists her hips, her trembling thighs gripping my hand.

"College, you know I can't come," she insists, but this is belied by an evident spasm of shudders and tight angry mewls from her throat, phlegmy, ragged, and burred. She says, "Hold me up," clasps her legs on my waist. "Put it in. This won't happen again." I wonder what she means by this but there's no time to think. My stomach is slapping on hers with an excess she courts and cajoles. Racked by a flurry of shivers, she stammers my name, says, "Jesus, don't lose it, go faster," then, "Stop now. No, don't," but I can't, and she lets out a long single sob that she's tried to hold in.

We disentangle our limbs. She won't look at my face as she turns off the taps.

"Bastard, you came inside me," Cassandra accuses again. Her look says not to contradict her or offer excuses. She squats, douches with slow-draining water she cups, splashes hard on herself.

There's no longer a towel. We dry ourselves off with my clothes. I sit on the folded-down lid of the toilet, watch Cassandra wiping the condensate clear from the glass with the heel of her palm. Her lips are drawn, bloodless. Her arctic eyes refract the candles she shifts to make room for her makeover kit.

"When I first arrived here," she says to her flickering reflection, "remember how good it all was?" She removes the cap from a jar, smooths moisturizer on her face. Cassandra daubs mannequin-tinted foundation onto her throat, forehead, cheeks.

"That isn't how I remember it," I answer, though this is what I'm wont to do, reinvent events, embellish, embroider until I see things as I want to. I don't mention the sight of her dangled by ankles outside of my window, her trick dress slightly torn, or the swing of her crinoline lei as she hung out there shouting on that summer day. I watch her powder-puff flesh-colored talcum, pat some on her tracks, apply Misty Pink blush with a black tufted brush like a small shock of mane.

"What's the matter?" she asks. "I thought you enjoyed this." She smears Plum Frost eye shadow onto her lids, aimlessly waving her free hand around in the polleny mist. "You know. How the other half lives."

Cassandra has always accused me of being a dilettante in her world. I study my arms in the mute candled glare. "I didn't know it would end in a habit," I say, though this is a lie. I trace the evidence of my veins with a nail.

Cassandra wields her eyeliner pencil like it's a baton. Her breath fogs the glass.

"Don't worry, College," she tells me. "You're almost done here." She dips a stiff caterpillar stick deep in its tube of mascara, brushes her lashes, her expression slack, artless, vague.

I search her reflection. Cassandra is talking about a final conclusion, more than the end of observing her preen of methodical makeup routine. She's easing the base of her Crushed Rose pink lipstick, applying a coup de grace slash to her moist pouting lips.

"You're not really with it and for it as you like to claim. You're not going to stay," she says, "you're too scared."

I want to say no. Her words are an actual hurt, a place in my chest where they burn, and she's aware of this. I watch Cassandra replace her cosmetics inside their soft see-through flower-decaled case. She uses her thumb and forefinger to pinch tight its Ziploc seal, to snuff the weak flames. Cassandra deserts me. I sit in the dark without clothes.

I want to come to a small understanding. I'm thinking there's any number of ways I could leave, down the stairs, through the wide double doors to the street, through the window like her or the overdose point of the needle's dulled tip.

I step on the carpet, observing the wet tracks I make to the overflow closet, see my hands select pants, arms tugging themselves into

Gary's striped acrylic shirt with its crescents of underarm stains.

Cassandra stands facing the window. She's striking a pose with her long arms akimbo, stripped to no more than her makeup, in rent underpants, their innocent stitching in cursive of yesterday's name near the crotch. Her ribs in the mayonnaise light are revealed in relief. Her collarbone slides under skin tinged a skeleton pale as she totters and leans down to pull on her scuffed go-go boots.

Together we cross to the couch. She straddles its armrest, reaches behind to the cinder block table, and picks up a Lucky. Cassandra blows smoke through her teeth as she slides up and down as if riding a Safeway's enamel paint nickel-buck horse.

"What if I wasn't being thrown out when you found me?" Cassandra suggests, her whispered singsong so unbearably calm it makes my scalp itch. "Consider that it was a put-up job right from the start. We figured you for the chivalrous, girl-saving type. We conned you so you'd let us stay."

I feel the blood drain from my face. If what Cassandra is saying is true, it was the one scam they've tried that has worked. It changes everything. "You did not," I manage to say, my voice adamant, shrill as a child's as I rap on the pane. "I saw you hanging out there."

Cassandra shrugs as she teases herself back and forth. "Believe what you want." She flounces her hair and touches my hand but I jerk it away. Her look is even, sustained. "Don't take it so hard. What's the matter, you going to cry?" She'd like that, her tone gives away. Cassandra stops her sofa-bound rocking, leans close as she can to my ear. "You got what you wanted, to see me in danger," she says, her breath Silver Satin and stale. "Can't play without getting it on you. That's the one lesson."

"You're not clever enough to have faked it," I tell her. "You're just a year older."

"And you can't be just an observer. I warned you. You can't live by watching." She climbs from the armrest and straddles my knees so we're face to face.

"So this is your payback," I say. It's what she extracts for letting me watch.

"You're getting smarter already," she taunts as she moves on my legs.

Behind her I see the room drift with its objects inducing abstraction, the uncovered mattress, yellowing pillow, the ash-dusted ball of the blanket, the needle, spoon, cotton, unlockable knob of the door. Her words surrender their meaning. I realize watching is also an act of volition bearing its own consequence.

It makes little difference if Cassandra's lying or telling the truth. It's beside the point. If she's inventing herself as she goes, this only enhances Cassandra's allure. She encourages, nourishes uncertainty, and this is exactly what I like about her, she knows. It is what Hanna was able to accomplish.

As if Cassandra is reading my mind she dissembles her features to how they appeared that first day when we stood in the bathroom. She's wearing the shade of atonement, regret, sublime longing, that Hanna tried on when she lied about where she was going, with whom, for how long, obscuring her motives yet making them plain. It was one of a number of looks she could choose when she willfully altered her gaze. Watching Cassandra's trick of expression I feel a dim fever, deep chill. Her role, after all, is effacement, creation. It's the reason I want her. It's her stock-in-trade.

Cassandra succumbs to a smile. "See how easy it is? It's my own special gift."

Her bare arms encircle my neck. Her hair's on my face with its smell of wine, bleach, cigarettes. "I've notched the ante between us. Now you won't take me for granted. Nothing is certain. This is what comes to the surface. It's good. It was worth it." Her fingertips brush the back of my head.

She's right and now everything's out of kilter and different. There are butterflies in my stomach that won't go away. If all that's occurred is open to reinterpretation, then there is also the chance for an outcome that's not been revealed, for change to take place. And then there's the thought that this also applies to the past.

Twenty-One

I don't want to come fully awake though I know it is morning.

I've dreamed Lincoln Park, where I went with the Catholic-school choir. In the logic of dreams, though I left her behind, I knew Hanna was near. I felt her presence around a green tent, a particular turn. I had to find her before the fair folded and took her. Already carnies were rolling up tarps, unstringing streamers of bulbs from the countstore, the pitch and toss booths, sprinkling the dust of the midway with oversized watering cans.

I couldn't call out her name or we'd be discovered, deported. Men ran behind me, bare feet slapping the packed, steaming dirt. I thought myself clever to hide in the fun house that inside was really a Byzantine church. The aisles were swarmed by a refugee shuffle caught in the revolt. I reasoned the soldiers wouldn't find me in the crowd.

I saw Hanna, kneeling, head bent to the back of a pew, something she'd never do. She'd somehow detached herself from the murmuring stagger force-marched under guard through the wide double doors past the Cross stations nailed to the wall. They filed through the part of the sacristy curtain, toward the barbed wire refugee border. My mother wore the sheer red-belted dress I liked best. She looked up and saw me, lifted an arm in a tentative wave, but this wasn't permitted. I let out a high soundless cry that nonetheless echoed.

Then we were shoulder to shoulder as I stood beside her. I realized I was much younger. I couldn't bring myself to touch her. Up close her resemblance grew fainter, her eyes less demure. She tipped her head to the side, slightly stooped in a posture I'd never seen Hanna assume. Nevertheless, it was overtly familiar. I was aware that a soldier had recently suckled the rings from her fingers. That's why she prayed, why they'd let her break off from the single-file throng that coursed through the church. She was a collaborator. By implication, I was one, too.

There was an aura of sex rising from her, a leftover smudge of pink lipstick and tear-marred mascara. A guilty yet gratified half smile of lust smeared her luminous face. She leaned on my arm, said my new name in English, a language she couldn't have known.

I wanted to tell her she needn't escape. I tried describing the other side's suburban pallor, since in a way I was already there, but my words came out garbled, unclear. I knew she thought of America as a country where dogs walked around wagging pretzels on tails.

I wanted to pull her to safety but couldn't remember the route. I reached out to grab her but Hanna's substance was weak. She called out an indistinct plea but already her outline was fading, her bed-tussle feminine odor grown faint, her gin and rose-blush aroma of lilium water transmuted to merely the dregs of my coming awake. I open my eyes and her infinite absence is palpably real.

We've nodded, slept, scratched ourselves quietly, past dawn. Gary's gone out to score, since we've run out of cottons. The girls sit on the tangled-sheet wreck of the bed. With unsteady hands they've already painted each others' toenails Wild Plum, fanned them dry. They've compared the tint of their skin, Cassandra's pale whey to Maria's burned cream.

The glass ashtray between them threatens to spill as they bend to tap glowing embers. Maria's boy's T-shirt is torn down the back like a hospital gown. The folds of Cassandra's sheer camisole capture the gold wash of slow, drifting motes in the room that's the color of tangerine wedges held up to the light. I feign sleep stretched out on the couch. I have covered my face, peek through fingers to watch.

Maria leans back on an elbow, legs casually splayed like she's practicing underwear lounging, serenely intact. She's been reading *Grendel*. "It's a comic book for adults without pictures" was her review. Cassandra is hugging a knee that's propped up to her chin. Her other leg tucked tight beneath her, she's rocking, impatiently blowing out smoke.

She's offering Maria a lesson on johns. "You don't have to pretend to like it. Sometimes they prefer it the other way, if you're mean."

"They all want to talk," Maria is saying. "I can't keep them from trying to kiss."

Cassandra is shaking her head. "You're in charge. Ward them off. Use your elbows and hands." She demonstrates, wielding her palm like a shield. "They want to be hurt, to feel guilty and bad. Then they'll return. Remember, they're nothing but pockets of money. It's no more than commerce with skin."

She picks at a fleck of tobacco that's stuck to her lip, changes tack. "Have you slept with Gary?"

Maria looks down at her feet. "A couple of times."

"It's all right, so have I," says Cassandra. "He's not into it. He'd rather get high." She's looking right at me as if she's sure I'm awake. I don't dare give up my act. She lights a new cigarette from the butt of the last. "What about College, have you balled him yet?"

Maria cocks her head sideways, demure. She stubs out her filter, looks down at her legs, shifts so she lies on her side with a cheek on her fist. Her backside is bared.

"I couldn't stand one more boy," she replies with a sigh.

I can't believe what has come from her mouth, that this is Maria's perception.

Cassandra is flicking her ash to the floor. "Believe me, I know. It's a chore."

I think she's saying this entirely for my benefit, to punish me more, to make some kind of point. She's not really serious, it's got to be some sick joke. Cassandra is doing this only because she must know I can hear. Her tone is disingenuous, coy.

Cassandra touches Maria's lean flank as if she might bolt. "Ever been with a woman?"

I see Maria flinch just a little but she doesn't answer or move. She allows Cassandra's ringed hand to remain on her thigh in repose.

"Don't worry," Cassandra is saying. "I won't seduce you, I already got my hands full. I just want to tell you how it was." A story is good, distracting, I'm thinking, there's been enough betrayal.

Cassandra turns wistful. "I learned about girls in the board-and-care home." She moves her hand to Maria's curved waist, caresses its crease of soft flesh with brief strokes. "It was those drinks Daisy made that started it all. She called them delirium treatments."

"When was this?" Maria asks, carefully removing Cassandra's palm.

She doesn't seem to notice, pausing to figure. "Christ, you were just two."

I subtract to that year. Gary Powers got shot from the sky and John Kennedy won. Connie Francis was singing her heart had a mind of its own. I saw *Ben Hur*, lived on Sno-balls and Cokes. The living room couch was covered in plastic. The father was working, the mother was cleaning, then they were both watching TV all night long. Wash your hands, time for bed, time for school. There were the nuns with keys on long chains, the hats of their habits like wings, my coarse brown uniform pants, white shirt, and dodgeball, the shrill recess bell, and my accent had long disappeared.

Cassandra is drumming her fingers across her thigh, looking at me every once in a while as if making sure I am getting it all. "It was shifty back then with no father, suspicious."

She says she told any who asked her he lived on a two-hundred-acre date farm in Spain, near Córdoba, sometimes a ranch on the Argentine pampas. Cassandra made up that her father bred sprinters she'd ride when he sent for her early next fall. She slides her palm to Maria's behind and lets it rest there. "Daisy worked as a freelance bookkeeper, a part-time cashier. She knew how to keep double books, short on change. 'I don't steal, you don't eat,' she would say."

Cassandra lies down face to face with Maria. "Relax and I'll tell you." The plume of her cigarette smoke rises toward the ceiling. "I was eleven, I wore what I chose."

I carefully listen as Cassandra recasts the past in her narrative tone. The tales we relate become what happened, I think. We remake, refashion, until it alters the present and colors the future as well. I pay close attention. I fill in the glossed over blanks as she goes. I'm memorializing Cassandra, certain somehow that this is the last story I'll hear. Our afternoon shower and her revelations have changed everything. My sojourn with her by the ocean is finite, I have to store up what I can.

One day like another Cassandra heard Daisy's eight o'clock alcohol swallow, her gagging on toothbrush and Pepsodent powder. Cassandra was trying on shorts she discarded for overalls worn with the bib hanging loose, a cinched-at-the-navel lime rayon blouse that would itch in the heat. After a while the front door clicked closed. Daisy did not leave a key.

"It was so I'd go to school," Cassandra explains. "I'd ditch anyway."

What she enjoyed when the school bus had gone was to sit at the kitchenette table, sip Daisy's reheated sugary coffee, peruse the newspaper like an adult.

She read that a ten-year-old girl had been found in a shallow sand grave only yards from her house. It said she was taken from bed in only her thin cotton nightgown, wrapped in a yellow bed cover. Cassandra savored this type of story with intimate details, snapshots of air crashes, car wrecks, and man-made disasters.

She scanned the rest of the headlines. Lana Turner had married again but so what? A Lancaster couple who'd tortured their baby were jailed. This item did not satisfy her. It wasn't explicit about what those parents had done to that child.

Cassandra refolded the paper and replaced the string. She

stepped into Daisy's white rabbit fur slippers so they'd collect burrs, went out in the yard with a number two pencil, a payables ledger. Once Cassandra pulled the knob shut behind her there was no return. Locking the house was a rule.

She sat on the split, canted bench, penmanshipped dirty words, bit the eraser in half, spit the dry nub in the dirt. Cassandra chewed on the yellow enamel until her teeth hurt.

Exceedingly bored, she strolled to the chain-link fence by the tall sticker bush. That's where her tackle box stocked with essentials was stored. She struggled it free of the gnarled, exposed roots, set it down on the scrub, worked the clasp, raised the top. Cassandra was still slightly thrilled every time at the way its compartments were hinged, like miniature Ferris wheel seats that rose straight, didn't tilt.

She fingered her thread wrapped on cardboard, her powder-puff compact, and red plastic beads. She rubbed for good luck the Tiny Tears evil eye gouged from its plastic-lashed lid, picked up and put back the Tareyton filter she'd try any day that had been there a week, tongued the flat blade of the dangerous knife for the rapist who'd been on the news. Cassandra hefted her soft pouch of ginger beer glossies and striped cat's-eye aggies, enjoying their weight and limp liquidy roll.

"Where did you pee?" Maria breaks in.

Cassandra looks up, her spell broken, annoyed. "Jesus, Maria, I'm not going to tell." The place where she used to squat dribbling drops on her pants, where she stashed the white toilet paper she dabbed on herself that turned crinkly and gray from dew and then sun, still holds its secret allure.

"I decided to put on a show," Cassandra continues. She recalls rigging a sheet between double-stacked kitchenette chairs. They were buckled from Daisy's quick grab for a drumstick, kernels of corn misaligned on her gums like gravy-stained teeth in new rows. Cassandra would not dwell on this. Instead she sliced the bleached fabric in half with dull pinking shears, parted the rent of the improvised curtain, and stepped center stage. She grasped the microphone-scissors, pretended to be Judy Garland, her fingertips curled just so. Cassandra announced her own name, spread a palm on her heart, raised her other arm toward the yard's useless pole, struck a balladeer's pose. Almost on key, overwrought, she sang "Put Your Head on My Shoulder" all the way through.

She threw herself onto the ground. Cassandra lay back in a sudden exhaustion on coarse twigs and blunt grass. She watched foam ticking sprout from a twisted up mattress, imagined the sky as an inverted ceiling on which you could stand looking up at the earth. Birds whooped, beat their wings in the dry trough of drainpipe, cajoled in the summer-scorched crowns of the transplanted birch. Occasional light planes droned, faded, droned. Their narcotic saw across blue must have put her to sleep.

A lackluster breeze raised goose pimples as Cassandra woke without dreams. She sat swatting her clothes and her arms because insects lived in the rustling lawn, even field mice or rats. From the pole and tree afternoon slant of the shadows Cassandra knew recess was over in school. From the sound of the car pulling up in front that Daisy was home way too soon.

Cassandra crawled to make sure. Sharp stickers stabbed, a beef-jerky scab on her elbow came loose. The slippers were gone, both sleeves torn. The brambles scratching her chin would inevitably make her sneeze.

The angle of drunk-driven Rambler was parked at a hypotenuse. She'd learned this word in class. The oblique arrangement of tires would usually make her remark about catching a cab to the curb when Daisy parked at the store.

Crouched on all fours Cassandra watched Daisy trying to force the wrong key in the lock. Her mother had probably bolted her lunch, all you can eat at the Bit of Sweden Smorgasbord, stopped at Lou's Twilight Lounge. There she'd have dosed her parched throat with the regular three B and B's Daisy claimed didn't count, they were ladylike drinks. This would be followed by one shot of vodka and one glass of ale for the road.

Daisy steadied herself on the jamb, cigarette in her lips, orthopedic hose bunched like pachyderm skin on her varicose shins. Her abbreviate lemony stretchpants were creased in the rear from the stick of a high burgundy plastic stool. Her too-tight white blouse was speckled with flecks of maraschino juice. Cassandra recalled sometimes Daisy would bring home the cherries wrapped in napkins imprinted with trivia riddles or goofy cartoons. In her words Daisy would "refresh" them in brandy. Her mother would hold on tight to the stems as Cassandra leaned over the post-dessert table to bite off the sweet, sticky fruit.

Now Daisy called out of habit, "Come help me."

Not thinking, Cassandra stood. Blood rushed from her head, the ground pitched and yawed. The sky tilted back where it had been before. Vertigo-struck, she stumbled through ragweed and swoonily managed the door.

"What's this?" Daisy asked as they stood on the living room's slightly manged carpet.

Cassandra looked herself over, picked shrubbery rye from her hair, pleased with her shirttail undone, her dirt-and-grass-kneed overalls. Daisy swayed in the unlamplit gloom. She pushed at the bridge of her nose as if wearing her office bifocals from Thrifty that made numbers bigger but blurred. She turned around, circumspect, as if something was missing, had been rearranged. But nothing had stirred, not the TV trays stacked by the wall or the portraits of Jesus, the glazed figurines that were carefully dusted each fifteenth and first. The monthly installment recliner still tilted at ease. The radio leaked Longine Symphonette "Claire de lune" mewls.

"Had a rough day?" Cassandra tried in a tone overheard from wives on the eight-thirty shows.

Daisy glanced at her watch with the expansion band that hash-marked her wrist. She shook it. "What the hell are you doing at home?"

"I failed air raid drill," Cassandra replied, unrehearsed. "I wouldn't get under the desk. It's that claustrophobia I had as a kid. You remember. It must have returned." Breathless, she knew she had gone on too long, because Daisy was calm, unperturbed.

"Come with me," Daisy ordered, yanking her arm. Her mother

was trailing a cough drop and beery aroma, damp talcum and Bene-
dictine.

Together they stood side by side in the kitchen, intent on the
yard, the sprung tackle box, the cast-aside shears, twinned chairs
and slit sheet. The tip of a rabbit fur slipper poked through a pile of
last-season raked leaves.

"You do all this?" Daisy asked, forehead bent to the glass.

"Not me," said Cassandra, raising her hands to her face just in
case. "Some kid must have climbed through the hole in the fence
while I was at school." The words sounded instantly lame.

Daisy invested her gaze with the faint captious cynical smile she
wore catching her child in a lie. It was dangerous, abrupt, disappeared. Cassandra leaned on the ironing board pantry. She flinched
as Daisy came too near to open the fridge, its rubber seal making
that sick sucking sound as it gave. Cassandra endured the *scritch* of
pried ice tray that stuck to your hand from the cold and the frost
wrench of cubes. She carefully eyed Daisy's reach toward the overhead cabinet to take down the half-gallon ice-cream container she
used for a bowl.

Cassandra knew what was coming. Daisy free-poured crème de
menthe, brandy, splashed in three fingers of under-the-counter
Fleischmann dry gin for the kicker, whipped the pistachio sludge to
a froth with the electric beater's thick blades.

Cassandra could not turn and run from the vision of Daisy trans-
fixed by the alcohol fumes. Then came the sequence of dipping the
I LIKE IKE mug in the muck, Daisy tipping the cup to her mouth,
teasing her tongue to the foam, draining the entire draft without
pause, wiping her lips with a palm. Daisy looked stunned as the
mentholated concoction hit. She wobbled a bit, her face florid and
splotched.

She tossed the mug carelessly into the sink, where it shattered.
"All right, Cassandra, since it's what you want, we'll both break the
rules." Her voice was hoarse. Cassandra stood lead-footed, caught,
dared not move. This had happened before.

Daisy's hands suddenly clamped on a shock of her hair, on her throat. Legs kicked out beneath her, Cassandra went down with a cry, pulled her mother along. The weight knocked the air from her lungs. Then Daisy was holding her face in a palm smelling faintly of graphite and slamming her head to the tile. Eyelids squeezed tight, Cassandra saw black punctuated with burst fireworks. She became giddy with screaming and biting but none of it did any good. She went limp, felt a tooth coming loose.

"Come on, fight," Daisy whined, grappling her onto her stomach, sitting astride her and ripping her blouse. Cassandra heard Daisy grunt, fumble for the beater, its tinny scrape on the Formica counter.

The first blow broke skin, she was sure. Daisy was pummeling the small of her back with the blunt metal prong. Cassandra tried passing out. Her flesh became hot, soft and mushed. Her blood smelled like rust.

"*Look* what you're *making* me *do*," she heard Daisy shout, beating time to the words.

The pain was so large it was somehow abstract. Cassandra was floating above it, removed. She saw Daisy's undulate fat, blouse soaked to the bra as tears and sweat mingled and strung spittle clung to her jaw. Cassandra observed herself pinned by her mother's broad buttocks, clenched by her hocks, overwhelmed by the jiggling hams of her thighs. The notion of how Daisy might attempt sex in this selfsame position crossed Cassandra's mind. She witnessed her own dull expression, severe, open-mouthed, head turned to the side, her cheek in a saliva puddle, arms spread like a crucified Christ.

Cassandra was mulling the notion of death at eleven, what that might be like. She pondered the concept of soul, was it solid and slow? Was it round? Would it sink like a stone in deep water or actually rise? It must be more like a wavery circumference, Cassandra decided, the shape of a ghost or a circle of light.

Cassandra considered the permutations of her afterlife. It was hard to make out. Her precise image got only as far as girls holding hands by a maypole, dizzy and heady from spinning around. Red, white, green crinoline streamers were clasped in damp palms. There was a papier-mâché bell on the pole that could nonetheless ring, and it did. It was a call to come home, to come in where there's frosting on slices of cake and each girl got a prize, and to sing her own special song as the others sat, rapt. Cassandra knew hers, its words on the tip of her tongue. "The tombstone told when she died. A virgin married at rest. 'I died before bedtime came.' More the thick stone cannot tell." Where did she learn this lament? Cassandra remembered. She saw herself mouthing the lines at an earlier time. She was seven or eight. It was a poem her uncle had read her one night in the sewing room's gloom before placing her hand in his lap. She expunged the rhyme from her thoughts. Then Daisy stopped, clambered off.

From her sprawled vantage Cassandra could make out the hands of the tile-inset hexagon clock. Only minutes had passed. Curling herself in a parenthesis like a baby, her thumb in her mouth, she watched the second hand parse round the dial.

Daisy had slumped on the cabinet nesting the garbage disposal's mechanical hive. Above her the dense air was strung with small blackheads of hovering gnats. A single moth battered itself on the pane of the window that leaked a weak calcium light. Daisy fanned herself, tugging the sop of her blouse, blew strands of wet hair from her brow. She exhaled a *whoo* like after completing some arduous task. The radio whispered the weather, confirming fair skies. It became drowned by an air force jet roving over the house, a car horn, a shout. Cassandra heard Daisy's breathing, exerted and harsh. She suffered the sandpaper buzz, the rivulet itch on her back. Cassandra touched herself there, brought her hand to her mouth, smeared red on her gums, and let out an overlong, distended sigh. She wanted her vision of heaven restored, nothing other than that.

Cassandra's no longer right next to Maria. They're tossed on the mattress, apart from each other. I've quit the pretext of pretending sleep, of watching the girls through my webbing of eyelashes, fingers like venetian blinds. I've been holding my breath. Listening to Cassandra is like being at the scene of a bad accident. You want to turn away, yet look harder instead. It's dirty and guilty, like masturbation. Still, you can't stop once you've started.

We're all getting nervous at Gary's incipient lateness. Maria is already sniffling and wiping her nose on the bare underside of her arm. Cassandra is smoking and anxious. She sits up and drinks from her half-full wine bottle, kills it with gurgly gulps. A thin stream of liquid runs down the side of her mouth. She gags, contemplates throwing up. I feel the familiar dope-yearning ache in my bones. Soon chills will start, nerves twitching the muscles, my spasmy gut making bile. Nothing is more relevant. It subsumes everything else.

"Tell the rest," says Maria. She also longs for distraction from coming down. Her forehead is perspired, there's a slight twitch to her eyelids.

Cassandra lies flat, legs stretched, her feet off the edge of the bed. "It was at recess that I was found out," she is saying, determined to get to the board and care part. "My shirt came untucked. Some kids saw the wound on my back."

The principal, nurse, had been called. The stains on her blouse were tinged pus. They made her bend over the first-aid room table and lower her skirt from behind. Though it was eighty the metal was cool on her chest. Cassandra made out a red rubber dodgeball's round bounce outside, runaround feet on the concrete, a chorus of shouts. She heard the no-nonsense back-to-class buzzer's alarm, the final unrestrained cries. Through the hinged windows came scraping-chair sounds. Cassandra thought she could even distinguish the squeaking and tapping of chalk, the click of a slide projector that flashed basic food groups, hygiene diagrams in health class. She savored the unspooling warp and the snap of a Mercator geography map. It was her favorite subject, she fleetingly thought. The coral and green to brown shadings, place names and latitudes, valleys and ranges, vistas of oceans that she made believe she discovered and christened, all calmed her. Cassandra liked to decipher the symbols for passes and ruins, run her fingers along the highways' red veins, the blue rivers' tributaries like leaf capillaries.

There was no time for this now. The medicine odor of bandages, gauze, disinfectant, were emblematic somehow. She knew this phase of her learning was done. They were asking her questions. Who did it? How often? With what?

She straightened, adjusted her skirt. "I'd rather not say. I fell down."

In the way of adults they exchanged knowing looks as if she wasn't present to see them. The principal scribbled something on a pad. He pronounced her name as if he'd never heard it, archly accenting each vowel. He studied her file, made an ah, recognized who she was from the jottings inside.

"You're the one lives alone with your mother," he said. He tapped the crinkly white paper. It explained everything. Clicking his tongue, he closed the mustard brown folder. The relevant clues had assembled for him, completing the picture.

"When you're finished here, you'll come to my office," he told her.

Cassandra noticed he combed his hair oddly, attempting to cover a bald liver spot on his crown. She thought this gesture was useless, transparently vain, a mis-stab at dash augmented by his collegiate tie clasp and synthetic breast pocket foulard.

"Will I be expelled?" The question hung in the air. It was greeted with silence.

"I'll have to phone," the principal said to the nurse as he turned to walk out.

Cassandra felt a welling inside but she wouldn't cry, give them that. She studied the nurse, who seemed held together by starch, tucked in her blouse, and stepped into the corridor, toward the light.

Outside the double glass doors she aimed left. She made for the ten-acre alfalfa fallow that shimmered with puddles of heat, the gouged sculpted blond distant hills. Cassandra considered her options. She started to run past the porcelain fountain, its rust-pitted metallic faucets, stepped off the edge of the crumbling school lot. She had to get home and then what? She had to make plans, to grow up. It was five miles away, there was time.

Wanting to seem inconspicuous she slowed to a walk. The asphalt was hot. It burned through her cheap plastic flats. There was nothing to see but a few stunted trees, clumps of sage, balls of tumbleweeds stalled. She kicked up dust that clung to her pores, made it harder to breathe.

Cassandra weighed destinations and modes of escape, knew she couldn't go back to the school. Daisy and she couldn't stay in this town. Maybe they'd go to Las Vegas, where Daisy had been, perhaps to the date farm in Spain that she had transformed from invention to real in her mind over time.

She passed a truck with its hood sprung like waiting for wrenches and pliers to devour, another one trailing a wake of old tires it had seemingly birthed from its rusted gas tank. She saw a protuberant elbow of pipe with no obvious function that poked through the ground, the incomprehensible six-wheeled machine with an awning, the haunted house with its hideout of yard hung with low weeping fronds. She passed the glade with lean trees where she used to play war with the kids after school.

They snapped spindly bows and forked branches for guns. It was Americans versus Germans but each side could win, lose, or draw. If you fell you were wounded and captured, got hit with a hand grenade rock you were dead. Then you had to count down from twenty real fast and join with the opposite side. Cassandra was made a lieutenant, bound a torn hem on her arm for her stripes. She got to say things like, "Cover me, men. Move 'em out."

Cassandra looked at the miniature woods and felt irretrievably beyond all of that, beyond the games of knockdown where you ran in a circle, broke loose, elbowed someone aside. She banished the thought of her marbles, the puggy, knucks games on her knees in the dirt, the allies she won playing potsies for keeps. As she walked that narrow sun-softened blacktop unrolling from Ulysees S. Grant Elementary to her stucco house, Cassandra made a decision, surrendering her childhood at last.

The day deepened to dusk. The sky leeched from russet to mud above the SEVERE DUST AREA sign. She pictured Daisy asleep with the radio, TV both on and once more broke into a run. She dashed past box hives, insecticide drums, the hand-painted sign of the shack selling humus and bark.

Panting, Cassandra arrived. Red and blue police car turrets were splashing the yard. A caricature of bent stealth, she snuck around back. She tiptoed inside. Cassandra bumped into an oversized cop whose paraphernalia clacked on his belt as he seized her by the arms.

"We've been looking for you. Are you hurt?"

Cassandra squirmed, kept her eyes on his gun. "Not until now," she replied.

By the kitchen door she made out the sway of her mother, arms pinned behind her, shoulders unnaturally taut. There'd been a struggle. Another cop propped her. The standing lamp had been toppled. Shards of figurines dusted the carpet. The La-Z-Boy recliner lay on its side. Cassandra was proud.

Then she was handed a WHITE FRONT–stamped sack and ordered to pack her essentials, her real ones this time. She gathered a toothbrush, a man's T-shirt nightdress, her wrinkled but clean pinafore. For good luck she dropped in her red plastic pearls.

Outside, in the driveway, a COMMUNITY SHARED SOCIAL SERVICES–stenciled green van had pulled up. It idled, wheezed blue puffs of acrid exhaust. A handful of neighbors had gathered, though they'd never bothered addressing Cassandra or Daisy before. One man held a red Labrador that jerked on its leash, choked, and barked. The rest stepped foot to foot, hushed, hypnotized by the cherry and cobalt sweep lights. She thought them too curious, rude. To each one in turn she gave her accusative, glowering frown, as if this was their fault, and somehow she knew that it was.

A cop boosted her into the van. So she could see better, Cassandra sat on the hump of the engine's warm cowl. The driver, whose name tag read HAZEL O. LORD, didn't greet her and made no remark. Together they watched Daisy muscled, half dragged, to the car. Cassandra could tell her resistance was no more than habit. She couldn't believe it. She'd never seen Daisy give up.

One of the bystanders actually waved as the van pulled away from the curb. She kept her eyes on the house, the receding yard that was now violated and sullied by strangers, a place where they couldn't come back. The last thing she saw was the crate still up-turned on the lawn.

They drove onto Highway 14, then the newly paved 10. Cassandra studied the undersea tint of the clock in the dash as it arced to-ward seven P.M. The temperature fell. A wax crescent moon slipped in and out on a sky that turned larded with high and dark clouds. She noticed their melanin-fleeced undersides.

"Where are we going?" Cassandra asked, but received no reply. The seam of horizon flared pink into black. They were three miles equidistant between the raze of Ravenna, the nowhere of Acton. Cassandra could tell by the signs and odometer count. They came to a headstonelike marker, aimed right on what read KEEP OUT, PRI-VATE DRIVE. The van rocked to a stop at a barrackslike building with two rows of opaque milk wire-meshed windows leaking a saurian light. There was no fence but two floodlights whitewashing each side.

Cassandra clutched her sack tight, refused the matron's stretched hand, took timid steps on the scrub. As she approached, the barred double doors as if by themselves opened out. Then everything hap-pened too ordered, rehearsed yet too fast.

A hand on her shoulder, Cassandra was steered down a hall lit by high-hanging canopied bulbs. The tiles were striped, the walls insti-tutional pink like her school, the shade of bologna left on a counter all night. Cassandra averted her eyes from the serious quizzical faces of children they passed. She knew she was being appraised.

"That place smelled like nothing before, just like the stuff they use to swab Trailways buses," Cassandra says now, wiping a perspir-ing palm on her thigh, recalling the odor of tart disinfectant, the linger of vomit through TSP powder, bleach, sodium fluoride.

They came to a shabby arrangement of office, a haphazard scat-ter of duct-taped green armchairs, a steel-bucket trash can, a single wood desk that was Bic-pen, knife-gouged. A gold-tasseled tatter of Golden State flag was flanked by a black-and-white glossy large-smiled Eisenhower who stared into space behind glass. Unlike the portraits that hung at the cleaners, she noted that his was unsigned.

Cassandra was handed a blunt nub of pencil, a five-by-eight card. She penned her name, address, height five feet three, weight seventy-nine, hair blond, and eyes brown. Did she wear glasses? She Xed the questionnaire yes, her first official lie. She flinched as her right thumb was grasped, an ink pad produced like Daisy had used to stamp checks. Cassandra was taken aback as the woman pressed down, transferred the whorls of her imprint onto a square. She'd seen this on TV and it was what criminals got. So this was a prison for children who told and that's who she was. Kleenex just smeared the ink smudge. She was turned around, her blouse lifted up, her skirt once more tugged. Evidence notes were cribbed on a clipboard's white chart.

"What have you done to my mother?" she asked, but Hazel O. Lord kept her silence intact.

Cassandra was led to an anteroom empty except for a high-sided oval steel tub. The woman motioned for her to undress and donned sleek yellow dish-washing gloves. There were no longer effective strategies left for how to behave. Cassandra climbed naked, embarrassed, into the clear tepid liquid that smelled like ammonia and rose to her waist. It made her want to go to the bathroom, but what if the water was spiked with the stuff that turns pee red she'd heard about? She saw her clothes dumped in a chute marked INCINERATE. The hands on her skin were sure, fast and rough. The scrub of the washcloth inside her legs was businesslike, matter-of-fact.

Cassandra was lifted out, handed a towel much too threadbare and small to do a good job. Her back was Mercurochrome daubed. It stung worse than the cuts. The woman unclamped a hosed, nozzled spray can contraption Cassandra had missed from the side of the bath. She'd seen one before removed from a truck parked in front of her house decaled with a top-hatted, waistcoated character bowed and obscuring a mallet, wagging his finger at what looked like Jiminy Cricket about to be squashed.

Hazel O. Lord finally spoke. "Hold your nose. Close your eyes. It's for lice." Cassandra thought of Anne Frank.

After, she fastened her pinafore dress, was led down the hall to a dorm where a girl stood on concrete affecting a yawn and a stretch. She was square-shouldered, squat, would grow up to resemble Daisy, Cassandra could tell.

"I'm Elena Ruiz. You missed supper," she said, extending her hand like a man. Baffled, Cassandra just shook it. The matron retreated. Cream-colored hospital cots on ball casters lined the long room head to foot in two single rows on each side. The glass-paned door at each end appeared locked. Magazine cutouts of junior high crushes were taped to the walls. The light was too harsh from the tall ceiling's even-set uncovered bulbs.

"That's where you sleep if you can." The girl tipped her chin toward a bed with a plain cardboard box underneath like the rest, this one printed with no felt-markered name as of yet.

"Let's see what you've got in that bag," she demanded, advancing, an arm held straight out. Her breath smelled like mint, Blackjack gum. Not thinking, on instinct, Cassandra struck her in the face, open-palmed. She was ready to hit her again but the girl reeled, staggered back, gingerly tamping her four-fingered reddening swell.

"You'll do all right. You'll be famous all over," she said. She bent under her bed, extracted a peach and a Mallomar bar, offering a choice to Cassandra, who took both at once. They sat on mattresses facing each other. Wary, the girl watched her pocket the candy, bite dribbling mouthfuls of fruit. Cassandra realized this was her first meal of the day and how hungry she was. She unwrapped the Mallomar, ate it as fast as she could.

The girl made slight *tsks* with her tongue on the roof of her mouth, gestured to pick at her nose, changed her mind. They both swung their feet, jogged their cots for the ratchet and squeal the springs made. Cassandra jiggled her tooth that seemed held by no more than a nerve's queasy thread. She twisted it loose, wiped its

viscous pink on the hem of her dress, handed it to the girl. Cassandra could see she was pleased.

"Where you from?" the girl asked.

"Pearblossom, near Palmdale," Cassandra replied, licking the soft
mushy gap in her gums like the pulp-textured pit she didn't know
what to do with that was staining her hand.

"I'm from Glendora," the girl said, tucking the bicuspid into the
cleft of her still-useless training brassiere.

Cassandra rolled the seed down the length of the aisle. "So why
are you here?"

Elena Ruiz chewed her raw cuticles for a while. She glanced left
and right at the blanks of the glass that reflected black as if someone
observed from behind, jammed both fists under her thighs.

"My father and I were found out," she whispered. "You know
what I'm talking about?"

Cassandra nodded. She realized with a start she was certain she
did. She was utterly sure of this fact.

So it wasn't just her after all. She hadn't told anyone all along because of the misconceived notion that she was alone in her damp,
furtive crime. How could she have been so wrong? Cassandra stared
at Elena Ruiz's puffed cheek, her hair also amateur-clipped and
rinsed bottle-blond, knew that she, too, was warned not to cry in a
guttural whisper on dark, recessed nights, pushed by a wall with her
mother nearby but so far. Maybe Elena Ruiz had also curled up on a
bunk in a sewing room locked from inside, saw the propped headless
dressmaker's dummy that nonetheless watched, the never-used
weights in the corner, the medicine ball, the dim subterranean bulb
that went out. Maybe she also gave in to the pleas, curt commands,
and the thing that once started could never be stopped.

Cassandra wanted to tell her how it even happened outside in
full light with shadows of leaves on the ground, on a crate in the set-
tling dust of the paw-stirred front yard with no witness around, only
her uncle guiding her hand to his lap, lifting her up, rubbing himself
on her shy secret parts until he came undone with a sob.

Instead, Cassandra asked, "Want to see a neat scar?" She stood, turned around, undid her pinafore dress's rear snaps, showed off the purpling lacerations marring the base of her spine that had started to scab, not a little bit proud.

She heard Elena release an admiring wow. Cassandra knew how it looked. She'd checked it out, reverential, unsteady, tiptoed on the bowl of the toilet, her back to the medicine cabinet mirror, turned from her silhouette cast by the bathroom's incarnadine glow on the next-to-last night in her house.

Cassandra scratches the top of a breast through her gown without qualm. As she's been talking our room's become bathed in a crisp winter sun. The curtain's not drawn, the window is shut. There's only the icebox's electric hum, occasional birds, and always, staccatos of one-block-away boardwalk drums.

Cassandra shifts on the bed so she's fully exposed, her knees far apart. "That place wasn't really so bad," she claims as she fishes in her purse for her compact, cracked vanity mirror, applies a blush of faint rouge to her cheeks with two swoops in the all around bright. By way of distraction she says to herself the rest of the girls had come back.

It was after lights out. There was no comforting under-door runner of gold once the bare bulbs were doused. Swatches of candescent pearl smudged the wall. Inside the under-bed boxes the clothes had been folded or carelessly flung. Empty shoes littered the floor like preparing for brief, aimless walks. Cassandra heard airy sounds, sudden coughs. She felt the accumulation of day like it was a pent-up, unnamed desire comprised of escape from the school, the cops in the house, the roll of the van, and the hands on her blouse, on her back, in her legs in the tub. More hands in a day than a lifetime, she thought, surrendering herself to the lozenge of curtainless windows that let in no view of outside.

After her eyes had adjusted she noticed in some of the cots there were too many limbs, in others none. She culled the subtle beds' racket, particular groans, sharp intakes of breath, sullen yowls. She had a yearning for something no words could describe in the fuzzed, muzzy light. She closed her eyes, heard the low sounds of mothers with fathers and others she'd overheard mimicked at recess. Cassandra invented a passion and touched herself lightly down there where it wasn't allowed.

She recalled Daisy's emanations released from behind the bedroom door partially closed when she wasn't supposed to be home. She'd seen Daisy spread on the chicken-greased sheet, legs splayed, nightdress hiked past her waist, in the TV's translucent blue light. Her mother was working a half-empty fifth of Kamchatka inside of her thighs. Cassandra could not look away, leaned closer and heard the booze slosh, her mother's intricate stutters, sighs, wheezes, and harsh exhalations that signaled a kind of unlocking. Raptly, she watched Daisy break into teeth-gritted spasms. Her flesh rippled, quivered. Her head tilted back as she rode the bottle she clutched by its neck with what seemed like alarm, her large hips impossibly rocking, a motion Cassandra did not think her capable of. Then she moved faster, relentless, unceasing, with lunges that couldn't go on, but they did until Daisy was seized by a series of shudders, contractions, and bucks. The headboard beat hard as Cassandra witnessed her mother, who barked like her uncle, released and unblocked. So women can do this as well, she had thought.

In the dorm on the bed on her back, knees slightly drawn, Cassandra slid two of her fingers inside. It tingled, slick, sticky warm. She'd done this before, but only for testing the depth of herself, and then she was dry. Now she felt vaguely ashamed and enlightened at once. She brought her juiced hand to her mouth, bewitched by the scent of her thick tarty brine, the rest of the smells, the effluvium of sweat and peroxide, a heady excitement that filled the whole room like a charge. She thrust herself into her touch, figuring the angle that made her best feel the unsubtle wave building up. She knew she was doing it right. Why, she could do this anytime! Cassandra thought of a palm on her thigh soft like hers and not blundering, rough, imagined her tongue being sucked, half listened to choked-off indelicate grunts and soft skin-slap response. She heard her own sound breaking loose, when suddenly someone was standing above her and clamping a hand on her mouth. Someone was parting her legs and climbing on top, the flesh like her own though a stranger's, familiar, a cool alabaster. Cassandra moaned, arms pinned to her side, gasped out loud as she couldn't hold back, smelled the odor of roller-set perm, felt soft breaths of words on her brow.

"Hey, new girl," she heard as the dorm and the world she had known up until then both dissolved in a shivery, throaty surprise.

Twenty-Two

Winter's officially started and we have no money for rent. This was bound to happen. I've mentioned that we'll be evicted. Cassandra and Gary are up in the room and they're fighting about it. She picked up an ashtray, preparing to throw it at Gary, who hefted his bottle of wine like a baseball bat. We had to get out.

Maria and I are caught in a shower that sizzles and crisps like a skein of electrical charge on the pocked, lunar sand. We're holding hands, don't mind that we're wet, watch the green roiling ocean's jade tubes. It can't go on like this, I think to myself, yearning for some kind of plan, but I don't know where to begin, what might be the first step.

The weather's chameleon, cooling. Mantillas of mist crown the crests of the peaks as the coiled waves roll in. A high surf has washed out the usual garbage, leaving the shoreline pristine. Orange-beaked sea gulls with polka-dot coverts idle away as we near. Their aimless, meandering arrow tracks curve on themselves. Plovers are dipping pipettelike bills in the foam, toothpick legs blurred as they dash among patches of tubers resembling the sex of Greek statues. The sea spills attenuate fingers that race up the shore, leaves shivering islets reflecting the sky's variegated, gray-layered pastel.

We're both dressed too light against a stiff wind that rises to blow out the rain. Jetliners lift from the airport in measured succession, bank over a slate of Pacific smeared clear. Catalina is visible to the southwest. SoCal Edison's power plant stacks string pearl distensions of vapor on smoke-colored air. Facades of miles-away oceanfront houses are whitewashed by a sun that's obscured from our view.

The waves become calmer, a juggernaut-steady advancing that puts me in mind of amphibious landings. We pass a ponchowrapped middle-aged woman hopefully stick-painting feathery flowers and leaves on the tideline's smooth certain erasure. Maria and I turn toward the snow-dusted San Gabriel Mountains and look at our row of squat buildings. Seen from this distance they seem to be somebody's quaint fantasy, a film set I have imagined, a playland arcade on which my wishes are projected. Slowly I've been disabused of my notions. Up close it isn't the same.

"Hold it a minute," Maria says, bending, throwing up where she stands.

"Dopesick already?" I ask.

"I'm fine," she replies, wipes her lips with the back of a hand, palms flecks of bile from her hair.

"But you've got the shakes," I tell her. "You should take a look at yourself."

"So? You look escaped from somewhere." She fishes her pockets, extracts a crumpled-up pack, lights a cigarette into the wind with unsteady, underage hands. She's learned that this is what kindles the flame. Maria lets out a laugh. "I can't get over the faces you made yesterday."

"Don't remind me," I say.

What happened seemed more horrible than our arms or the girls turning tricks. I had taken a can of V-8 from the fridge, I was taking a sip. There was something strange in my mouth. Reflexively, I spit it out. It was a dead roach. I let out a choked scream. The can fell from my grasp. Cassandra and Gary turned, startled. "I almost swallowed a cockroach." I pointed at the clump of brown and red mess on the tile. "It was in my mouth!" They fell on the bed, clutched their sides, rolled around. I thought I might barf. "It's not funny," I said, thinking this was the low point of my stay in the room.

Maria blows smoke through her nose as if to prove she inhales. "It was only an insect," Maria reminds me. "I've tasted much worse." She nudges my shoulder. "Come on. I have to go find a john. Pay the bills. Buy the junk. Cassandra expects it."

Her tone is bitter, resigned, as if she's ensnared by Cassandra's and Gary's demands on her flesh. I'd like to think we have a choice but her bearing, demeanor, disputes this. The soles of her sneakers are split, her frayed jean cuffs drag in the sand as she trudges and puffs on her Kool cigarette. Her eyes are too deep for her age.

We reach where we live but keep walking. Up there the radiator's stressed Geiger's repeating its incessant ticking, releasing an odor of wool and steamed leather much like the heaters at school. His silhouette startling the corners, the paraphernalia spread on the cinder block table, Gary is waiting for limp, sweaty money the girls must extrude from hasty-curbed cars in the Laundromat alley with up-and-down fists. The scheme of becoming dope dealers has given way to no more than this.

What we call our park is merely a bulge in the landscape, a short-winding climb. The ground's wet, so we have to stand. Maria is eyeing the corners and hugging her chest. Across Main bloated school buses shudder in neutral, fat tail pipes exhaling blue soot. Venice Elementary lets out with whoop-throated, lunchbox-bang gaggles disgorged in loose swarms. Red-zone-parked mothers lean over to unlatch their passenger doors. Children in multihued clothing disperse on the hopscotch-chalked yard. Maria could have been among them, running from a bungalow only last year, shouting and clutching a tabbed spiral notebook, a brown Peechee folder, excited by her show-and-tell.

She appears meditative, as if daring a recall of houses receding from dust-ingrained pickups, her sisters' names, Florinda, Inez, Magdalene, the angle of light on the walls, memories of music the radios played.

Instead, Maria says, "I've seen a stupid new girl working here. She looks like she also wants all the wrong things. She can take over. I quit."

I wonder if Maria means this or if she's bluffing or kidding herself. And if she does, then what happens next? Will I be the one to inform Cassandra? What will be the shape of the words from my lips?

Maria's eyes brim with tears she tries to hold back then allows to silver her cheeks. They waver and drip from her chin. Her face is contorted and red. She's never done this. I see how much effort it takes, how it hurts.

I say, "What's the matter? Don't cry." I think this is good, though, it befits her age, it offers release.

She touches my arm. "Don't tell Cassandra, she'll use it against me. You promise?"

"What, that you're crying?"

"Just swear!" she insists, and I have to agree.

Maria gets on tiptoes, cupping her palms to my ear. "I'm pregnant," she whispers, leans into my shoulder, relieved.

I'm suddenly giddy, too light on my feet. The sun appears just for a moment, compact and brittle, yet glazing the bricks of Oceanview apartments a rarefied mandarin tint. It washes the short crop of lawn to a bright lustrous green. It highlights Maria's thick hair, becomes obscured by clouds.

She pulls away, pats her belly. "It doesn't show yet," she says, like this makes it okay.

I'm thinking escape is geography factored by time. I ponder the unbidden nature of change. In under an hour Maria and I could be passing through Riverside County, past ordnance roads, feeder trails. I'd explain the meaning of SOFT SHOULDER signs. We'd distract ourselves from withdrawal by playing hangman and out-of-state plates. Maybe where freeway turns turnpike our fevers will break. Maria will unfold a triple A map, tamp its creases, circling the names of the towns she especially favors with gas station pens. We'll take cold showers in no soap rest stops, towel dry with our shirts. There may be enough money left for a Tuinal bought from a Harley-teed boy encamped in a van with "Stairway to Heaven" stereo speakers set out on the scrub. He might remind her of someone but she will be too old for him. As usual, I'm getting ahead of myself.

"We have to plan," I tell her. "For real."

She shakes her head, tries a lachrymose smile, doesn't say anything.

"I'll get my old job at the bookstore. I'll finish college. I know a place you could work."

I picture her two landings up in a high and white room in the city where winter semester is well under way. The bells of the square are releasing their sixteen-note peals, tones swallowing all other noise as they fall through the air. She'd sit in an unvarnished straight-backed wood chair, fingering the single-key necklace she wears. Maria would sip lukewarm Ovaltine from our single chipped mug, wait by the lightbulb-bleached lampshade, pullshades the same beige. I'd stand under our narrow scratched window, my rubber galoshes crunching the snow as I stepped foot to foot, my breath making dissolving cloudlets as I called her name. Hanna would have to approve.

"Cassandra is coming," Maria says, poking my ribs.

Sounds return as on waking, a Dopplering siren, the corner tattoo parlor's snap of taut awning. Raucous and wheedling gulls have swept inland for scraps. Cassandra's expression is full of a desperate insouciance. She's got a cut on her forehead, a purpling bruised cheek. Holding her elbows, she's tapping a foot on the mat, sodden grass.

"You two are a sight," she remarks. She points at Maria, "Expect many tricks dressed like that?"

"I hate you," Maria replies without rancor, her inflection flat.

"That's all right." Cassandra is unctuous. "I couldn't care less you exist."

Maria winces. "I'm not good for just making money," she says.

Cassandra affects a pained countenance. "Who says you aren't?" she replies.

Her answer I note is ambiguous on purpose, it could be interpreted either way. She is approaching the truth. She gives me a look of contempt that says I, too, am superfluous, no more than a college kid with a room where Cassandra is able to shoot up unbothered and sleep. She expects nothing of me after all. It's a relief in a way.

The air becomes fenny and leaden, too dense, as if it might start raining again. Maria and Cassandra contemplate each other's faces within striking distance. Cassandra is opening and closing her hands like in bed but more tense. Maria blanches but doesn't retreat. They remain still for the length of a Cessna traversing the line of our sight.

Then something ineffable transpires between them. Gestureless, wordless, it's made manifest nonetheless and I get to see it. Cassandra knows everything and Maria can tell. The standoff is altered, though Cassandra tries not to show it. Her posture's a studied indifference. Nothing's forgiven but somehow acceptance is granted. Some subtle feminine pact becomes forged, along with a tacit agreement that all of it remain unspoken.

They turn together, begin an acute descent. Cassandra's precarious heels break the turf, bracelets jingling, refracting the light to bright mica as she guides Maria by palming the small of her back. Their heads are conspiracy bent.

I stare at the trees that are lush all year round, at parallel candy puff contrails that ribbon the sky. I weigh the options. I don't want to wait for the girls to return, see them sullied but glad for the cash. I don't want to look for signs of Maria's new secret inside. I hate the room and all it implies. No, I won't go up there for now. I despise the park. This all has to end and it can't, but it has to somehow.

I cross to Pacific and get on the number two bus again, sit in the back where the rumbling's the loudest. The diesel seeps in. It mingles with scents of hard candy, shampoo, a faint reek of Lysol and vomit. I submerge myself in the windows' weak aquamarine, watch rectangle swatches of light roam the aisle. I am rehearsing for running away once again. This third time I'll do it right.

If Hanna was here, or even Maria, I'd show her the small things I notice, a puddling buckle of sidewalk, its narrow cracks tufted with

Icelandic poppies, a bush-swarming wrangle of thrushes. We glide
by a boy in a tetherballed yard. A blue waitress dress and incredibly
wide boxer shorts are hung from a wheel-and-spoke post in a circle
of uncut dun grass. I study the order of well-tended neighborhood
houses set close to the walk. We pick up passengers idling by stucco
apartments that offer no view of the sea, though with names across
their tan facades such as Vista Del Mar. All this would be lost on
Cassandra, who's too self-obsessed. She wouldn't care about culling
particular details, except as they relate exclusively to herself.

It comes to me how we once took this line to go cop, we were too
drunk to drive. It was still summer, our salad days, as Cassandra had
called them. She's dangerous when stranger-confided in a space of
this size. Maria was dancing a rubber dinosaur she had found in the
trash on her thighs. Cassandra played to the crowd. Her open-toed
heels and her flounce incited a nervous attention, an urge to both
stare and avert your eyes. She made you wonder where she had
been, what she'd done, what she might do next, if she had any underwear on. She swung from a vertical pole in an arc, daring anyone.

"You all want to help me and hurt me," she said loud enough.

"Quit throwing it up in their faces," Gary called from the back,
but she was past caring for how she performed in the public do-
main. Cassandra strode to the seats where men sat alone with their
parcels, insinuated herself much too close as they flinched, tried to
shy from her gaze. I knew she pleasured the smell of their fear that
was nonetheless mingled with intrigue and lust.

I pretended not to know her, that we didn't board with each
other. I studied the ads for dentists on credit, telephone numbers for
slip and fall Mexican lawyers, vocational schools. Gary had taken
three twist-off caps and the shrunken pea from his pocket. I was the
shill for the shell game con. It works like three-card monte. I "won"
ten dollars. Because Gary was conning students, he kept the bets
small. "Watch the bean, take a chance, pick the cap with the pea
underneath, it's not hard, use your eyes, common sense, win five
bucks," Gary chanted. Four students instantly lost. The trick is the
pea's in the con man's curled palm all along.

I saw Cassandra speak to the driver, nudging his thigh with her leg, felt a swerve. I went for the door as she turned, appeared regally blowsy, flamboyant.

"Best check your wallets," she called out as we disembarked. I saw the men patting their pockets in rapid and stiff pantomimes.

The rattling glass is my pillow. I'm falling asleep in my seat. I think of what Maria has finally told me about that lone father she wouldn't discuss. One day she was simply led up to his door. I'm not certain this is a dream. It has its qualities but because it's so close to the surface it seems exceedingly real. It rises, unbidden, nuanced, replete with details Maria has furnished, others I couldn't know, but I do. Maybe I've entered hers.

Mornings, he combed out her rich fulsome hair, noting the way it refused to conform to the curl of the brush. It put him in mind of black kelp at low tide, weeping willows at night.

He kept her fed on Dalmane mixed into her first orange juice of the day. It slurred her words when she'd tell him get back, get away.

He always said mornings were best, that tinkly silence, a car door slamming shut, the faraway whine of a two-stroke bike engine, the infantile wail of a cat making love.

For a while, but not long, he'd be content to simply observe her. He loved her. He knelt by her bed in the sun-drenched back bedroom they'd decorated together. She'd picked out the Crayola colors, he'd chosen the textures. He thought about shaking her head in his hands to witness the riot of fear on her face. That's how he'd remind her he'd do it again, inevitably committing the sin.

Inside where we've gone the man watched her. I see how he looked at her figure that lay there so calm, sleep-composed. He noticed her palms, the bare soles of her feet where the skin was incredibly subtle and tender. Maria's next-to-last father bent, pulled back the cover.

She slept not yet stained, uncovered, unbruised. The sheet that bunched like a shawl at her feet was ostrich and teal. The light in the room was flaring like sunflowers, drowning the corners, anointing the covers. It burned up the curtain's lime lace. Despite the abundance of bright he was frightened. It was only amphetamine kept him awake, made him brave. Because she lay there so smooth, unadorned, bathed in light, was why he could not bear to look away, why he couldn't be blamed.

He realized she was awake but pretending to sleep. He hated that worst, reached down to her stomach and so lightly touched it that though she was faking she still didn't quiver.

He went in the kitchen to grind up the pills for her powder. For this he had his own special mortar and pestle that no one could use. When he was finished, to take off his edge, he licked the brass bowl.

He thought of her almost toy bed so disheveled. She was his all-day salvation unless he was handling his pearl-handled .38 special. She must know he thought of his perfect, small house and how no one came close.

He returned to her still not sleeping.

"Wake up now," he told her, "there's no school today."

She shrank from the Yogi Bear tumbler he offered but drank anyway, didn't speak. He hated that, too.

"Sit up," he said tersely, though he didn't mean to, he loved her. Inside his mind he saw himself putting out lies like gasoline fires. She must have noticed the awed, abject dread in his eyes when he said, "Come on now, sit closer."

The drug opened her gaze into thick apprehension. In his bleached-pupiled, speed-scarred expression he knew she witnessed remorse, a blind, helpless, penitent rage. She couldn't stop him. She had to know he was ashamed.

"Do it or I'll pull you over," he said playfully, he thought. He sat on the edge of the bed and kiddingly kissed her. As if in wonder, she touched her mouth where his lips had just been.

She said, "I'm just a child."

"I know that, Maria," he told her. In one of the rooms a stereo played *Lucia di Lammermoor.* "What restrains me at such moments?" the tenor implored. Then he was certain she was relieved that all this had happened before. He saw her give up and roll over.

She also must have imagined the whole house in flames. He rose and went out.

She would have heard when he started the tub. Though his hands couldn't feel hot or cold because of the speed, he tested the water. He pictured Maria inside her room, the wind that came filling and folding the curtains, the ripple of sheets like sand dunes.

Maybe she heard him last night with his gun in the cellar, the small clicking noises it made, like slow, oily insects rubbing themselves on each other. He pondered if she might be thinking the name of the street where they lived and the city so if she got lost, she'd never come back to Valerio Lane in Pacoima.

The air was prodigious and clamoring with opera. He shot up the last of his stash in a hunger. He said to himself, "See it clearly, and you create beauty." He took off his clothes. He noticed one of her dresses hung from the rim of the round bathroom mirror and stroked its creased folds. Behind his shoulder, reflected by mirror, he saw the tattoo on his back of the face that resembled Maria's, its ink red and blue. Over the tub, like practicing voodoo, he pared his long, feminine nails.

He walked back to her room with a doped-up precision. It was always the same. Whatever she did made no difference. She moved to the wall. He sat down beside her. She studied his gender. Maria breathed his rubbing alcohol smell. He'd made himself smooth with a razor to match her. Because of his tremor he'd cut himself many times over. Thin welts of scars grazed his groin where he'd done this before.

He carried her into the bathroom and laid her down in the first-degree water. "No, it's too hot," she exclaimed.

He watched her hair floating free, how she burned, how she had to be clean. She couldn't be dirty, she was his baby. He thought her eyes were forgiving and meek. No matter, he held her under. His hands twitched like fish left too long on the shore. She also shook. He fully believed he could drown her, watch coils of her hair floating under the surface forever.

Instead he pulled her up, saved her. Using a washcloth imprinted with Bambis he wiped her all over.

"I washed your favorite towel," he murmured.

She smelled like the lavender balm he'd poured in the bath, but she was a make-believe sleeper, a liar. He felt himself an observer. That's what he wanted to teach her. He could tell she was starting to learn. Shyly, he wrapped her, then lifted her under the arms, held himself against her, letting the towel fall to tile. Now they were skin upon skin. His breath came too fast. She must have felt he was flaccid because of the speed.

In her ear, he said, "Honey, where is your mother?" He flashed his dentures, pretended hurt when Maria did not even smile at his joke.

He laid her back down in her juvenile bed and looked at his daughter. It was too late. Her eyes were too wide. The back of her hand when she shielded her face was too pale. He was weak, she knew he'd surrender. He lifted his scalded, spiked arms and parted the curtain to let in the summer. She wouldn't dare yell, even whisper. She was so helpless he'd take her.

He leaned over the little girl bed, touched her brow as if testing for fever. He noticed she saw he was out of control and that was too bad. She was just like him, bare, how he liked her. Now he could help her. He thought he knew how. He'd do everything for her and to her until she forgot her own name. He'd make her defenseless and glad.

Briefly he saw how she really was, hairless, like her doll. He shuddered. He thought of a consequence, then it was banished. He witnessed gradations of skin from her calves to the cocoa cream glaze on her thighs.

Outside, there were oranges rotting, the odor of freshly cut grass.

He couldn't stand what she made him do. He bent lower. He was certain that this was the thing she'd always pretend to put out of her mind.

It was just to distract him, but she said, "Last night I heard noises from under the house."

He looked at himself still unformed. His forefinger aimed at his temple, he told her, "I tried something out."

She must know how he wanted that pistol. He recalled the nomenclature of gun parts: sear, grip, cock, touchhole, hair trigger. He craved the rod, string cleaner, pull-through weights to fall down the length of the shaft. Liquid mercury rolled back and forth absorbed barrel leading. He remembered to best hold the cylinder firmly when cleaning the chamber. Cold liquid bluing helps keep a straight aim. Close-tolerant parts need constant attention. Bringing a gun from the cold to the heat makes it sweat. Soon moisture shows up on its surface and it's wet inside. To never let rust interfere is the way to gun health.

She made him remember last evening, the spread on his pants as the revolver rubbed on his member. She must have heard his private, discriminate groans in the cellar. The backs of his knees felt like after avoiding a car crash. He'd make her pay because he had to scare himself into it now.

She could see it would happen. He knelt on the bed, ran his hand through her winterleaf hair. He saw her sigh and surrender. Light poured in through the entire window. It made her face oddly cretaceous, her legs like marble and sad.

She frightened him so much he touched her. He thought he might vomit but he held it down. He felt like washing his hands so he put one inside her, realizing that she was a girl and still dry. He thought he'd help her. He moved his fingers around.

Outside, birds tittered and flirted among the mute, ready-to-drop avocados. The turntable howled lamentations. Ill-fated lovers were falling on swords.

He was still soft but tried force. She looked at the flat, flaring crystalline ceiling, pretended rehearsing an absence, but it wouldn't hold. It was when he used all his fingers to pry her that he heard her, sonorous, hoarse, a coarse moaning filling her throat that engulfed her and rose.

Once more he squeezed himself in her but this meant he would not anymore. After all, she'd discovered the game in the cellar. He heard how her voice surprised and scared her, some open-mouthed other's. He couldn't stand the inverse of pleasure that crowded her cries. Her fingers tore at his face and he let her. He relished the pain. Inside our confluent dream she screamed until he pulled out. Then he slapped her, pushed her to the floor. She looked up with an abject expression of loathing and pleading at once, a desire to be saved. But it was her teenager face and it stared not at him but at me.

I wake with a shudder, my shirt soaked through with the nightmare. I get off at Wilshire and 6th and study myself in a storefront. I'm in-corporeal, with smudges for eyes. My chin's sparsely stubbled with what could not be called a beard. There's a scar on my cheek I've ac-quired from some late-night scratch and my hair's sticking up. The soft blue plaid shirt Cassandra stole from a clothesline's untucked. I still wear the checkerboard pants without pockets, the white plastic shoes scuffed the color of pigeons in mud. If only the girls were here now they'd ignore me or laugh. I look like I need to be rescued at once. It is unlike summer, when this was a lark. I conveniently don't think of the tricks in the park, the pawning of my high-school-grad-uation-gift watch, which Gary cajoled from my arm. I put aside the Mexican apartment cries. It was adventure then, only good times.

I have an urge to recast the past now that it's strong as my habit. It heals and restores, gives me strength to go on in the present. It is a touchstone, a warm amulet. Unlike the capricious present, I can control it, bend it to my will until it's however I wish. It is my reli-gion. It's as necessary as taking a breath.

I have an idea, find a urine-stained booth with a telephone book. There aren't any churches named for Cassandra but one for Maria nearby. In the way of these things, its heavy brass clapper releases a round golden toll. The sky appears penitent, singular. Pinpricks of drizzle blow at an angle. I follow that sound.

It's nearly deserted. The stained glass is dull. The requisite mo-tions come back. I genuflect, cross myself, kneel on a pew's padded

runner. A hunched-over woman lights a memorial candle, a cha-
suble flashes behind a partition, an essence of incense lingers on
hushed, musty air. It's silent as intoxication in here.

I study Christ's dozen stations of passion. It could help, so I try
an Our Father. Removed from their commonplace rote the words
are avowals of God's breadth, dominion, a hope for the future, then
bartered forgiveness, a pleading for food. I don't like its implication
that we have to grovel.

A bough scrapes a gutter inducing a mild melancholia. The effi-
cacy of prayer delivers a vivid indulgence of Hanna and I also stepping into church to get out of the riot and weather. She is idealized,
beautiful, desperate. I feel free to take liberties with Hanna's radiant
appearance, to make her a saint. In this way she's reclaimed.

Hanna and I paused in the vestibule's dim arboretum of murk.
She wore her long-sleeved silk blouse, below-the-knee skirt. Its
matching lily-brooched jacket was spotted with rain. She shook out
her paisley-print kerchief, exposing peroxide hair and black roots,
retied it under her chin. The holy water was tepid, the font evapo-
rate-ringed.

"Don't touch it, you'll get a disease," Hanna cautioned too late.

We knelt on the hassockless runner. Attendance was heavy in
spite or because of the ferment that swelled the damp streets. The
priest wet his thumb on his tongue before turning the page of his
missal and raising his arms. The altar boys muttered their Latin re-
sponses, the smoking myrrh censer was lifted and swung. Stressed
benches creaked. Above the rococo frieze Eucharist shelter Jesus'
knees were bent on the Cross in effeminate, coy denial of his gender,
his eyes heaven-cast.

"Don't believe any of this," Hanna said, leaning close. The
Catholic religion was nothing redemptive but bloody and sad, she had
warned me before. She took in the murmuring, hand-folding rows.

"These are the people who tried to murder your father," she
whispered.

I didn't know how to respond, remained mute. He had been gone a long time, there were rumors. I realize I never liked him, disliked him, maybe because Hanna was always unhappy when he was around. He seemed always removed, a disembodied voice, a trail of faint smoke. I think in a way that man died in the camp and was never reborn. He made Hanna sad with his reproachful glances. Under his stare she believed herself perpetually accused. Of course she eventually gave him the reasons to find her guilty, thereby fulfilling her role.

Hanna had told me that nothing's forgotten and everything matters. She'd said he was slight but seemed larger, composed. Sometimes on evenings of gin and laudanum, Hanna would question herself in a quiet, singsong monotone. She'd lower her gaze to her carbonate flute as if it had the answers and sometimes it did, though, evanescent, they fled, would not hold.

Her face then was like a Vermeer, orange smudged by the lamp. The metronome tick of the grandfather clock in the hall was the sole accompaniment to her barely audible words: What was it in him that drew her? Why had she offered herself to a man so much older and haunted, dead many times over? Was it his dawn dreams of disinterred bones, the hair and skin plumes? The name of his previous wife on his lips who was limed in a pit while, as he slept, Hanna took him inside?

She shook her head. That couldn't have been what compelled her. She'd rest her brow on her arms, leave perspired marks on the gloss-polished living room table. No, she had said. It was the way he loosed the fall of her false blond hair dappled with sunlight and held by a colorless band, his pants folded neatly on the chair and his peppery, saltpeter smell. It was surely the stroke of his soft desk-bound hands.

"You're too young," she'd tell me. "You can't understand." She could have as well meant herself.

Here Hanna would pause, elbow-propped, unclasp the deep-sea pearl necklace he'd bought her, its beads like the perfect round teeth of some mythical fish. She'd let me hold it, rolling its beads in my palm. He kept his word, she would say, never wondered out loud why the rest went to flame, why not he. Never told.

Of course I looked it up later, Hungarians hunting their Jews in the street, at their places of work, in their homes. I read about the abstraction of transport, the days without water, death stacked in the corner, the meaningless names of the towns that lay over the northeast Polish border.

I saw a movie about it. Among the jerky-stride frames I wanted a glimpse of my father, though I had forgotten his features except as they mirrored my own. I looked for him in the queue toward the tall crematoria, his imprint on palettes they hugged side by side with the sick. I thought I'd recognize my father's mouth much like mine on a jiggling rimmed bowl of cold thistle soup. I searched for his grasp on the rail of a train that wandered the track for three weeks past the end of the war in the '45 spring.

In truth there was little to see in the film, long pans of the Ruhr and the Rhine, an aching rich quiet of forest, masonry crumbled, abandoned fences, night and fog, snow and stone. After a while, my mind filled the blank empty fields. I watched in rapt shame and fleshed in the scenes with staggering corpses all bearing the same gait we shared.

The light in the church, if this can be so, grew less dimmed. Hanna straightened my shirt. She had the odor of tissues she used to layer her pale camisoles.

"Let's take Communion, it's worth the chance," Hanna urged.

"You have to make an act of confession," I said.

Hanna ignored me and stood. Her hand on my shoulder, we filed up the aisle with the rest of the killers, pressed into the backs of their mumbling coats. No one was cutting their losses but hoarding them all for an afterlife proof.

The hands of the priest smelled like sausage and cheap cigarettes. The papery host to the body of Christ stuck to the roof of my mouth. I thought I would gag, teased it loose with a nail. Hanna turned. Her face in the votive flame glow was the color of pilsner set off by those pearls.

"I don't have to confess, I'm not guilty," she said, but I know now she was. Hanna preferred to remain unatoned for the sins she held dear, both collective and uniquely hers. Only like this could she live with the thought of my father, the sock in the drawer, buffed shoes the first time on the cover, his perfect starched collar, the tap water glass on the dresser, the curtain that blew with his ghost when she entered, the forever afternoon pills.

If I were Hanna I'd like to believe I, too, would have tried for the border. I think of us crossing together. I have to stop minding the difference between what has happened and what might have been. What good does it do? Nevertheless, I can't help it. It is a habit inured.

Only last year I'd sit by a Boylston Street bar's picture window watching pedestrians pass, some of them readied for weather, others with newspaper cover or bare-headed, chilled. Invariably I'd spread the square photo carefully clipped out of *Time* magazine. It was of an unnamed '56 Budapest street. There were two down-the-block tanks, their turret-sheathed cannons aimed at tall buildings enshrouded in what might be firefight fallout or mist. The foreground revealed a placard-sleeved tree, its twisted, rheumatic charred crown. Beside it a featureless body lay face up on tiles and cracked shards.

Beside this memento I'd unfold my portrait of Hanna, tamp its split creases. But it wasn't Hanna at all, a mere substitute of an actress resembling my mother who had the same eyes. They were slightly turned from the lens, lightly moist, longing for something that's lost, cannot be but once was.

Even my actual photo of Hanna was bogus, not to mention my memory, heightened and radiant, shot through with desire.

I realize Hanna must rest and succumb. I have to allow this, to cover her shoulders, to bathe her in petals of wishes and ashes, recite the litany comprising our past, touch her hair one last time, toss a rose, throw the dirt, and be done. This is the reason I've come to this church, to receive absolution, I'm suddenly sure. She is the person who stands at my side all the time, the one who I secretly talk to. It is her hand on my shoulder, her Hungarian lilt that now says,

"You know what to do." She's saying leave me alone and go on. I release you. Then her presence is gone.

"Hanna," I say out loud, but there is no response. So she doesn't want me to suffer like her after all. That was something I'd made up as a way of keeping her close.

I look around at the gloom. Soon it will be dark in this church, in our room, everywhere.

I rise and step out. The evening is spare, sentimental. I walk under mare's tail confections arranged on a nickel-gray sky. Newspaper pages are blowing, sidewalks running with scraps. The mom-and-pop storefronts are grated, the buildings grow glaucous and bold. Across the street in a window the locked melded shape of a man and a woman embrace, rise, and fall. The trees cast their diffident shadows. It seems like the streetlights leak milk on the trunks of the palms slightly bent with the weight of their pods. I finger loose coins in my pocket, the expired license, and out-of-state library card.

Today has a name and it scares me to say it. It seems like I'm walking beside me, perpetual stranger and witness. I say to myself it's all right, but it's not. I have to step into myself. The moon that seemed lit from within becomes exiled by clouds. The night is provisional, weak, no more than somebody's late errant thought. The ebbing of twilight is tinged by nostalgia for what might yet come. Whatever it is, it's something I'll have to make happen, without any help or applause.

I play a game of imagining the future. I must stop indulging myself like this but can't help it, just one more time, just for fun. On Sundays Maria and I will drive out to Lake Winnipesaukee. I'll teach her to row in an hourly rented and slow-leaking scull. I'll ask her to call her child Hanna or if it's a boy, after my five-numbered father. Would this be presumptuous, a curse? Trembling, I look myself over once more. I pretend again I'm her age.

When I was thirteen I slept with a transistor radio under my pillow, read World War II books. I wanted to be fully grown, to sit at a luncheonette counter and hear that the Dodgers were finally beating the Mets in a live doubleheader at Shea. I wanted to go see a

subtitled movie, drink one-third cream saccharin coffee, to lounge
in my car, heater on. Shoes kicked off, sludge-damped socks peeled,
I'd be tuning the radio dial to the news as I absently smoked. I still
want all this, and to ride the red line into Cambridge past seasonal
blooms on the sills, to be shaken awake.

I think of Maria right now in our room and its blue claustrophobia. I start to walk fast, almost run. I see her play with her Tiny Tears
doll, making it dance on her thighs. It's missing an arm, has stabs in
its near-hairless skull, bears swastikas Gary has carved on its flesh-
colored belly and back. Cassandra has pretend-fed it her bottle, and
none of us named it except for Maria, in secret, perhaps.

I see her learning to just tease the rouge on each cheek and how
to affect disregard. She could be pondering her baby, the thought of
a pink bassinet, the sounds of "abortion," "stillborn," that are crowding her mouth. She'll choke if she can't spit them out.

I see Maria wearing the cynical smile Cassandra has taught her. It
comes to me now that fate is a function of circumstance tempered
and forged by our will and desire. I know what has to be done, before it's too late for us, before we can't see our own gestures in front
of our faces because it's too dark.

Twenty-Three

Will my resolve flee in the balm of blue light or a spoonful of dope? This is what happens to all of our plans, they are lost with each shot.

Maria is lying in bed, her head hidden under the pillow, stiff mannequin legs sticking over the edge. I touch the fold of her blanket. She sits up rubbing her eyes, disoriented and sleep-dislocated. The dusk makes it appear like the ceiling's receded. The tables and chairs turn into caricature furniture pieces. Cassandra and Gary aren't here. It is the beginning of night and the air feels suspect. The windows are steamed. Maria and I are like children alone in a house by ourselves.

I tell her, "I'm leaving tonight and you're coming along." The words sound just right once they're out. I must have been secretly practicing them to myself without knowing since Maria told me about her child. The vision of Maria's next-to-last father has only confirmed it. All this is going to end as fast as it started.

Maria stares at the wall, shakes her head with what could be denial or assent, merely bewilderment. She tugs at the hem of Cassandra's trick dress. I can tell she, too, has been thinking about it.

It's been there all along in our gestures. They've become tactful. The tentative fit of our hands in each other's has grown meek, circumspect. Cassandra has noticed we've managed to fashion domes-

tic vignettes. She saw Maria sorting my clothes from the pile in the
closet, me grooming fleas from her ankle, and how our eyes met.
Maria had washed out our cup, warmed beans on the stove, served
them on a plate. She didn't allow me to swallow them cold from the
can standing over the sink.

Maria has voided her watery bile in the toilet as I held her forehead. We took time to make-believe carelessly troll the street where
the Fairlane is parked. She's remarked there's air in the tires, I've
said there's gas in the tank.

I squat by her feet. "How much did you make at the park?"

"Thirty-two dollars." I think of her hands on the men.

"That's all right, we'll manage."

She throws herself onto her side. "But we'll be so sick."

I rub my palm on her calves. "I hid some reds. This is our chance.
If we don't go now we won't ever leave and you know it. I'm not going to stay. It's something I've always been sure of."

"Yeah, right," she says, then, "Cassandra won't like it."

"I don't care what she wants. I've seen enough, no more dimebag
scams."

Maria plays with the edge of the blanket. "Why not just keep doing this?"

"Sure, I'll stick around to watch you miscarry. There'll be someone's certain OD, maybe mine. Gary will go back to prison, you'll
keep turning tricks, pick up a disease."

"You want to go, just like that."

I touch her arm. "Maria, it's come up before."

"I know where you'd take me. To Boston. It's cold."

I have a heady, adrenaline feeling akin to when I loaded the car
with my books and clothes and drove toward the interstate's west-
bound ramp.

"I'll take you, take care of you there."

"You've done great so far," Maria remarks. The trick dress rides up
as she lies on her side, cheek-palmed, elbow-propped, exposing Cassandra's pink underwear. This seems innocent, artless, obscene.

"Don't you want the baby?"

Maria sighs, covers her eyes. "I told you. I want to be older. To legally drive. Anyway, you and me, it won't work. I can't have nice men."

I'm thinking who says I am. "You sound like Cassandra. That can be unlearned."

She offers her well-practiced smile that means there's been too much spilled milk, water under the bridge, the purse of her lips a cliché. Still, in the tilt of her head is a vague possibility yearned. Maria takes in the room like she sees it can't help, it has never been safe. "I want someone who doesn't know everything. Who'll think I'm a good Catholic-school girl. Do you understand?"

"You couldn't live such a lie."

"Maybe I could, you can't tell," she replies, but wistfully, more to herself, like she doesn't really believe it. The blue light is grainy, dust-moted, ash-sifted. Maria won't meet my gaze.

"We could start over," I say. "We could change." I really want to believe it.

She looks away, wan, enervated. "You'd turn around if I asked?"

"In a minute," I lie.

Maria is tilting her head to the window and scrunching her face. "Oh, College, why all this now?"

"Let's just say I've had a vision."

"Oh?" she asks tauntingly. "Where?"

"In church," I reply.

She nods like this makes perfect sense. She keeps looking toward the window, the turgid slush wedge of the sky that it hides. Then there is the longest moment of silence and waiting I've ever had. "I'd like to see snow, and Christmas is almost here," she finally says.

As I fully register that this means yes, the door opens. Cassandra and Gary are back. They're carrying cookies and wine, cigarettes. They've gotten high where they went and I'm jealous.

Cassandra kneels by the bed and studies our faces. She looks at our down-tilted heads and the fold of our hands, at how we won't meet her gaze. "Something's up," says Cassandra. She looks toward the door, toward the street. She leans, takes my palm, and walks her two fingers across it like legs. I allow a slight nod. "So it's like that" is her comment. "I saw it coming. Don't think I'm surprised. You as much as gave it away in the park. Those doe eyes."

Cassandra glances at Gary. Her look says they both know our plans. He opens his hands, tilts his head in a gesture of "It can't be helped."

"This room is a mood. Didn't you say that one time?" Cassandra asks, changing tack. "College, let's sit on the couch."

I know she means to divide us but nonetheless do what she asks, it's a habit. I'm not sure I hope that she can or she can't.

Then we're side by side and Cassandra is combing my hair. She's never done this before and it's making me nervous. Gary is next to Maria, an arm on her shoulder. He says something firm in her ear. I see her mouth, "No," resolute. He tips her chin with his knuckles and says something more but still she demurs.

Outside, wind picks the silence apart, flings it into the eaves, blows the dust of the alley inland, away from the coast. Glass breaks below but we're used to it. It's a score for the end of the day, almost pleasant. Someone is shouting, "Hey, nigger," but without rancor, benign. Cassandra's and Gary's breathing is shallow and slow, synchronous. Maria's and mine is more like a pant. A lipstick-smudged cup, the charred, stem-bent spoon, another for eating, are scattered on top of the Formica table near makeup-smeared Kleenex and gouged cotton balls. Our clothes are draped everywhere, on the doorknobs and kitchenette chairs.

Cassandra's cast-off high heels are aimed like they're ready to walk anytime, as if they will accompany us. She's wearing a dress that's unbuttoned in front, revealing her ribs and bared concave chest, slit up the side exposing a leg all the way past her thigh to the hip. I study the mute evidence of her bruises, each yellow excess ringed by a blue aureole that fades into purple and black. Her sleeveless arms, like Maria's, provide their own comment. This close she smells like vanilla extract. Idly, she fingers my scalp, a smile of some willful distaste on her obdurate mouth. The Purple Smoke eyeshadow daubed on her lids is matched by the Brandywine pomade that graces her lips.

"This isn't what you counted on when you came," Cassandra pronounces.

"Maybe it is, exactly."

"Poor baby, you wanted to save me," she says, but unkind, sarcastic.

In fact, I don't think I did. Even when I pulled her into the room it was reflex. I wanted only to watch her, be near her, experience Cassandra's nonstop melodrama in which I got to play a part.

"You drew me in with those stories," I tell her. "You did it on purpose."

Cassandra yawns. "I've run out of them. Anyway, they might all be untruths."

"I know. You've said that."

"That's right," she muses. "I have." She looks toward the couch, doesn't mention my option to rescue Maria, though it lingers plain in her eyes. "Remember you told me we'd marry?" She raises a knee, revealing torn tan underpants. Her face grows devoid of its natural malice and idle contempt. "Remember the robe?"

I understand what Cassandra is doing. She knows my proclivity toward fantasy and invention. Now I'd like to believe that it's too late for that. Nevertheless, I can't help but conjure the robe and its red and white stripes. I say, "You kept it on for a while. You said, 'The little girl in me is finally having her way.' Then you took it off, got on top."

Looking for cigarettes she sweeps the couch with her palm. "I said that? I must have been loaded."

"You said, 'Pull my hair, pull it harder.' That I should hurt you a bit if I wanted, to tell you your name like I meant it. You promised I'd get to know you like nobody else."

"Well, you haven't," Cassandra replies. "That wasn't part of my plans. I acted like you were a schoolboy. I was breaking you in."

"I should have guessed."

"Lick my teeth, they're so sore," Cassandra had asked. She knew the timbre I wanted, the tone I desired, the taste of her mouth a moist, bitter velvet, hair sweeping my brow, her tongue a slight rasp. The room had an essence of pure possibility then when I did what Cassandra demanded.

After, we tented the blanket. She said, "See how you made my eyes bright?"

They were, I admitted. She waved me off. "They're the same as before. A trick of the light. It's you who's changed."

Cassandra is probably right. It has all been a sleight of hand on her part. It's been a game she has engineered from the start. Just because she could, I allowed it. I wanted it badly, and it has come out as Cassandra predicted. She did it on purpose.

I think of when I first arrived, the building imposing, exuding a palpable heat from its smooth, creamy tiles. The checkerboard lobby was sun-streaked, the double doors canted. I see myself grappling the box with my books up the stairs. Sometimes in sleep I open those volumes I lugged past the blood-handprint walls but can't make out the mutated alphabet print. Each letter's genetically altered, transformed so the meaning of words is achingly, vaguely familiar but cryptic, obscured.

I entered the room with its goldenrod glaze. The din of perpetual summer vacation rose from the street. A guitar and beach ball cantata joined with a disjointed solo of discordant notes from a horn. I had made my escape. I was sure this was it.

I catch myself doing it, tidying, shining events. The difference is, now I know it. It comes to me I have only moments remaining. We won't ever fall to the mattress, Cassandra's feet cold. We won't get to slide on each other still fully clothed. I'll no longer witness the tilt of her head or her rise-and-fall breath, rub her eyes' tender, translucent pouches like roe or the soft underside of a fish, suck on those cracked, blackened teeth.

I won't hear her say, "It feels great to be cheap," and "The world is a bed," as she picks at dirt from under her chipped crimson nails. There'll be the absence of her rare, indelicate laugh that puts me in mind of beer bottles on asphalt rolling away. I won't get to question her dreams. "No one has asked me that for so long," she won't say. She won't push me down on the tangle of sheet and scissor my legs, open and close her chapped hands, raise a wrist to her brow, say, "College, you know how I hate to be touched but now, please." There won't be a last exhalation of cigarette smoke occluding her split, peeling lips.

There isn't time left to loiter the corner, her hand on my shoulder, still taller, for Gary to call out, "Man on the line," as we duck in the alcove that says 5¢ SHOWER off Speedway and Breeze. I won't make it to watch for the tentative first girls of next spring in the foam of the surf to their knees, cupping water they'll gingerly pat on their breasts to get used to its chill. I won't kick the scalps of brown kelp alive with their thousands of fleas. There'll be only the memory. So be it. I'll think of all this as I think of Hanna, but maybe I'll know it's a comforting trick.

"Just stop now," Cassandra says. "Don't reminisce."

I parse and catalog sounds, the bark of the usual dogs and a transmission's grind, the clack of a latch and the incessant drumming describing the tone of the oncoming night.

Cassandra bites at a crescent of Tropical Passion forefinger's hangnail, pinches it free from the tip of her tongue, and flings it away.

It's the accumulation of gestures like this that endear her, that caused me to want her. I study the curl of her hand as she waves her Tareyton filter, her slack gaze where resentments linger, those practiced evasions begun with her uncle removing her jumper, refined in the longing for razors, perfected along the thin route of the pharmacy trail.

"Don't stare at me," says Cassandra. "Instead, take a good look around." Her tone is bitter, instructional, just like Hanna's when we neared the border. "This is the place you'll return to each night once you're gone."

Gary is combing his hair with his fingers and giving Cassandra occasional glances. I'm preparing myself for my absence. For me the room will always be blue just like this.

"Now look at your arms," Cassandra insists. "How far will you get? For once you should know what you're doing," she says, but I remain quiet. If I speak I might yet change my mind.

Cassandra is barren-voiced, hoarse. "It was an idea of me that you wanted."

"That's what we all want from each other," I tell her, but she's unconvinced.

"I invented myself just for you," she declares.

I think no falsehood's convincing if, at its core, it doesn't contain a tight kernel of truth.

Cassandra blows smoke through her nose. "Next time, don't pick a place numbered seven. There are seven attachments that have to be broken. It also stands for perfection that can't be attained."

Her eyes are entirely dry. The bulb renders her vividly pale. She makes herself appear invulnerable yet ensures I notice how inside she's frail. She knows it's how I like her best. It is how Hanna constantly looked before going out and turning a trick of her own. I shiver and startle. Of course that's what she did all along. That's how she paid for her lilium water, laudanum, and gin, for my favorite sheer dress and red belt.

"If you stayed I might let you help me. Let's face it, we both like to suffer. We'll do it together." Cassandra's words plant a doubt and a longing. She places a hand on my neck that prickles my flesh.

I look at Gary. "I can't. I'll turn into him."

Cassandra snorts, full of contempt. "You'll never come close. You're not properly damaged."

But damaged enough, I believe. "I will be if I stay."

She turns on the couch and stares at the orangy dunes, leaning palms. She raises the sash. Cassandra chews a limp strand of her hair and appears to be suffering the weather, the now empty bottle-swap, high-five pagoda, the char of horizon, the faint ravenous pink at the edge of the sky sublime with its pale band of ginger.

Wind ripples her dress. Her nipples are pinched by the breeze. Streetlights have come on and yellow rectangles appear on the opposite bricks. She reaches behind for the brush on the cinder block table, runs it through her slight curls with typical haphazard strokes. She swivels and sits with her legs tucked beneath her, unhurried and seemingly sober. Her profligate features reveal how many ways I don't know her. Her attributes won't be condensed.

"It's the last bongo sunset," she says.

Standing, she works herself free of her dress. The seams of her panties are strung with loose threads, the elastic is stretched from the stained shiny cloth. She looks from Maria to Gary and settles her seven-ringed hand on my head.

"One's too young, the other's too brutal," Cassandra observes as if they're abstractions, not present. She reaches into her purse with most of its white beads rubbed off, its fabric a mange, hefts her pint of Four Roses, unscrews the cap, releasing the burnt umber odor of late-night saloons.

Cassandra paces the room unsexed in her tan underwear. Once more I study the lines of her straight, boyish waist, the spade open space where the tops of her legs don't quite meet. She stops at the bed by Maria.

"Maybe you're carrying the baby I lost," she says, cold, no regrets. So she's known all along. "If it's a girl, what'll you name it?"

"Cassandra," Maria blurts out, unrehearsed.

Cassandra steps back as if struck, crossing her arms on her chest. "Don't you dare," she exclaims, reconsiders. "I don't know. Why not? Everything has to repeat, after all."

I don't want to agree about this. I hope it's wrong but our own examples tend to disprove it.

Maria looks up at Gary. "He says I should have it scraped out."

"That would simplify things," Cassandra replies. I'd like to believe there's some sympathy edging her tone but there's none.

Gary is flicking a strand of unwashed oily hair from his face. He's sidled as close as he can to Maria, reaches around her and squeezes her close. "We could have made lots of money on you," he says in her ear. Sure, open the dope enterprise, buy fedoras and guns, use an answering service, I think.

"You already have," she replies, her impulse to squirm no more

than a shiver because of the fathers and others, I think, a habit long
dormant, subsumed by the postures Maria's been forced to assume.

"Where's the runaway money you saved? I'll bet there's enough
for a pop. I can go score right now." Gary is anxious though feigning
lighthearted. He's always like this when smelling a shot.

Maria flicks me a question mark glance. She wants me to signal
both no and yes. Cassandra can see this. I look away.

"You're not thinking right. You won't get far, whatever you have,"
Gary says. "Eight hours at best. You know what happens then." He
moves his hand to her hollow of elbow, massages it there. Maria
swallows. All our insides are pulled tight exactly the same. There's
wires within us that grow taut and strum with an anticipation that's
trained. "You can go first, we'll let you have half," he cajoles with a
plea that is also a command.

"Another do-or-die moment," Cassandra is saying as Maria
stands, walks to the closet, extracts a brown paper bag, and starts
tossing in accouterments, a gold tube of Crimson Enchantment,
her white blouse, flats, nail file, barrette.

In two strides Cassandra's beside her, upending the sack. "Give
me my clothes back," she orders. "The pearls. You're not taking that
dress."

Gary throws himself onto his back. "No drama," he says, his con-
viction fled.

Maria removes the street corner shimmer, lifting it over her head
in one fluid unbothered motion, another Cassandra enticement
she's learned. She must have her whole repertoire memorized just in
case.

She carelessly tosses the metallic shiver that Cassandra catches
and clutches as if it was something that's been lost and missed. She
holds its limp sheen and fingers its folds like it offers solace despite
where it's been, what's been felt underneath it.

"My panties, too," Cassandra insists.

Maria shrugs, steps out of them, kicks them toward the bed. Despite the disrobing Maria appears unperturbed. She closes her eyes
and pirouettes, naked, her arms wrapped around herself.

I think Maria is dancing the dance of her houses on dry chaparral. She might be considering the nights she was stripped in back rooms of those difficult homes where the air was a stew of aftershave, hard-to-breathe cayenne, lard, cooking wine, sweat. She looks like she's making out words overheard from a half-open door as she stood in the tub, the water with salts rising hot to her calves. Behind the sound of the gargling faucet her next-to-last father was calling, singeing a lock of her hair he had clipped in the thin butane flame of a Zippo, grooming the nails of his obstinate fingers that felt her, haltingly, all over her skin. She lowered herself in the scald because it was safer to stall, to turn roseate pink in the burn.

Maria is clenching her fists like she's palming damp coins for a bus ride when all this began, her hope barely tempered back then, only a sizzle of sprinklers nearby for accompaniment. She touches her belly, not gibbous but already slightly convex. Maybe she's contemplating the baby, how big it will be, trying to guess its percentage to live. She might be thinking no one can help her, persuade her, dismiss her, wondering if she has sufficient resolve to get out of the room.

Gary and I should also remove our shirts and our pants. It would be a finalized rite, boy-girl-boy, the four of us shuffling counterclockwise on the carpet. Instead he's picking his teeth with the tip of his knife. Cassandra's slouched in skin-hued underwear. I'm sitting off to the side as if everything happens to somebody else. Cassandra has taught me this way to see clear. It's only the second time that I've instigated and willed a moment. I can only hope it turns out better than the first.

Maria stops twirling, turns goosefleshed, abashed. We're only children who've taken our clothes off in spite of, in front of, each other, I think. She tugs on her skirt, misbuttons my favorite plaid flannel, shrugs on our horsehide community-property coat that reaches mid-thigh.

"I'm not sorry," Maria is saying as she starts refilling the sack.

"You will be," Cassandra replies, resuming her place by my side on the dog-paw scabbed couch. I place a hand on her arm out of habit. She shudders and shies.

"You've touched me enough for a lifetime," she cries, balling and smoothing the dress in her lap. "You're not going to hack it. It's over, so I can say anything now."

"You always have," I reply.

Cassandra leans close. "It's too late to get smart." I smell her Four Roses breath as she narrows her eyes. "Listen, you're wasting your time with Maria. She's had a taste, she'll be back. You think you have what it takes to amuse a teenager? Don't kid yourself, College. Why, you haven't even had sex with her yet."

"How do you know?" I hear myself plaintive and hate how it sounds.

"Because she told me, remember?" Cassandra waves a frantic hand through the smoky blue tint. "Maria will think of all this, of the park. She'll grow heady and soft with nostalgia. She'll miss the high, the adventure. She'll be gone in six months. I'd stake my next fix."

I remember what F. Scott Fitzgerald said, that there are no second acts in American lives. I hope he was wrong. Anyway, I'm Hungarian.

"And what about me?" I venture. I think any possible truth from her mouth is incumbent upon the believer.

She hefts my palm, traces the mounts of Apollo, the planets, the lines of life, fortune, fate, heart. She presses the spot on the side of my thumb where will is revealed, rubs the heel of my hand where reason resides.

"You're so transparent," Cassandra decides. "You came, walked right up to the edge, you looked down, you stepped back. You think you can leave it at that." She drops my hand as if sick of me now past endurance and turns to the glass. "The first part, the going, is simple. It only takes desperation to run. I ought to know about this." She looks at Maria's reflection, still bending and filling her bag. "You'll set her up in a room by that school. You'll study. You'll get a small job. You might try to write some bad poems about me, about

Venice." She pauses to swallow, drops the empty pint. "You've told me this boring scenario before."

Cassandra studies the lights in the street as if they're hiding clues. "After Maria clears out you'll have your old consolations of sorrow once more. The bare trees. The white snow. The bells." Her voice becomes low-pitched yet strident. "You'll allow yourself the luxury of mooning her absence. Your suicide father. Your refugee losses. Your lost sainted Hanna. You talk too much when you're stoned. When all's said and done, it's me who knows most about you."

"I suppose that's your blessing," I tell her.

"Go ahead," she says, "have the last word."

Her face is a stranger's, revealed from a vantage of one year removed. I try my tricks to conjure the way that I knew her just yesterday, pretend it's my first time here. Nothing works. Betraying her namesake, in front of my eyes Cassandra becomes a mere girl. I see her now as she really is, stringy-haired, thin, tired, defeated. Watching her hair in the twilight I know I won't turn into stone. I'm being released from a dreamed-up seduction, a half-recalled song that cannot be sung except if you don't think about it at all. I'm thinking her new transformation is also an act, a secret letting-go gift that she offers, or maybe it's something I give to myself.

I know the Fairlane is parked on Andalusia, the street with my favorite sound, like seafaring, opera, the name of South Spain with its Guadalquivir and Sierra Nevada. That's where Cassandra invented a father who owned a date farm, a horse ranch in Argentina, who she said would send for her, rescue her from board and care.

Why do I think of this now? I'm suddenly swamped by the names of small towns, their private histories and hidden agendas, Maria's Tujunga, Covina. Cassandra's Ibbis and Java. Her tight homely alleys of Bannock and Homer with bus routes long canceled and smeared-off illegible scraps of blown paper, places for decades intact where nothing and everything mattered, where barns were the color of broccoli and rye while overhead clouds dragged their thunder.

I'm thinking how those towns comprise, compromised, her. They still crowd her features with distillations of two-dollar Benzedrine kisses, rolling through back roads surrendering no meaning, her mouth grazed by thistle as Cassandra slept in the back of a truck atop squat blocks of straw.

I hear her mouthing, "I'm dirty, I can't get it off." Not to me but to somebody else, hands rubbing a wall or a sheet or her dress. Her well-rehearsed stories will be rehashed, perhaps adding ours to the long repertoire. They'll be unique to the new face lying beside hers on pillow or floor. She'll soon be inventing herself for a man with his chin in his hands and a gimme-cap cocked on his brow in a bar's afterglow.

Cassandra's mythologies lift. They're no more than the sum of her tales and the places she's been. I have my own, my Osztergom foundries and Kecskemét prairies. The Budapest square and the train station name that translates to "Trouble" along the dun Danube that used to be blue. Swansea, West Brewster, the Agawam River, the towns with the Indian names. I see a field dusted white, the barren elms' gesturing arms, a riverbend piled with high drifts, a slow wooden sled being towed by a hand I'm certain is mine.

This room is used up for all four of us. I've been chastened on its couch, on its slipped-mattress bed. After I leave with Maria, Cassandra and Gary won't stay. I see her camped out in some sorry wobble-wheeled shopping cart nirvana, old clothes piled beneath her, her soothsaying flown while Gary dries out on a thirty-day lockup siesta and everything's spent. There'll be nothing to do but count flies, burble paper-bagged wine. She'll keep an eye on the public restroom for a six-dollar trick, pick at scabs on her shins, her wrists sticking out from the sleeves of an inside-out rabbit fur jacket that doesn't quite fit.

But this is only conjecture. There'll be time for it later. Right now I'm jumped up inside. I go to Maria, who's cradling the sack much too tight.

I lean down and say, "Don't be scared," but she isn't, I am. I see my own hand, not the scattering one, turn the knob. In lieu of good-bye, break a leg, I hear Gary saying behind me, "It's too close to call."

Maria and I do together what we couldn't manage alone. We

step out of there. We run through the hall, down the stairs, like a
fire's behind us, a blue conflagration incinerating the room. Then
we're past the wide double doors and no dime-store-charmed arms
raise the sash. There's no reprieve or a shouting for us to come back.

The evening is moonless. Ion-charged wind stirs the air, moans
among lampposts, swaying the power and telephone lines. It rustles
the palms' husky beards. Low damp fog swaddles the lights in round
halos of mist. The night is embalmed with this vapor, a wet tingling
moisture that rubs a raw blush on our cheeks. Milkweed mist settles
in whisperless patches on torn, thorny shrubs. It girds trees, trunks
of creosote poles. It mutes our walk, any possible radio playing, qui-
ets flutes, bongos, guitars. Maria is humming a lost little tune that's
making the evening seem careless, naive, mingling dread with a
sense of release and relief. I take her hand as Hanna used to take
mine. I consider the notion that Hanna purposely let go my grasp
on the night of the border, that she knew she could not ever leave
Budapest, that she'd stay, join my father, and pay. That Maria's fingers in mine are Hanna's blessing of this. They are the benevolence
of Hanna resting at last.

I think how nothing comes out as imagined, of how California
unfurled on the scrim of my wishes, beliefs. After all that has happened a few lines are spoken and something else starts, a new sequence begins. So this is how change takes effect, almost effortlessly.

At the familiar corner that now seems estranged we turn to the
thirteen green trees. This time Maria won't count them but I memorize the placement of each, which one's the fullest, which ones
grow reniform, obovate, conifer leaves, which has the toe-stubbing
roots.

We walk past the Post with its criminal loungers and no one we
know calls our names. We pass the Supersuds Laundromat lot
where Maria has parked to handle the men with her small hands,
round lips, breathing the flush of their alcohol pores and wiping
their cream from her chin. We glance at the rumble of tubs churning loads, don't pause for the comfort of Clorox, damp cotton, and
wool. Maria won't translate the posters once more, HUELLAS PELI-

GROSAS, ME ENCANTA HACE EL AMOR. We ignore the bending and folding, don't joke of the warnings that cover the walls, NO NUDE HERE. DON'T TAKE OFF YOUR CLOTHES. We ditch the spray-painted brick fascia that still begs for Joy Fosh to write, the phone being used for drug deals. We walk down San Juan, its regular-life squat spare houses, browned lawns.

The car is abandoned to husks of palmetto that cover the hood. They rise to the wheel wells like carapaces from which insects have crawled and then gingerly flown. The windshield is crusted with droppings, pollen the taint of dried honey, gash-colored petals, and curled, sun-cured leaves. The engine turns over three times, then it starts.

We mush the corners. The view from the glass is obscure. We lurch when the gas pedal sticks going fast. We drive on Cabrillo, Grenada, Córdoba, Mediterranean names I might later recite out of memory, a balm.

Inside the car it's as stuffy and warm as a palm on the face of a child. I look at my hands ten and two on the wheel and think I'll soon wash off the grime. Above us the heaven's a trampled, slogged, whey-colored yellowish cast. I drive by the room once more, put the car into park.

"This is it, then," I say to Maria.

She shifts in her seat so she leans on the passenger door, tucks her Catholic-school skirt in her thighs. She looks as if she's about to say something but I don't give her time. I touch my hand to my lips in a gesture for quiet.

I turn and look at the blue twitching shadows consuming the walls of the room I mistakenly thought of as mine. In there Cassandra and Gary must ready the needle, once more flex the tie, but this cannot mean anything to me now.

I put it in drive. I step on the gas, it's as simple as that. I look toward the ocean that's spilling, relentless against the dead sand, and up, where there isn't a star in the sky.

LES PLESKO was born in Budapest, Hungary, and studied creative writing at U.C.L.A. Subsequently, he worked as a cotton-shoveler, pool-cleaner, gas station attendant, furniture-refinisher, grape-picker, crop-duster's flagman, ditchdigger, farmhand, modeling school and cemetery plot salesperson, Catholic-school English teacher, trade-show consultant, dispatcher, boiler-room solicitor, country-and-western disk jockey, and freelance writer. Currently, he is editor of a medical journal. He lives in Venice, California.